Only
By
Moonlight

Lynn Emery

L'union fait la force

(In union there is strength)

Chapter 1

On a cold, windy February day, LaShaun sat across from Chase at her kitchen table as they had lunch. Chase had taken a break from being a deputy and chasing down crime to relax. She's fixed his favorite to lure him away for a few minutes: a sandwich made of tender roast beef on French bread with spicy Cajun mustard. She'd entertained him with small talk before telling him about her visit to the courthouse in Abbeville for her cousin's sentencing hearing. Chase said nothing as she spoke, but maintained a tight blank expression as he slowly ate. When LaShaun got to the end of her account, Chase carefully wiped his mouth with a napkin.

"Bad idea on like six different levels. My advice?

Steer clear of Azalei. She's seven different kinds of bad news."

"Azalei has her faults, but even I kinda felt sorry for her. Though I know she brought it on herself," LaShaun added thoughtfully.

Chase downed the last bit of ginger ale in the tall glass mug and crossed to the dishwasher. He stacked his lunch dishes inside it. Then he turned around, still wiping his mouth with a large paper napkin. "Bad news," he repeated.

"Well I..." LaShaun started and stopped when Chase held up a large hand.

"I'm just saying, LaShaun. We got enough on our plate. And what's with this mysterious 'It's not over' crap. Nah, ignore the dramatics. Bad news," Chase said.

"She could be finally willing to drop a few tidbits about Quentin Trosclair. He's been getting away with murder in Vermilion Parish for years," LaShaun replied and grinned when Chase let out a loud groan.

"If I have to deal with that spoiled rich asshole one more time, I'll be on trial for murder," Chase blurted out.

"I know, honey. Maybe Azalei means she wants to explain herself and try to make up for what she's done. Not that it will bring Rita back or..." LaShaun's voice trailed off. There was no arguing that Azalei's scheming lies led to their cousin Rita's death. "I know what it's like to set loose evil and be helpless to stop what you put in motion."

Chase tossed the napkin into the kitchen trash can and walked to LaShaun. He pulled her up from the kitchen chair to wrap both his brawny arms around her. "Come here. You believe that Monmon Odette would want you two to repair this big rip in the family. But,

2

sweetie, it ain't gonna happen. You got the land and the money they wanted."

"Well, that didn't end up being the warm reassurance I was expecting," LaShaun tossed at him with a sigh. Then she looked up into his dark Cajun eyes. "Okay, okay. You're right. We won't be having fuzzy family reunions any time soon. I get that."

"Just stating the facts, ma'am." Chase kissed her on the cheek, and then let go. He checked his phone for text messages. "For some damn reason, we got a rash of burglaries. Wait, let me check that. I know the reason; drugs."

"Meth labs and so-called 'bath salts'. Folks come up with some interesting ways to self-destruct." LaShaun shook her head.

Chase continued to scroll through messages. "Even in our pretty Cajun countryside, people get stupid or evil. Poverty and chaos are everywhere."

"Thanks for stopping by to share that cheerful thought, Deputy Broussard," LaShaun said.

Chase put his phone back into the case clipped to his belt. He grabbed her in a bear hug again. "Well, we've got some happy stuff to talk about, like our wedding in April. My brother says Adrianna is having a ball being your coordinator. She's dragged him to three different florists getting ideas."

LaShaun grinned. "Your sister-in-law is enjoying this way too much, and for the wrong reasons." Then LaShaun grew serious. "Your mother..."

"If she's not there then that's her problem," Chase said easily. "Hey, I said we were going to have happy talk. My sisters, my brother and Adrianna, and even my daddy will be there. She won't be thrilled about it, but she will. Grandstanding won't get Queen Elizabeth the attention she wants, so she'll come around."

"If you say so. You know her better than me," LaShaun said raising her eyebrows. Elizabeth Broussard didn't impress LaShaun as a woman who bluffed.

Before Chase could reply, his phone beeped. He took it out again and tapped the screen. "Damn, high priority; which means..."

She watched his expression. Chase walked away a few steps. When a law enforcement officer's cell phone went off, it usually wasn't good. Chase stood in the bay window that overlooked her back lawn. He spoke quietly for a few minutes before he turned around.

"Gotta move. People are crazy," he muttered.

"Somebody been stupid or evil? Which is it this time?" LaShaun followed him to the back door.

He leaned down and kissed her on the lips. "Watch the news. That's all I can say."

Moments later he drove away in his Vermilion Parish Sheriff's Department cruiser. LaShaun closed the door and went to the wall mounted television. She found the remote and tuned to the local station. A pretty blonde anchorwoman at the Lafayette station read the noon news.

"To recap, three teenagers were found two hours ago hanging from an oak tree near the small town of Kaplan. The Vermilion Parish Sheriff's Department is on the scene. We'll update this breaking story as details become available. Let's turn to the weather now. Clay Wilcox has our forecast. Can we hope for a warm up by Mardi Gras, Clay?" The woman lost her grim expression and engaged in light banter with the weatherman.

LaShaun hit the mute button. The chill moving along her arms had nothing to do with the cold temperature. Just as she was about to leave the kitchen, a soft sound of bells stopped her. She went to the wall mounted phone and lifted the handset. This time she wasn't surprised by the contralto female voice on the line.

***

LaShaun sat on one of four chairs around Mrs. Rose Fontenot's breakfast table the next morning. She could only imagine the number of curse words Chase would let out if he knew. LaShaun smiled at the image of Chase pulling one large hand down his face in frustration. Rustling to her left caused LaShaun to focus back on the elderly woman moving around the parlor. Sister Rose, as she was called by a lot of people, still stood tall despite her seventy-four years. People in Mouton Cove swore her apparent hardiness proved she had supernatural power.

Miss Rose fussed with a lovely china serving set with magnolia blossoms painted onto a white background. The scent of Louisiana dark roast coffee rose from the carafe. Matching cups, saucers, sugar bowl, and small cream pitcher were also arranged on a round honey oak Lazy Susan.

"Miss Rose, you don't have to go to any trouble. You know I'm not a guest," LaShaun said. She felt pleasantly full after eating fluffy scrambled eggs, and sausage.

"I'm from the old school as they say. You need to serve folks some refreshment when they drop by to visit," Miss Rose replied as she refilled two cups with the steaming dark brew.

"Yes, ma'am," LaShaun replied. She knew better than to argue with Rose Mouton Fontenot.

"I don't get over your way often; otherwise I would have been over to check on you." Miss Rose nodded as she placed a cup in front of LaShaun. "Have a slice of my banana bread. Perfect way to finish off breakfast."

LaShaun patted her mid-section. "No, thank you, ma'am. I'm stuffed."

Miss Rose chuckled. "Lord, I'm showing my age. This is how we used to eat before going out to the fields. Hard work, child. My daddy and granddaddy didn't have these modern combines to harvest that rice."

"No, ma'am," LaShaun said. She sipped more coffee and waited.

"Well, you didn't drive over here to hear an old woman ramble on." Miss Rose chuckled again.

"You can ramble all you want, Miss Rose. That's the privilege of elderly ladies," LaShaun said and grinned at her.

Miss Rose wagged a forefinger at LaShaun. "Smart mouth just like your mama and Odette." Then she sighed. "I miss my friend and our long talks."

Miss Rose and Monmon Odette had met when Miss Rose taught school. Francine, LaShaun's mother, had stayed in trouble right up until she dropped out of high school. Monmon Odette frequently declared that Miss Rose was the best teacher around. Their efforts to keep Francine on the right path forged a decades-long friendship. The two women had something else in common; the gift of second sight.

"I'm back, Rose," a gruff voice called out.

The thump of a door slamming shut sounded a few seconds later, and then he walked in. Miss Rose called Pierre her "young" husband. He was, but only by four years.

"Alright, you don't have to tell the entire parish," Miss Rose replied loudly. Then she lowered her voice. "Every Wednesday he meets his men friends down at the local diner for breakfast. They flap their lips like they know what they're talking about."

"Me and Mack going down to look at the river, see how the water is running. Might be able to tell what the fishing will be like come spring." Mr. Pierre stopped short when he noticed LaShaun. "How you young lady?"

"I'm fine, sir. You look well." LaShaun crossed to him and pecked him on the cheek.

"See, Rose? You better treat me right. I can still catch the eye of pretty women." Mr. Pierre laughed harder at his own joke than either of them. A car horn blew. "Y'all don't be talkin' 'bout me when I'm gone. I'll be back around lunchtime."

"Bye. That man," Miss Rose said as if she didn't need to explain anything else. She listened to the door open and close, and then she turned to gaze at LaShaun for a few moments. Her amused expression faded away.

"So, you called me for a reason," LaShaun said. She felt a familiar prickle on her arms.

Miss Rose walked over to a beautiful pine kitchen cupboard. LaShaun guessed it to be at least one hundred years old. Miss Rose opened one of the drawers and returned to the table with a worn scrapbook.

"The children they found hanging; that's a bad sign, cher. I've been watching the news. They talk about how kids have been dabbling in devil worship and such out in the woods." Miss Rose suddenly seemed to feel her age. Gone was her sprightly demeanor. She moved stiffly as she sat down again.

"Kids acting stupid. We both know they don't have a clue about what they're doing," LaShaun said. When Miss Rose pointed to the scrapbook, LaShaun opened it. The first page had four small leaves in wax paper envelops taped to it.

"Never mind those," Miss Rose turned the pages and tapped the fifth. "Look here."

"Okay, you've been collecting articles... from the eighteen hundreds?" LaShaun raised an eyebrow as she glanced at Miss Rose.

"I'm old, but I ain't that old, girl," Miss Rose wisecracked and then grew serious again. "Where did they find those silly youngsters?"

"Off Highway 694 on Indian Bayou Road," LaShaun replied. She knew that Miss Rose wasn't asking the question because she didn't know the answer.

Miss Rose nodded slowly. "That land used to be part of the Sweet Olive Plantation. Read the top article."

"Horror at Metier Mansion," LaShaun read the dramatic headline.

"Now look at this." Miss Rose turned more pages.

"Another article from 1937, another in 1956, another in 1967. Couple found dead, murder-suicide suspected," LaShaun said and looked at her. "Scrapbooking is a nice past time, but Miss Rose, you've got a creepy hobby."

"Look at the location, cher."

"Sheriff Henry told this reporter that Deputy Bill Fontaine found Joseph and Eliza Ducommon on the dirt lane locals called Duck Lane just off... Highway 694." LaShaun shuddered when the prickle spread up her arms again. The sensation was more intense, like a combination of a static shock and pins sticking into her skin.

"Your monmon and me been watching for many a year, child. We kept hoping this thing, this evil, would be banished. We tried our best. I'm afraid you'll have to fight it now. After Odette got so sick, I went to see her. You hadn't come home yet. She knew."

"That she wouldn't live much longer," LaShaun whispered as though talking to herself.

"More than that, cher. She knew that you would have to face down this evil." When LaShaun looked at her sharply, Miss Rose put a hand on LaShaun's arm. "Yes, the spirit in the woods. Odette called it a loa, from the Voudoun religion. A spirit called up by your ancestors. Greed drove Isidore LeGrange to call this fiendish force into our world. Arrogance convinced him he had the strength to control it."

"But Loa are strong, unpredictable. They always have their own agenda. They will turn on their human guide just for amusement," LaShaun said, repeating what she'd read.

"Malicious loa may be a different culture's name for Satan's demons," Miss Rose replied.

"You think these kids acting stupid stumbled onto a real ritual that called up this spirit again?" LaShaun looked at her.

"And have paid for their stupidity in blood, cher," Miss Rose said in a bleak tone.

"Coincidence, Miss Rose." LaShaun gave the older woman an indulgent pat on the hand.

"I know you thought, or more likely hoped, that thing was gone for good, child," Miss Rose said, her voice soft and sympathetic.

"No, ma'am. I prayed and prayed hard," LaShaun replied. She smiled at the older woman, squeezed her hand and stood. "Thank you, Miss Rose. But this time I'm sure that we don't have to worry."

Miss Rose stood with her. "I feel better hearing you sound so confident. But if you need me, call. I'm old,

9

but I still pack a punch if I do say so myself."

"I couldn't ask for a better sidekick, but I won't need that help," LaShaun replied and hugged Miss Rose.

"You come over here anytime, cher. I'll whip up some blackberry cobbler, and we'll have us a good old time," Miss Rose said and hugged her back. "One more thing; Odette didn't want you to be bitter against your family. The evil infected your family bloodline, she said. Greed and the hunger for power crossed generations."

LaShaun turned to leave, but then stopped short. She stared at Miss Rose. "Wait a minute. What is the connection between those murders over decades?"

"I'm sorry, cher. I wish I could tell you. Odette and me couldn't figure that one out. We just sensed the pattern. Same as when I saw the news last night." Miss Rose shook her head. "So much death."

"I'll search archives online and let you know what I find out," LaShaun said.

"Email it to me." Miss Rose grinned at LaShaun's surprised expression. "My granddaughter bought me a tablet computer and taught me how to use it. Child, I'm hooked on that thing. Let me get it." She went to a shelf on the same cupboard and came back with it.

LaShaun sent an email to herself from Miss Rose's tablet. Miss Rose wrapped up slices of banana bread for LaShaun to take with her. After repeated assurances that she would keep Miss Rose informed and it was probably nothing, LaShaun left for home. On the ride to Beau Chene, LaShaun rehearsed breaking this latest news to Chase. Once again, the supernatural mixed with human stupidity played into Vermilion Parish crime. Chase and M.J. Arceneaux, the acting Sheriff, would not be pleased.

"Maybe I can figure it out. It's not like I'm keeping

secrets. All Miss Rose has is a faded newspaper article and intuition," LaShaun mused aloud as she turned onto Highway Eighty-two. Still, a tiny prickle argued with LaShaun's attempt to stay grounded in the natural world. Miss Rose was no ordinary septuagenarian holding on to hundred-year-old superstitions.

LYNN EMERY

Chapter 2

That evening, LaShaun didn't need paranormal powers to know Chase would be working late. The body of a local drug dealer had been found in a local farmer's crawfish pond. LaShaun watched the six o'clock evening news on the kitchen television as she picked over her supper. The perky young brunette seemed excited. She had the air of suppressed glee as she reported one more crime in the Beau Chene area.

"Javon Collins had been in the parish prison on a drug charge and being a convicted felon in possession of a firearm," the reporter said. "He was out on bond. Authorities found two bags of marijuana in a car parked along the road nearby. The car was stolen last week."

"I'll bet the locals will have a party criticizing M.J. now," LaShaun muttered.

As if she'd heard LaShaun's words, the reporter put on an affected solemn expression. "Tune in to our ten o'clock broadcast. Channel Six News will have a special report. Three teenagers are victims of a bizarre attack, only two of them survive. Is our Sheriff's Department prepared to deal with twenty-first century crime? We'll examine the issue of rural settings with big city crime. Next, we'll have our forecast." She smiled into the camera.

"Damn, don't sound so happy about it," LaShaun complained.

She got up from the counter, covered the small bowl of gumbo, and put it in the fridge. Just as she started to wash her few dishes, the front door chimes trilled. LaShaun glanced at the clock, wondering who had driven out so far at night. She went to a window in the formal parlor and peeked out. Her friend, attorney Savannah Honoré, stood on the porch in the soft yellow porch light. Her husband Paul was with her, which shocked LaShaun. Paul was polite whenever they happened to meet, but LaShaun knew he had qualms about the wisdom of Savannah being friends with the infamous voodoo woman of Beau Chene. The fact that LaShaun kept getting pulled into gruesome and weird crimes didn't ease his mind. LaShaun unlocked the front door.

"Good evening. Come in and satisfy my curiosity," LaShaun said with a grin at Savannah and a nod to Paul.

"Hello. I tried to talk Savannah out of dropping in without calling. Cell phones make it easy," Paul said and gave an exasperated grunt.

Savannah locked the front door like she was at home. Then she gave LaShaun a quick hug. "Oh will you stop. I had a weak signal on my wonderfully advanced smart phone, so I couldn't call. Hey girl. How y'all doin'?" Savannah asked.

"Come on back to the kitchen. I was just in there watching television. I made gumbo today. Y'all welcome to have some," LaShaun said and led the way down the hallway.

"Nah, we can't stay long. We gotta go pick up the kids. You remember Charice, don't you?" Savannah hopped on a stool and patted the one next to her. Her husband sat down obediently.

"Yes," LaShaun replied.

Savannah and Charice had been best buds since the third grade. Now they both had a set of twin girls, and even more in common. Charice's girls were older than the Honoré eleven-year-olds, and more like older sisters the girls idolized. LaShaun smiled as she imagined the combined energy and noise four girls would make. A wave of longing swept over her as she thought about having a family. Paul's deep voice broke into her thoughts.

"Nice kitchen. I like the red and brown color scheme, makes this large space look homey." Paul rubbed a palm over the granite countertop in appreciation.

"Why thank you," LaShaun said. She watched in amusement as he studied the rest of room. "No eye of newt and tongue of dog. Just chicken and sausage gumbo in the pot," she joked, making a reference to the witches brew from Shakespeare's play Macbeth.

Paul blinked for a second, then burst out laughing. "Okay, okay. I deserved that. I was thinking how... um, normal the placed looked."

"I hid the jars of dead black cats and goofer dust," LaShaun replied laughing with him.

Savannah slapped her husband's shoulder playfully. "Don't come in here embarrassing me. Oh, wait a minute. You've never been to LaShaun's house before."

"And he wasn't sure what to expect, so he came to protect you from eee-vil," LaShaun intoned in a deep, horror movie tone of voice.

"Well, I wouldn't put it quite that way," Paul said with a sheepish half-grin at his wife.

"Oh Lawd have mercy, Paul." Savannah shook her head.

"No, he's got a good point, especially with everything happening around here lately. I don't blame him for worrying about you wandering around at night these days," LaShaun said.

Paul and Savannah glanced at each other. As if on some silent cue they'd agreed on beforehand, Paul stood and pointed to the television. "I'm going to watch the sports channel if y'all don't mind."

"Sure," LaShaun said.

She watched him cross the open floor plan to the family room area. He found the remote and moments later seemed engrossed in reports on scores. Ex-athletes exchanged banter about upcoming games and made predictions. LaShaun turned back to Savannah with her eyebrows raised.

"So now you're going to tell me the reason for this visit, huh? You guys have been married long enough that you've got the secret signals perfected," LaShaun joked.

"Yeah, and I'll bet you already have the same connection to Chase. I've seen you two together. I'm so looking forward to your wedding." Savannah grinned at LaShaun. "Girl, y'all the talk of Beau Chene. My daddy is happy for you, too. He says your mama and Miss Odette would be so proud."

Antoine St. Julien had always been kindly toward LaShaun. LaShaun smiled. "Tell him I said hello. Now back to the subject of you dragging poor Paul out here. You took a detour out to my house because..." LaShaun sat down and crossed her arms.

"Allison Graham asked me to come out and talk to you," Savannah said low.

"Who is that?" LaShaun blinked at her.

"Her son, Greg, was one of the teenagers found hanging from three different oak trees," Savannah said with a grim frown.

"No," LaShaun blurted out.

"Greg is the only survivor who's talking. The girl, Rebecca Saucier, is still in shock. She won't say a word. The third kid, a boy named Elliot Dubois, was pronounced dead at the scene." Savannah spoke quietly as she glanced over at her husband. Paul seemed engrossed with the sports report and took no notice.

"Tell his mama I didn't have anything to do with it," LaShaun retorted. She cut in before Savannah could reply. "No, I'm sick of people around here saying I'm involved in every freaky act their kinfolks get into."

"LaShaun, she--"

"I don't care what she's heard, Savannah. It's her fault she didn't know what her darlin' boy got up to in the woods."

"Just shut your mouth for ten seconds," Savannah said through clenched teeth. She sighed when LaShaun crossed her arms.

"I'm listening." LaShaun glared back at her friend.

"She's not blaming you for anything. In fact. she came to my Abbeville office and--"

LaShaun leaned forward. "Wait a minute. You have an Abbeville office? Ms. Big Time Attorney got multiple offices."

"Yes, I'm practicing with another attorney in Iberia and Lafayette Parishes," Savannah said. "Now for the last time, stop interrupting me, damn it."

"Promise to tell me about your plan to rule the legal world later." LaShaun grinned at her. When Savannah squinted back, LaShaun sighed. "Alright, alright. Go ahead. Allison Graham snuck out of town to consult you."

"Exactly. Oh she tried to play it off. She claimed she was going to be in Abbeville anyway and that meeting there would be more convenient, so I agreed to the cloak and dagger stuff. Came in with a scarf wrapped around her face, dark sunglasses, and her hair tucked into a knit hat," Savannah said.

"Can't say I blame her with all the sensational talk going around the parish," LaShaun replied.

"Luckily, M.J. has kept details from leaking to the media, but we have a short window of opportunity before the hounds are released." Savannah got up and went to the fridge. She found a bottle of cream soda and then turned to her husband. "Honey, you want something to drink?"

"If LaShaun doesn't mind, a beer would be nice," Paul called back.

"She's fine with it," Savannah replied and found a bottle of a locally brewed beer. She talked as she found tortilla chips and poured them into a large bowl. She filled a smaller bowl for herself.

"No problem, Paul. Obviously your wife knows where everything is in my kitchen," LaShaun quipped as Savannah took a wooden tray and carried him the snacks.

"Shush, I'm going to keep him happy so I can tell you this story," Savannah whispered as she walked past LaShaun. "There you go. We'll be ready to leave in a bit."

"Um-hum," Paul answered without taking his gaze from the television. When Savannah put the tray on the end table near his elbow, he picked up the beer. "Thanks, ladies."

Savannah sat down next to LaShaun again. "Anyway, Mrs. Graham is afraid Greg got involved in some kind of Goth group at school. They started off playing one of those spooky role-playing games, Wizards and Witches or something. She's not even sure what it's called. The kids made it up."

"Lovely. Violent video games got boring I suppose," LaShaun blurted out. When Savannah gave her a mean look, she raised a hand. "Sorry, sorry. Keep going."

"Mrs. Graham wants to know if you and Chase have been investigating any... Ahem, demonic activity or something equally silly. I told her I would ask, but honestly, I thought you'd get a kick out of this. Ha, ha." Savannah gave a weak laugh and studied LaShaun as though looking for a sign. "Please laugh this off with me and tell me it's absurd."

"Hmm." LaShaun frowned.

"Oh hell," Savannah muttered and glanced over at her husband. "Paul is talking about us moving out of the parish, not just the town. I mean, serial killers, gossip about loup garou, and now this."

"Ah c'mon, he won't insist on moving. Would he? Your father and aunt are getting on in years," LaShaun said. Not to mention LaShaun would miss her friend.

"He's worried the girls could get sucked into some crazy peer group. I can't argue with his reasoning. Look at what Allison Graham and her husband are going through. They're an upper-class family. One day her blonde-haired boy next door is playing little league baseball. Then he's a teenager hanging out in the woods at night dressed in black from head to toe."

"Being a parent can be scary, huh?" LaShaun blinked hard at Savannah.

"You best believe it. So..." Savannah gazed back at LaShaun.

"The last three or four crimes were plain old human sin. Maybe these kids got carried away with this role playing. The news reports say there were possibly other kids involved. What did Mrs. Graham say about that?" LaShaun asked.

"She's talked to the sheriff's deputies for sure, one of Chase's guys on the criminal investigation team.

They're also talking to the kids at school," Savannah said and munched on a chip.

"Chase hasn't said anything to me, but then, he doesn't routinely bring his work home. We've got more stuff to talk about," LaShaun replied and ate a chip from Savannah's bowl.

"Sure, like the wedding plans and which house you're going to live in." Savannah smiled at the more pleasant topics.

"Yes, and how his mother probably won't be at the wedding. She'll probably try to guilt the rest of the family to boycott." LaShaun shook her head.

"Well, at least you know which house to pick; whichever one is farther away from her," Savannah wisecracked in a graveyard humor tone.

LaShaun burst out in a loud laugh. Paul pulled his attention away from the sports channel for a second before going back to it. She had to wait a few moments before regaining control. "That was a good one. I needed a laugh about the Broussard family drama. Whew."

Savannah grinned. "Girl, please. You've faced down demons. A mean mother-in-law will be like a day at the beach."

LaShaun gave a snort. "You've never met Chase's mother. We'll deal with her tantrums. Now back to Mrs. Graham and her wayward boy."

"Yeah, them," Savannah replied and lost her expression of good humor. "Mrs. Graham is hoping to blame somebody other than her son."

"Chase's investigators think he did it?" LaShaun looked at Savannah with interest.

"Greg was injured, but not as severely as the other two kids. He was released from the hospital a couple of days after being admitted that night. I mean, the other two can't talk. And he won't."

LaShaun faced her fully. "So you're going to be his lawyer because you expect the investigators to consider him a suspect eventually."

Savannah shook her head. "Mr. and Mrs. Graham hired a lawyer while Greg was still in the hospital; a top criminal defense attorney from Lafayette. A couple of their friends recommended me; because I know you. Remember I was involved in that adventure with," she dropped her voice low, "The Blood River Ripper."

"Oh my good Lord." LaShaun rolled her eyes. "Reassure Mr. and Mrs. All American that Greg slipped into no-good all on his own. The devil didn't make him do it."

"I have a feeling that won't reassure them," Savannah said.

"That's all I got." LaShaun shrugged.

"You can't blame her for asking after some of the stuff that's gone on in Vermilion Parish," Savannah said and stood.

"Yes, I can as a matter of fact. They're looking to build a defense. Well sorry, I'm fresh out of supernatural beings to give them a hand," LaShaun retorted. "Now you and your hard-working hubby go collect your kids. I'll send you home with a big container of gumbo, some potato salad and jalapeno corn bread. You won't have to cook, and the kids can get to bed on time. That way they'll be fresh tomorrow morning for school."

"Don't go to any trouble," Savannah replied.

"I've got a big pot and more than enough." LaShaun got up and got busy fixing their take home food.

"Aw, look at you. You're already preparing to feed

21

a family." Then Savannah's eyes went wide. "Hey, are you...?"

LaShaun paused in the act of scooping up gumbo with a ladle and filling a plastic container. "Am I what?"

"You know," Savannah said and nodded at LaShaun."

"Huh? No! Don't you start gossip about me being pregnant either."

"I wouldn't," Savannah protested and wore an affronted expression. Then she giggled. "Wouldn't that chap Mrs. Broussard's behind!"

LaShaun grimaced. "You'll be the first one to get a famous Rousselle curse in one hundred years."

Savannah waved a hand. "Relax. I'm only going to tell a few close friends. I'm kidding, just kidding." She let out a squeal when LaShaun pretended to swing the ladle at her head.

"Y'all need to quit playing around. Hey, we gonna have gumbo tonight," Paul said as he strolled in. "Babe, we better get a move on. Thanks so much for the good food, LaShaun."

"You're quite welcome. Now take your troublemaker wife home." LaShaun pretended to swing at her again.

Savannah burst out laughing. "Don't spill my gumbo."

Ten minutes later, Savannah and Paul were on their way out of LaShaun's front door. Paul carried a canvas tote bag with all the fixings for a down home Creole supper. He went ahead to load the car and Savannah turned to LaShaun.

"I'm going to assure Mrs. Graham that she needs human legal advice only, no demon hunter intervention," Savannah said. She stared at LaShaun hard.

"What? I said there's nothing paranormal going on... that I know of." LaShaun squirmed under Savannah's sharp-eyed legal gaze.

"Oh hell naw. Here we freakin' go again with the spooky stuff," Savannah spat out in a harsh whisper. Then she turned to Paul who was already sitting in their car. "I'm coming, sweetie."

"I swear I'm telling the whole truth and nothing but the truth," LaShaun said. She raised her right hand as though taking an oath on the witness stand.

Savannah started to walk off then came back. "Anything changes, you let me know ASAP, especially if it means you'll need a lawyer again."

"I'm staying out of trouble," LaShaun assured her. After exchanging goodbyes again, LaShaun shut and locked the front door. "I hope."

***

At two o'clock the next morning. LaShaun came awake. She instinctively threw out an arm to feel for Chase. Then she sighed and rolled over. Determined to get back to sleep. she tried to ignore the blue glow from her digital clock. Watching the numbers change would not help her go back to sleep. She closed her eyes and let her mind drift away. The light seemed to pulse through her eyelids. LaShaun bolted upright into clear thinking from the soft haze of drowsiness. She got out of bed. When she drew aside the curtains of one of the windows that faced her woods, her heart thumped. A soft silvery blue fog pulsed behind a stand of trees to the west. LaShaun glanced up at the full, lustrous moon against the night sky. A wispy cloud drifted across the pearl white disc and then drifted down to the woods.

She blinked at the sight and rubbed her eyes. Was her imagination playing tricks? With quicksilver motions, LaShaun got dressed in jeans, waterproof boots, and a heavy flannel shirt. She pulled on an insulated rain jacket and retrieved her knife and grandmother's rosary. She whispered a fervent prayer, and then headed down the hallway to her back door. Then she stopped and went back to her bedroom.

"Might as well be well armed," she murmured.

LaShaun found her Remington derringer. The lovely scroll work on the barrel made it look like a fashion accessory; it was a deadly fashion accessory with silver bullets. Then she pulled on supple leather gloves she'd special ordered. They would keep her hands warm but not interfere with her grip on the knife or gun. Loaded and ready for a fight, she went outside. Moonlight washed across the backyard, competing with the security light to the west of her house. She listened to the night.

Leaves rustled as the cold wind blew through the trees and bushes. Furry creatures did not creep out in the wintery night. Instead they hunkered down in burrows or hallowed out tree trunks. So LaShaun didn't expect to hear the kind of night sounds that came with spring or summer. The blue mist strangely retreated deeper into the woods. Suddenly the swish and whispery noise of the wind changed. A sound like breathing filled the air around her. If she hadn't known better, LaShaun would have thought a huge giant animal crouched' nearby... a hunter stalking prey, waiting in the dark to strike at just the right time. LaShaun started at a realization of something different. The mist floated beyond her woods, away from the historic Rousselle family cemetery. A sharp chill raced along her arms and down her back. If this demon was no longer tethered to her woods, where else could it travel? She walked backwards until the heel of her right boot hit the back steps. LaShaun continued to scan her surroundings as she opened the back door with her key. Once inside. she wrapped both arms around her to stop the shivering. A thumping sound made her jump. When she heard footsteps, LaShaun moved away from the door. The footsteps caused a crunching sound on the fine gravel driveway. Suddenly the sound moved away.

LaShaun let out a sigh of relief. She hurried to the bay window in her kitchen. Her heart skipped when she recognized the tall figure walking from the circle of illumination from the security lamp toward darkness, following the retreating blue light.

"Oh no."

She raced to the solid steel door styled to look like dark wood. Precious seconds ticked by as she clicked the set of three locks that usually made her feel safe. Moments later she'd pushed through the screen storm door. Too scared to call out, LaShaun's legs pumped as she ran to catch up to him. Chase strode along, not seeming to be in a hurry. His long-legged stride easily increased the distance between them with each step.

"Chase. Chase!"

LaShaun spoke in a hoarse whisper, as though that would help keep some malevolent beast from noticing them. When he kept walking, she felt a surge of panic. To hell with stealth, she decided. LaShaun skidded to a halt, pulled out the small gun, and fired two shots in the air in rapid succession. Chase stopped in mid-stride. Oddly, he lowered his leg slowly, like a robot that had suddenly been turned off. Seconds later his head turned from left to right looking into the night. Then he faced

LaShaun.

"Hey girl. What the hell..." When he walked into the circle of light, Chase blinked rapidly.

"Are you okay? Are you hurt?" LaShaun ran to him as he walked to her. Panting, she still held the gun above her head. Then she stepped to her right and pointed it at the landscape bathed in gloom beyond the beam of the security lamp.

"No, I-I'm okay," Chase replied, but his voice sounded unsure. He rubbed a hand over his forehead. "I thought I heard something, and plus this night air seemed so sweet I..."

LaShaun got close to him. He wore a puzzled expression. She looked past him again. The blue mist faded away. She engaged the cross bolt safety on the derringer and put it into her jacket pocket.

"Let's go inside; get out of this frosty air. I'll fix you something warm to drink."

As she walked with him, LaShaun rubbed his cold hands while glancing over her shoulder. No trace of blue or anything out of the ordinary appeared against the night sky. The full moon looked down on them like a placid face giving no clue about what he'd seen. Chase remained silent as LaShaun kept up a stream of chatter. Her nerves became even more rattled by the odd blank expression he wore.

"You're shouldn't be wandering around in the dead of night. It's almost three o'clock in the morning. Why didn't you come on home or go to your place to get some rest? Talk to me, sweetie," LaShaun said, her voice breaking with anxiety. She fought the urge to cry, to shake him violently until he lost that look on his face. Something in her tone must have gotten through to him.

"Hey, girl, you sound upset. Nothing happened out here, did it? There's been some wild stuff going on." Chase pulled her tight against his side.

"No, nothing." LaShaun said no more until they were inside the kitchen.

Chase removed his thick, dark brown jacket with the words "VP Sheriff" on the back. He glanced around as though checking for threats. Then he took off his felt hat with The Vermilion Sheriff's Department emblem. He hung both on wall hooks near the back door.

"You're not telling me something, like why you out in the backyard with a gun. It sure as hell ain't hunting season, and that little pistol ain't legal for hunting." He placed both hands on his waist and waited for an answer. His dark eyebrows pulled together in a severe expression.

"I heard a noise and... I know, I know. You think it's a bad idea for me to go outside," LaShaun said cutting off his lecture.

"Yeah, darlin'. Especially since we don't know what particular kinda freaks are roaming around," Chase replied. Only then did he take off his duty belt. He carefully put it in a locked drawer of the wooden cabinet next to the small desk in her kitchen.

"I thought you said drug dealers and burglars. Just the garden variety lowlifes. You want something to eat? It's breakfast time now." LaShaun pointed to the clock.

"Nah, I'm good. Don't wiggle out of answering my question. What did you hear or see outside?" Chase followed LaShaun to the bedroom when she headed off.

LaShaun put her derringer and knife in the drawer of a small table and then got undressed. She still wore her pajamas underneath her clothes. "Some kind of rustling, like maybe one of Mr. Marchand's horses got loose or something. I took the weapons for safety, like you would have told me to do."

"I told you not to even go out, but to call the station and they'd get word to me." Chase gazed at her hard, and then took off his shirt.

"We got to go through this again? I'm no scary little girl who can't protect herself, so just relax. I don't want you worried about me while you're out chasing bad guys. Concentrate on them, so you'll stay safe." LaShaun walked to him and planted a kiss on his lips.

"You're trying to get me off the subject," Chase murmured and brushed a hand through her hair.

"I can't think when you're looking so hot, Mr. Lawman." LaShaun kissed him again, slowly and more passionately. She tugged at the zipper of his jeans.

In seconds, they were definitely distracted. Chase covered LaShaun's body with kisses that left her weak. By the time they were joined, LaShaun would have told him anything he wanted to know. Chase's only conversation consisted of how much he craved her in every way. After long, luscious minutes of pure pleasure, the electric pinnacle to their desire left them panting. They lay side by side locked in a loving embrace.

"Nice breakfast," he murmured as he nuzzled her neck.

"I love you, Deputy Broussard," LaShaun whispered.

"April I'll be saying 'I love you Mrs. Broussard'," he replied. His eyes closed, but before he drifted off to sleep, Chase added softly, "When I wake up we're going to talk about what you really thought was outside."

"But--" LaShaun began but broke off.

His soft regular breathing stopped her. With the long hours and stress of the last few days, LaShaun knew he needed rest, not arguments. She snuggled closer to him, knowing very well he'd keep his promise to get answers. LaShaun also knew he'd be quite dismayed when he got them.

She kissed his forehead. "Be careful what you ask for."

***

The next day, the residents of Beau Chene buzzed with the latest news. Over a late breakfast, or early lunch since they didn't eat until eleven o'clock, Chase watched the news. The Channel Six early morning broadcasts were replayed on a local access cable channel until noon. The grim set of his jaw tightened as a young male reporter talked.

"What's he doing on my crime scene? Dave is supposed to be in charge of keeping folks outta there," Chase burst out after a commercial came on. He pointed his fork at the television. A chunk of sausage danced crazily on the end of it.

"Stop getting all worked up, honey. Looked like the reporter was a good distance away from the crime tape," LaShaun replied calmly.

Chase wasn't in the mood to be reassured. "I can't wait for this damn election to be over. Dave is probably kissing up to the media. If I hear any stuff that's from a 'source inside the sheriff's department' I'm going to kick his--"

"Whoa now, you can't be beating on your opponent. That is not video you want going viral on the Internet. Calm down," LaShaun insisted. "Besides, you don't know that Dave is talking to the media or giving them inside tidbits."

"He's seen the polls. I'm ahead by two points. Dave

is determined to be the next sheriff." Chase sighed and dropped the fork onto his plate. "I don't know why I ever thought running for sheriff was a good idea. I hate all this political crap!"

"Sheriff Triche and M.J. both schooled you on what to expect. Sheriff Triche said being a lawman is only fifty percent of the job," LaShaun said in a deep gruff voice in imitation of the older man.

"Yeah, yeah, I remember. I don't mind working with people in the community, making policy and administrative decisions. but dealing with the mayors and other local politicians... gonna take a lot of gettin' used to." Chase gathered up his plate and LaShaun's and then went to the sink. He started the faucet and poured liquid soap into the sink.

"It's going to take diplomacy, so start practicing. By the way, thanks for the delicious breakfast. Can I expect regular service like this after we're married?" LaShaun teased. She grinned at him.

"Washing dishes and doing other chores relaxes me. You most certainly can expect plenty of service after we're married," Chase quipped, wiggling his dark eyebrows at her before returning to his task.

"I'm gonna hold you to all promises, stated and implied," LaShaun said with a laugh. "Seriously though, Chase. You're going to make a wonderful sheriff.

"So M.J. keeps telling me. I think she's just itching to let me sit in the hot seat. I'd rather have her as an opponent. At least I'd know we wouldn't have a brown-nosing fool running the department."

M.J. Arceneaux had made history by being the first black person and first woman appointed acting sheriff. More than a few citizens had urged her to run for the office. M.J. stood firm in telling everyone 'no way'.

Privately, she'd confided in LaShaun and Savannah that she wasn't ready to face the constant backlash. She felt sure every decision she made would be questioned. Any missteps would be amplified because of her race and gender.

"There would be a lot of pressure on her, and she's a single mother. Besides, she'd rather be one of the tribe than be the chief." LaShaun giggled when Chase rolled his eyes at her.

"I get it. M.J. is part Indian and you're so clever," Chase shot back as he rinsed soap from a plate.

"Thank you," LaShaun said, ignoring his playful sarcasm. "Anyway, you're going to win. I've seen it in the stars."

"Don't be saying stuff like that in front of folks. They'll swear you worked a mojo or something equally stupid." Chase scrubbed the cast iron skillet he'd used to fry up eggs and sausage.

"Us voodoo queens routinely use gri-gris to get what we want," LaShaun replied. When Chase let out a loud groan she giggled. "I won't kid about it outside these walls. I can count the number of folks on one hand who'd know I was joking."

"Humph, fortunately, we have a lot of new blood in the parish now." Chase stacked plates onto the drain tray.

LaShaun joined him at the kitchen sink. She grabbed a fluffy towel to dry them. "They'll vote for you. Dave has the solid, good old boy thing going on. But you have the young, fresh twenty-first century look. Not to mention you're sexy as hell. Women will flock to the polls to vote for you."

"Oh please." Chase shook his head.

"I'm serious, babe. Take a picture with your shirt

off, hat pushed back and with those brawny arms crossed. Put that on a billboard and Deputy Godchaux's campaign is dead in the water." LaShaun grinned when he winced.

"Luckily you're not my campaign manager," Chase said with a scowl.

"You don't have one," LaShaun replied.

"And now you see why," he retorted. Chase wiped his hands dry and leaned against the counter. "Speaking of your gift for seeing stuff in the stars, what exactly did you see in the woods at two o'clock this morning?"

"Ahem... I saw, hmm, it was a strange light." LaShaun concentrated a little too much on drying the last coffee cup. She turned away from his scrutiny to put the dishes in the cabinet.

"A blue light like the times before?" Chase stood straight and frowned.

"I was still half asleep. It could have been just moonlight reflected on mist rising from the ground." LaShaun worked on making her tone of voice matter-of-fact.

"You wouldn't have gone out there locked and loaded if you thought it was just moonlight. You had your grandmother's rosary in your jacket pocket. It fell out when I hung up your coat."

LaShaun let out a long sigh. "Okay. Okay. I talked to Miss Rose over in Mouton Cove. She taught my mama way back in grade school. She was good friends with Monmon Odette."

"Your grandmother didn't have many friends, so Miss Rose must be...special," Chase said.

"At odd times she sees, I don't know, pictures of the past because they're tied to something happening in the present." LaShaun held her breath for a few seconds. She watched his expression. When he didn't groan or grab his head in despair right away she exhaled.

"She couldn't just be a regular retired school teacher. Nope, that wouldn't make life quite as interesting." Chase rubbed his forehead for a few seconds and then sighed. "Okay, so you talked to her and then saw that thing, whatever it is, floating around. Now what?"

"Truthfully I don't know. It could be nothing supernatural at all," LaShaun said with a shrug.

"Uh-huh. You told me that before. I ended up fighting off a demon."

LaShaun rubbed his shoulder. "Not everything is hocus-pocus."

"Let's get back to you being outside," Chase said and gazed at her steadily.

"The light, night mist or whatever it was, just kind of faded away. Now I have questions for you." LaShaun stepped close to him. "You seemed out of it when you were in the yard this morning. It was like you didn't see me at first, and you just stared off into the woods. Did you feel, I don't know, strange?"

"What I felt was tired and keyed up at the same time. I probably just paused to enjoy some clean air after dealing with crap all day," Chase said. He smiled at her. "Don't' worry."

"Okay," LaShaun said and smiled back. She proceeded to worry.

Chase easily switched to everyday topics. He ran through errands and chores he'd do before he went back to work. LaShaun worked at paying attention, but she couldn't stop thinking about their early morning encounter. His odd behavior coupled with the

33

reappearance of the blue light meant she should get started on that research. Now.

Chapter 3

"Well come on in." Pete Kluger, the director and curator of the museum, waved LaShaun into his office.

LaShaun had driven over to the Vermilion Paroisse Musée only minutes after Chase left her house. Located in a nineteenth century three story building donated by a local, wealthy family, the museum housed a varied collection. Some of the items, like voodoo dolls, were controversial. Luckily for Pete, a transplant from the mid-west, the museum board supported him. Monmon Odette had donated furniture and books. LaShaun carried on the tradition as well. She'd donated three antique books and pottery after her grandmother died.

Pete, tall and lean with thick silvery gray hair, chattered on about museum events and other local gossip. "Oh, and we're going to have a fantastic Mardi Gras exhibit opening next Saturday, the twenty-second. Did you get your invitation to the reception?"

"Yes, but I confess I've been preoccupied. It's still sitting on my desk in the kitchen. Sorry I haven't sent in my RSVP." LaShaun sat down at the round antique table in the seating area of Pete's office.

"No problem. You can tell me now, and I'll put you and Chase's name on the guest list. The deli from Mayor Savoie's grocery store is catering. I may have my quarrels with the man, but he's got some of the best local cooks making his dishes." Pete bustled around making hot chocolate, his favorite. "We're going to have jambalaya, crawfish pasta, boudin balls, the works. Mrs. Grenier is going to make the king cakes. Yum."

"Sounds wonderful," LaShaun replied and accepted

a mug with the museum logo on it from Pete. She sipped a little of the hot chocolate. Smooth and rich, Pete prided himself on making it from an old Creole recipe. LaShaun let the delicious liquid slide down her throat slowly to savor it. "Perfect, as usual."

Pete beamed with pleasure at her appreciation. He sat down in the chair next to her at the table. "Thanks, dear. Much as I agree my chocolate is worth a trip over here, I don't think that's why you came."

"No, I'm doing some special research," LaShaun said.

"The last time you did 'special research,' scary things were happening. Please tell me we're not infested with rougarou again," Pete replied with a grimace.

"No," LaShaun said and drank more hot chocolate.

"Thank the Lord for small favors," Pete murmured with a relieved sigh.

"At least, I don't think so," LaShaun added.

Pete's eyes widened. "Help us sweet Lord."

"Calm down. I'm pretty sure Chase and I cleared out the last pack. I'm thinking this is something else. I need anything you have on the Metier family."

"Of course, we have quite a few books on local families. I started a list of common surnames in the parish fifteen years ago when I first took over. Then I cross referenced those names to public documents from the historical records," Pete said. His mug of liquid chocolate forgotten, he went to the computer on his desk.

"You've done an excellent job digitizing the collection." LaShaun took his mug and placed it on the desk at his elbow. She knew he'd be reaching for it soon.

"Hmm," was Pete's distracted reply.

LaShaun sat back down and kept quiet while he searched. As she expected, Pete picked up the mug and sipped a few times. His gray eyebrows pulled together as he concentrated on his task. Minutes later his expression relaxed and he grinned.

"You're in luck. A descendent donated furniture from the kitchen of the mansion outside Abbeville. Let's see, according to my files, Mr. and Mrs. Lawrence Volant made the donation in 1946. Mrs. Volant was the great-great niece of one Felicity Metier," Pete said, and he continued to use the wireless mouse to click on icons.

"See if you have anything on a Clarissa Metier and Vincent Metier; anything about a murder in·1837 in the family's papers," LaShaun said.

"Hmm," Pete said once more and searched for a few minutes. "I've found copies of a Vincent Philippe Metier's last will. His widow finally assumed possession of the estate in 1840. Seems there was some family dispute, but it's only mentioned briefly. The entry says after a protracted court battle the matter was resolved."

"I'll bet there was plenty of drama," LaShaun said.

"When a large inheritance is involved, things can get real ugly real fast," Pete agreed.

"You don't have to tell me. I lived it," LaShaun muttered. She thought about the bad feelings in the Rousselle clan about Monmon Odette's legacy. It still bubbled just beneath the surface.

"Vincent Metier owned a little over one hundred acres, the mansion, a successful business, and more buildings. I'm sure whatever fight she had must have been intense to last so long. I suggest you look at the parish court archives." Pete hit a key and the printer hummed.

"Transcripts will tell me who contested the will and the arguments," LaShaun replied.

"You'll get an account of the entire family feud in their words. It's the next best thing to stepping into a time machine and being there," Pete said, his eyes gleaming with excitement. He handed LaShaun the pages he'd printed.

"I bet you'd mortgage everything you own to get a real time machine." LaShaun took the pages.

Pete sighed wistfully. "Sylvia would stop me, but what a prize that would be."

"Your wife is very sensible," LaShaun murmured as she read through the pages in her hand.

"She can be quite adventurous, but when it comes to the house, I'm afraid she put her foot down. It was built in 1896 you know. We've had several offers," Pete said.

LaShaun glanced up at her friend and laughed. "Gee, Pete. Sounds like you've given this buy a time machine thing some thought. Lucky for Sylvia one hasn't been invented."

"She insists that our grandchildren should have fond memories of visiting us during summer school breaks. Oh well, maybe someday," Pete replied with a shrug and sigh.

"You really want to experience war, pestilence and outhouses? No thanks. I'll settle for reading historical records. Thanks for the starting point. I sure wish they'd mentioned Vincent Metier's murder though." LaShaun stood.

"I'm not surprised they didn't want to air dirty laundry in public. You might strike gold if you find personal journals from family members. I included the names of some descendants still living in the area," Pete said and pointed to the papers LaShaun held.

"Hmm, I see what you mean. I'll contact some of the descendants and ask if they could help complete our collection. Maybe they found family journals in an attic or something." Pete grinned as he rubbed his hands together.

"If they haven't tossed them in the trash," LaShaun said with skepticism.

"It's possible, but people in these parts place a lot of value on family memorabilia. I love my job," Pete exclaimed and started scrolling through pages on the computer screen again.

"You're almost as good as a time machine the way you pull tidbits from history," LaShaun replied with a grin. "I'll wait for your call. Thanks again for that wonderful mug of hot chocolate."

"You're very welcome, but I get something out of this as well. You keep life very exciting for this old guy. Except for the evil supernatural creatures bent on spreading death and destruction part of course," Pete added matter-of-factly without taking his eyes off the computer monitor.

"Um, yeah. Right. Later." LaShaun shook her head and left.

****

Two days later LaShaun sat across from Chase's younger sister, Katie, and his brother's wife Adrianna. Piles of catalogues covered the kitchen table in Chase's kitchen. The former family home stood on two acres of Broussard property.

"We've decided on all this stuff. Do we really have

to go over this again?" LaShaun said wearily.

"Every detail must be checked and double checked," Katie replied crisply. She had the tone of a general preparing for a huge military operation.

"The wedding is going to be pretty simple," LaShaun protested. "At least, that's what I'm fighting for anyway."

"Of course it's going to be a simple yet elegant wedding. Now, I've confirmed that we have tents for the food. Mrs. Trenton has the arches ordered with the flowers we selected. It'll be set up under grandmother's oak tree." Katie sighed and pointed through one of the kitchen windows. "Such a lovely setting. Oh, and Mrs. Trenton and her employee are going to wrap flowers around the trunk of the trees."

Adrianna gave LaShaun an encouraging smile. "It's going to be beautiful the way Katie sketched it out. We'll have an arch of flowers on the patio with a little raised platform for you, Chase, and the preacher to stand on."

"And chairs for the guests on the lawn. Adrianna's brother will use his lawn care equipment to do a perfect manicure of the grass," Katie added.

"We'll save money on chairs for the guests. Most of the Broussard family and their friends aren't coming," LaShaun murmured.

Adrianna and Katie exchanged a glance before Katie spoke up. "Concentrate on the people who will show up. They're the ones who really care about you and Chase."

"Right." LaShaun slowly turned the pages of a travel catalog.

After an awkward silence for a few seconds, Adrianna cleared her throat. "I see you looking at romantic honeymoon destinations. So speaking of that, what about a magical island paradise getaway?"

"Or the big city for a change?" Katie put in. "New York can be so exciting. That's where Jeremy and I went on our honeymoon. We saw Broadway plays, strolled in Central Park, and went to posh restaurants."

"No," LaShaun cut into their excited chatter. "Either way, Chase says he won't be able to leave for a while. If Chase is elected Sheriff, he'll have to get right to work almost immediately. If he doesn't win, then the new sheriff will need his support, so it's got to be someplace close."

"Like how close," Katie said with a frown.

"Someplace in easy driving distance I'd think. We'll take a four day weekend at the most. Then a few months later we can go on a longer trip," LaShaun replied and shrugged again.

Adrianna pouted. "Well shoot. That's no fun! I was picturing a welcome home party and seeing video of you guys enjoying an exotic place."

"Or walking hand in hand in Times Square," Katie put in. "Wait, maybe you can go to Paris or the south of France. We all have French ancestors."

"Like I said, a big trip isn't in the cards right after the wedding. That's the life of a dedicated officer of the law. Honestly, I don't care about a honeymoon. We'll have each other, and that's the most important thing to me."

"A honeymoon serves a true purpose. You get to extend the romance until you settle into a routine home life. These rituals can be very important," Katie announced with a crisp nod, sounding like her bossy mother. "Now where's a romantic place close by?"

"The swamp? They can hold each other close while

they listen to the adoring grunts of gators mating," Adrianna joked. She and LaShaun burst out laughing. They stopped when Katie crossed her arms and squinted at them.

"Besides, Chase and I have been lovin' on each other for months, so the honeymoon can wait." LaShaun winked at Adrianna.

"We need to focus ladies. Time is short. As the chief coordinator, I plan to have everything be perfect for the happy couple," Katie snapped. "Now let's get serious and think."

"What about a romantic bed and breakfast close by? A friend's husband treated her to one in New Iberia and she loved it," Adrianna said.

"That's it!" Katie blurted out with such fervor that Adrianna and LaShaun jumped. "The Metier House is close by and perfect.

LaShaun had been forming an argument to forget the idea, but the name brought her up short. "What did you just say?"

"It's called The Sweet Olive B & B. A couple from Vermont bought it two years ago. But everybody local still calls it the old Metier House. I hear they've done so well, they now have spa services, a guided tour of the restored gardens, and made the restaurant bigger." Katie whipped out her smart phone and tapped the screen. A few minutes later, she showed a picture from their website.

"Wow, that's looks dreamy," Adrianna said.

"Yeah, dreamy," LaShaun murmured and took the phone from Katie.

The house had three stories with porches that wrapped around the first and second floors. Large round columns supporting the porches made the house live up to its description as a mansion. Dark pink, lighter pink, and white azaleas bloomed against the pristine white structure. A wide packed earth driveway led up to the first floor porch steps. An impressive front door painted dark green had beveled glass windows on either side.

LaShaun grabbed her cross-body bag. "Okay, let's go. Katie can drive since she knows the way. Or we can follow the GPS on one of our phones."

"Wh-what? But we still need to make up the final menu for the caterers." Katie blinked rapidly and shuffled through the catalog until she found her tablet computer. "We should have some fancy appetizers. Now I think these bacon wrapped shrimp would be perfect. Also..."

"Sure, I agree with everything you suggest. I trust your taste completely. Let's get moving," LaShaun started to stand, but Katie pulled her back down.

"We can't just march over there and expect a tour with no notice," Katie said in a scandalized tone. "These people are running a business, LaShaun. We have to make an appointment. Besides, Chase should go with you so he can be part of the decision."

"I'll take him later. Now let's get shaking. I'm so excited about this idea I don't want to wait. That house looks like a dream come true, dripping with history and atmosphere."

"I'm game. Anyway, we don't need to do anything but go in and look around. LaShaun can make reservations while she's there. I mean, like you said, Katie, the wedding is right around the corner. It might already be too late depending how popular they are in the spring. A lot of these old houses have fascinating stories about the former owners." Adrianna stood and picked up her purse. "Oh c'mon, Katie. Wedding planning should be spontaneous and fun."

"Good gravy, LaShaun. You went from not caring about a honeymoon to practically giddy. Let me just organize all my materials so I'm not lost when we get back."

Katie fussily arranged the catalogs in her own system to help her remember details. Then she insisted that LaShaun and Adrianna wait while she made final notes. Finally, she called her husband to update him on where she would be. Adrianna grabbed her left arm and LaShaun grabbed her right arm. They marched her out of the house. LaShaun set the house alarm and locked the front door. Minutes later, Katie sat behind the wheel of her Jeep Cherokee grumbling. She ordered Adrianna to call ahead to the bed and breakfast. The wife answered the phone and cheerfully informed them they were more than welcome.

"Thank the Lord for small favors that they don't mind us barging in on them," Katie said when Adrianna ended the call.

"Don't be silly. They're innkeepers for goodness sakes," Adrianna replied. "Welcoming strangers is their business. So they have a spa you said. I may convince Bruce to come with me one weekend. We can drop the kids off with his parents."

"The website said they have a couple of hot tubs and a masseuse. She uses those warm stones to help relax the muscles. The walking paths through the restored gardens lead to a pond with geese. They even have peacocks on the grounds. The new owners re-created the way the estate was kept over a hundred years ago," Katie said.

Adrianna gave a low whistle. "Dang, the original

owners must have been loaded with bucks."

"The first Metier got a land grant back in the mid 1700s. He made his fortune trading in furs in New Orleans. Two of his sons moved to the area around 1806 I think," LaShaun said, reciting the history Pete had e-mailed her from the museum.

Katie took her gaze from the highway for a few seconds to glance sideways at LaShaun. "I thought you didn't know about this place."

LaShaun blinked back from her musings. "Oh, well. I've been studying the history of the parish for a while. You know my family came to Louisiana generations ago. I just happened to remember a few facts about the Metier family."

"Right," Katie replied as she gazed ahead again.

"They were very prominent. Their names are throughout a lot of historical documents. Two of the Metier sons founded small settlements, but they don't exist now," LaShaun went on.

"Okay," Katie said.

Adrianna and Katie became quiet. LaShaun could almost hear their thoughts. She started to assure them that there was nothing spooky about the house, but in truth, she couldn't guarantee any such thing. Not from what she'd read in the old newspaper article Miss Rose had showed her. LaShaun decided not to make promises she couldn't keep. Not until she walked onto the property. Who knows what kind of aura had been left behind after at least one bloody incident? The murder seemed to have been grisly enough to have left some trace behind. LaShaun just hoped it wasn't in the form of wandering spirits. Or at least, none that showed up to scare the crap out of her future sisters-in-law. She had few enough allies in the Broussard family as it was.

Thirty-five minutes later, they arrived at the Metier Mansion. The pictures had done the historic structure justice. Except for the flower shrubs having no blooms yet, the house and broad driveway looked just like the photos on the website. Sunshine made the white paint of the wood columns gleam. They parked in the lot adjacent to the house. Katie snapped a picture of the house with her cell phone once they got out of the car.

"Okay, now we'll check availability first and make a tentative reservation in case you fall in love with what you see. This place is very popular. Ready?" Katie tucked her phone into a side pocket of her leather purse.

"Yes, ma'am." Adrianna snapped a salute.

"Should we march in single file double time, ma'am," LaShaun added standing at attention.

Katie heaved a long suffering sigh. "I feel like I'm herding a group of thirteen-year-old girls on a school field trip. Stop giggling and let's go. Sheesh."

LaShaun and Adrianna smothered laughs as they followed Katie up the front steps. A wreath made with weathered wood and draped with Spanish moss decorated the front door. The word "Bonjour" was painted on a half moon sign above it. Katie opened the front door and strode in. A waist high desk served as the check-in area on the left. Four stuffed chairs covered in fabric with blooming roses and camellias were arranged against two walls.

"Bienvenu, ladies. Welcome to Sweet Olive." A woman with her dark hair cut short in a page style beamed at them from behind the desk. "I'm Marion Saunders, owner and happy hostess of this establishment."

"So nice to meet you. We're wondering if you have

a bridal suite and if it's available April twenty-sixth through April thirtieth," Katie replied looking around.

"Let me see. We have quite a few reservations so we may not have anything." Marion lightly tapped the keys of a computer on a lower shelf of the desk.

"You don't have an old fashioned book?" Adrianna asked. She peeked down to see the sleek monitor.

"We keep it kind of hidden to preserve the nineteenth century ambiance," Marion replied with a smile. "But we need twentieth century reservations software since we've become so popular. Ah, here we go. No, sorry. That month is booked solid."

"Well, I guess there's no point in looking around. Thank you anyway," Katie said. She pulled out her phone and began her search again.

"Not so fast," LaShaun said quickly. "I love old homes. I'd like to take a tour anyway."

"What's the point? They don't have any dates available in April. There's another B&B near New Iberia. I can call them right now." Katie was already dialing.

"Fine, you work on that. I'll look around," LaShaun said.

"I want to come, too," Adrianna put in.

"Excellent. This is my husband Harry. Watch the desk while I show these ladies around," Marion said to a friendly looking man who walked in. His thin hair had gone from blonde to mostly gray.

"Sure thing. Nice to see you, ladies." Harry nodded at them and stepped behind the desk. Just then, a couple descended the lovely carpeted stairway with a burnish stained oak railing. Harry was soon busy showing them tourist brochures of area attractions.

"You know, we very well could get a cancellation or two. So you should have your friend leave her contact information. We love hosting newlyweds," Marion said as she led the way through an arched entrance. Moments later they were in a lovely dining room.

"Katie is already married. LaShaun is the blushing bride," Adrianna replied.

"Congratulations. You're from the area?" Marion smiled at LaShaun warmly.

"Born and raised in Vermilion Parish," LaShaun said.

"Oh I really hope someone cancels," Marion said in a low confidential tone. "Of course, we value out-of-town guests, but I have a special fondness for Louisiana folks. Harry and I have loved it since we moved here. People are so open and welcoming."

"The restaurant has a lot of historic charm," Adrianna said. She fingered a lace linen napkin on an antique buffet table.

Katie came in. "My, but I love this room," she said.

"Was this the original formal dining room?" LaShaun walked around pretending to admire the decor. She tried to pick up any vibrations left from previous residents.

"Actually this was the formal parlor for entertaining. A smaller ladies parlor was over there, and then there was a music room. Through this arch was the formal dining room," Marion explained.

"This house is huge," Adrianna murmured aside to LaShaun.

"We expanded the room to make two smaller dining areas. We can use those for private parties or a reception. Of course, you can rent the entire restaurant if needed. We can turn what was the library on the east side into a restaurant for other guests. There's no private party booked on your wedding day."

Marion's perky voice faded into the background for

LaShaun. Katie and Adrianna became absorbed in Marion's sales pitch. LaShaun walked across the lobby. She entered what had been the library, where Vincent Metier was brutally murdered one hundred and seventy-six years before. Harry Saunders smiled at her and nodded as he talked on the phone at the front desk. LaShaun smiled back. She entered the long room. Beautiful floor to ceiling bookshelves were on the north facing walls. A fire place had two large stuffed chairs arranged in front of it. An archway led into a smaller area. LaShaun started to walk out again but stopped, pulled to turn back toward a seating area. Four chairs were arranged around a teakwood table. Four sofas, large and small, along with chairs were arranged in different parts of the room. Guests could easily find a comfy corner for conversation, or find a spot to be alone. Several chairs near windows or in two corners offered seclusion. Suddenly a strong smell of cigar smoke and whiskey hit LaShaun. She swallowed hard.

The sunny room faded as though a dark storm cloud had descended. Gas lamps on the fireplace mantel and tables lit the room. Instead of the modern setting, LaShaun watched as the room traveled back in time. A man sat slumped at a massive dark oak desk. A still smoking cigar rested in a massive bronze ash tray at his elbow. A dark figure wearing a wide brim hat and long black coat stood over the man. LaShaun couldn't see the person's face. The figure regarded the motionless man calmly, puffing on a long cigar. Blood pooled on the desk blotter. Spots had splattered heavy light brown draperies covering a window behind the desk. After a while, the figure lifted the man's head. One of the victim's eye sockets leaked gore. LaShaun felt a wave of nausea that made her gasp. She clapped a hand over her mouth. The figured laughed softly as he examined his handiwork. A yawning slash across the victim's throat caused his head to flop to one side. More blood flowed and the man made a gurgling sound.

"My God, he's not dead," LaShaun moaned.

She grabbed for the phone in her cross body bag. Silk fabric rustled under her fingers. Looking down, LaShaun found she wore a deep green taffeta floor length dress. When she touched her hair, it was pulled back into a prim bun.

"Don't worry, my sweet. He will be dead soon enough. Consider yourself free," the dark figure said.

He turned to face LaShaun. Only bright red eyes glowed against a coal black face. Not skin, and no facial features; only a blank void. Suddenly, an opening appeared in the shape of a grotesquely grinning mouth full of razor sharp teeth. Dizzy from the sensation of the room spinning, LaShaun grabbed for a chair nearby. She whimpered as a wave of that horrified remorse washed over her. When a hand touched her shoulder, LaShaun pushed away. She stumbled forward looking for a way to escape the horrendous scene.

"We better call 911. She's about to pass out," a female voice said. "Honey, sit down. Can you walk?"

"I've got her," Harry Saunders replied as he circled an arm around LaShaun's waist.

"What?" LaShaun sucked in air and let it out in an effort to recover. With a jolt she bounced out of her trance into the present again.

"Don't worry, we're calling an ambulance to get you to the hospital," Katie said in her in take charge tone.

"I'm okay. Just let me have some cold water and sit down for a while," LaShaun blurted out forcefully. "No hospital."

"You look positively green," Adrianna said with a worried frown.

"I haven't eaten since last night. That's all it is." LaShaun allowed Harry Saunders to support her across the room. He eased her into a cushiony chair.

Marion handed LaShaun a glass. "Here you go. I put a little peppermint in the water. It settles the stomach. Now sip slowly."

"Thank you." LaShaun forced a smile she hoped would reassure them all. Worried and skeptical gazes told her they weren't convinced.

"I still say you should get checked out," Katie insisted. She blinked at LaShaun rapidly.

"I'm a retired nurse. Give me your hand, dear," Marion said. She placed two fingers on LaShaun's wrist, and then looked into her eyes. "Her pulse is normal. Pupils not dilated."

"I'm really feeling much better. I just got a little woozy, no big deal," LaShaun said. "Let's see the upstairs rooms and cottages."

Adrianna spoke up before anyone else. "Not a great idea, LaShaun. We can always come back."

LaShaun shook her head hard but she stopped, afraid the faint sensation would return. She needed to find out more, see more about the dark figure and the woman in the taffeta. Just as she was about to argue why she should stay, her cell phone rang. She pulled it out. Chase's picture and cell number was displayed.

"It's Chase," LaShaun said.

"Her fiancé," Katie informed Marion and Harry.

"Hi honey," LaShaun answered the call in a cheerful tone.

Adrianna murmured to the others and they moved away to a discreet distance to give LaShaun privacy.

Katie seemed the most reluctant to leave, but Adrianna cupped Katie's left elbow and forced her to move.

"You okay? You sound funny," Chase said through the phone.

"I'm fine, baby," LaShaun assured him. Once again she wondered if Chase had some psychic ability. Or maybe, as Monmon Odette had told her once, those who truly love connect soul to soul. She hoped it was the latter. If he was open to the spirits... She shook off that thought and said, "What's up?"

"I need to come get you. I know it's crazy, but I'm in court in Abbeville and the DA wants you here just in case. We've recessed for lunch. I'll explain when I get to the house." Chase spoke in a rapid pressured voice.

"I'm a short ride outside Abbeville," LaShaun replied.

"I thought you were with Katie and Adrianna at my place to go over..."

"We changed plans. I'll explain once you get here. What does a court hearing have to do with me?" LaShaun asked, lowering her voice.

"Manny Young hired an attorney. He's filed to have his conviction for murder overturned," Chase replied. "He's got a unique defense. We'll talk in a few."

"Okay." LaShaun gave him directions and hung up.

Manny Young, the serial killer known as The Blood River Ripper, could be released? Evidence against him had been strong. His DNA had been on at least two of the dead women found near Blood River. He was linked to ten other deaths, bloody corpses found in three Louisiana Parishes and one east Texas County. LaShaun wondered what kind of madness had been set loose that had convinced anyone Manny Young should be on the streets again. Apparently, she would find out soon.

The image of the dark figure with fiery red eyes and saw-like teeth from the Metier library flashed into her mind.

Chapter 4

LaShaun had explained three times that Chase was on his way to pick her up. Katie huffed about the strange turn her day of planning had taken. Chatterbox Adrianna became quiet. LaShaun could tell she was afraid that more spooky events were happening. Chase pulled up in his Vermilion Parish Sheriff's department cruiser and her future sisters-in law weren't the only folks staring. Marion and Henry wore expressions that held equal parts anxiety and curiosity. Marion spoke up first before Chase even got out.

"Um, I hope there isn't a problem," the innkeeper said. She looked at all three of her visitors with curiosity.

"No, ma'am, nothing for you to worry about," LaShaun said in her best cheerful tone. Not unless you call possibly having a serial killer for a neighbor a problem, she thought grimly. But she kept her smile as Chase exited from the driver's side.

Katie turned to the woman. "You know how it is. He probably got lonesome for his one true love, and since he was close by..." She winked at the older couple.

"Hey, everybody. This place is pretty nice," Chase said with a grin and planted a kiss on LaShaun's mouth. "I hope y'all don't mind me runnin' off with my lady for a bit. She said y'all were about to wrap it up anyway."

Adrianna wore a slight frown of skepticism. She shot a glance at LaShaun with an eyebrow raised. "We haven't seen the rooms or the cabins for your honeymoon. I'd say that's pretty important."

"I was going to suggest that Chase come back with

me for that part of the tour anyway," LaShaun put in before Chase could speak again.

"Yeah, that sounds like a plan. So, let's go baby. Nice to meet y'all," Chase said and nodded graciously to Henry and Marion.

Henry strode forward with a hand out. "Nice to meet you, Deputy Broussard. You're a real hero around here."

"Thank you, sir. Just doing my job," Chase said and shook hands with him.

"You've done more than just an ordinary day's work on those cases, Deputy. Honey, he's running for sheriff, and he's got my vote. I know a lot of people who feel the same." Henry grinned at him and motioned to his wife. "These folks are famous for catching a load of killers around here. Wow, this is fabulous."

"Oh my," Marion blurted out. "You're LaShaun Rousselle. I watch Ghost Team USA all the time and James Shaffer says you're a psychic. Is it true those murders were linked to the supernatural?"

LaShaun cleared her throat loudly to cover the loud groan from Chase. "No, ma'am. There's very little reality in that reality show."

I've really enjoyed meeting you folks, but we have to leave," Chase said and grabbed LaShaun's hand. "We'll see you later, Katie and Adrianna."

"Come on, Marion. We've got dinner to plan and rooms to clean while the guests are out sightseeing. Great meeting you folks," Henry said.

Marion kept talking as her husband nudged her back to the B&B. "You know, I think we can finish renovating that cabin near the pond by the time of your wedding. That's it. You be sure and call me back."

"Thanks. We'll be in touch," LaShaun replied with a

wave.

Katie stepped forward with Adrianna beside her. "Why did you really drive miles over here?"

"Yeah, what's up?" Adrianna added. Her Latina accent grew deeper. "I know you didn't just happen to drop by this way. Don't even try it."

Chase waved a forefinger at his sister and sister-in-law. "Official business I can't discuss. Thanks for understanding." He tugged LaShaun's hands until she trailed behind him.

"Sorry, girls. I promise we'll get right back on the wedding details. Call you." LaShaun blew a kiss at them.

"Yeah, we want to know more than wedding details," Katie shouted.

LaShaun got into the passenger side of the cruiser. The imitation leather interior was such a deep brown it looked black. The tough vinyl could stand up to heavy use, but the seats were comfortable. She sat in the bucket seat. A console between the passenger and driver held a compact laptop computer, a wide band radio, and other tools of the cop trade. Chase slid smoothly into the driver's seat behind the wheel.

"We still got forty minutes left of the recess the judge granted the DA. Good thing we're so close to the courthouse." Chase checked for traffic and pulled onto the road. He soon had the cruiser going up to a speed of fifty miles per hour.

LaShaun waved a hand in front of her nose. "What is that trace of stink?"

"Sorry, I don't even notice it now. Had a real smelly robbery suspect in here about three days ago. Guess I better get one of those little scented trees to hang from the rearview mirror, huh?" Chase grinned.

"What did he steal, road kill? Phew!" LaShaun hit

the button and the car window rolled down.

"Hey, this is way better than it was. I had it scrubbed out," Chase chuckled at LaShaun's pained expression. "I can see you wouldn't like police work. We deal with a lot worse smells, believe me."

"Speaking of dealing with the dirty side of crime," LaShaun said and lost the playful expression. "Manny Young is trying to get a new trial?"

Chase frowned. "Yeah, and trust me, there is no clean side of crime. Not in my experience. Killers like Manny Young and his grandfather make funky smelling petty crooks something to look forward to."

"He was convicted of a bloody killing, and there's solid evidence linking him to at least eleven other murders. What lawyer in his right mind would take his case and work on an appeal for the Blood River Ripper?" LaShaun stared at Chase. "It's unbelievable."

"That's where you come in seems like," Chase replied with a tense set to his handsome jaw. "One of the hot shot professors from Tulane Law School and his top students. They take on cases with 'unique circumstances' is how they put it. I read up on them."

"What?" LaShaun glared at him and slapped his arm. "How long have you known Manny was trying to get a new trial?"

Chase heaved a sigh. "Only about two weeks. We've both been happy for the last few months, even with the political crap that goes with the election. I didn't want to spoil it, especially for you. You've been so relaxed, like... I don't know, like just a normal nervous bride."

"Yeah, about as normal as you can get with the notorious LaShaun Rousselle, right?" LaShaun said and smiled at him. "I wish I could give you even more normal, honey."

"Hey, I got what I want. Darlin', if I wanted normal, I could have gotten a job in a local plant and married some girl next door. Instead, I chose to join the sheriff's department and fell in love with a beautiful woman who had me with her first 'Hello'." Chase took one hand off the steering wheel and rubbed LaShaun's thigh for a few seconds before letting go again.

LaShaun laughed as she slid as close as the divided seats would allow. "I'd like to see the day Chase Broussard let any woman rule him."

"Trust me, baby. You got me body and soul," Chase said quietly as he pulled up to a four-way stop intersection. When the car stopped moving, he took the chance to kiss LaShaun.

When their lips parted, LaShaun brushed her fingers through his hair. "Me, too, Deputy Broussard."

Chase put both hands back on the wheel and took a turn for the final two miles to the courthouse. "I don't want anybody messin' with you, and that sure as hell includes Manny Young."

The warmth from their kiss faded as LaShaun remembered the serial killer. "What's the lawyer's theory, and how does it involve me?"

"He says because Manny had an abusive childhood, his grandfather had control of his mind. At first the DA thought he was going for an added twist on the insanity defense. But I don't think so." Chase pulled up to a stop light on a few blocks from the picturesque downtown of Abbeville. "I think the lawyer is going to say Manny didn't kill anybody, that he may have been present but..."

"His granddaddy actually did the killing," LaShaun finished for him. An intense prickle like electricity coursed down her arms. Orin Young had been a kind of human evil that could make even an atheist believe in Satan. "Orin Young did destroy his oldest son and turned Manny into a monster," LaShaun replied.

"Humph, that's exactly what his legal team wants to convince the judge. There's the DA. He's not looking too happy," Chase said and nodded toward the lovely old courthouse.

As they got out of the cruiser Scott Hazelton strode toward them. He seemed on edge, unable to wait until they crossed the pavement to reach him. At six feet four inches tall, the DA made a big impression during trials and before media cameras. His thick dark hair, slightly gray at the temples, helped as well. LaShaun could sense that he had a mixture of annoyance and relief to see her. After all, he'd come close to trying her for murder less than a year ago.

"Ms. Rousselle; thanks for coming on such short notice," Hazelton intoned and stuck out his hand.

LaShaun took it briefly and let go. "I'm very surprised to be here, to say the least."

"I can well imagine. I..." Hazelton's voice faded away as he glanced past them. "We've got company, this way."

Chase followed his gaze. "Damn it. How did Schaffer get wind of this?"

"Tell me you're kidding," LaShaun muttered.

Hazelton jerked a thumb for them to follow to a side door a few feet away. "At least he won't be able to follow us."

The DA's long legged-stride made LaShaun almost jog beside him to keep up as Chase brought up the rear. Schaffer called out to them as he hustled from almost a block away to get closer. His videographer stood still shooting footage for a few seconds longer, no doubt using a zoom lens. Then he moved when Schaffer yelled for him to follow. Both were too late. Hazelton got them through the door and inside long before Schaffer could catch up. The entrance wasn't for the public, only for official use. A chunky male Abbeville police officer checked LaShaun's small cross-body bag and waved them on. Then the solemn middle-aged cop scowled at Schaffer, who stood outside tapping on the glass with the words "Employees Only" clearly painted on it. The officer opened the door.

"This isn't a public entrance sir. If you have court business, please go to the new building across the parking lot."

"I only want to speak to the DA and Ms. Rousselle. I'm with the Fox Network and--"

"Sir, you can't come in," the officer repeated in a monotone that implied he was used to repeating those words.

LaShaun looked back only briefly as Hazelton led them deeper into the historic old building. Schaffer's attempts at impressing the officer fell on deaf ears. LaShaun smiled as Schaffer's voice rose in frustration.

"You can bet he'll be waiting for us," Chase said with a grimace.

"Who is that clown anyway?" Hazelton said. He waved them into a small conference room. A younger man dressed in a dark gray suit entered and shut the door.

"The lead investigator of spooky happenings on a show called Ghost Team USA," LaShaun started.

"My wife loves that show," the younger man said. He shrugged when Hazelton sighed. "Sorry, but it's kind of popular. I'm Josh Labadie by the way, assistant DA."

He grinned at them and nodded. His honey blonde

all-American-boy-next door good looks contrasted with Hazelton's dark, somber facade.

"Nice to meet you," LaShaun said. He seemed less keyed up, and more accessible than his boss. Yet she also sensed he used his charm as a weapon to disarm. "So why am I here gentlemen?"

"Right to the point, eh? I like it," Labadie said, the good-humor radiating from him.

"Emanuel Young's new lawyers intend to argue that his grandfather or someone in his grandfather's gang did the killings," Hazelton said, just as direct.

"They haven't come out and said as much, but based on comments they've made so far..." Josh added and looked to his boss.

"That's where they're headed. Neal Montgomery is one of the top defense attorneys in this state, in the country even. He teaches part-time at Tulane Law School and started the True Justice Project. He selects six students from the top two percent of the class." Hazelton's dark eyebrows went up. "And that's saying something, because all the students at Tulane are top notch."

"Full disclosure, sir. You're a Tulane alum," Josh quipped. "I'm from LSU. We hold our own."

Hazelton's grave expression cracked for a second when one corner of his mouth lifted. Then he grew serious again. "Back to the reason you're here, Ms. Rousselle. Montgomery has you on a list of potential witnesses. I know you visited Young at the forensic facility twice. Tell me what you discussed."

LaShaun glanced at Chase. His dark Cajun eyes gave no clue as he sat across from her. Still, she felt a wave of protectiveness from him. The DA and his assistant glanced between them as though trying to read body language.

"Your exchange isn't covered by any kind of professional privilege," Josh said quietly. When Chase shot a sharp look at him, the young attorney cleared his throat. "In case you're wondering."

"I know that, and I want to help. I sure don't think Manny should be out, or even in a minimum security setting," LaShaun replied with a frown.

"How did you know that he's..." Josh's voice trailed off. He turned to his boss.

Hazelton continued to gaze steadily at LaShaun. "Ms. Rousselle?"

"We didn't talk about his conviction. Mostly we talked about his family, a little about his childhood. I'm surprised he would go for an appeal. He mentioned that he knew the evidence against him was solid. He even implied that he needed to be locked up." LaShaun shook her head. "Then there's the other side of him."

Hazelton sat forward on the edge of his chair. "Tell me more."

LaShaun thought back to the lightening quick change Manny could make. She switched off from her surroundings as she relived sitting across from the serial killer. "Manny can be charming, even look totally harmless. But he's a cunning, ruthless predator. He enjoys the physical sensation of overpowering his victim. Emotionally he feeds off their struggle to survive, like a psychic vampire. Manny even likes the taste of his victims."

"He's a cannibal?" Josh asked, eyes wide with repulsion.

"No, not eating their raw flesh, though I suspect he bit several of them. He likes licking their sweat. The flavor excites him sexually." LaShaun's stomach lurched as she pushed against making a telepathic connection to the monster. Her skin tingled and itched so intensely that she rubbed her arms hard. "I don't think bringing Manny outside for court is a good idea. At all. He's a master manipulator."

"Baby, calm down. Manny ain't even in the parish. I promise you," Chase said quickly and put an arm around the back of her chair as he moved closer.

"He's at Feliciana Forensic Hospital, ma'am," Hazelton said.

"But he's been watching the hearing using video conference equipment we set up," Josh added. "His attorney insisted. Look, is it true he's got some kind of paranormal abilities?"

"We're not going down that mumbo jumbo path," Hazelton clipped back before LaShaun could react. "I don't give a damn what some crew of boogey-man chasers say. Manny is a sadistic killer. Human evil exists. I've seen enough of it to know."

"We don't want to sensationalize this case anymore than it's already going to be. Manny lured his victims in and murdered them. Plain and simple," Chase added in his deep, firm voice as he gazed at the assistant DA.

"Sure. I was just asking," Josh replied and sat back in his chair. He avoided the stony look from his boss. "So, any clues from his childhood with Orin Young?"

"Manny was abused physically and emotionally by his father," LaShaun replied carefully.

Josh flipped open a soft leather briefcase and took out a folder. "Ethan Young disappeared years ago. He had an arrest history, mostly drugs. But he did have a couple of simple battery charges."

"Orin Young was just as vicious to his family as he was to the strangers he killed," LaShaun said with force.

Her rage at the agony one man inflicted flooded her veins like fire. She slapped the surface of the table.

"Damn," Josh mumbled and blinked at his boss.

"Look, we're pretty sure Manny's legal team is going to say he was abused. They're more than likely also going to say he was controlled by his grandfather and his father," Hazelton said.

Josh glanced at his smart phone. "We've got about five minutes left of this break."

"Did Manny mention his grandfather or his father leading him to become a killer? Was Orin or Ethan Young with Manny when he killed any victims?" Hazelton said, getting to the point.

LaShaun glanced at Chase and then back at Hazelton. "Manny never mentioned them being together."

"Which doesn't mean they weren't," Hazelton answered and stared at her hard as though willing her to remember more.

LaShaun shook her head. "But he didn't talk to me about the murders."

"Okay then. That's good." Hazelton stood and smoothed down his dark green silk tie. He buttoned the deep blue jacket of his suit and nodded to his assistant. Josh rose and hastily stuffed the folder back into his briefcase. Chase and LaShaun stood as well.

LaShaun looked at Hazelton in surprise. "Really?"

"Yeah. Manny's lawyers are probably hoping you can tell a gruesome tale of how Orin forced his poor grandson to witness a bloodbath," Chase answered for the two prosecutors.

"Deputy Broussard has been down this road before," Hazelton said with a tight smile.

"Nothing pisses me off more than the 'Poor me'

defense," Chase grumbled.

"Manny's sister told me Ethan and Orin beat him when he was a kid. He suffered psychological abuse as well." LaShaun stopped short of saying how learning he was a product of incest had twisted Manny's mind even more.

"More reason he needs to stay locked up. That makes him less likely to respond to short-term therapy," Josh put in.

"Which makes him a threat to public safety; that fact along with the physical evidence linking him to the murders means the jury got it right the first time. The death penalty was made for guys like Emanuel Young," Hazelton said.

"Sounds like you've got your closing argument half-way finished," Chase said with a half grin.

"Just about," Hazelton answered. "Judge Barrow is known to lean toward extenuating circumstances and the bad childhood argument."

"Crap, Patricia Barrow is your judge?" Chase rubbed his forehead.

"What's wrong?" LaShaun asked and tapped Chase's arm.

"Judge Patricia Barrow isn't exactly a fan of law enforcement procedures. She views some of our routine practices as going over the line to trap suspects." Chase scowled as he spoke.

"I wouldn't go that far," Josh said. "Judge Barrow has handed down her share of convictions in bench trials."

"Mostly in trials of misdemeanor cases though. She also thinks the system is stacked against minority defendants." Hazelton shook his head.

"I happen to agree with her," LaShaun said more

sharply than she probably should have. "And more than a few studies back that up." The three men grew quiet for several seconds. A knock on the door broke the silence.

A court deputy stuck his head in the door. "Court is about to be called back in session, guys."

"Thanks." Hazelton nodded at him. "Well, the issue of bias on the basis of race won't come up with Manny anyway. That's something. Look, Ms. Rousselle, I realize you came to feel a certain empathy with his family, maybe even for him."

"I know exactly who and what Manny is, Mr. Hazelton." LaShaun spoke calmly as they walked out of the old court building and toward the more modern version. "He needs to stay in a secure setting for a long, long time."

"LaShaun doesn't have any ammunition that's going to blow apart the case against Manny," Chase said.

"What about you, Deputy Broussard?" Hazelton shot back. "You were at those interviews, and you brought in Orin Young."

"And the rest of his gang, too," Josh added with a serious expression on his fresh, young face.

Chase grunted. "His lawyers sure as hell won't get any traction from anything I have to say. Manny may be nuts, but he knew exactly what he was doing; same goes for his granddaddy. They killed because they liked it. Nothing supernatural about that."

They reached the entrance to the courthouse. Another court deputy checked LaShaun's purse. He also made sure Chase wasn't carrying his service hand gun before he let them go to Court Room B. More than three dozen spectators were seated on the two rows of long wooden benches. LaShaun guessed at least a third of those were reporters. Hazelton and his assistant strode down the center aisle and took their places at a table. The court officials were separated from the audience section by a three-foot-tall solid wood gate with little swinging doors at both ends. A tall man with jet black hair stood talking to a woman.

"That's Neal Montgomery." Chase was about to go on when he let out a hiss. "Oh hell, look who's here."

James Schaffer waved to LaShaun when she glanced around. She ignored him and went back to studying Neal Montgomery. He stood at least six feet tall. His skin had the olive tone that implied he had Italian ancestry mixed in with the Irish, but it was his intense violet blue eyes that made Montgomery stand out. Suddenly, he turned from talking to the woman next to him. He gazed directly at LaShaun without looking around at anyone else. He smiled and nodded a greeting to her as though they'd met. LaShaun's heart beat fast. Something was wrong.

"You know the guy?" Chase asked with a frown.

"Never met him before," LaShaun said.

"Well I already don't like him," Chase muttered and stared back at Montgomery. The tall man gave a nod and went back to his conversation. "What the hell was that about?"

"I have a feeling Mr. Montgomery knows all about us right down to the size of our shoes," LaShaun whispered.

The police officer on duty pointed them to a bench close to the front that had space that he'd reserved, right behind the prosecution table. "Y'all come up to this front bench. How you doin', Sheriff Broussard?"

Chase gave him a collegial clap on the shoulder. "Not yet, but keep a good thought on that, Danny. This is my fiancée."

"Nice to meet you, ma'am." The man gave a respectful nod then went back to his duties. He studied the audience before going back to stand against the wall to the right of the judge's bench.

LaShaun sat next to Chase. She waited to see if Montgomery would look at her again. She intended to do her own research about the striking man. He gave off a different kind of aura than she'd expected. Yet LaShaun couldn't quite put her finger on what it was or why it felt so odd.

Chase leaned close and spoke softly. "You got a funny feeling about Manny's lawyer. I can tell."

"Yes, but..." LaShaun sighed. "Maybe it's nothing. Some people are so strong-willed they affect me that way. It doesn't happen often though."

"So did I knock you back a few steps?" Chase grinned at her.

"Yes, you did, Deputy Broussard. And in a very good way," LaShaun quipped with a grin. Before she or Chase could continue flirting, the bailiff's voice broke in.

"All rise. Court is now in session. The Honorable Patricia Robertson Barrow," Danny boomed.

"Thank you, officer. You may be seated," Judge Barrow said without looking at the audience after she sat down. "Mr. Montgomery, the court has taken your request for a new trial into consideration. I find no evidence to suggest the first conviction would have been different had the jury known about Mr. Young's history of childhood abuse. Further, none of the facts surrounding the investigation of his grandfather's crimes show evidence that Orin Young committed these crimes. Therefore, your request for a new trial is denied."

"Yes!" Josh blurted out. He winced when the judge glared at him.

"Your honor, we wanted to question a witness. Ms. Rousselle might have shed some light on the entire facts surrounding the murders Mr. Young's grandfather is alleged to have committed. At the very least he seems to have instigated them. Those would constitute mitigating circumstances that might change his death sentence, or support the need for a new trial."

"Mr. Montgomery, I read your arguments and your petition. According to the records, Mr. Emanuel Young never implicated his grandfather. Mr. Orin Young never confessed to the earlier string of murders. Request for a new trial denied," Judge Barrow spoke sharply as though her patience was being sorely tested. She banged her gavel as a symbolic and emphatic end to Montgomery's attempts to debate.

The audience in the courtroom set up a growing buzz of conversation. The officer on duty firmly invited people to find the nearest exit or keep quiet. His expression clearly communicated he'd help them find the doors if they didn't comply. Chase gave him a wave. He and LaShaun followed the two prosecutors out through a side door and into a side hallway.

"Put one in the win column for the good guys," Chase said and gave a sigh of relief.

Hazelton tucked a large expanding folder under his right arm. "Judge Barrow surprised me."

"Surprised? I about broke my jaw when it hit the floor," Josh put in.

"I'm just happy LaShaun didn't have to testify," Chase said. His relaxed smile was back.

LaShaun started to answer him when Montgomery pushed through the doors. His female colleague came right behind him. She had dark red hair that contrasted with her strikingly pale skin. She followed Montgomery's gaze and studied LaShaun. The woman nodded at LaShaun before they strode off, hand in hand. Both seemed to say they would meet again on their terms.

"This issue isn't over," LaShaun said, her voice cutting off the conversation between Chase and the two men.

"Sure. It's routine for lawyers to file an appeal, but we have a solid argument, especially if even liberal Judge Barrow didn't buy their attempt at a new trial," Hazelton replied with confidence.

"Yes, and the important thing is Manny will stay locked up for years while they fight a losing battle," Josh added.

"Even more good news," Chase said. Still he glanced at LaShaun. "You okay?"

"Yeah."

LaShaun watched the handsome couple stride down the hallway and turn a corner. Both left behind traces of their strong auras, two powerful personalities not easily discouraged from a path once chosen. Their efforts on Manny's behalf weren't over. LaShaun somehow sensed that it went beyond the court case.

"This isn't over," she repeated softly.

Chapter 5

Two days later, LaShaun sat in the den off her large kitchen enjoying a second cup of strong Louisiana coffee. In her lap was a book of legends, but the morning news had distracted her. The election campaign had turned hectic. Between his duties as a chief investigator and visiting with civic groups, LaShaun had not seen Chase since they'd been in court. All she'd had of his time were a few telephone conversations and one video chat. For a mostly rural parish with a relatively small population, folks in Vermilion Parish seemed up to a lot of no-good deeds lately. LaShaun tried not to believe there was more to it than the usual rowdy, randy and stupid human nature.

Chase's opponent hardly let a chance slip by to mention the latest crime wave, and hint that a lack of proper leadership was the problem. Dave Godchaux was giving an interview to the leggy blonde host of a local television morning show. This was his third appearance in the last five months. Supposedly, Godchaux was there to talk about a Knights of Columbus pancake breakfast fundraiser. LaShaun frowned at the TV screen when good old Dave talked about the importance of good family values.

"We believe that our program to mentor young men has an affect not only on their lives, but on the lives of others. We save one young man, and quite possibly we save someone from becoming the victim of a crime."

"So true, Deputy Godchaux," the host said. Then she beamed at the camera. "Once again, the breakfast

73

will be held on March 22nd at the Our Lady of Lourdes Recreational Center. For information on tickets call the number on our screen."

"That's right, folks. Come out and help us help our community," Dave intoned. He gave off the right mixture of caring and determination to do good works.

"On to a less pleasant topic, tell us about the crime statistics in Vermilion Parish. I hear that we've had a slight decrease in burglaries, but a sharp increase in murders." The blonde tried to look like a tough journalist and failed. Maybe it was because she spent most of her time interviewing garden club members about roses and giggling over cute pet videos.

Dave's expression grew somber. "Sadly we've experienced a string of brutal crimes. The good people of this parish can rest assured that your Sheriff's Department is ready to respond and protect our citizens. We could use more resources, which is why I've helped our legislative delegation draft several bills that help tighten certain laws."

LaShaun tapped a button and switched to another station. "Stick a pancake in it, Dave."

When the doorbell rang, LaShaun went to her front door. LaShaun gazed through the peephole. She didn't recognize the nut brown woman standing on her porch. The woman glanced around as though examining her surroundings. When LaShaun swung open the front door, but not the storm door the woman jumped. Only then did LaShaun see the man standing beside her.

"Ms. Rousselle, I'm Candy Wilkinson from WFTK Television in Lafayette. I'd like to talk to you about..."

"I didn't invite you here, so please leave my property. Now." LaShaun crossed her arms and gazed at them through the glass top half of the storm door. The young man raised a compact video camera with a microphone attached in one hand. "And you don't have permission to take my picture."

The young man wore a grin. "Don't need it."

LaShaun shut the door. She would have favored them a long list of colorful words, but LaShaun didn't want the little creep to be rewarded with audio they could use. After ten minutes LaShaun heard the rumble of a car engine. She looked out the window in time to see a dark red Chevy Traverse back up, turn around, and head down her driveway.

"Better not come back either," LaShaun muttered as she watched the car disappear.

Determined not to let them rule or ruin her plans, LaShaun went out to the garden and fertilized the three beds of roses her grandmother had planted some thirty years before. As usual, being out in the sunshine and surrounded by the lovely Louisiana countryside improved LaShaun's mood. Two hours later she'd not only finished with the roses, but she completed a few indoor chores as well. By eleven thirty, LaShaun participated in a video conference with her accountant about the assets and investments her grandmother had left her. The accountant had LaShaun's attorney, and friend, Savannah Honoré join them online. Savannah delivered the unwelcome news that LaShaun did indeed have to attend the board meetings of three local companies.

"We'll need to talk later," Savannah said from her office in Beau Chene.

"Why? I mean, it'll be boring, but I'll do it. The rest of the family will squeal like little piglets if they even think the money faucet will turn off." LaShaun said.

She let out a humorless laugh as she gazed at her

business advisors through the webcam. Monmon Odette had not only left LaShaun a substantial legacy, but did her the favor of leaving her in charge of doling out profits to her aunt and uncles. Calling it a thankless job was a laughable understatement. Monmon Odette's children had fully expected to spend time fighting each other for control of her money. They constantly complained about "going to LaShaun hat-in-hand" for what was rightfully theirs. Never mind that they got enough money to fund their expensive tastes and those of their greedy adult children.

Savannah raised an eyebrow. "Quentin Trosclair is also a major shareholder in Southwest Louisiana Bancorp. He's started attending the quarterly meetings."

"When the hell did that happen?" LaShaun blurted out.

Quentin Trosclair, LaShaun's former lover during her wild days, was once again bad news. The man had gotten her involved in two murders, and suspected of being the killer in both cases. Rich, handsome, and used to getting his way, Quentin had escaped paying for his sins too many times. Now it seemed Quentin had turned up to poison her life once more. LaShaun thought back to what her cousin Azalei had told her. Quentin wanted to get back at LaShaun, and most likely hurt Chase as icing on the cake. Despicable weasel, she thought darkly. LaShaun would just have to spoil his payback party. The accountant's monotone voice broke into her daydream of slapping Quentin around.

"His uncle died, and the uncle's daughter sold her shares to Quentin. He knows you're likely to attend the meeting. I don't see a problem," Clarence Baker, the accountant, blinked through his black-framed eyeglasses. "Let's see, Katherine Trosclair Worthington did sell her shares to her cousins. They haven't taken an active role in the company, not since her father became too ill to travel fifteen years ago. The Trosclairs have managed two hugely successful businesses for three generations at least. I can only see them becoming majority stockholders as a good thing."

"I don't like the sound of that one damn bit, Clarence," LaShaun said sharply. She looked at Savannah. "What can we do about it?"

"You could sell your shares and cut ties with the company," Clarence said promptly. "I wouldn't advise it. Word on the street is Quentin is courting Mrs. Veronique Delacroix."

Savannah glanced at LaShaun. "She owns fifteen percent of stock in the company. He wants her to sell, to him of course."

"Typical Quentin strategy then," LaShaun retorted. "Charm her into bed because she's of use to him."

Clarence looked embarrassed. "I don't usually listen to gossip unless it relates to business, but the talk is they're having an affair."

"What about his second wife? Or is she his third? Hell, I can't keep up," Savannah said.

"Being married doesn't stop Quentin from seeing other people," LaShaun quipped.

"He'll own a big part of a company you have an interest in if his plan succeeds. If there's history between you two, some bad blood... That could be a problem." Clarence rubbed his chin and blinked behind his eyeglasses. "Of course you could have me attend as a proxy. I have business in Houston, so it wouldn't be a problem at all."

"Skip it, just sell the damn stock. I'll invest in

something else," LaShaun said. She wanted no connection with Quentin Trosclair, not even a remote one.

"I'll look into it and get back to you. Goodbye, ladies." Clarence gave a nod and signed off as though eager to get to other business.

Savannah remained online. "How are you doing?"

"Missing Chase, and ticked off that a reporter showed up on my porch this morning. I hope that's not a trend. Could I get away with shooting one of 'em? Well, shoot at them. That should put the word out not to come on my property." LaShaun said.

"Hell to the double hell no. But on private property, they do have to leave when you ask them to."

"Okay, let me put a reminder in my smartphone; don't shoot the damn reporters. At least until after Chase is elected Sheriff." LaShaun laughed out loud when Savannah rolled her eyes.

"I'm not going to be your lawyer in a criminal matter again, LaShaun. So stay out of trouble. I have an appointment in twenty minutes and I need to prepare."

"Let's do lunch next week sometime if you have a break in your schedule," LaShaun said. The friends agreed to firm up meeting on Tuesday and signed off just as LaShaun's doorbell rang again. "That reporter is about to test my self-control."

LaShaun marched to the door and yanked it open. Instead of the reporter, a tall slender blonde stood on her front porch. She wore a yellow sweater twin set and brown tweed skirt. Pearl stud earrings completed the wholesome look. The conservative outfit didn't disguise a great figure. Her only indulgence seemed to be her hair, which she still wore long as she probably had when she was in high school and college.

"I'm Allison Graham," she blurted out and blushed a deep pink.

"Hello Mrs. Graham," LaShaun said.

"Good morning. Well, it's almost afternoon now, isn't it? I'm sorry for showing up here without calling, but it's so hard for me to get away. I mean I'm so busy these days, and I just wanted to..." Her voice trailed off and she looked around at the azaleas and rose bushes. "You have a beautiful yard."

"Thank you. Mrs. Graham, I--"

"Call me Allison. The police and district attorney say that over and over when they call. 'Mrs. Graham' this and 'Mrs. Graham' that. My husband is no help. He seems to think this is some passing phase and he just won't listen. He's as bad as Greg, and what about Sherri? That's my ten year old. And..." Allison burst into tears. She cried so hard her body shook.

LaShaun quickly unlocked the storm door and opened it. "Mrs. Grah-- Allison, you need to calm down."

"I can't do this anymore. I-I just can't," Allison wailed and covered her face with both hands.

"Come in so we can talk. I'm sure it can't be that bad."

LaShaun gazed at her in dismay and wished Savannah was there to help. LaShaun had no skill dealing with emotionally over-wrought soccer moms. Not even those who suspected one of their kids was possessed by Satan. She led the weeping woman into her living room and sat her down on the sofa. Allison continued to cry, though not as loudly. Fumbling with her purse, she finally managed to find a few tissues, but those became a sodden mess in no time. After a few seconds of patting her shoulder, LaShaun tossed out the gentle approach. She went to her bedroom and came back quickly with a box of tissues. LaShaun snatched a wad from the box and handed them to her.

"Allison, snap out of it," LaShaun said sharply. "Falling apart won't help you or your family. If your son is out of control and your husband is out of touch they need you more than ever."

After a series of rapid gasps for air, Allison nodded. She dropped her purse on the floor and put a hand to her throat. Her mouth worked as though she wanted to speak but couldn't. LaShaun went to the kitchen, filled a glass of water and came back in a matter of seconds. She sat next to Allison and handed it to her.

"Thanks," Allison said in a scratchy voice. She sipped the water. After a few seconds more she put the glass down on the coffee table. "I'm sorry for getting hysterical like that. I've been on edge for so long it just... came out."

"You've been through hell," LaShaun said quietly.

"I'm still there. To my husband's family appearance is everything. I mean look at me. I'm the picture of a wholesome small town wife with a perfect small town family. I even dress like a clone mass produced from a factory." Allison wore a grimace of distaste as she glanced down at her skirt and blouse. "Sometimes I think there's a label somewhere on my body that says, 'white female, blonde, model number 81WF'."

"Are you okay?" LaShaun eyed her closely for signs of more hysterics.

Allison stared at LaShaun wide-eyed. "Lord, I can't believe I'm talking to you like this. Are you psychic like they say, you know, have special powers?"

"Sometimes it's easier to talk to strangers, and you've pent up your feelings for weeks."

Allison gave a bitter laugh. "No, for years. I thought Jonathan and I were holding it together well enough. Our marriage is... problematic. I suppose it was foolish to think the kids wouldn't notice."

LaShaun felt a flush of heat on the back of her neck. Her arms tingled. She could clearly "see" the true picture of what those few words meant. The Graham's "problematic marriage" meant both had had several affairs over the years. Harsh accusations, shouting matches and slamming doors played out like a weird stage play inside LaShaun's head. Allison startled her back to the parlor and the present by touching her hand.

"I've tried taking Greg to several therapists over the last two years. He won't talk to them. Now they're saying he killed that boy Elliot and he raped Rebecca. It's all lies of course," Allison's protest sounded mechanical, rehearsed even. She twisted the tissue in her hands to pieces.

"Greg has been keeping secrets from you, getting in trouble at school. Do you believe he's innocent?" LaShaun cut her off with the second question when Allison opened her mouth to speak.

A tear slid down Allison's face. "I didn't want to get pregnant. Jonathan kept at me until I gave in. I wanted to consider having a baby, but after I finished college. Greg was an irritable baby, and I'm afraid I wasn't very patient. I never hurt him," she added quickly and glanced at LaShaun.

"Go on," LaShaun said.

"He always pulled in the opposite direction on everything. Always rebelled on anything I tried to do for him. It was like he knew I didn't want a baby. That made me feel even more guilty."

LaShaun studied her for a time. "You indulged him."

"Yes, but not as much as Jonathan. He loves having a son, a little mini-Jonathan. Greg looks a lot like his father." Allison shrugged as if that was a mystery to her.

"I think Greg looks a lot like you."

Allison smiled. "When he was five, I realized how much I loved that boy. I guess our battles kind of drew me to him. Greg likes to go his own way no matter what anyone else says. He didn't get that kind of independence from me, I can tell you that."

"So what do you want from me?" LaShaun asked.

"I'd like you to talk to Greg. He's willing," Allison said quickly when LaShaun frowned.

"What does your husband say about it?" LaShaun waited. She knew the answer when Allison glanced away.

"We'll tell him later maybe."

LaShaun looked through a window at the expanse of freshly mown grass of her front yard. Beyond a set of three magnolia trees she could see a car or two drive past on Rougon Road. The Graham family seemed a potent mix of pent up emotions, and none of them healthy. LaShaun knew what Chase would say. Stay out of it, especially because of the criminal investigation. When LaShaun turned around, Allison looked at her expectantly.

"No, Mrs. Graham. I won't talk to Greg. I'm sure your son's lawyer advises against it. My fiancé is a police officer investigating the case. I can't promise confidentiality or anything close to it."

"You talk it over with Deputy Broussard. With our help he could break the case, and get elected. Our family has a wide circle of influential friends. Some other person is responsible." Allison Graham's voice lost its trembling weepy quality. The tortured mother seemed to be replaced by a cold realist, one more than willing to point the finger at someone else.

"I'm sure the Sheriff's Department intends to follow wherever the evidence leads," LaShaun replied quietly.

"Thanks for your time." Allison Graham gave her a controlled smile and walked out.

Surprised at the odd twists and turns of the woman's behavior, LaShaun followed her to the front door. She watched Allison walk to her tan Volvo SUV and get in. She turned the vehicle around and drove off. LaShaun shook her head and went back inside. For hours later, she replayed the odd conversation in her mind.

At eight o'clock that night, Chase called to say he'd be at LaShaun's house in twenty minutes. LaShaun smiled when she ended the call and hummed a love song. She got busy. The late February weather had continued to be cold and damp. She took out a container of catfish couvillion she'd made earlier that day, one of Chase's favorite dishes. After she put rice in the steamer, LaShaun sliced up a half loaf of French bread. Soon she had Zydeco playing on the sound system and the house smelling of the savory dish. Chase arrived an hour later. He'd pulled his truck down the driveway to the back yard and came through the kitchen door using his key.

"Hey, cher. Don't shoot, it's me," he called out as he hung his brown felt cowboy hat on a peg near the door.

LaShaun crossed from the stove quickly and wrapped her arms around him. She ruffled his dark hair and gave him a long, passionate kiss. When they came up for air finally, both sighed. "I'm so happy to see you."

"Well, damn, if I'm gonna get this reception, maybe

I better stay away more often," Chase said and claimed another quick kiss.

"Don't you dare," LaShaun replied with a scowl. "Missing you is a miserable feeling, even if I know you're only a few miles away. Now get comfortable so we can forget the rest of the world exists outside these walls. I'll fix you a plate.

"Yes, ma'am," he said with a grin. Chase gave her bottom a pat and walked past the stove, but doubled back. He lifted the pot. "Hmm, my favorite. You're spoiling me, girl."

"Yes, and get used to it," LaShaun quipped and winked at him.

Her reward was the wonderful sound of his deep, rumbling laughter as he continued on to the master bedroom. Moments later she heard him singing off key in the shower. LaShaun smiled with affection. Soon she'd be able to hear that lovably discordant music more often. The thought of their wedding brought on a flash of jitters. Katie and Adrianna had already scheduled another preparation session... As though LaShaun's thought had reached out to her, the phone rang and it was Katie. Chase's sister briskly ran through their agenda for Friday. Then she dropped a hint about where Chase and LaShaun would live later on. LaShaun managed to distract her by changing the subject back to the reception, urging Katie to follow-up with the bed and breakfast again.

"Yes, Katie. I promise I won't skip out on you this time. I've been looking at the catalogs you left from the florist. I'll give you my choices Friday." LaShaun rolled her eyes and pointed to the cordless phone when Chase came back into the kitchen. "You're brother is here. Say hi."

He took the phone with a comedic grimace. "Hey, baby sis. How ya doin'? Oh yeah, you whipping the bride into shape, huh? Keeping her on task. Good job."

LaShaun turned from spooning rice onto a plate and hissed at him. "Hey!"

Chase laughed. "Yeah, LaShaun is giving me a dirty look. Okay. Tell Dale I said hey, and kiss my baby nephew and my niece for me. Bye."

LaShaun finished filling both plates and put them on the table. She turned to face Chase. "I'm thinking we need to skip the wedding and just get married."

"Okay, baby." Chase nuzzled her neck. Her words became muffled as his lips grazed the line of her chin.

"I sorta let Savannah, Adrianna, and Katie talk me into making it fancy." LaShaun rubbed his shoulders as she tilted her head. She pressed against him and sighed. "We're already like one soul and body."

Chase tugged her long sleeved dark red t-shirt over her head. "Uh-huh."

He clearly wasn't paying attention to her complaints. In seconds he peeled off her lacy bra. Chase kissed her so deliciously hard that LaShaun forgot everything else as well. By the time he'd taken off his shirt, she felt hungrier for him than anything she'd cooked for supper. Chase pulled her to the sofa in the open den adjacent to the kitchen. He removed her soft yoga pants and moaned at the sight of the pink lace panties she wore. In minutes his clothes were off. LaShaun pushed him down to a seated position and straddled him. Slowly, still kissing him, she moaned as he filled her. They both shuddered at the flash fire of being physically united.

"Are you through working tonight?" She whispered and wiggled her hips until he gasped her name twice.

"I... I gotta go back," he managed to get out before licking one of her nipples before taking it into his mouth. Then he moaned, "Yes."

LaShaun gasped a few times before she could speak. "Then we better make this a quickie.

Chase rested his head against the sofa back. "Do it."

LaShaun rode him wildly, pausing to tease him with him kisses until he moaned for her to move again. Up and down, she savored the sensation of being in control. She ignored his pleas for her to go faster at one point. Going slow drove her to the point of madness. Nothing else mattered as waves of pleasure ruled them. When he was finally able to speak, Chase let out a long hissing breath.

"This is the best work break I've ever had," Chase mumbled.

"I'll take that as a compliment," LaShaun quipped. She got up from his lap and motioned for him to follow her. "Let's take a quick shower. We're gonna have to heat that food up again."

"I doubt it cooled off with the fire we had goin' in here," Chase joked with a grin.

They teased each other, enjoying the happiness of being in love. Twenty minutes later they were dressed and back in the kitchen. Chase wore a pair of sweat pants and t-shirt as he devoured the plate of food.

"This is what I call home. Loving on my soon-to-be wife and eating some down home cooking. I'm ready to catch me some bad guys and call it a day." Chase winked at her.

LaShaun laughed as she rose from the table. "You're feeling mighty powerful."

"Did you really mean it about no wedding, honey?" Chase looked at her, his long legs stretched out.

"Actually, yeah. We could switch gears without too much trouble." LaShaun shrugged and started washing the few dishes. She liked doing it by hand even though she had a high tech dishwasher.

"Sure. I guess Jessi won't mind not being a flower girl. Katie will get over not watching her big brother get married. The people who love us will survive not watching us vow before God to be together forever..."

LaShaun spun around to face him, suds flying from her hands. "Stop already. I get it. I didn't realize you were so romantic about the ceremony."

"At first I thought, who needs it? But then I saw how happy it made Jessi, my sisters, and you. Oh, no," Chase said and pointed a finger at her. "Don't tell me you weren't enjoying the whole idea of your special day dressed like a princess."

"It's our special day," LaShaun replied softly and walked back to him. "I love you."

"And I love you. Will you marry me?" Chase pressed his face against the cotton fabric of her pink t-shirt.

"I seem to recall you already asked and I answered." She kissed the mass of dark softly curled hair on top of his head.

"Say it again so I'll know it's not a dream," he replied and looked up at her.

"Yes," LaShaun said.

"The wedding is on? I don't want to be the one who has to tell my niece she won't get dressed up and toss rose petals. Uh-uh. Not to mention my sisters and Adrianna." Chase affected a shudder of fear.

"We're going through with this production because you're scared of the Broussard females?" LaShaun burst out laughing.

"Damn right," Chase replied promptly. He was

about to say more when his cell phone played a Cajun two-step tune. He crossed the kitchen to retrieve it from the counter top. He glanced at the display and answered. "Yeah, boss."

LaShaun continued cleaning up the meal. By the time she'd scrubbed the cast iron pots clean of rice and catfish couvillion, Chase had hung up. She smiled at him, but his serious expression chilled the moment of loving warmth still in the kitchen.

"What's happened?" LaShaun asked.

"Becky, girl that was with Greg, has disappeared. Her mother is down at the station pretty much out of her mind with worry. I could hear her screaming while M.J. was talking to me."

LaShaun stood rooted to the floor as waves of terror crashed into her. "She slipped away to meet Greg tonight, Chase."

Chase froze in the act of pulling on his favorite old scuffed leather work boots. "You know where they are right now?"

LaShaun closed her eyes. She swayed for a few seconds. "Resurrection fern," she whispered.

Chapter 6

Moonlight barely touched the darkness of the early morning hours. LaShaun walked slowly through the woods. She watched every movement of the leaves and tuned into the sounds. They had arrived at the scene around midnight. Chase, M.J. and other deputies had spread out in the opposite direction. After two hours, they'd been too busy to notice that LaShaun had headed north. The scent of wet foliage tugged her to Blood River. Birds and squirrels scrambled through the trees or scurried in the thick shrubs. LaShaun heard plenty of sounds, but none of it connected to a human. Her cell phone hummed against her hip. She pulled it out of her jeans pocket and glanced down. Chase had texted "where r u?????" LaShaun paused to answer him so he wouldn't worry. "i'm ok knife and gun with me."

LaShaun had taken time to get her favorite weapons. The denim jacket she wore had three inside pockets. She'd sewn them just the right size. One long one held the sterling silver knife she inherited from an ancestor. In the other pocket was the small derringer pistol loaded with silver bullets. They would kill human or demon if the need arose. LaShaun wasn't sure which one she might face in the shadows that moved between sunset and dawn.

Most folks assumed demons and spirits only did their dirty work in the dark. Big mistake. The most powerful supernatural forces could move at any time, though darkness did appeal to them more. LaShaun sensed that the missing teenage girl had no clue about the danger she was in. Like most parents, Becky's

89

mother and father blamed "hanging with a bad crowd." They chose to ignore one fact, Becky had seemed more than willing to follow where Greg and the others led.

LaShaun's cell phone hummed again insistently, but she ignored it. She saw ahead with her third eye. LaShaun walked quickly through the brush without making a lot of noise. She wasn't worried that Becky would hear her and bolt. In her vision, LaShaun could see that the girl was preoccupied. Unlike what most people thought, having paranormal abilities didn't mean all was revealed; or even if revealed that LaShaun would understand what she saw. LaShaun moved cautiously since she didn't know if Becky was alone.

Moments later LaShaun arrived at a huge oak tree. Massive branches as thick as trunks of other smaller trees curved to the ground. Spanish moss draped several branches farther up. Resurrection Fern grew along others. Humming an odd discordant tune, Becky sat on the grass brushing her fingers through the greenery. Her voice would rise high and then dip into hissing. LaShaun stepped behind another large oak tree and listened for a few moments. Her cell phone buzzed again, vibrating insistently as though to communicate Chase's agitation that she wouldn't answer. So she did. A short text, "found her". He texted back that he would follow the GPS tracking app on her phone. LaShaun slid her phone back into her pocket and started to show herself but paused. Becky had stopped humming. A breeze picked up, but only seemed to center around the tree where LaShaun stood. Then she heard a whispering voice near her ear.

"I have returned. This girl and others are mine. These young ones are quite a delight. Why not join us?" the voice said.

The last word was drawn out to a long hissing sound that grew louder. The familiarity of the lilting male voice sent a jolt through LaShaun like dozens of electrified needles. She strode quickly toward the still seated teenager. Becky had a serene yet vacant expression on her smooth young face.

"Rebecca Saucier, you stand up right now young lady. You've put your family through a horrible night of worry," LaShaun said sharply. The hissing sound intensified as though a nest of giant snakes had arrived.

Becky blinked a few times as though she had trouble focusing. Then she slowly looked around until her gaze found LaShaun. She smiled. "Don't be ridiculous. There was no need for them to worry. Besides, what I do is none of their damned business."

"You're going home now," LaShaun barked at her. "You're going to listen to me, and you're going to listen to your parents from now on."

Becky, still smiling, stood. The lovely white dress she wore had leaves and a small twig stuck to the lace hem. She put her hands behind her back. "Fine, but only because I'm ready to leave anyway. I'll come back here whenever I want to. No one can stop me."

LaShaun examined the ground as she walked around Becky in a circle. Becky moved in a circle as well so that she always faced LaShaun. The girl showed no fear, not even a faint trace of anxiety. The white dress looked delicately beautiful, a style from a different era. She looked like a bride from the nineteenth century.

LaShaun took a step toward Becky. "Whatever they told you, whatever he told you is a lie." His promises come with a terrible price."

"I don't know what you're talking. You're just a crazy lady wandering around in the woods," Becky said in a musical childish tone.

"I know your name," LaShaun murmured and then stepped back.

"Who sent you?" Becky blurted out. The smile disappeared.

"Don't experiment with evil, Becky. At first it feels so good, right? You feel strong and free from everyone telling you what to do, when to do it, and how you should live. Then horrible things start to happen. Like your friend Elliot. He's dead." LaShaun recited a prayer Monmon Odette had taught her, the same prayer from a Rousselle family journal written in 1801.

"Elliot's not dead. Look up. That plant is brown and looks dead, doesn't it? Under the right conditions it comes back to life, green and vital." Becky pointed to a high thick branch of the oak tree. "Resurrection fern is what they call it. Water, that's all it takes because it's not really dead."

"You listen to me," LaShaun snapped and grabbed her arm. "Elliot was a human being, not a plant. He was your friend. His parents had his funeral three days ago. That's reality."

"No. No. You're the one full of lies." Becky shook her head.

"You don't think his mother wanted him to be alive? She had to see him lying in the hospital morgue. If she even thought he was still breathing, Mrs. Dubois would never have let the coroner..."

"Stop it," Becky shouted.

"Cut him up doing an autopsy," LaShaun continued fiercely.

"LaShaun, what's wrong?" Chase called out as he ran toward them.

"You'll pay for touching me, bitch," Becky spat at

LaShaun. Her hazel eyes seemed lit with the fire of her rage. "You don't know who you're fucking with. I'm chosen."

"You silly fool," LaShaun shouted back at her.

"Becky!" a woman yelled. "Becky, are you okay?"

"Ma'am, stop." A female deputy tried to pull the woman back. Mrs. Saucier moved faster. She brushed past Chase, making a wide arc around him so he couldn't stop her either.

"What the hell..." Chase shot forward and managed to grab the woman's checked flannel shirt and pull her back.

"This woman has my daughter. You should be manhandling her. That's my child she's attacking!" The woman shrieked and struggled to get free.

"Calm down," Chase replied in a steady voice. "LaShaun isn't trying to hurt your kid."

"Mama, she slapped me. She wants to hurt me," Becky wailed. "Help me, mama!"

"You let go of my child or I swear I'll..." Becky's mother fought against the hold Chase had on her.

Four more deputies arrived along with a tall dark-haired man. M.J. marched through the growing crowd and took in the scene before her. She looked at Mrs. Saucier. "LaShaun helped in the search. You need to settle down."

"Jody, stop it. Just stop," a dark-haired man said. Chase let her go only when the man was close enough to take his place. Mike Saucier put an arm around his wife's shoulders.

"That's the Rousselle woman, Mike. God only knows what she's gotten Becky into." Jody pointed a finger at LaShaun.

"Please, don't make things worse," Mike Saucier

said in a shaky voice. Still he grimaced when he looked at LaShaun.

Becky glared at LaShaun in triumph. She raised a hand to strike her and LaShaun shoved her back. The teenager fell to the ground in a melodramatic fashion with a shriek. She cried hard and curled into a ball. Her mother shouted profane threats toward LaShaun. Finally between M.J. and the other deputies, the Saucier family was hustled yards away. Deputy Dave Godchaux, Chase's election opponent, seemed able to get the parents to listen after a few minutes. LaShaun couldn't hear them, but Jody's dark glances shot in her direction said a lot. Mike Saucier finally helped herd his wife and daughter down the path toward the road a quarter of a mile away. After a moment Dave strode over to them. M.J. gave directions to a group of deputies to step carefully and look for any possible evidence. Three deputies began walking an arm's length apart, their heads down scanning the ground.

"Everybody move back but step carefully," M.J. said. "Just move away from this area. It's a long shot because we're not even sure which way she came."

"Don't know what we're lookin' for, Sheriff," a thin older deputy said in a thick Cajun accent. "Ain't no crime far as I see. That little gal run off on her own."

"Not much to see in the dark either," Chase put in.

Still they tried a preliminary search using the beams of their powerful flashlights. M.J. wiped sweat from her forehead with a bandanna. "All we need," she grumbled.

"I don't think getting your woman involved was a good idea, Broussard," Dave said gazing at Chase. His twin bushy black eyebrows went up.

"LaShaun is my fiancée," Chase snapped back.

Dave turned to M.J. "That Schaffer guy is in town, too. He's still sniffing around after Louisiana spooky stuff. I say we concentrate on real police work. Reporters will definitely make a big deal outta this."

"Right after you make a beeline to tell them," Chase muttered.

"Let's make sure Greg Graham wasn't involved," M.J. said quickly and shot a warning look at Chase.

"Is Becky his girlfriend? That would explain her slipping away to see him. Their parents were advised to keep them apart," LaShaun said.

"Why is she involved in this case? She shouldn't have knowledge that might be material to an on-going investigation." Dave shot a glance at Chase and then back to M.J. "I convinced the Sauciers not to discuss this incident with anybody. But reporters will be jumping for joy to find out the local voodoo woman is hooked up in another murder. I say we..."

Chase pointed a forefinger at Dave's nose. "If you insult LaShaun again I'll turn you upside down and use your head to dig a hole in the dirt."

LaShaun moved quickly to pull him away from Dave. His muscular bulk made that task impossible. She didn't even succeed in moving Chase an inch. "Those are just words. Don't let him push your buttons."

"More proof you're not the man to take over the sheriff's office, Broussard. Hot-headed and too willing to make the wrong choices. Your fiancée has been involved in weird killings since she got back to town. You think the voters will look past her and just see your smiling face? That slick campaign talk won't work." Dave's voice held the edge of more insults he could have said, but held back.

"You slimy son-of-a..."

"Chase!" M.J. shouted.

Dave sprang back. He swung a fist that gave Chase a glancing blow. Chase called Dave a couple of colorful names. Two male voices grew animated. LaShaun turned to see them pointing. One raised a hand, no doubt to record video. LaShaun used all of her force to push Chase in the opposite direction away from Dave. The older man huffed and puffed in rage, but didn't try to follow.

"You chose one helluva time to pick a beef, Dave," M.J. said in a voice tight with anger. She kept her voice low. Then she spun around to face the two deputies who had observed the action with amusement. They lost their grins under her hot scrutiny. "Get those damn reporters far away from here. You two, keep looking, and Dave will help," she barked at the remaining men. They nodded and went back to work.

Dave opened his mouth to object, but when M.J. glared at him he backed up. He cleared his throat then strutted off with a take charge attitude. "Keep sweeping the area guys. Not likely we'll find anything useful, but we need to be thorough."

"Lord," M.J. said. She rolled her eyes as she watched him.

Chase took a deep breath and let it out slowly. "I'm okay. I'm okay."

"You're supposed to respectfully disagree, not beat the crap out of each other," LaShaun said.

"He had that coming, and more. Dave's been dropping slick little remarks for weeks around the station. I'm sick of him and his phony ass Mr. Church-Going Good Guy act." Chase seemed to be getting worked up again.

M.J. marched over to them. "Great, just damn

96

freakin' perfect. Two senior Vermilion Parish deputies who also happen to be running for sheriff get into a brawl, and with reporters sitting ringside."

"Yeah, right. Sorry." Chase's scowl in Dave's direction implied he had no regrets.

"Go talk to the girl and her parents. Try to remember we're working a case, not having a bar fight," M.J. growled at him.

"Okay." Chase glanced briefly at LaShaun and then left.

LaShaun turned to M.J. when he was a few yards away. "Any chance those reporters didn't see what happened?"

"No such luck. I want to shove this job off on Chase as soon as possible. I'd appreciate if he didn't screw up my plans by losing the election," M.J. said firmly.

"You're preaching to the choir, so give him this lecture, Madame Sheriff," LaShaun replied with a shrug.

She stared ahead. About a third of a mile through a stand of trees, the Saucier family stood near a circle of sheriff department cruisers. Dave draped a blanket around Becky. LaShaun tried tuning out the activity around her, to use her extra senses as a sort of feeler. But the adrenalin and tension from everyone was like static that drowned out the psychic signals.

M.J. looked around as if making sure they had privacy. Even so, she pulled LaShaun farther from the scene. "Have you noticed anything... different about Chase lately?"

"What do you mean?" LaShaun continued to focus on the teenager who'd caused the frenzied search.

"He's got a hair trigger these days around the station. I thought he was going to slap that Graham kid when we questioned him a few days ago. He gave the father a tongue lashing that had the man shaking in his shoes." M.J. shook her head. "I've never seen him act like that before."

LaShaun forgot about the Saucier girl and focused on M.J. instead. "Chase has always taken his job seriously."

"Yeah, he has. But Chase is typically the good cop in the old 'good cop - bad cop' routine. Hell, I'll be glad when this election is over." M.J. observed her deputies while tapping a fist against her thigh.

"You hit the target; M.J. Chase is under more stress than he wants to let on with this campaign. And he's been working long days lately," LaShaun said.

"The last couple of months have been brutal. Greg and his little crew having a party that turned bloody just about capped it," M.J. said and grunted.

"Yeah," LaShaun replied with a grimace.

"So far, we haven't found any of the usual signs they're experimenting with Satanism or witchcraft." M.J. crossed her arms. "I'm lighting candles at mass that Vermilion Parish gets back to everyday old crime. You know, common stuff like guys cutting each other up over a woman or drug dealing," she quipped.

LaShaun raised an eyebrow at her friend. "I hope you're not implying that I brought some bad mojo with me when I moved back home."

"Of course not," M.J. said promptly. Then she gave LaShaun a sideways grin. "But you gotta admit..."

"Here we go," LaShaun sputtered. "The Rousselle family legend lives on, huh? I'm not inspiring these folks to act crazy."

M.J. turned somber again. "And Manny Young is trying to get out of prison. He's almost as much trouble locked up as he was out killing folks. The fun times just keep rolling."

"Hey, boss lady. We found a few things you wanna take a look at," Deputy Ricard shouted from a distance. She waved her super-sized flashlight as a guide.

"On my way. Whoa, where you think you goin'? This is an official investigation. Bye." M.J. pointed the way for LaShaun.

"But maybe I could help..."

"Look, I appreciate the offer. But we can't give any defense lawyer reasons to say we tampered with evidence, if anything comes of Becky's little trip. Dave isn't going to let it drop that Chase brought you along. And those reporters will have a great time bringing up your past adventures." M.J. held up both palms when LaShaun started to speak. "I'll have one of my guys take you home."

LaShaun studied the determined expression on M.J.'s smooth brown face. Standing five feet eight inches in her socks, M.J. cut a formidable figure. She looked more than able to handle trouble, even if her uniform accentuated her female curves. M.J. Arceneaux took her job just as seriously as Chase.

"I promise to get in Chase's truck and stay there. Just let me know what you find." LaShaun nodded to M.J.

"No way," M.J. shot back.

"Okay. Wait a minute. Make a big show of ordering me out of the way."

"Huh?" M.J. raised both eyebrows and then a smile tugged her full lips up. "Might make Becky and her folks more talkative if they think we're putting you in your place."

"LaShaun winked at her. Then she affected a scowl and raised her voice. "Fine, stumble around this case on your own! Just don't come begging me for help later."

"I can promise you that won't happen, LaShaun. You need to leave the crime scene," M.J. replied just as loudly.

LaShaun strode off wearing a stony expression without looking left or right. She passed a few feet from where the Saucier family stood with Chase. When she went by, Mike Saucier shushed the giggling Becky.

For two hours, LaShaun sat patiently waiting. Finally Chase joined her. He got in the truck, slammed the door, and started the engine. They drove along for ten minutes. Unlike his usual habit, he didn't turn on the radio or CD player. Listening to Cajun, blues and Zydeco music seemed part of his routine to help him sort through facts. LaShaun had watched him tap his fingers to a tune while mulling over case reports many times. Instead he wore a frown and stared straight-ahead at the road. The dotted yellow painted squares that divided the two-lane highway whizzed by.

"You're real quiet, honey. You okay?" LaShaun said, breaking the silence.

"This job is starting to wear on my nerves I guess. Kids barely out of diapers dying and getting their kicks in freaky ways... I don't know. If I wanted to deal with that crap I'd work in a big city department." Chase let out a long breath.

"That 'crap' is all over these days, including rural parishes like ours. But at least we get it in small doses," LaShaun replied in an attempt to console him.

"I'll bet Elliot's mama doesn't think it's so small. This stuff is even giving me nightmares." Chase shook his head.

LaShaun felt a familiar sensation, like an army of ants with tiny electrified feet marching up both arms.

Her stomach tightened as she resisted the urge to claw her own skin. She glanced down to reassure herself and saw nothing on the back of her hands or on her forearms. Instead she centered all of her attention on Chase. Suddenly, a curtain dropped between them. Like a television monitor, the image of a wooded area appeared. A soft blue haze pulsated within it. Then the vision flicked off as though someone had hit the "Off" button. LaShaun rubbed her forehead.

"You look a little wobbly, cher. You okay?" Chase frowned at her, concern on his handsome face.

"What kind of nightmares, Chase?" LaShaun said sharply.

"Never mind about that now, you..."

"I'm fine. Tell me about the dreams you're having. It will help you to talk about them," she pressed. When he slowed the truck and looked at her hard, LaShaun put a hand on his arm.

"Most of them I don't remember clearly. They start with me falling into a dark hole. While I'm going down, weird symbols flash by. I can hear voices, and then it's only one voice. I can't tell if it's a man or a woman." Chase paused to grin at her. "I'm not cheatin' on you in my dreams, cher. I swear."

LaShaun forced a smile back at him. "You better not be. What happens next?"

Chase didn't answer immediately. He concentrated on turning east at the intersection of Highway 35 and onto Highway 14. "After a while I get this sensation of being lost, like I'll never find my way out of a dark place. It's kind of hard to describe, but all I can remember is fighting to hold on."

"Like you're lost in the woods or something?" LaShaun's heart drummed in her chest with such intensity she winced.

"Not exactly. I don't know. Pretty crazy, huh?" Chase gave a nervous chuckle.

LaShaun winced a second time. The powerful anxiety he felt seeped into her pores as well. She squeezed his arm a little tighter. "You're the most steady, feet-on-the-ground guy I know, Chase Broussard. The stress of the election and working double shifts would give anybody nightmares."

"Yeah, well I need to get it together. Going after Dave like that was a stupid move. M.J. is right. I need to take off a couple of days to re-charge, and do some damage control for when that story makes the rounds." Chase smiled at LaShaun. He took one hand off the wheel to give her thigh a quick pat. "That means you'll be stuck with me."

"I look forward to it," LaShaun said and smiled back at him.

For the rest of the ride to her house they shared a comfortable silence as the dark countryside slipped by. She would make Chase's time off from work as relaxing and enjoyable as possible. LaShaun knew Chase's real worry, that post traumatic stress episodes from three tours in Afghanistan would cripple him. She actually hoped his behavior and nightmares came from PTSD. LaShaun feared the cause came from a more sinister source, one not from this world. Had the evil called forth by her ancestors returned?

Chapter 7

For two days LaShaun monitored every move Chase made, every expression and every mood he displayed. Not even the newspaper and television stories of "a heated exchange between the two candidates for sheriff" seemed to bother him. Friday morning, Chase woke LaShaun from a sound sleep in a most delicious way. Wrapped in flannel sheets, LaShaun had made her master bedroom his sanctuary.

"I'm going to be pulling more over time in the next few days," Chase murmured as he nuzzled LaShaun's neck. "I need a nice, hot memory to get me through the chilly nights of fighting crime."

"Candidate Broussard, you're supposed to be motivated by a passion for justice," LaShaun replied and wiggled against his hard body.

"I've got a passion for a lot of things; justice is only one of 'em, cher."

Chase slipped his hand between her thighs. He stroked her flesh and moved his hand up. With a light touch, he caressed her mound for a few seconds before using his fingers to slowly drive her insane with desire. His tongue circled first one nipple and then the other, back and forth as his fingers worked a kind of magic she'd never felt before. Within the next hour Chase thrilled her with three different positions, each one more exotic. At last he stood above her as she lay on the edge of the bed, her legs stretched up against his chest. The rhythm of his thrusts kept time to her moans. As she grew more frenzied, Chase would slow down. When she couldn't stand it any longer, LaShaun tried to take control, grinding her hips to satisfy a cavernous hunger. She clawed to hold onto him when Chase pulled out. But she was rewarded moments later when he pulled the comforter to the floor. On his back, he guided her to sit in his lap. LaShaun wrapped her legs around him as Chase lifted them both. His tongue circled both nipples again until she screamed with pleasure. Waves of ecstasy seemed to go on forever as she moved up and down, faster until nothing existed except the motion that satisfied her cavernous need.

"Take control, baby. I'm yours," Chase whispered, urging her on with his own intense thrusting.

"I need every inch of you," LaShaun gasped and dug her fingers into the hard flesh of his shoulders.

Her moans answered his shouts urging her on. Their voices intertwined in the special language of love and sexual pleasure. When Chase exploded inside her LaShaun came again, every nerve ending on fire. When her movements slowed and stilled, LaShaun let out a shuddering sigh. After a few minutes he used his powerful legs to stand up with LaShaun in his arms. He eased them both back onto the bed. LaShaun blinked away tears as she trembled against him.

"How did I exist without you?" she whispered softly. "I will be yours forever."

Chase gave a deep chuckle and stroked her hair as LaShaun drifted into a semi-conscious dream state. A vision of them lying on a wide bed with a beautiful rattan headboard in a room with an ocean view popped into her head. Eyes closed, LaShaun smiled and savored the floating sensation. A beach breeze made gauze curtains framing a window flutter, their private tropical paradise.

"Mwen vle viv andedan ou," a deep voice said

softly, wrapping around her. ("I want to live inside you")

"J'taime," LaShaun replied.

She gazed up into fiery almond-shaped green eyes. Her feeling of joy turned to panic. LaShaun tried to pull away, but her body seemed numb. Her limbs would not move. She tried to cry out but no sound came from her lips. The eyes sparkled, and then darkened into a light brown that gradually grew darker.

"Hey, sleepy girl. I know how irresistible I am, but loosen this death grip on me. I gotta go to work."

LaShaun's eyes popped open to find Chase smiling down at her. She blinked at him as her heart beat so hard her chest ached. Pushing him away, LaShaun stared at him. "What did you say?"

Chase got out of bed. "I'm going back to the grind of being a peace officer. I can't lay around lovin' on you all the time."

When he started for the bathroom, LaShaun caught him by the arm. "No, I mean before. You were speaking Creole."

"Honey, with the moves you made I wouldn't doubt I was speaking French and every other kind of language." Chase winked at her and then kissed her hand. He turned away and opened a dresser. "With all the clothes I've left here it makes our decision easier 'bout which house we'll live in, huh? I feel right at home."

LaShaun jumped out of the bed and pulled him back around to face her. "Chase, you were speaking Haitian Creole, and, and your eyes changed color."

"That was some crazy dream," Chase said with a laugh, but it died away as he gazed back at her. He wrapped his arms around LaShaun. "Cher, you're shivering."

"We were in a house on the beach, but it wasn't any place I've ever been. I can still hear the sound of waves." LaShaun looked up into Chase's eyes desperate to see the familiar, the man she knew. "I want you to be safe."

"Baby, you're kinda freakin' me out here. Like I said, you had a weird dream, that's all. You've had them before." Chase spoke in a soothing tone as he gently rocked her.

"And we know what happens, too. I get those visions and then..."

LaShaun swallowed hard. She took having visions in stride, even when she saw horrible things. Sometimes she could almost start fires as heat flowed from her finger tips. Monmon Odette had taught LaShaun early about the Rousselle family legacy. Her grandmother had schooled LaShaun on how to direct her 'gifts', marveling at how strong they became with time. None of those skills had ever frightened her, not even as a child. But this was very different. Never had a vision come so close to home.

Chase kissed her lightly on the tip of her nose and slapped her rear end. "Baby, you were sound asleep. That was a dream, a really weird one, but still just a dream. Now I'm gonna shower and get down the road before my boss calls asking why I haven't shown up. We're going to interview one of Greg Graham's friends. See if we can find out what the hell these kids are playin' at out in the woods."

With a shake of his head, Chase padded on bare feet to the master bathroom. He continued to talk about routine matters. LaShaun didn't answer him. Instead she sat on the edge of the bed thinking about the "dream" as Chase insisted. He seemed to be himself again, a fact that helped LaShaun not totally come unglued. For the first time in months she felt the sharp pain of not having her grandmother in this world. Monmon Odette would be a source of strength, and knowledge right now.

"So I'm hopin' we can wrap up this case and figure out who killed that poor Dubois boy. To top it off, the coroner says he could have had a fall. But I don't buy it. Nope, that kid was murdered and..." Chase stood wearing only his briefs. He gazed at LaShaun with a grin. "You're still sitting here naked, babe?"

LaShaun sat blinking rapidly and looked down. She was sitting in the middle of the queen-sized bed in a lotus position as though meditating. "What? Oh, I was just giving you some space to get ready."

"Thank you, darlin'. The last two days did wonders clearing my head, that's for sure."

Chase pinched her cheek. Then he sat down on one of the stuffed chairs, pulled on his socks, and stood again to step into a pair of black denim pants. Five minutes later, he was fully dressed. LaShaun took a shower. She quickly dressed in jeans and a soft flannel shirt. When she went to the kitchen, Chase was already on his phone getting an update. He liked knowing what had been happening at the station even before he walked in the door.

"I'm going to fix us breakfast," LaShaun whispered to him.

"Don't worry about it. I heated up one of those frozen sausage biscuits and made some coffee to go. I'm running behind as it is." Chase kissed her mouth. "I'll see you later."

LaShaun put her arms around his waist. "Hey, I noticed you're not being specific. I guess that means I won't see you for a few days."

"It's crazy, honey, so I can't make promises. I just talked to Bo. He says we got more trouble, but said he'd let M.J. and Dave tell me." Chase stepped away. He pulled on his department issued jacket and zipped it up. The Vermilion Parish Sheriff's Department emblem was stamped on the back.

"Show 'em what you got, but be careful. In a few short weeks, you'll be in charge. M.J. will gladly hand you the keys to that place," LaShaun said with a laugh.

Chase shrugged. "We'll see. Old Dave has more than a few friends in this parish. You get back to planning our wedding." He headed for the door.

"Oh Lord, don't remind me. Katie and Adrianna have sent me at least fifteen e-mails, a piece. I don't think the royal wedding in England was this much trouble." LaShaun groaned. "And we're running out of time, at least that's what they keep telling me."

"It's still only February, sweetie. Don't let those two gang up on you. Keep it simple. We both agreed." Chase pointed a finger at her. "If you need back-up, just let me know. We'll face those two down."

"Thanks, cher. We have the location, under the historic oaks of Broussard ancestral lands. We'll have the reception right there on your patio and..."

"Our patio, sweetheart," Chase corrected her, but looked at his smart phone again reading a text.

"Gotta get used to that, and so does your mama," LaShaun quipped in a soft voice.

"Huh?" Chase tapped out a reply to someone at the station.

"Nothing. Go make Vermilion Parish safe from crazed teenagers."

Chase gave a grunt. "Bye."

With one last kiss, LaShaun sent him out of the door. She waved at him through the kitchen window as he turned the new Dodge Ram truck in a circle and drove away. LaShaun ate a light breakfast while she watched the morning news. Relieved not to hear more weird developments in Beau Chene or Vermilion Parish, she pulled up the to-do list on her tablet. She stared at it for a good ten minutes without enthusiasm. Her thoughts were still on her "dream". The doorbell startled LaShaun out of her reverie. When she went to the front door she got another surprise.

LaShaun opened the solid wood door, but left the storm door locked. She gazed through the glass at Neal Montgomery. "What is the lawyer representing the worst serial killer in Louisiana history doing on my doorstep?"

"Good morning, Ms. Rousselle," Montgomery said, ignoring her lack of a cordial greeting. "I apologize for not scheduling an appointment, but my mission to save Emanuel Young is rather urgent."

"How does that concern me?" LaShaun shot back. She didn't like him. Every one of her senses, normal and paranormal, seemed to kick in shouting something was off about the man. "The DA wouldn't be happy to know you're talking to a witness without telling him."

"I'm investigating on behalf of my client, which is legal and in fact my ethical duty. You haven't been called as a witness. Yet." Montgomery let an eyebrow slip up briefly after he said the last word.

LaShaun gazed at him for a few seconds. "Uh-huh. Court rooms don't scare me."

"So I've heard. I won't take much of your time I promise. I just have a few questions." Montgomery wore a look of patience.

"Come on in. I knew you'd appeal Judge Barrow's decision." LaShaun clicked the locks back and let him in. "Can I get you anything?"

"I'm good." Montgomery smiled.

LaShaun led the way into her formal living room. She sat down in a chair and Montgomery sat in another one across from her. He looked around. She could feel him assessing what approach to take. Montgomery wanted her off guard, but had to figure out how to rattle her. LaShaun waited him out. Finally he looked at her again.

"So what got you interested in trying to free a sadistic psychopath?" LaShaun said before he could speak. She titled her head to one side.

Montgomery let an easy smile slide across his handsome face. "Our justice system--"

"Our legal system is built on the principle that everyone deserves a good defense. Yeah, I know," LaShaun cut in. He blinked in surprise, but he recovered fast.

"We don't think he got the best defense the first time around. By 'we' I mean our team at the True Justice Project. We very carefully review cases before we take them." Montgomery stood and walked around the room gazing at antiques. He leaned forward to stare at a miniature painting of a Rousselle ancestor. "Your family goes back several generations in Vermilion Parish I hear."

"Five to be exact. Manny's family has been here almost as long," LaShaun said. When Montgomery straightened and faced her again, she raised an eyebrow.

"Of course, the point of my visit is not to explore your family tree. Rather, let's talk about Manny's family.

Orin Young was suspected of being a uniquely vicious person." Montgomery sat down again.

"His partners in crime were more than eager to give him up," LaShaun said.

"Once they knew he was dead. He seemed to inspire great fear in people. Manny has told me the way Orin and Ethan treated him. His descriptions of the physical abuse he suffered are chilling, to say the least." Montgomery sat forward, elbows resting on his knees, hands clasped. "Obviously this shaped Manny's personality and behavior."

"Which doesn't mean he should be let loose on the world again," LaShaun replied mildly.

"If he's innocent?" Montgomery sat back against the chair.

"You won't prove that Manny didn't kill anyone, Mr. Montgomery. There is physical evidence that put him with at least two of the twelve victims. He was in the area where the murders occurred."

"He hung out with those people. They were all transient, living a high risk life-style." Montgomery rubbed his chin. "We can show evidence that Orin Young met some of those victims on his property, the house on Black Bayou."

"What?" LaShaun felt a tingle up her arms. The mention of the house where Orin Young acted out his depraved urges triggered images in her mind.

Montgomery smiled with satisfaction at surprising her at last. He nodded. "Yes. Manny told us of Orin's sick parties."

"You mentioned evidence." LaShaun gripped the arms of her chair, fighting the compulsion to gag. She felt buffeted by waves of emotions; craving for liquor, lust, greed and terror. With great effort she pushed against the gut wrenching sensation from horrible deeds committed in that place.

"Are you feeling alright, Ms. Rousselle? I don't know why we need to be so formal here in this lovely setting. Call me Neal, and I'll call you LaShaun. Not La-La, which is what your grandmother used to call you as a little girl. That would be too familiar." Montgomery's voice seemed to float far away and then back, getting louder.

LaShaun took in deep breaths. "I don't understand..." her voice trailed off.

"It's quite simple really. Emanuel Young took the blame for Orin Young's depraved crimes, a terrible miscarriage of justice, LaShaun." Montgomery stared at her steadily.

"I... I don't believe," she said, her throat feeling tight as she tried to go on.

Suddenly the atmosphere in the room shifted. Air rushed in as though several windows had been opened. A solid series of thumps sounded. LaShaun whispered a prayer she'd read in one of six old family journals. Once she managed to steady her breathing LaShaun's thinking cleared. When she stood so did Montgomery. He wore a wary expression, but covered it quickly with a smile.

"You looked a little green there for minute. Maybe you should get a glass of water with a little mint to settle your stomach," he said.

"I'm feeling fine. Thank you, Mr. Montgomery," LaShaun said firmly in control again. "So if you had this evidence, why didn't you present it in court the other day?"

"We got some leads we didn't have then, thanks to a friend of yours," Montgomery replied.

"Mine?" LaShaun frowned at him.

"The well-know journalist James Schaffer. He did a series of investigative reports on the events surrounding your capture of Orin Young."

"I didn't capture anybody. I helped search for a little girl. Deputy Chase Broussard, Sheriff Arceneaux, and their officers brought those guys in." LaShaun frowned. "If he's your source then I'm afraid Manny shouldn't get his hopes up. James Schaffer is a reality show ghost chaser, not a journalist. He'd turn a squirrel hunt into a battle with Big Foot to get ratings."

"It's not just Schaffer's theories. As I said, we're gathering real evidence," Montgomery replied.

LaShaun focused her energy on him, imagining it as a laser. She pushed the heat out to him. "Why do you really want Manny to get out of prison?"

Montgomery's flared nostrils were the only sign he felt anything. "Orin Young was the true monster. Manny was his victim."

"That's only part of the truth." LaShaun felt a throbbing pain start at the base of her neck and move to her temple. She broke off the focus of her gift. "Manny won't leave prison alive, Mr. Montgomery."

Montgomery leaned forward in the chair. "You're a fascinating woman with an amazing presence."

Krystal Hardy appeared suddenly in the archway leading into LaShaun's formal parlor. She shot a brief glance at Montgomery, a chilly smile on her thin face. "The woods around here are lovely, Ms. Rousselle."

LaShaun glanced at Montgomery sharply. "So you distracted me to give your partner a chance to search my property. If you've been in my house looking around..."

"I needed to stretch my legs after a long drive from New Orleans. I assure you I wasn't in your home or snooping around outside. I was merely admiring your property," Krystal Hardy said before Montgomery could speak.

"I see," LaShaun drawled.

"Quite interesting that your family cemetery is on the property. That was quite common in rural areas in the eighteenth and even into the nineteenth century. I could almost feel the spirits of the Rousselle and LeGrange ancestors." Krystal Hardy gazed around at the paintings on the walls as she spoke.

"Yes, I wouldn't doubt you could sense the power of the old ones, Ms. Hardy." LaShaun walked to her slowly. "They were strong people in life. The story of Louisiana and my family are quite unique."

"So I'm told," Krystal Hardy replied.

LaShaun sensed that the woman had a fierce love, even an obsession, for Neal Montgomery. Despite her cool exterior, Krystal didn't like that Montgomery had been alone with LaShaun. LaShaun faced Montgomery and brushed back her thick hair. Montgomery smiled as his bold gaze swept over her.

"Are we finished here, Neal?" Krystal said.

"Did Orin Young give you any indication that he'd committed those murders, the ones poor Manny was convicted of I mean?" Montgomery seemed not to notice his colleague's soft hiss of displeasure.

"No, he didn't," LaShaun replied mildly.

"Did Manny ever mention that his father or grandfather was present during the crimes or might have been responsible?" Montgomery asked.

"He never mentioned anything like that," LaShaun said. "I won't help any effort to release him. Now if you'll excuse me I have things to do."

"I apologize for showing up unannounced. Next

time I'll make an appointment." Montgomery started for the door with Krystal head of him.

"Don't bother. I have nothing else to tell you," LaShaun said. She followed them to the front door.

Krystal was already on the porch as though eager to leave. "Goodbye, Ms. Rousselle."

"Goodbye. You should be careful wandering around people's property out here, Ms. Hardy. Us country folk are likely to shoot first and then find out who we plugged." LaShaun grinned when the woman took a step back.

Montgomery laughed out loud. "You certainly live up to your reputation. Thank you for being patient with us, Ms. Rousselle. Goodbye."

LaShaun watched them drive away in the silver Mercedes Benz SUV. She spent the rest of the afternoon doing research on Neal Montgomery.

Chapter 8

Wednesday morning dawned bright and cold. LaShaun's to-do list still flashed reminders on the calendar app of her tablet. Yet she'd been too glued to her desktop to take notice. When her phone rang, she fully expected to hear Chase's deep sultry voice telling her he would once again have to work and wouldn't see her that day. Instead her friend Savannah's voice surprised her.

"Girl we got trouble," Savannah said.

Twenty minutes later LaShaun stood in M.J.'s office, too keyed up to sit down. M.J. waved aside the deputy who acted as her assistant when LaShaun rushed in without asking or knocking. Still the young woman stood outside her boss's office on alert. Only the second black female officer in the Vermilion Parish Sheriff's Office, Toni Ferdinand seemed eager to prove her worth. LaShaun nodded to Deputy Ferdinand. She got a nod in return before Deputy Ferdinand closed the door and went back to her desk. LaShaun turned back to the acting sheriff. M.J. spoke in a clipped tone into her cell phone.

"I'll update you when I know more, Mayor. Yes, of course." M.J. hit the off button and dropped the phone onto her desk. She looked up at LaShaun. "Damn, you got the word fast. CNN ain't got nothin' on the small town network of gossips."

"Savannah called me. Is Chase okay? What the hell..." LaShaun glanced around through the glass that made up one half of the office walls. The other officers seemed to be carrying on as usual.

"He's fine. Wish I could say the same for the witness he was interviewing," M.J. snapped and scowled ahead. "Remember I asked you if something was different about Chase?"

LaShaun sat down slowly. "Yeah, out at the scene where we found Becky."

"He tried to take Dave's head off out there. Now he's slapping around suspects and witnesses." M.J. nodded when LaShaun gasped. "Kid was cussin' everybody in sight and was stupid enough to get in Chase's face. Chase knocked him on his ass; kid was out for about ten minutes."

"Oh my God," LaShaun blurted out.

"Doctor at the ER says it was a minor thing, mostly stunned him. But they're keeping him in the hospital overnight just to be safe. His mama is already screaming about a lawsuit, racism and police brutality. Yeah, the kid is black. Like we don't have enough crap to shovel," M.J. said angrily.

"I'm sure Chase felt threatened, M.J. You know Chase doesn't go around beating up kids, or anyone else for that matter." LaShaun rubbed her forehead as though that would help her get answers. "He's more stressed out than I realized."

M.J. tapped an ink pen on the surface of her desk for a few minutes. "You think maybe he's having some problems from his time over in Afghanistan? PTSD is very common for veterans."

"No," LaShaun said quickly. "I've never seen him act like he's having flashbacks or any other symptoms."

"Sometimes it can be delayed. I took classes because PTSD affects cops, too. We see a lot of bad stuff."

LaShaun shook her head. "I would have noticed,

M.J."

"The thing is Chase, doesn't talk about his time over there, so you don't really know the details of how rough it was for him."

"Look, this is one instance--"

"He talked tough to a couple of suspects a few days ago. Then he went after Dave, and now this. I'm worried about his career, but more important I'm worried about him." M.J. gazed at LaShaun steadily.

"I know you care about Chase, M.J.," LaShaun replied. "Is he suspended?"

M.J. sat back. "We caught a break. Two residents of the trailer park back up Chase's account that the kid made physical threats. That helps. But two local reporters were already in town. I hear they've been talking to this kid's mama already."

"Where is Chase now?" LaShaun stood.

"He's out on another case. Look, this wasn't a shooting or anything like that," M.J. added when LaShaun showed surprise. "Except for Chase running for Sheriff, I doubt anyone outside the department would take notice. Definitely most of the guys don't see the big deal."

"But we know differently, M.J. We know Chase." LaShaun sat down again and frowned with worry. "Chase wouldn't shove around a kid because he was black, suspect or not."

"Let's face it; this department has a reputation for being a less than sensitive group when it comes to race and gender." M.J. let out a humorless laugh when LaShaun rolled her eyes.

"I'm shocked to the core," LaShaun retorted.

"Humph, I had it rough fifteen years ago when I started. Toni is getting the same blow back. Things haven't changed as much or as fast as we'd like. Most of the guys gave him props for messing up a perp." M.J. wore a stern expression. "I'm not included in that number, and my vote outnumbers them."

"M.J., give him a chance to explain," LaShaun said.

"I did. He said the law-abiding citizens expect us to hold the line on low lifes." M.J. broke off when the door to her office opened.

Chase smiled at LaShaun easily, as if his day was going as usual. "Hey, baby. What are you doing here? Gonna treat me to lunch I hope."

LaShaun stood. "I was just... I came down because... I got a call that you might have been hurt."

"If you're talking about that little dust up out on Post Oak Lane, forget what you heard. I'll bet by the time the story gets around town, folks will say there was automatic gunshots and dead bodies everywhere." Chase laughed. He glanced at M.J. "We got a three car accident with injuries out on Highway 35. Bo and Larry are working it with the State Police. I'm going to wrap up my report on the kid. Oh, and I'm going to interview Greg Graham again at three this afternoon. I'll bet you money he got Becky to run off. Crazy kids."

"You best postpone that talk with Greg Graham," M.J. said firmly.

"No reason. I'm fine," Chase replied mildly and then placed his hands on his waist. "Are you saying you don't trust me?"

"I don't want a repeat performance of you deciding to knock answers outta some smart ass kid. We both know Greg fits that description," M.J. shot back.

"You don't have to worry unless Greg comes at me like that other punk. Or would you like deputies on your watch to get beaten or shot so we can be politically correct?" Chase snapped.

M.J. stood up. "You better watch it, Chase. I'm willing to give you the benefit of the doubt. But acting like a loose cannon commando around this parish is not how we enforce the law. It wasn't that way under Sheriff Triche, and it sure as hell won't be while I'm acting Sheriff."

Chase and M.J. stared each other down. Despite the itch to jump between them, LaShaun kept quiet. Not only was M.J. the boss, but she had a right to be angry. Nor would Chase appreciate her acting like his mother showing up to defend him in the principal's office. Tense seconds ticked by as LaShaun held her breath. She let it out when Chase's stony expression softened.

"Okay, you got a point," Chase said.

"Oh yeah," M.J. retorted, still steadfast in asserting her authority. "We get more information by treating suspects with respect, and even courtesy."

"The kid in the trailer park really did come at me. I could have used my training a little better, but he grabbed at me like he was going for my gun," Chase said in a calm tone.

M.J. seemed to relax at his words. "I believe you made a solid decision based on your professional judgment."

"Thanks, Sheriff." Chase's usual easy smile pulled up his lips. "Look, I'm on notice to keep it cool. I'll be the perfect gentleman lawman even when Greg or his daddy mouth off."

Deputy Ferdinand knocked and came in. "Sorry to interrupt, but Patrick called. That's deputy Anderson," she said to LaShaun in explanation. "They found scales, two bags of weed, three thousand dollars and two Glocks in the kid's trailer."

"Damn kiddie crooks," M.J. grumbled to no one in particular.

"Good job, Chase," Deputy Ferdinand said. "If we're lucky, the DA will charge him as an adult. I'd like to see him locked up before he uses one of those guns to kill another kid."

Chase nodded with a solemn expression. "I didn't know all that when I knocked him down, but I had a feeling the kid was dangerous. So, I'm good to go with the Grahams today, boss?"

"Yeah, just remember..."

"He's only a person of interest, not a suspect. Gotcha." Chase grinned widely.

"I was going to say behave yourself so you can win the damn election. I sure as hell don't wanna be in this job longer than necessary. You and Dave keep clean, and stay healthy." M.J. gave a grunt and sat down.

"You can't want Dave Godchaux for a boss. The guys a self-righteous..." LaShaun stopped short when Dave appeared and tapped on the glass section of M.J.'s office door.

"We're having an action packed week, huh?" Dave said.

"Doing what we're paid to do, Dave. The action comes from crooks," Chase said. His smile stretched tight across his face. When Dave glanced at LaShaun, Chase's eyes narrowed.

"Afternoon, ma'am," Dave gave LaShaun a courteous nod. He glanced at M.J. "I'm going to make a loop around Black Bayou and a few miles down Highway 85. Call if you need me."

"Thanks," M.J. said evenly.

With a final curt nod, Dave closed the door again and strode off. They watched him turn down the hallway that led to the exit used by deputies and other employees only.

"Call if you need me," Chase said, mimicking Dave's officious manner.

"Dave isn't the enemy. Sure he's got his ways, but we all do." M.J. slapped open a folder. "I'm sure there are stories going around about me being a pain as the boss. Now go. I've got work to do, and a mayor's jumpy nerves to soothe about legal action."

"We're getting out of your way, boss," Chase said. "I'm taking you up on that lunch treat, lady."

"I didn't mention treating you to lunch, Deputy Broussard. You came up with the idea," LaShaun tossed back at him.

"It's a mighty good one, too. I'm hungry. Knocking sense into gangsters really works up an appetite," Chase quipped.

"Hey!" M.J. cracked at him and pointed a forefinger. "Not funny."

Chase held up both hands. "I won't repeat it outside these hallowed walls."

M.J. sighed deeply as she shook her head. "The election can't happen soon enough for me."

Chase opened the door and let LaShaun go first. "I'm right there with you, boss lady. Win or lose, I'm ready for the whole thing to get done. See you later, and don't worry. With the election everything gets blown way up."

"Yeah, yeah, yeah," M.J. said softly. She flipped through a report as though she'd already moved on to more important matters.

Chase and LaShaun walked three blocks toward a new downtown restaurant. Mardi Gras was only a week away. February would be gone, and March would roar in with more cold weather according to the forecasts. They would be married in just a few short weeks. LaShaun shivered even though the day had turned warmer with the temperature in the mid sixties. She stole sideways glances at Chase. He walked with confidence as though life was normal.

The shops and street lamps were decorated with purple, gold and green, the traditional colors of Mardi Gras in Louisiana. Giant masks hung on doors. Each lamp post had a fleur de lis made of glittering ribbon. They reached the shop owned by Savannah's father, Antoine St. Julien. His storefront stood out among all of the Fat Tuesday finery. Mr. St. Julien was skilled at carving wood. LaShaun had no doubt that the Mardi Gras float replica so elaborately decorated was his handwork. Tiny dolls had been arranged inside it, some holding beads. A small crowd of admirers gathered around. Mr. St. Julien appeared in the window. He smiled and beckoned them inside.

"Welcome. I haven't seen you in a long time. How've you been?" Mr. St. Julien said warmly and gave LaShaun a hug.

His paternal attention always slightly embarrassed LaShaun, but made her feel happy as well. The soft burr of his Creole accent could soothe the most jangled nerves. She smiled at him shyly. "I'm doing good, Mr. St. Julien. How're you feeling now? Savannah says you've been sick."

"She makin' a big deal over a little arthritis. Old men gonna creak like old houses." Mr. St. Julien laughed at his own joke. He turned to Chase. "How's our soon-to-be sheriff?"

Chase grinned. "Can't complain, sir. I hope you been lookin' in a crystal ball. If so, I won't spend any more money on campaign signs."

"Naw, I ain't got the sight. I just hear good things being said 'bout you round town, son. Y'all fixin' to get some lunch at that new place?" Mr. St. Julien pointed west, the direction they were headed.

"Yeah, figured we'd give it a try," Chase said.

"They got good burgers I hear. I got to avoid beef these days and eat heart healthy." Mr. St. Julien lowered his voice and leaned forward. "But try the fried alligator tenders with tartar sauce. Owwee, that's good eatin'. But don't tell Savannah or my sister Marie."

"My lips are sealed. We guys gotta stick together," Chase said with a wink.

"Follow medical advice," LaShaun broke in. "You're needed."

Mr. St. Julien waved a hand. "Ah, I'm gonna stay around for the children and grandchildren," he said, referring to Savannah, her husband Paul and their twin girls.

"Also take you heart medicine," LaShaun pressed.

She put her arm through his as though encouraging him. What she really wanted was to see if she sensed that he might get sick any time soon. LaShaun had known when her beloved grandmother was moving on to the other side. To LaShaun's relief, nothing came to her. She relaxed, patted his forearm and then let go.

"Pooh, I'll be here to stir up trouble for awhile yet. Deputy Dave been puttin' the word out that he's more level-headed." Mr. St. Julien frowned. "I say we need fresh blood."

"No comment." Chase smiled all the same.

LaShaun cleared her throat. She felt uncomfortable with the direction of the conversation. "That float in the window is gorgeous. Are you selling it?"

"I keep that for the store. I made two special order for Quentin Trosclair. Yeah, I know what you're thinkin', cher," Mr. St. Julien said when LaShaun grimaced. "But he paid good money, too good to turn down. Five thousand for the pair."

Chase let out a low whistle. "Whoa. I would have delivered those bad boys on my back for that price."

"Nah. I carried 'em in my truck right to his doorstep though." Mr. St. Julien shared a laugh with him.

"Just like Quentin to suck people in," LaShaun retorted. Quentin used money and charm to get what he wanted.

"Don't worry. I know what he is. Trosclair is having a big Mardi Gras ball at that big mansion of his this weekend. That's how the Trosclair family did it back in the day, you know. All the way back to the turn of the century they been havin' those fancy shindigs. Spend a fortune." Mr. St. Julien frowned. "I hear them parties get wild, too."

"Well at least he doesn't have the power his grandfather and great-grandfather had around here. Like you said, it's a new day," Chase said. He pulled LaShaun closer to him. "The Trosclair name doesn't send folks running to do their bidding anymore."

"Right," Mr. St. Julien agreed.

The folks they called "Old Beau Chene" knew well about LaShaun's intense affair with the rich man's son years before. LaShaun was barely out of her teens, and using her gifts in all the wrong ways. She saw Quentin as a way to gain a fortune and power. The legends about LaShaun's ancestors said the Rousselle clan had done the same for generations. LaShaun pushed aside the familiar weight of the dark family history.

"You should make a few more, Mr. St. Julien. I'll bet

you'd pick some more wealthy pockets if you did," LaShaun joked to lighten the tone of the conversation.

"You might be onto something, little lady. Y'all go enjoy your lunch." Mr. St. Julien gave Chase a handshake. "You keep these criminals in line."

"I'm working on it, sir. You have a great day." Chase gave him a pat on the shoulder.

"Bye-bye." LaShaun accepted a peck on the cheek from the older man.

"You take care. I'm so happy you're going to have a wedding and a family soon." Mr. St. Julien beamed at them both.

"A wedding yes, but if you mean..." LaShaun blushed and blinked rapidly.

"I'm going to consider them my grandchildren, too," Mr. St. Julien said, taking the thought even farther.

"You sure can," Chase piped up. He grinned when LaShaun poked his side with an elbow. "What?"

"You gonna have babies. Your Monmon Odette told as much," Mr. St. Julien said. His sister, Miss Marie, came out of the back of the store talking to an employee. She joined them.

"Who gonna have babies?" she said, and waved hello to LaShaun and Chase. Then she looked at them again. "Oh, are you?"

"No," LaShaun said fast, loudly and firmly.

"All young couples have them some babies, it's natural as rain and sunshine. Why we'd have an empty, sad world without babies," Mr. St. Julien went on, oblivious to LaShaun's blushes.

"Antoine, shush. You just have to forgive my brother. He don't know better than to say what's on his mind." Miss Marie shook a finger at her brother.

"Oh shoot, I'm just tellin' the truth. Bye, darlin'."

Mr. St. Julien winked at LaShaun.

They exchanged more goodbyes and walked two more blocks to the cafe Lagniappe Cafe. Chase teased LaShaun all the way. Mr. St. Julien's warmth, and his sister's down home sense of humor, had brightened the day. Heads turned when they entered the cafe, but LaShaun felt the positive waves sent toward them. The pretty waitress with blonde highlights worked hard not to stare as she led them to a table. She clearly found Chase attractive, with his handsome Cajun looks. One man gave him a thumbs up sign.

"You're pretty popular around town," the waitress, Jenny from her name tag, said with a smile. She seemed not to notice LaShaun. "Everybody is talking about how you arrested that drug dealer and helped keep a serial killer from getting out of prison."

"Thank you, ma'am," Chase replied with a gracious nod.

LaShaun cleared her throat when the woman kept gazing wistfully at Chase. "I'll have a glass of sweet tea."

"Uh, yeah. Right." Jenny reluctantly acknowledged LaShaun's presence. "And for you Deputy Broussard?"

"I'll have cola, Jenny. Thanks."

"Sure thing. I'll be right back to take your order." Jenny rushed off as though she couldn't wait to serve Chase.

LaShaun gently kicked him under the table and rolled her eyes. 'I'll have cola, Jenny'," she said, her voice pitched low mimicking him.

"What? I can't help being popular," Chase joked.

"At least this time the town gossip is in your favor for the election," LaShaun quipped. She started to say more, but stopped in surprise.

Neal Montgomery and his sidekick Krystal sat at a

table on the other side of the cafe. He nodded to LaShaun. Still looking at her, Montgomery dropped money on the table and headed toward them. He seemed to have forgotten Krystal. She called out to him, but Montgomery merely lifted a hand in response without breaking his stride. The young woman shot an angry scowl at his back, but then followed after a few seconds. They arrived at LaShaun and Chase's table at the same time the waitress returned.

"I'll come back for your orders in a few," Jenny said and left again.

"So you haven't left town yet," Chase said as he stood and shook hands with Montgomery. He nodded to Krystal, who in turn murmured a soft hello.

"We're on our way to New Orleans now. I'll be back this weekend, but not on business." Montgomery transferred his smile from Chase to LaShaun.

Krystal wore an annoyed expression. "We'll be back this weekend."

"Funny. You don't look like the outdoors type," Chase said mildly.

LaShaun's skin started to tingle like crazy as Montgomery's smile widened. He radiated satisfaction. Montgomery relished being able to spring an unexpected piece of news on LaShaun. Her vision sharpened as if her surroundings had been switched to high definition.

"You're going to be a guest at the Trosclair Mardi Gras ball," LaShaun said.

Krystal hissed in shock. Chase looked at LaShaun with a baffled expression. Yet Montgomery's smile didn't waver, nor did he seem perturbed by LaShaun's declaration. With her senses enhanced, LaShaun noticed those around them, town residents, were paying close attention.

"Quentin throws the best parties. The Trosclair social events even get talked about in New Orleans circles. Isn't that right, Krystal?" Montgomery did not look at her despite his question.

"Hmm," Krystal replied.

"Ah, we've interrupted your lunch long enough. Goodbye," Montgomery said when the waitress approached again. He started to leave but turned back. "Wait a minute. Why don't you two come to the ball? Deputy Broussard could do his campaign some good making contacts."

"Quentin Trosclair might have a problem with us showing up without an invitation," Chase quipped. "Besides, I'm pretty sure he's not one of my supporters."

"I happen to know Quentin has no horse in this race." Montgomery took out his cell phone and tapped the screen. "Hello, Q. Yes, we're about to get on the road now. Listen, I'm here with Deputy Broussard. What about sending an invitation to the leading candidate for Sheriff of this fine parish?"

Montgomery tapped the phone again. Quentin's laughter bounced from the small smart phone's speaker. "I should have thought of sending Chase and LaShaun an invitation. Brilliant idea. I'll have it delivered to the Sheriff's station within the hour!"

"Excellent, Q. See you Saturday." Montgomery ended the call and beamed at them. "We're going to have a wonderful time. Well, we better get going. Goodbye."

Krystal merely glared at LaShaun as she swept past them to follow in Montgomery's wake. The tall, good looking attorney attracted admiring glances from the women in the cafe. Krystal radiated resentment. Montgomery's charisma would continually attract women, a power he savored. LaShaun suspected he used it regularly. His lover had years of misery ahead.

Jenny cleared her throat to get Chase's attention. "Sir, your orders?"

Both ordered sandwiches with sides of coleslaw. They watched the waitress leave again. The other diners shot glances at them, and the buzz of conversation hummed through the air. LaShaun could imagine Beau Chene would get an update on the couple that kept them all talking, the latest episode of the deputy and the voodoo priestess.

"Humph, that's a strange development." Chase drank from his glass and gazed out of the wide window onto the street.

"What an understatement. You have my permission to be rude and send a 'Hell no" as your RSVP," LaShaun retorted. When he didn't respond, her skin tingled again. "You're not seriously planning..."

"I think we should go. Like Montgomery said, it's a great chance for me to make nice with the rich and powerful." Chase looked at her. "You're curious about out how those two got to be friends. Admit it. Here's your chance to find out."

LaShaun gazed at him in fascination. Chase seemed the same, but different in a way that disturbed her, a lot. What's more he was dead on target. She definitely wanted to see Quentin and Montgomery together to glean a sense of what was going on.

"So I guess we're going to the ball." LaShaun shivered at the smile Chase gave her in response. She also wanted desperately to find out what was happening to Chase.

:

Chapter 9

Saturday morning LaShaun went to visit Miss Rose again. The elderly woman had been delighted to get her call. The drive to Mouton Cove was lovely. Even with the cold of winter holding on for one last bite, Louisiana fought back. Green leaves mixed in with the bare gray branches of leaves stripped by frosty winds of early March. Fluffy clouds, light giant cotton balls, hovered against the blue skies. Yet the bright March sunshine hadn't worked on LaShaun's dark mood. By the time she reached Miss Rose's lovely old Creole Cottage, it was barely seven-thirty in the morning. LaShaun drove down the driveway around to the back of the house. The older woman waved at her from a window.

Miss Rose opened the kitchen door. "Hello, sweet daughter. This is a fine morning, eh?"

"Good morning. Yes, the weather is nice." LaShaun pulled her jacket closer against the sharp March wind. "Whew, I'm looking forward to spring though."

"Warmer weather and a wedding. You have good reason to look forward to spring."

LaShaun took off her jacket after she entered the cozy kitchen. Miss Rose chuckled as she closed the door firmly against the chill. She slipped on an oven mitt and took a cast iron skillet from the oven. She placed it on the stove. The smell of fresh coffee, biscuits, and sausage filled the air. Miss Rose placed the food on two plates. LaShaun poured two cups of coffee, and both of them sat down at the table.

"You need something hot in your stomach. You shouldn't miss breakfast."

"Thank you, Miss Rose." LaShaun didn't need to ask how the older woman knew she hadn't eaten. "I'm sorry for bothering you at this early hour."

"Child, I get up at five o'clock every morning. Old people don't sleep well. My husband is already up and gone. He went to his friend's farm to help him put out hay for his cows. Fred's kids have all moved to the city. Young folks don't want to live the old ways, eh? Well I don't blame 'em. Who wants to walk through manure all day?" Miss Rose chuckled again. "Ah, but I miss the old days. My first husband had a ranch."

"Yes, ma'am," LaShaun said respectfully. She knew the story of Miss Rose's first husband. Loris Mouton had been a handsome Creole cowboy. In the forties and fifties he'd competed in rodeos.

Miss Rose sighed. "I've been blessed with two good men, Dieu merci. But you didn't come out here to listen to my dusty stories from the past."

LaShaun smiled at her with affection. "There is more wisdom in your ramblings than most could hope to have in a lifetime."

"So, it's old woman wisdom you need, eh child?" Miss Rose lifted a dark eyebrow at LaShaun.

"Counsel from a woman who understands that there is more to this world than what we see with our eyes," LaShaun said, her smile now gone.

Miss Rose drank her coffee in silence for a few moments as she seemed to ponder LaShaun's words. "Eat your breakfast."

LaShaun had skipped dinner the evening before, unable to stomach food. She spent most of the night watching the eerie blue light dance in her woods. Its return taunted her that prayers had not been enough to banish the demon. Or maybe her prayers had not been strong enough or pure because of the things she'd done in her past.

Miss Rose's maternal attention consoled LaShaun. Suddenly at ease, LaShaun felt hunger pains for the first time in hours. The fluffy buttered biscuit melted against LaShaun's tongue when she tasted it. Miss Rose nodded approval and nibbled on at piece of sausage, still thinking. The two women shared the morning meal as though they were having a normal visit. After a time Miss Rose stood slowly. She tugged the sweater she wore a bit closer as she left, slippers shuffling across the tiled floor.

"I'll be right back, cher," Miss Rose said over her shoulder.

True to her word, Miss Rose came back a few minutes later. She carefully laid a thick book on the table. She tapped a forefinger on the dark green leather cover with gold letters. A border of more gold, in the shape of leaves laid end to end, decorated the book. LaShaun gazed at the book for a second. She carefully wiped her hands on the cloth napkin before picking it up.

"Warriors Against Evil: The Battle Rages Quietly, by Father Leonce Gautier," LaShaun read aloud. She admired the workmanship of the book for a few seconds before opening the pages. "Wow, written in seventeen ninety-nine."

"He wrote the second edition and published it in eighteen forty-seven. Father Gautier came to Louisiana in seventeen eighty-nine. He was twenty-two years old. He went to Natchitoches first. You know it's the oldest settlement in Louisiana. Anyway, he eventually made his way to Vermilion Parish. He's not as well known as Father Maigret in the history books, but those of us who know understand. This is an English version. I donated the French version, second edition, to Xavier University. Four of my ten grandchildren attended there you know."

"You're right to be proud, too," LaShaun said. Afraid Miss Rose would veer off to brag on them, LaShaun gently prodded her back to the subject at hand. "But the book."

"Hmm, ah yes. You know me too well, cher. In a minute I'd be showing you pictures of my beautiful babies." Miss Rose laughed, and then turned serious again. "This book talks about Father Gautier's encounters with people who did terrible things. He eventually concluded that some were possessed. Others, while not possessed, had simply decided that committing evil acts would benefit them more than following the scriptures."

"Satan worshippers?" LaShaun flipped to the first chapter.

"No, not exactly. He spoke of those who had scorn for Biblical instructions to turn the other cheek, resist the lure of fleshly desires and so on. They followed Satan by their deeds, choosing to lie, steal, commit adultery with whoever they wanted to as often as possible. You name a sin, they committed it." Miss Rose wore a grin. "Not that different from today, eh?"

"No difference at all, Miss Rose," LaShaun agreed.

"According to Father Gautier, there are those among us who choose evil. While they live, they prey on the weak-minded. The worst of these may come back as demons once they die. Father Gautier calls these weak ones "dupes". They're seduced by the truly evil ones, who tend to be charismatic and good-looking. Finally there are those who are possessed by demons. They don't seek to be taken over, but a strong evil spirit can seize a chance to become even more powerful. " Miss Rose leaned back against her chair. She looked tired, as though speaking of such wickedness sapped energy from her.

LaShaun refilled Miss Rose's empty cup with more coffee. "We can put off this talk for another time. I think you need rest."

"No, we talk now. You will tell me why you're so afraid for the young man you love." Miss Rose nodded slowly when LaShaun put a hand over her mouth. "Tell me, cher."

Her voice trembling at first, LaShaun began the story. LaShaun told her about her ancestors first, and how the loa had been called on to help them again. Every detail documented in the journals tumbled across LaShaun's lips. She hadn't spoken to anyone of the accounts of family misdeeds that spanned just over two centuries. Monmon Odette had been her only confidant. Now Miss Rose filled a void. LaShaun could speak of these things with not only someone who shared her Creole heritage, but who had "the gift". LaShaun finished with the account of her long ago affair with Quentin Trosclair.

"I feel like my ancestors brought on this evil. Including what happened at the Metier House in 1837." LaShaun let out a long sigh. Some of the weight of her family guilt lifted from her soul. But by no means all of it.

"Cher, there is something very deep going on here. Father Gautier attended the trial of Clarissa Metier. He was her spiritual advisor. I found an account that doesn't name her, but I'm sure this is the same incident from the way he describes it. But..." Miss Rose paused dramatically. "Father Gautier describes much more than that old newspaper article."

"The murder was more gruesome," LaShaun said softly.

"Yes, her husband's throat was cut so deeply his head almost came off. 'Only a slender thread of flesh held it close to the poor wretch's body', is exactly how Father Gautier put it." Miss Rose gave a shudder. "He talks about what he calls depravity. Mrs. Metier was rumored to have had many lovers."

"Was she one of the truly evil or a dupe?" LaShaun flipped the pages of the book.

"Father Gautier could never figure her out. Maybe she was possessed," Miss Rose said quietly. "Now, cher, tell what has happened to Deputy Broussard?"

LaShaun felt a stab of ice cold fear in her chest. "The blue light in my woods is back. And Chase is acting... not like himself. He's more aggressive than I've seen him before. It's not like he's on edge or losing his temper. No, he's cool and calculating about using violence to enforce his will. No remorse, and no apologies."

"Ah, you know him much better than me, child. Your gift will guide." Miss Rose sipped more coffee and sat deep in thought.

"Here's another thing. Just the mention of Quentin used to make him practically spit in disgust. The other day he was joking about him, and we're going to the Trosclair Mardi Gras ball," LaShaun said.

"Mon dieu. That doesn't sound like a good idea, cher," Miss Rose exclaimed.

"Sometimes you have to track a predator instead of waiting for him to come to you, Miss Rose," LaShaun said with a voice of steel. "I want to know how Quentin is connected to any of this. He's one who has chosen evil. Unfortunately I know him well, too."

Miss Rose gazed at her. "Quentin Trosclair would have chosen his path even if he'd never met you." Miss Rose went back to sipping coffee and thinking.

LaShaun read a couple of pages before she closed the book. "I don't know what to do."

Miss Rose gave LaShaun's hand a maternal pat. "Ah, cher, you must let go of your past. You hug it much too close. As for what to do, you have your grandmother's good sense and your mother's fire. You'll find your way.""I would gladly let go of my past, Miss Rose. But it keeps rising up like a zombie to follow me," LaShaun said, her voice heavy with a dread of what might come.

***

Saturday night at eight o'clock Chase picked her up at home. Despite all of his long hours, he made time to attend the famous Trosclair Mardi Gras ball. He looked magnificent in a black suit. A black top hat and a silver mask was his only costume. Yet he managed to look like a gentleman from a bygone era. The heavy gold chain of a watch swung from the pocket of his suit jacket. LaShaun chose to wear a lace shift dress the golden color of the finest champagne. Her hair was in a French roll, and she wore a gold headband around her head. She wrapped a fancy bronze colored brocade cloak around her to keep warm against the chilly night. When she opened the door, Chase let out a long whistle.

"You look so beautiful," Chase said. His dark eyes shone bright with desire.

"Merci, monsieur. I'm a lady from the nineteen twenties ready to slip into a speak-easy and shake my shimmy to some hot jazz." LaShaun batted her eyelashes at him.

"We'll hold off on the shakin' until after this party," Chase replied. "For now, I'm going to shake hands to get last minute votes."

LaShaun's amusement faded quickly when she remembered where they were going. "Why don't we forget about this party? Since we're all dressed up we could drive to Club Francois in Lafayette for their Saturday night jam. We'd have a much better time."

"Yes, but nobody in Lafayette can vote in Vermilion Parish. Now come on so you can make all those rich women jealous." Chase kissed her lightly on the forehead, and then swept a hand out with a flourish. "Your carriage waits, princess."

"My prince calls his pick-up truck a chariot. Yep, you're a true Cajun," LaShaun quipped. She followed instructions and went ahead of him out of her back door.

Despite her effort to match Chase's good mood, LaShaun's unease grew as each mile slipped beneath the truck tires. They drove toward the outskirts of Beau Chene to the Trosclair family home. The moon glowed in the night sky like a giant white mother of pearl disk. For once, LaShaun hoped Chase would get a call that he needed to report for work. His phone remained annoyingly quiet.

Chase brushed a finger against LaShaun's cheek. "Beautiful night, huh? The moon looks like it's so close."

"There are a lot of myths associated with the moon. For instance, in some African legends the moon and the sun are lovers. The solar and lunar eclipses happen when they make love." LaShaun shrugged when he glanced at her. "It's true. Look it up if you don't believe me."

"You're my moon. Let's make an eclipse right now. I can pull off under those trees over there."

"Don't you dare," LaShaun said quickly and pointed ahead. "You keep this truck on the road."

He laughed hard for a few seconds. "Okay, okay. Guess we'll have to stick to the plan."

LaShaun relaxed at the familiar playfulness that she enjoyed. Maybe it was all in her imagination that Chase was different. Still the reality of where they were headed poked at her. "Honey, I'm really shocked that you agreed to attend a party given by Quentin. You're not exactly a fan of his. In fact, you threatened to shoot him once." (Read A Darker Shade of Midnight)

"I'm willing to use his curiosity about me to be more visible with high rollers." Chase grew serious. "I did some research. A lot of the society types that accept his invitations don't really like him. But his family still has a lot of power all over the state."

"Really? People don't like Quentin? I'm so totally shocked!" LaShaun fell back against the leather truck seat in melodramatic fashion. "Maybe the fact that he's a selfish, backstabbing snake has something to do with it."

Chase let out a bark of laughter. "Anyway, you know the old saying about staying even closer to the enemy."

"Yeah, well sometimes it's better to handle a snake with a really long handle," LaShaun retorted.

"We can debate it later," Chase replied. He turned the truck off the four lane highway that led to Beau Chene. A wide street curved around until it ended. "Wow."

Belle Oaks Drive ended at the Trosclair family home

driveway. Yet "family home" didn't begin to describe the three storied structured. Four Ionic columns graced the wraparound porch on all three floors. All were lit up. The first floor had golden hued lights, the second floor had green lights, and the third floor had lavender lamps. The Mardi Gras colors made the house glow. Garlands in matching colors had been wrapped around the railing of each porch. A giant set of Mardi Gras Masks hung on the huge double doors leading into the house. Valets kept busy parking luxury cars that arrived.

"Damn, I should have put some Mardi Gras beads on the truck to fancy it up," Chase joked.

"Humph," LaShaun said with a snort. "You look mighty fine in this truck any day of the week."

"Guess I won't worry about you wanting to run off with some guy in a Jaguar then." Chase looked around at the professionally landscaped grounds.

"All the glitter doesn't impresses me. Remember, Quentin has scales beneath those thousand dollar suits he wears." LaShaun placed a hand on his arm and squeezed firmly. "I don't miss those days at all."

Chase gazed at her. "I don't doubt your love, darlin', and I'm not jealous."

"You have zero reason to be," LaShaun said and kissed his cheek. "Now let's get this over with."

A burly young man hurried to the passenger door. "Let me help you, ma'am. Sir, I'll need to see your invitation.

"No problem," Chase replied. He pulled the envelope from his inside jacket pocket and handed it to him.

"Thank you, sir. Now if you leave the keys we'll safely park your vehicle."

"I hope they're paying you well tonight," Chase said as he handed the young man a valet key.

"I'm doing good," the valet grinned back.

LaShaun put on her mask as she waited for Chase to finish small talk with the valet. She listened to music coming from inside. Chase joined her and they walked up the brick path to the steps. As they crossed the porch, the doors swung wide as though they'd been expected. A middle-aged woman took LaShaun's cloak.

"Here, ma'am. Put this ticket in your purse. Not that I won't remember you wore this lovely thing. Is this fur collar real?" The woman held up the cloak.

"Thank you. No, it simulated seal fur." LaShaun smiled at her.

"My oh my. Y'all go on in and get some refreshments." She blinked at them. "You make a handsome pair, if I'm not being too familiar."

"Thank you, ma'am. All compliments like that make you darn near family," Chase said. The woman hustled off when a stern looking man glanced their way.

"Well, let's mingle with our betters," Chase murmured. He walked close to LaShaun.

"Trust me, no one here is better than us. They're all people with the same flaws. They just get to display them in a more elaborate way with all their money."

Chase chuckled. "You're very cynical tonight. So, does the place look different?"

"I've never been here before." LaShaun raised an eyebrow at him above her golden mask. "Sweetheart, I was not the date Quentin could bring home to meet the folks."

"What a naughty girl you were back then. Save some of that for me later." Chase put his arm around her waist.

"Stop," LaShaun whispered, but giggled. "Someone is going to hear."

"No one has noticed us. They're too busy drinking expensive wine and eating this fancy food." Chase waved to a passing waiter with a tray of goblets.

"Don't let these folks fool you. We're being discreetly examined. Once they warm up we'll get some interesting questions. I give it maybe five minutes before the ice is broken." LaShaun smiled as she took a sip. "Yes, only the best."

A woman with reddish blonde hair glided over to them. She wore a floor length cream silk gown that draped her slender figure perfectly. The long sleeves ended in a bell shape at her wrists. Perfect white teeth sparkled when her blood red lips parted in a smile.

"I'm Janine Trosclair. Welcome to our little gathering. I don't believe we've met."

Janine Trosclair gave Chase an appreciative head to toe look. Then she turned to LaShaun. Her smile faltered for a second, but she recovered quickly. Her exclusive private-girls-school manners took over. An artificial smile stretched her thin lips up at the corners.

"Deputy Chase Broussard, and this is my fiancée Ms. LaShaun Rousselle."

"You're running for sheriff of Vermilion Parish. How wonderful that you could be here. I don't care what some of my husband's friends say. I think you're just as qualified as Mr. Godchaux." Janine's velvet tone delivered the zinger as though she was merely making polite conversation. Still her eyes glittered as she waited for a reaction.

LaShaun knew instantly that the woman relished manipulating tense, even explosive scenes. "Why thanks for your confidence, Mrs. Trosclair."

"Please call me Janine, LaShaun. Now that we're friends, Chase, let me introduce you to Bill Ambrose. You might have seen his name in the papers as William J. Ambrose. He's the CEO of the southeast division of Pantheon Corporation. His grandfather was one of the founders." Janine paused. "You don't mind if I borrow Chase for a moment. This is a golden opportunity for him to make connections."

"Of course not. I'm going to make new friends myself over at the buffet table," LaShaun replied with her own killer smile firmly in place.

"Perfect, dear. You have fun over there." Janine's tone managed to communicate that it might be best if LaShaun not go with them. A mixed couple might test the facade of tolerance of the most supposed liberal among her set.

Chase's dark eyebrows drew together. "I won't be gone long."

"No need to rush on my account." LaShaun waved at him.

Chase left with the hostess. Janine chattered away as they moved through the crowd in the large foyer. LaShaun gave him another smile of assurance when he glanced back at her over his shoulder. Once they disappeared, LaShaun took time to notice the interior of the home. Marble floors the color of rich cream gleamed beneath a chandelier in the foyer. A curved staircase led up to the upper floors. On the western facing side of the house was another arched entrance. The oak frame of the open double doors had carvings of magnolia blooms. The dining room beyond had been set up with a long table filled with gold plated trays of food. The center piece was a large paper mache harlequin figure. It sat in the center of a king cake.

"I'm glad you convinced Deputy Broussard to come."

LaShaun spun around at the sound of the silken seductive voice so familiar to her. She gazed into the icy blue eyes of Quentin Trosclair. He held a large champagne flute in one hand. He laughed and took a long gulp of the golden wine.

"Hello, Quentin. Thanks for the invitation," LaShaun said in a distinctly ungrateful tone.

"Well don't fall over with delight, darlin'. I was just kidding about you convincing 'The Candidate' by the way. He's quite the political climber. Neal says he was eager to come."

"How exactly do you know Neal?" LaShaun ignored his dig at Chase.

"We were at Princeton together. Before they kicked me out that is. The men in our respective families have attended since before the Civil War. Anyway, he graduated and came to Tulane law school. I was there work on my MBA. Grandfather whipped me into shape and made me finish college." Quentin lifted his glass. "Here's to grand old granddad."

LaShaun eyed him closer. He swayed ever so slightly. "So you two stayed in touch."

"We've been great friends for years. He's considered a legal genius across the country. He's even given lectures at international conferences." Quentin sidled up close to LaShaun as though they were on great terms. "But he still knows how to have fun, too."

"Odd he happens to be in Vermilion Parish representing a serial killer, since he's such a prominent man in the legal world," LaShaun said. She noted with satisfaction the brief glint in Quentin's eyes. He wasn't as drunk as he pretended.

"Neal doesn't take on battles he can't win. So there must be solid evidence the man is innocent." Quentin nodded slowly.

"That's bull," LaShaun said bluntly.

"I like how you deliver an opinion. Straight, no chaser. Brings back the old days when we were... close, remember?"

LaShaun rolled her eyes. "Yes, unfortunately I remember more than I'd care to."

"Now darlin', don't be like that." Quentin's gaze swept over her body.

Jonathan Graham stumbled around and through other party goers until he got to them. He gave Quentin a look of contempt. Dark beer sloshed over the side of the large glass mug he held in one fist. "Well, I see you're still chasing other men's wives. Slimy son of a..."

"Drink my liquor and insult me. Isn't that what the perfect guest should do?" Quentin replied mildly.

Allison Graham stood across the room. She didn't move to intervene or stop her husband's behavior. Most of the other guests kept right on partying, as though they were used to drunken confrontations on the subject of adultery. A few shook their heads and headed off to get more food or drink.

"Stay the hell away from Allison you bastard. Screwing half the population of Louisiana doesn't keep you busy enough?" Jonathan shouted.

"Mr. Graham, maybe you should give the drinking a rest and go get some fresh air," LaShaun said quietly.

"And what the hell is she doing here? Her man must not know about the history between you two. I'll bet you're going to give him a couple of earfuls, huh Quentin?" Jonathan lurched toward LaShaun. "Yeah, bet he's got some stories to tell about you."

"Making a scene won't help your family at all, Jonathan," Quentin said in a reasoned tone. "Your son is in quite enough trouble. That's where your focus should be. Not on baseless accusations."

"You don't know a damn thing about my son," Jonathan snapped. He pointed at LaShaun. "And you stop filling my wife's head with a lot of bullshit jungle magic."

Chase strode up. "Just what the hell does that mean, Mr. Graham?"

Chapter 10

LaShaun's heart pumped double-time in fear at the wildness in Chase's eyes. He stood gazing at Jonathan; his hands flexed open and then into twin closed fists. Every muscle in his tall powerful body seemed poised to spring on the man. A circle of Quentin's guests seemed keen to witness a smack down. Jonathan Graham looked at Chase for a full minute without saying anything. He must have seen the dangerous line he'd crossed.

"Forget it," he mumbled and pushed his way through a knot of costumed party guests.

"What do you expect? He's only two generations from being like those swamp characters on television," a woman said quietly to her two companions, her patrician southern drawl damning him for not having true blue blood.

"I don't know why Jon is complaining. He's been banging Missy Edwards forever, and Allison knows it," her male companion replied. All three wandered off laughing.

"That was... interesting. Remind me not to cross your lover, lover," Quentin whispered in her ear. Then he turned to Chase. "I apologize for that unpleasant spectacle. I certainly didn't invite you here to be insulted."

"No problem," Chase replied. Still he watched Jonathan Graham walk to the bar set up in a corner of the living room.

"Maybe we should..." LaShaun stopped when Chase raised a hand.

"I gotta take this." Chase pulled out his vibrating cell phone, glanced at the display and answered. The crowd parted to let him through.

"Now that's what I call a real sheriff. He takes no bullshit," an older man said in a gruff voice. "We need somebody that will kick ass with these trashy types around here. Hear that, Quent?"

"Yes, Uncle Hugh. I hear you." Quentin gave LaShaun a sideways wink. He lowered his voice and guided LaShaun away. "That's my mother's youngest brother. Uncle Hugh is a crusty old bastard, but he's rich as sin. I try not to disagree with him."

"How fascinating," LaShaun murmured. She watched the front door swing shut as Chase went onto the porch. Then she walked toward a window. Chase leaned against one of the huge columns, still on the phone.

"I'm sure he'll be just fine," Quentin said over her shoulder. "You really are into him."

LaShaun turned to face him. "I love him fiercely."

Before Quentin could answer, Neal Montgomery appeared out of nowhere. "It seems Deputy Broussard is taking a serious business call. Trouble somewhere has flared up."

"A lawman's work is never done," Quentin put in.

Something pricked LaShaun's senses. She stared at Montgomery. "What do you..."

"LaShaun, I've got to leave. I'll get your wrap," Chase said.

Quentin smiled at LaShaun without looking at Chase. "I'll see LaShaun gets home safe and sound, Deputy Broussard. That way you won't be delayed answering an important call."

LaShaun took Chase's hand. "Lovely party, thanks

for inviting us."

"Come again," Quentin shot back.

Janine walked up next to Quentin and put a hand around his shoulder. "Yes, please do come back. We'd both love to have you."

LaShaun tilted her head to one side. No, she hadn't imagined the sexual innuendo in the woman's tone. "Goodbye."

Chase nodded and tugged on LaShaun's hand to urge her along. The woman who'd taken the coats saw them coming and disappeared into the living room. Minutes later she came back with LaShaun's cloak. She helped wrap it around LaShaun's shoulders.

"I told you I'd remember. Thanks for spicing up this gig," the woman whispered to LaShaun. "You made even the best of these ladies look like hags." She chuckled as she stepped away.

"Thank you," LaShaun said with a laugh.

"You're welcome ma'am. Thank you, sir," the woman said with delight when Chase handed her a ten dollar bill as a tip.

As they left, LaShaun looked back to see Quentin, Janine, Neal Montgomery and Krystal Hardy watching them. They had the look of hounds observing potential targets for a hunt. LaShaun moved closer to Chase, gripping his hand tighter. They waited a few seconds for the valet to get his truck since Chase had already talked to the valet. As soon as the truck doors shut and they were alone, LaShaun turned to him.

"What's happened?" she asked.

"A guy was found wandering around Black Bayou Road. He was all beat and mumbling nonsense." Chase turned on the heater when LaShaun shivered. "It'll warm up soon enough, honey."

LaShaun nodded, but the chill she felt wasn't because of the weather. "Okay, so some drunk guy got into a fight. Why is that an emergency for you?"

"Because the deputy followed a trail of blood and found a body. They can't tell if it's male or female." Chase wore a grim expression.

"I don't understand," LaShaun replied.

"The body is so cut up we'll have to wait for the corner to tell us."

***

An hour after Chase had dropped LaShaun off at home, she had taken off her finery, and was curled up on the sofa of her den off the large kitchen of her home. She wore her favorite Southern University sweat suit and slipper socks. She cupped a mug of chamomile tea with honey in both hands as she waited for news to come on. A local access television channel showed a replay of the ten o'clock news broadcast every two hours. When the credits rolled at the end of an old detective series from the 80s, LaShaun turned up the volume. After a commercial advertising a furniture store, the news show graphics flashed on.

"Good evening and thank you for tuning in to KATC. We start with breaking news out of Vermilion Parish. A state police spokesperson tells us that a body has been discovered on a rural road near Black Bayou. Few details have been released, but sources tell KATC news that the sheriff's department and state police suspect foul play. This is based on the condition of the body when found. We'll bring you updates when we learn more. In other news..."

The blonde anchorman's voice faded when LaShaun

turned down the volume again. She stared ahead without seeing the images of annoyed politicians squabbling. Instead she thought of other events in the parish. LaShaun did not ponder if they were connected. The familiar tingling beneath her skin confirmed it. Now she waited for a vision or image to come, but she felt nothing. She had no more than the unsettled feeling that more bad things were on the way. After a time, LaShaun went to the bay window looking out over her back lawn. Despite the dread in the pit of her stomach, she looked at the woods. No blue light. Yet she wasn't comforted by its absence. The thing was off stalking human victims. In fact, LaShaun had to face the possibility that the spirit had begun to influence Chase. Such dark thoughts made her mind freeze with fear. She began to tremble. Chase could handle himself against any threat from a human criminal. What could he do against an attack on his very soul?

The ringing telephone startled her into spilling tea on her sweat shirt. She ignored the feel of the hot liquid and the stain. Instead she put the mug down on the table and rushed to the phone. Snatching up the handset, she noticed what the caller ID displayed.

"Hey, babe. I figured you watched the news. Just checking in so you won't worry. Gonna be a long night of dealing with this latest mess we got." Chase let out a long sigh.

"Thank God you sound normal," LaShaun blurted out.

"What's that?" Chase's puzzled tone came through the receiver.

"I mean, I'm glad you're okay," LaShaun put in quickly and cursed at the slip.

"Humph, okay as I can be after what I've seen. Feels

153

like somebody has been rubbing sandpaper on my eyes." Chase sighed again.

"Come home to me when you finally wrap up. I'll fix waffles and andouille sausage, your favorites. I've got that new local blend coffee you like, too."

"You're too good to me, girl. Is that why I'm so crazy about you?" Chase joked.

"I don't know, soon-to-be Sheriff Broussard. You can list all the reasons for me, cher." LaShaun went back to the sofa and sat down again. "I'll have a fire lit for you."

"I'll have a fire for you, too," Chase said with a chuckle. "I gotta go, babe."

"Wait a sec, just tell me you're coming by," LaShaun said quickly.

"I don't know. Let me call you in another couple of hours or so. You might not want me to, not with the smell of death on my clothes," Chase said, the light joking lilt gone from his Cajun accent.

"Bad, huh?" LaShaun knew the answer even as she asked the question.

"Worse than they say some of the bodies Manny Young left behind," Chase replied.

"My Lord." The doorbell rang and LaShaun stood. "Somebody's at the door..."

"Do not answer it, LaShaun," Chase barked into the phone. "There's a crazy person running loose. Just let them assume you're not home. LaShaun, are you hearing me?"

"Calm down. I can handle myself." LaShaun darted into her bedroom. She took her antique silver dagger from the nightstand drawer. "I've got a couple of extra shotguns in the case thanks to you, honey."

"We'll debate your self-defense skills another time.

Just let the doorbell ring. I can get to your house in ten minutes. Stay away from the door." Chase spoke fast, the words shooting through the phone like bullets.

"You're upset because of what you've seen. I'm going to be fine."

LaShaun nodded as though Chase could see her. She walked down the hallway and looked out of the window. More words of reassurance dried up in her throat. Greg Graham stood on her front porch with a young girl next to him. His clothes were rumpled. An ominous stain smeared the front of his jacket.

"I know you're in there looking at me," Greg shouted.

The girl next to him jumped every time he moved. LaShaun glanced down. Greg held a long butcher knife in one hand pointed down. "We've got a problem. I have to go outside."

"Like hell you do. Look--"

"Greg Graham is on my front porch holding a knife, and he's got a girl with him," LaShaun whispered. "I'm going to put the phone on speaker. Get here. Fast."

LaShaun slipped the phone into a pocket in her sweatpants. "Uh, hey Greg. Give me a chance to put on some clothes, okay? I wasn't expecting company."

"Open the damn door and quit stalling. We need your help," Greg shouted back. His voice went high, almost into a shriek.

The desperate sound of his voice brought LaShaun up short as she started down the hallway. She couldn't risk taking too much longer to retrieve a rosary Monmon Odette had worn for decades. The silver cross had been passed down for at least four generations. Power came from such a holy symbol.

"No time," LaShaun said as she hurried to the front

door. Instead she whispered a prayer her mysterious childhood mentor Jean Paul taught her. "Angel of God, my Guardian dear, to whom God's love commits me here, ever this night be at my side, to light and guard, to rule and guide. Amen."

When LaShaun opened the front door Greg took two steps back. He pulled the girl by the arm to keep her close. In the light of the porch the girl's skin looked pinched and pasty. Greg's gaze slid sideways at his companion and then back to LaShaun.

"Good evening. Hope everything is okay." LaShaun spoke in a calm tone as she unlocked the storm door separating them and pushed it open.

"I didn't know where else to go." Greg faltered as though trying to gather his thoughts. He looked around him as though just realizing he'd traveled to her house. "You alone?"

"Yes." LaShaun looked to the girl for some sign. "Hi, what's your name?"

"Jenna, but my friends call me Jen. It's getting late, and I should go home," the girl said in a shaky voice.

Greg snapped back to the present. "I thought you wanted to be with me. We're having fun. Didn't you like the party we went to?"

"My mother doesn't know I snuck out. She'll be worried," Jenna said. She sniffed, and her eyes pleaded with LaShaun for help. "There was a fight, and those guys were a lot older than us and..."

In an instant the girl's voice faded. Images flashed into LaShaun's head, a story of what brought them to her house. Jenna foolishly allowed her teenage crush to blind her. Convinced that everyone was wrong about him, she'd snuck out of her house to be with Greg. And this wasn't the first time. LaShaun had to prevent this youthful mistake from being fatal.

"Jenna is right. It's really late, and I'll bet she needs to get up early for church in the morning," LaShaun said.

Jenna nodded quickly. "Yes, ma'am. I sing in the choir. I have a solo tomorrow." Tears slid down her face. "I really need to go home."

"Shut up about church. I told you that's a bunch of bullshit they're feeding you. My parents go to church and look at them. Dad screws anything that moves. All the time he's faking the all American family man act." Greg gave a throaty laugh. "I can show you what's real."

"What does that mean, Greg?" LaShaun watched for any sign he might lift the knife. She'd try to get between him and Jenna if necessary.

"Turn the other cheek? Love your enemy? Yeah, right. Only if you want to be somebody else's bitch." Greg spat as though just talking about the scriptures fouled his mouth. "If you've got brains you take control."

LaShaun looked at him closely. His speech wasn't original. Someone had been feeding Greg a twisted doctrine. Teenagers drifting in life, feeling isolated and rejected would grab at some form of philosophy to belong. Cults had been born that way for centuries.

"How exactly do you get control in a world that's out of control?" LaShaun calculated that staying still might keep the girl safe for a little longer.

Greg's eyes narrowed as he smiled at LaShaun. "We have a plan. You should join up with us. We're going to rock the foundations of the world one day. But things take time. I'm one of the stronger ones. I'm going to have a lot of kids, and they'll rule one day."

"You're establishing a dynasty then." LaShaun felt a

prickle along her arms. Greg believed what he was saying, and she knew he wasn't alone in his thinking.

"Yes." Greg rubbed the knife against his thigh as he stared at LaShaun. "With your voodoo skills we could do some damage, make faster progress. I'd even give you a baby or two. Yeah, my women will give birth to a master generation."

Jenna tried to pull away from him. That's disgusting. She's old enough to be your mother."

"Shut the hell up. You're nothing special. Just because your daddy has a little money, so fucking what? The kids at school make fun of you all the time. Your family is only a step up from trailer trash," Greg said and laughed.

"No!" Jenna covered her ears.

LaShaun sensed that Greg had touched on Jenna's weak spot. The girl had deep insecurities about her family background. No doubt the privileged kids at their expensive private school let everyone know who was "in" and who was "out".

Greg pulled her close and spoke in her ear. "Your daddy is vice president of nothing at a company nobody cares about. All I wanted was to sample that tight little pussy, and you gave it up fast. Didn't you?"

"No, no," Jenna cried. The heartbreak dripped from her quivering lips. "Why are you saying these things?"

"Because it's true," Greg shot back.

LaShaun heard the keening sound of sirens, but Greg hadn't noticed yet. He was whispering insults into Jenna's ears until the girl seemed about to collapse. "Greg, you need to put down the knife and let her go. I'll take her home."

"Hell no. We're going to party. I feel like a threesome tonight. Right, Jen? Just like with me, you and Elliot that time." Greg laughed when Jenna responded with a wail.

"I never, I never did," she sobbed.

"Oh yes you most certainly did, babe. I've got the cell phone pictures to prove it." Greg cackled. He stopped laughing and tilted his head to one side. "What's that sound?"

"Listen to me, Greg. Deputies are on the way here. Put down the knife so nobody gets hurt," LaShaun said slow as calmly as she could.

"Sneaky bitch, huh? You were in there calling the cops. Not that it matters. They can't touch me." Greg seemed to relax instead of becoming nervous.

"Let Jen come stand by me."

Greg pulled Jenna tightly against his body making her whimper. "You still don't get it, do you? We're rulers.

"Dear Lord in Heaven, loose the evil binding his mind. Pull the demon's veil from his eyes so that he may see clearly," LaShaun prayed, her words barely audible.

"That won't..." Greg blinked rapidly for several seconds as though waking up from a hypnotic trance. He looked around. "My... my head hurts."

The screech of the sirens sliced through the night getting louder. Flashing blue lights flashed through the trees as headlights swung down Rousselle Lane. The first cruiser turned onto LaShaun's long driveway seconds later.

"Just let Jenna come over here to me, Greg. We'll get you some help." LaShaun glanced over to see Chase step carefully out of his official car. She held up a hand hoping he'd give her time to talk Greg down.

Greg followed her gaze. "They should leave me the

alone."

"I'll call your mother, and then we can all sit down to talk," LaShaun said. She deliberately didn't mention his father since Greg seemed to have a lot of anger toward him.

"She's here?" Greg sounded, and for a second looked like a little boy who'd wandered away from his mother. He half turned as though looking for her.

"Not yet, but we can get her here fast." LaShaun could feel the adrenalin of the growing number of law enforcement professionals arriving. The night air crackled with tension. Her stomach dropped when Greg's expression changed again.

"You're lying, bitch. You called them to stop us, but you're too late." He jerked Jenna with him while backing away.

"You don't wanna do that, Greg," Chase said, his voice made more menacing by the loud speaker atop his cruiser.

"Of course I want to, you dumb fuck. You think I'd be here otherwise?" Greg shouted back.

"You came to talk to me for a reason," LaShaun said quickly to buy time. Waves of anxiety and the need for action came to her from Chase, but also from the other five officers in the dark.

"I thought you would understand. Don't pretend you're my friend now. I know about you. Everybody knows." Greg twisted around. "Hey, I see you out there."

"Greg, listen to me." LaShaun mustered the authority of a maternal authority figure into her voice. "Put down the knife. Jenna is not worth going to jail for, right? You said so a minute ago."

"Greg..." Chase barked.

"Give us a minute. Please," LaShaun yelled back at Chase. "Those deputies will shoot, Greg. There's no need for that. I do understand."

His face softened into a look of tortured despair. "I don't want to be damned, but my life is already a kind of living hell."

"What does that mean, Greg? Put down the knife and let Jen go home. Then you can tell me about these people who got you into something bad," LaShaun replied holding her hand out. "You need to give me the knife."

"No, LaShaun! Back away from him," Chase called out. He was about to say more when M.J. stepped up and spoke to him. He hesitated, but after a few beats handed her the handset.

"Son, we're willing to listen. You need to drop that weapon so this can end peacefully. I know that's what you want. It's what we all want." M.J. spoke in a reasonable tone.

LaShaun still held out her hand. "C'mon, Greg. Let's call it a night and talk without all this drama, huh?"

Greg looked at her hand, his lips quivering. When Greg inched two steps closer to LaShaun, he stretched out his arm and extended the knife to her. When he took another step, so did LaShaun.

"Give it to me handle first." LaShaun stopped moving closer to him. Something shifted in his expression. "Okay, put it down on the floor instead. Move slowly."

"Yeah," Greg said still gazing at LaShaun. He bent forward and down, taking Jenna with him.

"Let go of me you freak," Jenna screamed. She jerked out of his grasp and scrambled away to jump off the porch.

Greg howled out his rage. "I'm going to finish off that bitch," Greg screeched.

He slashed LaShaun's forearm with the knife. She felt no pain, only the warm flow of blood. When she kicked a leg from under him, and Greg sank to one knee. Before he could recover, LaShaun stomped on the arm holding the knife. His expression registered shock and confusion. The world slowed down like a stop action video as deputies charged forward with Chase in the lead. LaShaun started to yell at them not to shoot, but Chase moved fast to protect her. M.J. made it to the porch at almost the same second as Chase. She pulled LaShaun down to the ground. The scene blurred into chaos with shouts, curses and flashing lights.

Gunshot cracked through the voices and Greg fell silent. Everyone froze in place as if someone had hit the pause button on a horror movie. After a few seconds the spell broke, and the cops sprang into action again. Jenna wailed in terror as she crouched on the ground behind a gardenia bush.

"Stupid little shit," Chase grumbled.

LaShaun woke from her daze to stare at him. What she saw frightened her more than the out of control teenager with a knife. Chase had no trace of sympathy for the young man bleeding on the porch floor. She watched as he stepped back to let his fellow law officers follow procedure.

"You need to give me your gun so it can be examined," M.J. said in a muted tone. She gazed at Chase with a troubled frown.

"It was a clean shoot. He went after two hostages with a knife. He even wounded one," Chase said as though practicing his speech for the interview to come, since any police shooting required a review.

"Yeah," M.J. replied and then turned to LaShaun. "I've got paramedics on the way. Deputy Ricard, find something to wrap LaShaun's wound."

Chase seemed to notice LaShaun for the first time. "I'll do it. C'mon, baby. You're gonna be okay. At least that kid won't be taking out anymore victims."

"Chase," LaShaun said sharply. She glanced at M.J. who shook her head slowly.

"I'm just telling the truth. Now let's make sure you don't bleed out before the medical cavalry gets here," he replied without bothering to look at Greg or ask if he was alive. He led LaShaun into the house while whistling a jaunty Cajun tune.

Chapter 11

The next two days sped by LaShaun in a dizzying whirl of answering questions from deputies, and dodging questions from reporters. Greg was alive, but just barely. Chase had taken aim with deadly precision, a single shot to the head. Greg lay in a coma. He'd been transferred from the small hospital outside Beau Chene to a trauma center in Baton Rouge once he'd been stabilized. By the end of the week, LaShaun simply wanted the world to stay out of her way. Savannah came over for lunch Thursday morning. They didn't dare try to eat out, not with all the attention. Cameras clicked like crazy when LaShaun showed up anywhere. A reporter would pop out of nowhere like a magician.

By twelve thirty, LaShaun had homemade chicken salad, coleslaw and raspberry lemonade set up on her back porch. The stitches and thick bandage on her left arm didn't keep her from regular tasks. The early March day had turned warm, though a breeze kept it cool. Savannah drove around to the back of the house and blew her horn as a greeting. She climbed out of her Toyota Rav4. She kept talking on her cell phone as she pushed the SUV door shut with a foot.

"Hey, girl," LaShaun called to her.

"Okay. I'll call you next week. Bye." Savannah ended the call and dropped the phone in her jacket pocket. She heaved a sigh as she climbed the back steps and took a seat. "Damn, can't I just have lunch without anybody getting sued, disinherited, or arrested?"

"Don't complain. If folks clean up their messes, you wouldn't get paid," LaShaun retorted.

Savannah perked up. "Good point. How's your arm, and how are you doing out here in exile?"

"The arm's fine. Just itching like crazy because it's healing. And I don't give a crap about reporters or gossip. I've got a real problem," LaShaun said, her taste for food drying up on her tongue. She poured a glass of lemonade for Savannah from a glass pitcher.

Savannah sighed as she climbed the steps to the porch. "This isn't just a chance for girlfriends to get together type lunch, is it? This is a 'I need a lawyer' lunch."

LaShaun smiled at her friend despite her troubled thoughts. "Stop trying to make me laugh, crazy woman."

"From the look on your face, you need it," Savannah replied. She accepted the lemonade, took a long sip, and squared her shoulders. "Okay, talk to me."

"I'm not even sure how to explain it." LaShaun paced instead of sitting down.

After a few seconds of watching LaShaun walk the length of the porch and back, Savannah shrugged. "Take your time. I'll just help myself to some food."

"Uh-huh." LaShaun continued to pace for a few moments longer. Suddenly she stopped, turned her back to Savannah, and gazed into the distance. Sunlight and blue skies made a stark contrast to the dark subject she had to broach. Then she faced her friend. "I want to make sure Chase isn't elected sheriff."

Savannah froze in the act of bringing a fork full of chicken salad to her mouth. "S'cuse me?"

"I'm not sure I can save Chase from the demon trying to take over him in time. The election is less than a month away and..."

"Back the hell up." Savannah dropped the fork in

her hand. She didn't notice it bounce from the plate onto the floor. "Please tell me you didn't say something about demon possession. Please."

"The signs are clear, Savannah. I... I'm losing him slowly." LaShaun's legs felt weak. She finally sank onto a chair.

Savannah pushed the food away. "I don't think either of us is in the mood to eat right now. Keep talking."

"Do you think they'll charge Chase for shooting Greg?" LaShaun asked.

"Unlikely. Greg had a knife, he held two women hostage, and injured one of them. Some may question that he overreacted," Savannah replied.

"Greg's parents for sure," LaShaun broke in.

"Oh yes, there is going to be a lawsuit. Here's the odd thing, that lawyer trying to get Manny Young out of prison is advising them." Savannah nodded.

LaShaun blinked hard as that news rattled around her brain. "What is going on?"

"He's not representing them. One of his pals from New Orleans is the attorney of record. He's a top civil litigator in the state, too. If I had to guess, I'd say they're going to argue that the use of deadly force wasn't necessary. But we know better. Right?" Savannah stared hard at LaShaun.

"I knocked the knife out of his hand, Savannah. Chase saw the knife on the floor, but he shot Greg anyway." LaShaun shuddered at the words she hadn't dared to speak aloud. She had only whispered them in prayers offered up for guidance on what to do.

"So Greg surrendered?" Savannah said in a steady, measured manner. The friend had transformed into the experienced attorney.

"What?" LaShaun stared back at her.

Savannah sat on the edge of her chair. "Chase faced a dangerous situation. Things moved fast, I mean like a high speed train bearing down on him. Any cop will tell you that once a hostage is hurt, the plan is to neutralize the threat. There's no time to say, 'Gee, I sure hope he doesn't get his hands on that knife again'."

LaShaun gazed back at her friend in silence for several moments. Finally she let out the breath she'd been holding. "I was there, Savannah. Chase didn't have to shoot Greg. He wanted to hurt him."

"Of course he wanted to protect you, and the girl. Don't forget he had two people at risk," Savannah insisted.

"I'd pretty much kicked that kid's ass and Chase knew it, Savannah! He's seen me defend myself before. I'm no damsel in distress in a fight."

"Hmm..." Savannah eased back in the seat.

"M.J. asked me about Chase's personality change. He's more aggressive on the job. Look at the kid he arrested a week ago or so."

"A known drug dealer," Savannah countered.

"I know, I know." LaShaun massaged the tight muscles in her neck. "On the surface he's just a tough cop getting the job done, the perfect man to be sheriff."

"He's moved ahead of Dave Godchaux in the polls according to the newspaper this morning," Savannah replied.

"I feel like I'm going crazy."

"Ahem, you said it," Savannah murmured. She held up both hands when LaShaun glared at her. "Will you listen to yourself? Chase is saving lives, and you call it demon possession."

"No, that's not what I..." LaShaun stomped over to

the chair and sat again. "Okay, pay attention. This is me, the girl who stirred up some seriously dangerous supernatural shit back in the day. Remember? I have visions of things that have happened. I don't usually see happy ever after events either, so this is no fun for me."

Savannah leaned forward. "You're right. I need to listen to you. Lord knows you used that voodoo stuff on me enough when we were kids. You hated my guts back then. Whew!"

"So can we stop debating if I'm just imagining things please? I need your advice," LaShaun snapped.

"Legal advice I got, but don't ask me about paranormal phenomena. They didn't have a course on that in law school," Savannah said, totally serious. When LaShaun squinted at her, Savannah smiled. "You haven't described Chase doing anything more than being a zealous lawman. And you're sure Chase knew he didn't have to shoot Greg?"

LaShaun turned to stare into the woods, land that had been in her family for five generations. She knew every inch, every leaf and every tree still standing. "Chase is good at what he does. He could have taken control of Greg without pulling out his gun. That wasn't the man I know and love."

Savannah stood. "Then honey, you don't need a lawyer. You need a powerful voodoo woman, and that's you."

"I'm too close to Chase to be of any use. I can't concentrate because I'm so scared for him. Besides, the fact that I brought it here ties my hands for some reason," LaShaun said quietly.

"You've got to at least try," Savannah insisted.

"Odette LeGrange Rousselle would know what to do. Only she can advise me," LaShaun said.

"Yeah, except she's..." Savannah took a step back from LaShaun. She put a hand over her heart. "You're not going to do something creepy like..."

LaShaun faced her friend with a somber expression. "Try to communicate with the dead. That's exactly what I'm going to do."

***

LaShaun drove to Mouton Cove. She rehearsed her speech over and over, both logical arguments and emotional appeals. By the time she reached the sprawling ranch home, LaShaun had her lines down pat. But she might as well have saved herself the trouble. After a few moments of chitchat she made her pitch. Miss Rose looked at her in horror.

"Non! Not even for Odette's child would I agree to such craziness. Haven't you learned the dangers of calling on the spirit world?"

"But Miss Rose, it's not..."

"I said no," Miss Rose cut her off quickly.

LaShaun held up a hand when Miss Rose opened her mouth again. "Miss Rose, at least let me finish a sentence."

"Um-humph," Miss Rose retorted. "You gonna hafta to make this argument real good."

"Our family journal, the oldest one from my ancestor Jacques LeGrange, has a lot of... guidance about connecting to the other side. I'm not as strong as Monmon Odette was, even in her later years," LaShaun said.

"You mean when we both got old. That's a strange way to try and sweet talk me." Miss Rose squinted at her.

"Monmon Odette tried to banish the spirit when she was young. Only she didn't. For almost two hundred years our ancestors have been calling this thing forth. As she lay dying, Monmon Odette tried to tell me what to do, but... she ran out of time." LaShaun paused as the memory of seeing her beloved grandmother slip away. She blinked as her eyes filled with tears.

Miss Rose's expression softened. "Oui. We all run out of time eventually. You're monmon is gone, child."

LaShaun wiped a stray tear from her cheek. "I'm not using this as an excuse to cling to Monmon Odette. Miss Rose, what's happening to Chase is just one part of the threat. I think more is at stake. Do believe in coincidences?"

"Life can be random you know," Miss Rose said cautiously. "What are you talking about?"

"Manny Young has a high powered lawyer out of New Orleans trying to get him out of prison. This same lawyer is friends with Quentin Trosclair, and shows up at a party with Greg Graham's parents. They all know each other."

"Not too many folks live in Vermilion Parish, so it's natural they would. The old families have close ties. As for the lawyer, bet he went to school with one of them. Am I right?" Miss Rose asked.

"Yes, I believe he's from an old New Orleans family as well. You heard about Chase shooting Greg." LaShaun let out a long slow breath. She still couldn't say the words without feeling a chill.

"The whole state has heard, cher." Miss Rose shook her head. "Boy has gone wild."

"The lawyer representing Greg's family was recommended by Manny's lawyer. Savannah referred them to someone else, but they switched. Still believe in coincidences?" LaShaun watched the older woman's expression for signs.

"Go on," was all Miss Rose replied.

"I did more research. The land Greg and the other kids were on used to be part of the Metier Plantation. But it was first owned by Jules Octave LeBrun." LaShaun sat forward. "His daughter married Georges Trosclair. The couple got it as a wedding present and..."

"Sweet mercies in heaven," Miss Rose muttered and stood abruptly.

Startled by her behavior, LaShaun jumped to her feet as well. "Are you okay?"

"Cher, you know I've researched family lines in Vermilion Parish for over forty years." Miss Rose looked at LaShaun.

"I know it sounds crazy, but--"

"Therese LeBrun married Georges, this I know. They also got more than land as a gift. Her daddy gave her a fourteen year old slave girl named Chloe to take with her. She was one of your ancestors." Miss Rose sat down hard again. "Odette never told you this story, eh?"

"No. Are you..." LaShaun waited for her to go on.

"I'm not sick, child. Don't worry about me," Miss Rose said, answering the question on LaShaun's lips before it was uttered. "I know who we need to call on for this task. I don't like doing it, but I've needed their help twice in the past thirty years."

"I don't understand."

LaShaun's entire body tingled. The stinging intensified, like a thousand tiny electric needles stabbing her skin. Miss Rose grabbed LaShaun's hand and held it for several minutes until the feeling began to subside. When LaShaun sighed with relief, Miss Rose let go and left the room. She came back carrying a beautiful book with a bronze leather cover. A copper clasp held it closed. Only when Miss Rose placed it on the table did LaShaun realize the clasp was a lock. Miss Rose placed a small key beside it.

"Odette loaned this to me years ago, one of your family books, for research. She teased me about how much I would owe her in fines if she charged late fees like a library." Miss Rose did not smile despite the joke. Instead she wore a subdued expression as she stared at the book.

"This is lovely craftsmanship." LaShaun used the key to unlock the clasp. She opened the book with care and read the inscription on the second page. "Une étrange histoire de notre famille, the strange history of my family."

"Start on page seventy-seven while I'm gone. I'm going to call them."

"Wait, call who?" LaShaun spoke to the older woman's retreating back.

"The twins, and I hope they've stopped their infernal bickering," Miss Rose muttered as she left.

***

Two hours later, LaShaun was still reading, seated comfortably in an overstuffed chair in what Miss Rose called le parloir. The modern world and those who no longer spoke Louisiana Creole French could jump in the lake, to quote her. She wasn't giving in to time or the lack of respect for traditions in Vermilion Parish.

In the time waiting for "them" to arrive, Miss Rose had been too preoccupied with preparations to answer questions. LaShaun gave up trying to figure out why she was being so mysterious. Instead, she allowed the older woman to rummage around in an old trunk stored in an extra bedroom. Besides, the book pulled LaShaun into the long ago world of her ancestors. Soon she was engrossed in the tragic story of Chloe.

At fourteen she was torn away from her parents and twelve siblings. Her tearful pleas not to leave them were ignored. After all, she was no more than property. Why would her feelings count to those who owned her? So she ended up on what would later become the Metier Plantation. The account of her life would be whispered for decades. Raped by the drunken Monsieur Trosclair and his equally drunken friends, she became pregnant. The young girl never recovered from the trauma of that awful night. Enraged and jealous, Madame Trosclair declared the baby would be sold immediately. True to her word, Madame Trosclair contacted a slave trader though her husband resisted. At the prospect of losing her baby, Chloe went insane. She smothered little Estelle and hung herself. Chloe's mother, known to be a woman of magic, cursed the Trosclair couple. Over the next three years the young Trosclair bride had three still born children. Madame Trosclair died at age twenty-seven from a strange fever after suffering for three days, her body covered with sores. It was said that she kept screaming for someone to stop the baby from crying. Yet there was no baby in or near the big house.

"Wow," LaShaun murmured as she rested the open book on her lap.

"Now you know of the chilling tie between your family and the Trosclairs," Miss Rose said as she set up three long white candles on the coffee table. She then arranged a circle of small cloth bags around them. Next she placed a rosary on a lace shawl that she draped on one side of the long table.

"We are related, and I had an affair with Quentin back in the day," LaShaun murmured in shock.

"Non, cher. Chloe's baby died. It's said that the baby had a shock of red hair just like the Scotsman, one of the beasts that violated her. It's fairly certain his seed is the one that took root in the poor girl."

LaShaun felt a burning hot hunger for vengeance. "Were they all cursed? Those men I mean."

"Legend has it that none of them ever prospered." Miss Rose turned to LaShaun and shrugged. "Their names are lost to history, so we can't be sure."

"Why did the Trosclair family become rich if they were cursed?" LaShaun picked up the book and turned pages to read more.

"The tale passed down says Chloe's uncle, Theodore LeGrange, made a bargain with Trosclair. He would not curse his generations, and in return, the LeGrange family would be freed from slavery. Not only that, but they would be given land and livestock." Miss Rose started to continue but the doorbell chimed. "Let's get this business done with the least damage."

"I wish you'd explain..." LaShaun broke off when Miss Rose waved a hand at her.

"No time. Watch and learn." Miss Rose went to the foyer.

Moments later came the sound of the door opening and closing. When Miss Rose returned, LaShaun thought she was alone. Then Miss Rose swept out both arms in a flourish. The enigmatic "they" walked through the archway into the parlor side by side.

"This is Odette's grandchild." Miss Rose turned to LaShaun. "Justine and Pauline Dupart, LaShaun.

"Nice to meet you," LaShaun said. She blinked at the dizzying feeling of seeing double.

The identical twins both wore their hair in thick braids. One had hers pinned up. The other wore a tignon, or elaborate scarf, with several of her braids hanging to her shoulders. Though they looked ageless, LaShaun guessed them to be in their late fifties or early sixties. One wore jeans and a tunic styled tie-dyed t-shirt under a bright red jacket. The other wore a maxi dress in vibrant colors and a dark green ankle length coat. They both eyed LaShaun with great interest.

"I'm Justine," said the twin with her hair uncovered.

"Which can only mean I'm Pauline. Glad you said something, sister. Sometimes we don't even know which of us is which." Pauline tittered. This earned a rolling of the eyes from her sister.

"That joke is older than our grandmother," Justine retorted.

LaShaun laughed. "I liked it."

"Don't encourage her," Justine replied. She put her large quilted floral purse on one end of Miss Rose's sofa. "Are we going to have to beg for something to drink? That's a long drive from Mermentau, Rose." She sat down heavily on the sofa.

"Pooh, stop your complaining. You drive farther than that to see that old man you chasing," Pauline replied with an impish wink at LaShaun. She sat down on the other end of the sofa.

"That is none of your business." Justine snapped. "You keep flapping those loose lips and I'll..."

"I was only remarking on how wonderfully faithful you are to Henry, dear sister," Pauline said. Her large brown eyes widened innocently.

"How you have time to mix in my affairs is amazing.

Your unruly herd of a family can't keep themselves out of trouble more than a few days at a time."

"My boy went to jail one time and you never stop talking about it," Pauline said heatedly.

"Stop it right now," Miss Rose cut in. "I don't have time or patience for this nonsense today. You should at least learn to curb this bickering in front of someone you just met.

Pauline cleared her throat. "Absolutely correct, Rose. I'm sorry, sister. I shouldn't tease you."

Justine shrugged. "Well, I should be used to your ways by now. I'm a little sensitive about my Henry," she said to LaShaun in a whisper as though they were alone. "My husband died ten years ago. A woman gets lonely you know."

"Henry's a good enough man, Justine. But you could do better," Pauline butted in as she accepted a cup of coffee from Miss Rose.

"Now don't you start with that again." Justine grimaced at Pauline.

"Enough," Miss Rose said loudly. "We have a serious situation on our hands, ladies."

"I'll say." Pauline turned to gaze at LaShaun intently, so did her twin sister. "We got to stop Satan from being elected sheriff of Vermilion Parish,"

Chapter 12

LaShaun shot to her feet. "What the hell..."

"Exactly, girl. Straight from hell," Justine said in a grave tone.

"Miss Rose, I'm gonna need you to start explaining right now," LaShaun said. For the first time in years she felt unnerved.

"Surely Miz Odette prepared her?" Pauline turned to Miss Rose.

"LaShaun was living in Los Angeles when Odette got sick. LaLa ran out of time, my dears." Miss Rose sat down one of the upholstered chairs that faced the sofa.

"LaLa?" LaShaun asked. "That was my nickname when I was little."

"Oui," Justine said. For the first time the serious woman wore a smile. "We called you Petite LaLa. But your grandmother was LaLa first. Her grandmother used to call her that. You know LaLa was what the old folks called house parties."

"They say nobody could party like your great grandmother, and you from what I hear. You got it honest," Pauline added with another wink. "I hear you had Quentin Trosclair wrapped around your finger at one time."

Miss Rose spoke up before a stunned LaShaun could recover enough to answer. "We didn't come here to gossip. What do you think about this idea of reaching out to the spirit world?"

"No biggie. We've done it before," Justine said promptly.

Pauline put a hand on her sister's arm. "But only in

very serious situations."

"Well I'd say trying to fight the devil qualifies, sister," Justine replied mildly.

"You keep talking about the devil. My family stirred up a minor spirit. I mean, he's evil enough. Loves chaos and causing trouble, but I didn't think..." LaShaun's voice trailed off as the full weight of their assertion sunk in.

"When you call on any spirit, even God's angels, there are consequences, child," Miss Rose said quietly.

"That's why we use our ability sparingly," Justine added, and looked at her sister.

"Yes, we're careful to keep a low profile. Folks from miles around would show up on our doorstep wanting us to contact their dearly departed." Pauline sighed.

"For good or questionable reasons. Sometimes you can't tell the difference because people lie," Justine said. "We're not telepathic that way, so we can't sort out motives."

"Only a few know what we can do. We've learned through the years that's best," Miss Rose explained, and the twins nodded with her in agreement. "Back to the business at hand."

"LaLa was a strong woman, so she might be still connected to this world," Justine replied. "But she may not want to communicate. Spirits can be moody."

"Tell me about it," LaShaun retorted. "It's no fun having them bust in on your life uninvited."

"Rose explained what's happening. We've been watching the news. I don't like what I'm seeing." Pauline looked at her sister.

"Pauline can see connections and patterns in events," Justine explained.

LaShaun glanced at Miss Rose. "See? That's what I

was trying to explain. Wait a minute. If Satan has taken an interest in this, then there is a plan. Oh Lord."

"What?" The twins said in unison and both leaned forward.

"This is going to sound crazy, but what if someone wanted to get serial killers released to start even more chaos?" LaShaun looked around the three older women.

"Pooh-ya, child," Miss Rose blurted out. "They got enough lowdown criminals running loose. Satan doesn't have to recruit."

Pauline studied LaShaun for a few moments. "Most are wicked, that's true. But they aren't all that special, or smart come to that. What are you thinking?"

"Manny is all three. He's smart, wicked and special. He has paranormal abilities," LaShaun said quietly. "What he can do is limited because he's cut off from society. And they keep him on medication to control his rages."

"Okay," Miss Rose and the twins exchanged glances. All three shrugged.

"What if the rest of the cases Montgomery works on are the same? Serial killers with paranormal skills?" The tiny pricks along LaShaun's arms confirmed she was on the right track.

The twins made the sign of the cross while Miss Rose murmured, "My oh my."

"If you're right, then that settles it. We need to call in reinforcements," Justine pronounced solemnly.

Pauline and Justine rose as one. They moved the candles around to fit some shape they wanted. Justine pulled out matches from her pocket and lit the wicks. Her sister whispered as they both moved.

Miss Rose stood back and watched them. "You need

me to do anything?"

"We brought what we need." Justine pulled a large wooden cross and a Bible from her floral tote.

"Just like that you've decided we should try?" LaShaun watched them in fascination. She'd never had contact with any others with "the gifts", only her grandmother and Miss Rose. Then she shuddered. And Manny Young.

"This is the most serious situation we ever been called on," Pauline said and looked at her sister.

"Yes, now let's get started. Stand up, dear," her sister said.

She and Pauline joined hands and walked in a circle around the table. As the sisters walked, the flames of the candles danced. They called Monmon Odette's full name as they recited prayers asking for divine guidance and permission to communicate with her. LaShaun was startled at a touch on her shoulder.

Miss Rose handed LaShaun a knit shawl. "Wrap up, cher. It's going to get cold in here."

LaShaun did as instructed. Sure enough ten seconds later the warm cozy room took on a distinct chill. Not knowing what to expect, LaShaun waited for one of the twins to start speaking in her grandmother's voice. Instead they continued walking in a circle repeating prayers in perfect sync. Pauline would start one and they'd end it at the same time. Then Justine would start up and they'd repeat the process. Ten minutes went by. LaShaun felt no shift in the atmosphere. Not one of Miss Rose's many knick-knacks moved. Only the flames wavered. Suddenly the twins stood still in identical listening poses.

"What the--" LaShaun stopped when Miss Rose pressed a finger to her lips.

"You'll know soon," Miss Rose whispered ever so softly close to LaShaun's ear.

The antique clock in the hall chimed ten times. After a while the tick-tock coming from it seemed amplified throughout the house. This is dragging on way too long, LaShaun thought. Ten minutes and still the only thing moving in the house seemed to be the hands on the clock. Another sound of chimes signaled fifteen minutes had gone by. LaShaun started to express impatience that nothing had happened. Before she opened her lips to speak, the twins shushed her.

Pauline gestured, moving her hand in a circle. "Turn around, and keep going," she whispered.

"But..." LaShaun stopped when three pairs of dark eyes gazed back in reproach. "I hope Monmon Odette shows up sometime this decade."

LaShaun followed instructions. After a few seconds the walls spun past like she was on a merry-go-round. Suddenly she saw flowers everywhere framed by blue skies. Shades of pink, white and violet azaleas bloomed. A warm breeze brushed through her hair. She heard humming, a song Monmon Odette loved to sing. Shading her eyes against the bright sunlight, LaShaun saw a straw hat floating above the leaves. She followed it until she came to a clearing.

"Humph, took you long enough to get here, girl." The voice to her right had a playful lilt to it that LaShaun recognized. Her grandmother stood fanning herself with the straw hat. She wore denim overalls and a red shirt. Her hair was swept up in a blue and white bandanna, but flowed into a thick ponytail.

"Monmon Odette," LaShaun said, her voice shaking. She put a hand over her mouth as tears fell.

"Now none of that. Do I look like I'm suffering?"

Monmon Odette waved a hand as if dismissing her sorrow. "I wouldn't come back to earth for nothing. Just look at my garden."

In spite of her tears LaShaun burst out laughing. "You could at least pretend to miss me, you rascal."

"Ah, just like the living. It's all about you," Monmon Odette quipped. Then she winked at LaShaun, which made her laugh again.

"Okay, Monmon. You got me on that one." LaShaun ran to her grandmother and hugged her tightly. "I thought you'd tell me we couldn't touch or maybe I'd be grabbing at air."

Monmon Odette kissed LaShaun's cheek and then stepped away. "Just this once, cher. But after..."

"I won't be able to speak to you and touch you again, will I?" LaShaun gazed at her in wonder.

"Oui. Most don't get that much. So you best have a good reason for waking the dead," Monmon Odette teased, then laughed hard at her own joke.

LaShaun felt a bit disoriented. At once Monmon Odette seemed both close and far away. The colors surrounding sharpened as though lit from within. A sense of urgency pushed LaShaun forward.

"The loa is back, Monmon. I didn't call on it this time, but it seems even stronger," LaShaun started, but stopped when Monmon Odette raised her palm.

"Abiku," Monmon Odette said firmly. "His name is Abiku, as told to me by one of the ancient ones. But... this is very important, girl. Say his name only at the right time or he will grow even stronger. He'll take what you love."

"He's already taking someone dear to me, Monmon. I will fight back though," LaShaun replied with force.

"You must. Or he will take someone even more precious." Monmon Odette's voice echoed ominously, and the sunshine dimmed.

"Please tell me more," LaShaun pleaded. She felt as if a powerful fist had closed around her heart.

"Remember to fight smarter, not harder like I taught you." Monmon Odette looked around on the ground. "Now where did I put it?"

"You have herbs, or some talisman to give me?"

"Ah-ha, here's my hat." Monmon Odette wore a wide grin as she put it on her head. She started off between the shrubs humming again.

"But wait, Monmon," LaShaun called out. "You didn't tell me when to say Abiku's name or how to fight smarter. Is there some special prayer? Which saint will help me?"

"These days y'all got all them fancy machines like computers, tiny phones in your pockets and such. You'll find out." Monmon Odette faced LaShaun. "Your strength comes from the journey, cher." The azalea shrubs quickly grew larger until Monmon Odette disappeared.

"Come back," LaShaun shouted repeatedly, except her voice sounded no louder than a whisper.

The sound of a rushing wind drowned her words. She opened her eyes to find Miss Rose and the twins standing over her. Miss Rose stroked her forehead. Pauline held one hand, and Justine held the other. LaShaun realized she was lying on the sofa with a pillow under head. She tried to sit up, but Miss Rose pushed her back.

"You stay put a few more minutes, child," Miss Rose said. She wore a look of concern.

LaShaun grew fearful when the three older women

exchanged glances. "What happened to me?"

Justine said, "Let her sit up, but take it slow. Young ones always think they strong as a rock."

"Oui," Pauline agreed. They helped LaShaun sit up.

Miss Rose appeared with a glass of water. "Drink."

After she took three sips, urged on by the women, LaShaun finally put the glass down. "So tell me what happened, please," she added.

Pauline sat down next to LaShaun while the other two took chairs. "Reaching out to the spirit world is risky for more than one reason."

"You see what they have in the movies and on them stupid reality shows--" Justine said with a grimace.

"Child, don't get me started," Miss Rose blurted.

"The living person who wants to reach out has a much stronger connection to the dead. So the spirit comes to them, sometimes even through them. Not us," Pauline explained.

"All that nonsense about spirits speaking through the mouth of a so-called medium, pooh! That rarely happens. Only le bon Dieu has the power to move like that," Justine broke in. She stopped when Pauline squinted at her. "Sorry. You go on, sister."

"The last time I reached across the divide was over twenty years ago." Pauline looked off as though distracted. Her sister took up the tale after a few moments of silence.

"A woman, Bettina Hebert was her name. She wanted to speak to her deceased mother. Something happened. We're still not sure what kind of spirit took control. Bettina was never the same after that night. A year later she killed her husband and then shot herself in the head. Their eleven year old daughter found them. She sat with the bodies for days until a relative found her."

"You think there's a connection?" LaShaun shivered.

"We know there is," Justine said quietly. She gazed at her sister. "Pauline blames herself."

Pauline sighed when Justine put an arm around her shoulder. "I'm all right."

"LaShaun, what did your grandmother say?" Miss Rose asked. The three women studied LaShaun.

"She teased me, just like she always did," LaShaun said with a smile. "She looked so content that I can't be sad, not anymore."

"Good, good. This is better than we could have hoped. You weren't harmed, and your grief has been eased." Miss Rose sighed with relief. "Go on."

"She called the spirit Abiku, and said he would take someone even more precious. But that doesn't make sense, nor what she said at the end, that the journey will strengthen me." LaShaun glanced around at each other women in turn. "I don't understand at all."

"Rose, you're the history expert," Justine said.

Without hesitation Miss Rose became a teacher once again. "Abiku is the Yoruba name for a type of demon. It comes from the myths of the old Kingdom of Dahomey. This kingdom had a female army unit called the Dahomey Amazons. They were said to be just as fierce in battle as the men."

"Give us the short version," Justine cautioned before Miss Rose could go on.

"I was getting back to the subject," Miss Rose cracked in reply. "Abiku is cunning and deceitful, like all demons."

When the normally talkative women said nothing, LaShaun leaned forward. "Tell me everything."

"There is a lot we don't know..." Miss Rose's voice

trailed off. She looked at the twins as though seeking back-up.

"The more often a demon is called on, the stronger it gets," Pauline said softly.

"Feeding on the human vices; greed, envy, hate, and other emotions; can give power to wickedness," Pauline added.

"And why we're hesitant to call on spirits. These demons wait for portals to open up so they can jump through," Justine said.

"Then we're in serious trouble. Look at all these psychics and reality show ghost hunters calling on 'em," LaShaun said. "No wonder all manner of evil is bustin' loose in the world."

"Most of that stuff is fake," Justine retorted and waved a hand dismissing her worries.

"A few get messages from beyond, but they don't have the true gift to make an opening between the worlds. They just talking to spirits that haven't moved on yet," Pauline said.

"Merci le bon Dieu," Miss Rose murmured. (Thank the good God).

"Idiots," Justine added as additional commentary.

LaShaun looked at Miss Rose. "So Abiku is the real name of this loa or spirit?"

"He's probably called himself many names through the ages. No matter the name, he's a menace to our world," Miss Rose replied gravely.

"What did Monmon mean when she said the journey would make me stronger? LaShaun felt even more confused.

"Finding the answers and stretching your gifts to the limit will give you the power needed to beat this demon," Miss Rose said, with the twins nodding agreement.

"Okay. Then there's her riddle about Abiku going after someone even more precious to me. I don't understand. Monmon Odette is gone, and so is my mama. That just leaves Chase." LaShaun gazed at the older women.

Miss Rose sighed. "Cher, there is another part of the Dahomey legend about Abiku. He steals children."

"But I don't have children," LaShaun said.

"Are you sure you're not pregnant, child?" Pauline said softly.

LaShaun instinctively placed a hand on her lower abdomen. "I'm not pregnant."

"Sister, could it be?" Justine looked at Pauline.

"Sure could," Justine agreed with a nod. They both stared at LaShaun.

LaShaun felt cold fear creep up her spine. The familiar tingling sensation started at the base of her neck and spread over her body. "Monmon Odette told me not long before she died that I'd have children one day."

The women started chattering in Louisiana Creole French all at once, hands flying as they gestured to each other. They spoke too fast, and LaShaun wasn't as fluent as the older generation. Besides, LaShaun sat too stunned by the realization of a deadly threat to her unborn babies to demand they translate.

"Stop, stop!" Miss Rose commanded. Her friends fell silent. "You're right, LaShaun. There is more at work here than one demon stirring up a bit of mischief."

"Wheels within wheels," the twins murmured in unison and gazed at each other with matching grim expressions.

LaShaun thought about all that was at stake, and

not just for her. She stood with both hands on her hips. "I fought him once, and sent him away. I'm going to do it again."

Justine jumped to her feet. "That's the way, girl. We can't let the devil's stinky minions run amok."

"We'll be your back-up team, especially if we need to have a prayer circle. I know two others we can call on." Miss Rose grinned when LaShaun's eyes went wide. "Oui, cher, we network with others who have special gifts."

Justine clapped her hands with glee. "We're usually so isolated, well except Pauline and I have each other."

"When you're not squabbling or giving each other the silent treatment," Miss Rose quipped.

"We always make up. Eventually," Justine said with a wink.

Pauline still wore a grimace of anxiety. "There is something else you must know, LaShaun. Remember I told you that Bettina Hebert had a child, a daughter?"

"Yes," LaShaun replied.

Pauline turned to LaShaun with a look of expectation and waited. Seconds ticked by marked by the old clock in the hallway. "Bettina Robillard Hebert, from a fine old family out of Natchitoches Parish. Her daughter's name is..."

"Allison, and now she's Allison Graham. Greg's mother," LaShaun said.

"Wheels within wheels," the three older women whispered in sync.

Chapter 13

That night Chase gave a satisfied sigh and swiped his mouth of crumbs. "That was some mighty fine meatloaf, darlin'. Good old-fashioned comfort food after a hard day."

LaShaun sat across from him at the table in her kitchen. Right outside the soft yellow curtains of the bay window, nightfall had covered her property in darkness. Yet she felt no foreboding presence. That wasn't assuring. Abiku, or whatever he called himself in this century, was out rambling around stirring up trouble. LaShaun stared at Chase for at least the fifth time since he'd come in, looking for signs.

"I'm glad you liked it. You don't seem to have lost your appetite. You wiped up just about every drop of tomato gravy with that garlic roll."

"Correction, with three garlic rolls," Chase joked with a wink. "I went six hours without sitting down. Only food I had was a cup of weak coffee and half a biscuit. I rolled non-stop."

"You must be exhausted then." LaShaun said. He didn't look the least bit worn out. His eyes shined with alertness, too bright for her comfort.

"I feel great. Must be this home cooking you're feeding me," Chase said. "Nah, I'll probably crash in a little while. You'll be jammin' your elbow in my ribs 'cause I'm snoring on your sofa."

"You can snore on my sofa or anywhere else you like. You work hard. Just go relax while I clean up." LaShaun stacked his plate on hers.

Chase picked up the serving dishes with fresh snap

beans, more slices of meatloaf, and roasted new potatoes. He balanced all of them with the grace of a waiter. "Well it doesn't matter. I'm not going to be one of those men who expect their wives to do everything around the house."

"I appreciate the gesture, cher. Now go on and park in front of the television this time. I'm just going to load the dishwasher. No need to feel guilty." LaShaun got busy filling containers with leftovers. "I can make you a sandwich for lunch tomorrow. Maybe put a little green salad in with it."

"Sounds like a plan. Thank you."

Chase watched LaShaun work for a few seconds. He played with the satellite radio awhile until he found an all news station. Perched on one of the stools on the long granite countertop, he flipped through the local paper. Anyone observing would have thought it a normal, warm domestic tableau. Yet LaShaun kept darting surreptitious looks at Chase. Once she loaded the dishwasher, LaShaun made him a meatloaf sandwich and a small bowl of salad. She placed both in the fridge and turned to find Chase standing near her. He put both large hands on her shoulders.

"You wanna tell me what's bothering you?" Chase said quietly.

Something in his voice gave LaShaun chills. There was a foreign and not quite warm tenor to it that caused her to pull back. Chase moved with her. "I worry about you working so hard, and all the craziness you're dealing with. I think..."

"Go on." Chase placed a forefinger beneath LaShaun's chin and made her look up into his eyes.

"You've changed, a little," she said.

"M.J. has been talking to you, maybe even my

sisters?" Chase looped a strong arm around her shoulders. "Ain't nothin' wrong with me that more time off with my baby and less time with knuckle-heads wouldn't cure." Chase led her to the sofa and they sat down. He picked up the remote control for the television, but didn't turn it on.

"Are you finding that your temper is short lately? Do you think differently about your job, like the people you work with and the suspects you arrest?" LaShaun warmed to the subject now that he'd opened it.

Chase laughed. "You sound like a commercial for some kind of herbal tonic."

"Answer the questions, please," she said firmly. "There are strange happenings around here lately, Chase. I have to ask."

Chase startled her when he jumped to his feet. A deep scowl transformed his handsome face from the mirth he'd shown only seconds before. Then he paced in a circle. "I just wish everybody would leave me the hell alone. I've got a job to do, and I'm doing it better than any damn body in the whole Sheriff's station. A bunch of freakin' idiots, and that goes for M.J. for listening to Dave or whoever else is after me."

"Chase, listen..."

"No, I'm not going to let you or anyone stop me from taking over. This parish needs a strong hand. Why are we chasing down petty crooks anyway? Let 'em kill each other. Who cares if a bunch of whores are hanging out in those dump motels along Indian Bayou? We got more important things to do like lettin' everybody know who's the damn boss in Vermilion Parish." Chase stopped, leaned forward and planted both hands on the sofa back on either side of LaShaun. "Are you on my side or against me, with them?"

LaShaun breathed hard at the aggression in his dark eyes, and the demand in his question. She whispered a two line prayer in Creole French that Monmon Odette had taught her. Then she stood, forcing him to back up. "I'm always for you, cher. When did you start doubting me?"

Chase blinked rapidly, and the color drained from his face. He closed his eyes for a few seconds. When he opened them again his breathing seemed labored. LaShaun braced her body against his as he seemed about to topple over. Somehow she managed to ease his six feet two frame onto the sofa. She rubbed his cheeks. The cold feel of his skin terrified her.

"What the hell is..." Chase couldn't go on. He blew out air in sharp puffs as he tried to catch his breath.

"Think about your family. Remember who you are, connect to good memories."

LaShaun hated to leave him, but she needed her grandmother's rosary. She kissed his forehead and both sides of his face. Then she hurried into the small parlor. There she retrieved a Catholic prayer book published in nineteen twelve. Monmon Odette had found it at a plantation estate sale. She'd told the six year old LaShaun that it had power. If ever she needed the power of goodness, LaShaun needed it now. In two seconds she retrieved her grandmother's rosary from its resting place beside the family Bible. When she returned to the den, Chase sat doubled over. LaShaun ran to him and dropped to her knees.

"I bind this evil one with the same bonds our merciful Lord bound the gates of hell. I call on our protector, our creator to deliver his child from the chains of this demon, for he has no power in the face of our Lord," LaShaun spoke the words rapidly as she cradled Chase's head against her neck.

"What in the world are you mumbling? Stop it!" Chase said with effort. The stranger in his voice had returned.

"No," LaShaun replied and continued praying. She stayed on her knees holding Chase for what seemed like hours. Yet when she finally looked at the wall clock only ten minutes had gone by.

Chase pulled LaShaun into a tight embrace. "I'm okay now. I promise to eat better and get more rest."

LaShaun burst into tears and molded her body against him in relief. The tender voice, gaze and touch belonged to Chase alone. "Thank you, thank you, thank you."

"Shh..." Chase rocked her in his arms, no trace of the stranger left. "I didn't mean to worry you so much, cher."

He kissed the top of her thick hair. When she looked into his eyes, Chase kissed her forehead, and then captured her lips completely. LaShaun felt all the fear drain from her body as his hands caressed her. He stepped back, took her hand and they went to her bedroom. There they slowly undressed each other in between kisses. When all the clothes had been stripped away, they stood holding each other and savored the sensation of flesh on flesh. Finally, Chase backed LaShaun up until they reached the bed. Without bothering to take off the covering, he eased LaShaun onto her back. For a few moments, he gazed at her as his hands traveled the length of her body. With an assured touch, he stroked her breast. Long fingers trailed down her stomach and teased LaShaun until she gasped. Unwilling to wait, LaShaun pulled him to her. She guided him inside her and moaned at the pleasure of how he filled her up so completely. As they moved in a steady rhythm of passion, LaShaun let go of any thought, their bodies becoming one. His hardness pushed her close to the edge, but then he'd gently decrease the pace. With unhurried motions, Chase pleasured her into oblivion. As her hunger for him increased, he lovingly intensified his movements as she pleaded for him to go faster and deeper. Their union absolute, they cried out together as both crashed into an explosion of ecstasy. LaShaun dug her fingers into his back, clawing for every bit of his body and soul he offered up. Their cries echoed in the room. After what seemed like a blissfully long time, they lay still.

Chase pressed his face against hers. "Will you marry me, cher?"

LaShaun gave a throaty chuckle. "Haven't you asked me that twice already?"

"I want to make sure you still want me," Chase whispered.

"Of course I..." LaShaun realized that what she thought was sweat were really tears on his cheeks. She held him tightly, her own tears coming. "Darlin'? Oh baby, what's the matter?"

"I don't know what's happening to me, LaShaun. I couldn't admit to you for a long time, but M.J. is right. Maybe it's this rash of crimes and long hours. I'm thinking of ways to hurt people when they cross me. I never thought wanting to be Sheriff would make me that kind of man. Sometimes I... maybe I need to withdraw from the race." Chase's words tumbled out in a trail of misery.

Unsure what to say, LaShaun cradled him in her arms for a few moments. She hummed a Cajun song about finding happiness in the simple things of life. Eyes closed, LaShaun planted kisses on his face every few moments. Deep inside she knew that to speak too soon would be a mistake. She wanted his words to sink into them both, and truthfully give her time to regroup. The dramatic shifts in his mood and behavior had left her just as confused as well. Chase should know, shouldn't he? She owed the man she loved the truth about the danger he faced.

"Honey, I need to tell you something," LaShaun started. Her voice less shaky, she searched for a way to say the unspeakable.

A soft tapping made her open her eyes and look at one of the bedroom windows. Through the sheer curtains a large white moth fluttered against the glass. A soft silvery glow like moonlight seemed to surround its delicate wings.

"He is not equipped for this battle. You must use faith, love, and resolve to fight for his soul," the words floated around her like wind brushing through dry winter leaves. LaShaun watched the moth as it floated in circles, the movement hypnotic in a way that stilled her tongue.

"Um-hum," Chase mumbled.

"I didn't say anything. Are you okay?"

She pulled away to gaze at him. Chase rolled onto his side and nestled against her, his face dry and his expression peaceful in sleep. LaShaun eased out of his embrace. With soft murmurs she encouraged him to get beneath the covers. She slipped between the flannel sheets and spooned him. Without waking, Chase pulled her back against his body. His breathing was steady.

"Thank you again," LaShaun said. She sighed and drifted off to sleep.

***

The next morning, LaShaun jerked awake by the ringing landline phone on the nightstand. She mumbled for Chase to answer it, then turned over and realized he wasn't there. A note on the table lamp said he'd gotten a call to report for duty early. The soft blue numbers of her digital clock read just before six o'clock. LaShaun said a prayer that more bad things weren't happening. She stumbled out of bed, shivering at the chill against her bare skin. In one motion, she snatched the cordless handset, hit the button, and then rummaged in a dresser drawer. She pulled a sports bra over her head.

"Hello," she blurted out and went to her closet. She grabbed her favorite old red plaid flannel shirt. With the phone in one hand, she put an arm in one shirt sleeve.

"Hey, I have to talk to you," Azalei said. "All kinds of shit is about to hit the fan. So..."

"Azalei, I'm in no mood to hear gossip," LaShaun said, her mind still on Chase. "I've got things to do, important things. So if you'll excuse me, now is not a good time for a chat."

"What I got to say you need to hear in person. Besides, I don't trust these phones," Azalei said with melodramatic flair as she dropped her voice low. As usual, her cousin only thought of what she wanted.

"This isn't a good time for a visit either." LaShaun pushed her other arm into the shirt. With the phone tucked in the crook of her neck she worked on getting into a pair of corduroy jeans. "Where the heck is my belt," she muttered.

"Say again?"

LaShaun huffed in frustration a few seconds longer

until she found the belt on the shelf. She tucked in her shirt and slid the belt through the loops of her jeans. "I'm going to get some things done. I'm not waiting almost an hour for you to drive over here and rant about Quentin Trosclair."

"What I have to say won't take long, LaShaun. Trust me, you need to know what a certain person is up to," Azalei replied.

"Did you hear me? I'm not waiting for you to drive all the way from..." LaShaun paused. She couldn't remember where Azalei lived. "Wherever you are now."

"You won't have to wait. I'm in your driveway," Azalei said dryly. "Now open the door and put on some coffee."

"What the?"

LaShaun stuck her feet into fuzzy slippers and went down the hall to the kitchen. She jerked back the curtains of one window. Sure enough, Azalei sat outside in her yellow mustang. When she opened the driver's side door, LaShaun let go of the curtain and muttered a curse word. Before she completed the turn toward the back door, the doorbell was ringing. LaShaun stomped to it, clicked back the locks and jerked it open.

"Don't press your luck." LaShaun opened the latch on the screened storm door.

"Well good morning to you, too. Excuse me for dragging out here almost before the crack of dawn to help you out," Azalei said. She followed LaShaun down the short hallway and into the wide kitchen. "Hmm, you've updated the place. Granite counter tops, big den opening up from the kitchen. Stainless steel appliances. Guess you're making good use of Monmon Odette's money."

"Say what you came to tell me, Azalei," LaShaun

said. She clenched her teeth to keep from spitting out a more colorful comment. She measured fragrant coffee grounds into a filter. Many in the unruly Rousselle clan still felt raw about her inheriting the bulk of Monmon Odette's estate. She had no intention of rehashing that drama.

"Monmon knew you would take care of her legacy in more ways than one. I probably would have ended up broke. But I would've had a damn good time doing it," Azalei wisecracked.

LaShaun glanced at her over one shoulder briefly, and then finished pouring water into the coffee maker. "Okay, just remember I wasn't the one who said it."

"You could have. I wouldn't argue." Azalei dropped her purse on the counter and sat on one of the bar stools. "You know the judge ordered me to get therapy?"

"No, I didn't." LaShaun faced Azalei. She could only pity the poor therapist that had to deal with her hostile, sarcastic cousin.

"After a bumpy start, I got into it. I've learned a lot actually," Azalei said and nodded. "You got something to eat?"

"Yeah." LaShaun found a bag of croissants and buttered two. She took bacon from the fridge. In seconds she had it sizzling in her one of her grandmother's small case iron skillets. Soon the rich smell of coffee and bacon filled the kitchen. "So what have you learned?"

"Hmm. Now this reminds me of being over here when Monmon was cooking. Remember those days? We'd all be in here with her telling stories, singing while she whipped up the best food in Vermilion Parish." Azalei seemed lost in memories for a few moments. She shook her head slightly as though coming back to the present. "I should have picked up more of my daddy's habits than mama's."

"He tries to do right by folks," LaShaun replied. She could have added that it was a mystery what her uncle-in-law ever saw in Azalei's razor-tongued mother. Maybe it was true that opposites attract. Shy and polite Uncle Henry hung in the background while Aunt Leah demanded to be the center attraction.

"Daddy is quiet, but he's always liked Mama's fiery side. I guess it gets hard to take after so many years," Azalei said, leaving unspoken that her mother's temper flared against her quiet husband. "Well, I can't help it. I'm like mama. Look how it worked out for me. I'm on probation and earning minimum wage."

"At least you're alive," LaShaun said.

Azalei winced, and seconds later tears pooled in her hazel eyes. "If I'd ever thought they were going to kill Rita... I swear I didn't know."

LaShaun wanted to blast into her, but her own past was a reminder not to cast stones. Azalei's tears seemed genuine. LaShaun put food on two plates and sat next to Azalei on a stool at the long counter.

"I made a few mistakes back in the day."

Azalei went from remorseful and back to her usual obnoxious self in a hot second. "Did you! Folks still talk about you and Quentin Trosclair. Did you really help him hide his granddaddy's body like they say? C'mon, give me the real story."

All sympathy dried up as LaShaun scowled at her. She briefly considered snatching back the plate of hospitality and dumping it in the garbage. "Get to the point of your visit."

"I got up with the chickens and drove all the way

out here 'cause I'm trying to help you. I have to go into work once I leave here, and I can't be late again. That bitch of a supervisor is looking for a reason to get me fired. She'd love to see my probation revoked." Azalei gave an angry hiss.

"I told you not to take a job working for Quentin, Azalei. You're just asking for trouble," LaShaun shot back.

"I didn't have many options. Don't lecture me about how I should have stayed in school. I've heard enough of that already. Anyway, I don't work for Quentin. I work at one of his companies. They have an office in Lafayette." Azalei stuffed bacon into her mouth and spoke between chews. "I hear you went to his Mardi Gras party, so why you hanging with him?"

"I went with Chase so he could make connections for his campaign. If it's any of your business," LaShaun snapped. She pushed her plate aside, appetite blunted by her cousin's bad company. "So how is getting on my damn nerves this early going to help me?"

Azalei patted her mouth with a napkin. "He came in for a meeting last Thursday in that big fancy conference room on the seventh floor of the building. I managed to sneak up there. I think he's making a move on some of Monmon Odette's assets. You better be careful. Back when y'all were... close, Monmon Odette got prime property. Remember?"

"Yeah," LaShaun said.

She definitely remembered how she used her red hot affair with Quentin to her advantage. With his help, Monmon Odette had acquired land and stock in Trosclair family corporations. Several of the companies had been sold, making Monmon Odette a healthy profit. Once again, she cooled her judgment of Azalei.

What kind of role model had she been for her younger cousins?

"Geological studies have been done on land right next to it. Seems there could be natural gas or something they can mine." Azalei's eyes glowed with greed.

"They drill for gas, Azalei," LaShaun replied, absentmindedly correcting her as she considered her cousin's revelations.

"Drill, dig, whatever. It means big money, but only if we head off Quentin from buying up that land," Azalei said eagerly.

"I'm not selling any property, so his plan won't work." LaShaun gazed at her cousin. "You could have sent me this in an e-mail. Finish up and go to that job you love so much."

"If you weren't family..." Azalei grabbed a croissant. "Quentin still thinks I want to stab you in the back any chance I get."

"Is he far off on that one?" LaShaun retorted.

"He is as a matter of fact. Now I want to stab his lying dog ass in the back," Azalei said with a nasty smile.

"But you're still pissed off that I have Monmon Odette's money. Giving me this info could mean that I'll make more money. Don't tell me you only want me to get richer. Please."

"I deserve a commission or something since I helped you. Well, it should," Azalei protested when LaShaun gave a snort. "Okay, fine. Be that way. Screwing up Quentin's little plan will be reward enough." The stiff expression on Azalei's face told a different story. She wanted the money, too.

LaShaun took a sip of coffee and put down the mug. "Monmon put me in charge of a trust that increases from certain holdings. Royalties could be shared with family members."

Azalei grinned at the prospect. She picked up the last slice of bacon. "That's what I'm talking about. Maybe I can stick it to Quentin and make enough money to quit that job. But we have to stop him first."

"I told you, Azalei. I'm not selling any asset to Quentin. He should have the brains to know that. So once again, you drove out here for no reason." LaShaun picked up both plates.

"I sweet talked him into to telling me one crucial detail, cousin. Monmon Odette put land in a company name, not hers. So if he gets control of the company..."

Her meaning slammed home for LaShaun. She remembered the phone conference with her accountant and Savannah. "So that's what he's up to."

"I didn't trust talking on the phone. You know how the government monitors phone conversations. The Trosclairs have connections, too." Azalei stuffed one last bit of croissant into her mouth. She stood and slung her purse over one shoulder. "Same for e-mail. The local internet company is one of their businesses you know."

"You've got some wild imagination going, Azalei," LaShaun quipped. "Look, thanks for giving me the tip. I'm sure between my lawyer and accountant, Quentin won't be able to damage Rousselle family assets."

"Quentin wants to get back at you, LaShaun," Azalei said. She nodded slowly, her expression grave. "His lawyer pals are helping him, the same one trying to get that psycho out of prison. Quentin wants you broke. Not to mention he hates seeing you with Chase."

"He needs to get over it and live his life." LaShaun tried to brush off her words, but something in what

Azalei said rang true.

"Quentin wants to hurt you in more ways than just money. What's that about?"

LaShaun thought about Miss Rose's warning. "You don't want to know the details. Trust me."

"If it has anything to do with voodoo, ghosts, and scary crap like that you're right. I do not want to know. Just tell me when to come get my check," Azalei wisecracked. She dug in her purse until she found a lipstick tube and compact mirror. Gazing at her reflection, she swiped her mouth until the cherry red color covered her lips again.

LaShaun walked toward her with a stony expression on her face. "Don't kid yourself that you can escape. The Rousselle-LeGrange legacy is more than just money. We're all touched by spirits. A visit to the historic family cemetery just a short walk out my back door will prove it to you."

Azalei froze. She looked around as though expecting their ancestors to appear. After a few beats, she stuffed the lipstick and compact into her purse. "I- I gotta go to work. I'll call you for news next time."

"Sure. Better yet, come to dinner one evening. Chase works late a lot, and I get lonesome way out here at night," LaShaun said.

"Yeah, uh, I'll let you know about that. See ya."

Azalei scurried for the nearest exit. Seconds later the door slapped shut. By the time LaShaun walked onto the back porch, her cousin was in her car. Azalei turned the mustang around. Gravel kicked up from the tires when she gunned the engine to escape. LaShaun laughed hard at the fun of scaring her shady cousin. Then she grew serious again at the thought of Quentin and Neal Montgomery.

LaShaun looked at the woods surrounding her home. "More wheels within wheels."

Chapter 14

Azalei left at seven o'clock, so LaShaun did research as she waited for normal business hours. LaShaun had read through her business files. Her cousin possessed the skills of a private detective, except her motive was revenge. Yet the facts backed up her paranoia about Quentin. LaShaun owned a small realty company managed by an outfit based in Shreveport. The land in question was owned by her company. Pelican Reality, Inc. had rental houses and two condo complexes. But included was undeveloped land. LaShaun remembered having a meeting with the chief of operations to discuss plans for additional development. Though she was sure Pelican not only owned the land but the mineral rights, LaShaun checked anyway. Her company owned the rights as she expected. No doubt Quentin knew it as well.

By eight o'clock LaShaun decided not to wait. She left messages on Savannah's and her accountant's office voice mail. By the time they returned her calls, LaShaun had a game plan mapped out. She instructed them to buy the land from Pelican for her immediately. That done, LaShaun spent the rest of the day on mundane tasks. By late afternoon LaShaun came back from errands in town. A trip to the grocery store and hardware store resulted in a load of bags in her SUV. Still restless, even after a day of activity, she decided to do something she hadn't done for a while. As it was close to three o'clock, late afternoon sun slanted across the pasture she crossed. A brisk quarter of a mile walk along a path of flattened grass brought her to an outbuilding. Her neighbor, Xavier Marchand, stood outside his bright red barn next to a small tractor. His wife sat in an off road buggy talking to him.

"Afternoon," LaShaun called as she approached.

"Hi there," Betty Marchand said before her husband could reply.

"How you doin' today, LaShaun." Mr. Marchand pulled off work gloves and stuffed them in the back pocket of his blue jeans.

"I was wondering if you wouldn't mind me taking Sunflower out for a little exercise before the sun goes down. Won't be gone long." LaShaun enjoyed riding the calm chestnut Tennessee walking mare. In return, LaShaun paid for bales of hay to feed Sunflower.

"No problem. My boy just finished grooming her matter of fact," Mr. Marchand said referring to Xavier, Jr. and headed into the shadowed barn interior.

"Great." LaShaun smiled at him.

Mrs. Marchand studied LaShaun. "Why don't you buy yourself a horse? We'll stable it for you, no problem. Life gets mighty complicated sometimes. Riding is a good way to settle your mind and work out problems."

LaShaun ignored her attempt to probe. "I'm thinking about it, but I'm not sure I'd get much time to ride. Didn't this day turn out beautiful?"

"Yep, warmed up real nice. Should be even prettier in time for your wedding. How's the planning going?" Mrs. Marchand's eyebrows went up.

"Fine, but it's not that big a deal. We have the flowers and food nailed down. Since we're getting married outside, decorating is easy." LaShaun smiled at her.

"I hear the Broussard land out there is beautiful.

Lots of history," Mrs. Marchand went on. "His mama probably told you about it."

"I know about the famous oak tree planted over two hundred years ago, yes ma'am." LaShaun almost laughed when Betty Marchand blinked rapidly at her.

Disappointment creased Mrs. Marchand's brow, but she gamely tried again. "I'll bet you're having a good time with his mama. She's helping you pick out your dress and the bridesmaids dresses, huh?"

"I'm wearing a lace gown my grandmother wore when she married my grandfather. The sleeves are handmade of Alencon lace from New Orleans... A lot of family history is attached to it from what I understand," LaShaun said in a dramatic tone, intentionally feeding into Betty Marchand's fertile imagination.

"Really?" Mrs. Marchand's eyes went wide.

"Here we go, LaShaun. Hope Betty didn't bend your ear too much." Mr. Marchand cast a knowing glance at his wife.

"We were just chatting is all," Mrs. Marchand replied, a bit on the defensive.

"Uh-huh." Mr. Marchand let his tone communicate how much he believed her protest. "Now you have a good time with Sunflower. Be careful to get back before dark though. We don't wanna have to send a search party in them woods at night."

"I'll be fine, Mr. M. The moonlight will lead us. Isn't that right girl?" LaShaun gave the horse a pat of affection on her flanks.

"Yes, I'm sure being in the woods at night isn't scary for her at all," Mrs. Marchand mumbled aside to her husband.

"Shush," Mr. Marchand hissed at her.

"No, ma'am, Sunflower is the brave one. Aren't you

sweetie?" LaShaun said as she smoothed a hand on the horse's long head.

"I, uh..." Mrs. Marchand stuttered. She glanced at her husband who crossed his arms. His expression clearly said, "Serves you right!"

LaShaun mounted Sunflower. The soft leather of the saddle felt good. She waved to the couple and set off at a leisurely trot. "I'm going to stop neglecting you my friend."

For the next thirty minutes, LaShaun let herself get lost in the pleasure of riding. Sunflower seemed to be enjoying the ride as well. They followed a well worn riding path through prairies and around the occasional oak tree. After a time, LaShaun circled back toward her property. She reached the outer limits of her property line. A movement to her left caught LaShaun's attention. Long shadows fell. Almost four o'clock, evening still came fairly early. Still LaShaun estimated she had another twenty minutes before dark. As if to back up her words to Mrs. Marchand, the moon shimmered in the early evening sky. LaShaun softly pressed her right knee against Sunflower and tugged on the reins. Sunflower turned west smoothly as though she and LaShaun were of the same will.

Following the movement she was sure she'd seen, LaShaun guided Sunflower into a sparsely wooded area. Tall pine carpeted the ground with soft needles. The scent seemed to please Sunflower. After another few yards, they came to woods with trees closer together. Massive oak trees that had to be well over a hundred years old stood as if they were the elder statesmen of outdoors. Just as LaShaun had decided she'd seen a fox or a rabbit, a distinctly human like form separated from a large tree trunk and darted into the brush.

"Now that can't be somebody running around in the palmettos and palms, can it Sunflower?"

LaShaun smiled when the horse gave a spirited snort as though agreeing with her. The sharp, spiny leaves of the palmettos alone would discourage romping around. Yet there it was again, someone moving through the brush. With a soft reassurance that she wouldn't be long, LaShaun looped the reins around a small tree branch. Sunflower gave a shake of her head, which LaShaun interpreted as "Take your time". The horse nipped at blades of grass as LaShaun walked around the low bushes. There were signs that something heavier than a rabbit had crossed the ground. In just a few steps, LaShaun had left behind the relative light of late afternoon and entered the dusky world of a Louisiana forest. Someone or something circled behind her once she got deeper into a thickly wooded area. After few seconds LaShaun heard a low growl and her heart rate jumped. Suddenly her surroundings seemed foreboding. She could only see tiny patches of dark blue evening sky through tree branches overhead.

"Why do you keep interfering?" a whispery female voice said it from somewhere to LaShaun's left.

"Because she's a nosy old witch," a squeaky female voice replied from behind. Giggling followed.

She recognized the scent of pubescent females, their hormones signaled they were excited. And dangerous. LaShaun had been like them at that age. At fourteen, suddenly the smell of males slammed into her, giving her heated dreams. That they found her attractive made LaShaun feel powerful. That was the time she'd opened herself to her gifts in all the wrong ways. The belief that she could have whatever she wanted was like a potent drug. Like any junkie, her addiction led LaShaun to death. Not hers, but the death of someone else. Now these kids were on the same road.

"You girls don't know the rules of the game you're playing," LaShaun shot back.

"You're the one who doesn't know the fucking rules, old lady."

"I'll just have to show you who you're dealing with, Becky." LaShaun barked out the name. The rustling stopped.

"How did she know?" the squeaky voice whispered.

"The same way I know your voice, Regan Williams," LaShaun snapped.

The stunned quiet that descended in the brush confirmed her guess. Chase told her that Regan and Becky were best friends since the fourth grade. LaShaun figured Jenna, the other member of their circle, was too terrified from her ordeal with Greg. She no doubt had abandoned the clique. One other boy's parents had shipped him off to a fancy boarding school. Only Becky, Regan and Greg remained of the original clique.

Becky emerged from behind a tree. She wore a long-sleeved black t-shirt under a black denim jacket and tight blue jeans. "Don't be too impressed with her psychic skills, Regan. Her boyfriend is that hot deputy running for sheriff. He told her."

"My grandmother says when Rousselle women speak folks just shrivel up," Regan's voice became even more high-pitched, and seemed to grow fainter.

"Don't you dare leave," Becky commanded. "Regan, do you hear me? I summon you to step forward. If you face her we'll be the strong ones."

"Haven't you had enough of running around wild?

You better quit this mess before you end up like Elliot or Greg." LaShaun took a quick look around and then back at Becky.

"See, Regan? If she was so psychic she'd know about Greg." Becky smiled at LaShaun. "He's out of intensive care. I saw him last night. He even got a hard on when I stroked him good."

Regan squealed and giggled. She stepped into the clearing. Her dark green over-sized sweater matched olive green cargo pants. "Becky, you're so terrible. I wish the boys were here right now. We could all party. Hey, she doesn't look that old."

"Shut up, Regan," Becky shot back. She put both hands on her hips. "Now what should we do with you, huh? Out here snooping around where you got no business."

"Thanks, girls. You just told me something important." LaShaun grinned at Becky.

"Not really." Becky's voice didn't sound quite so confident.

"Sure you did. I'm close to your gang's hang out," LaShaun replied mildly. "All I have to do is follow your trail. I hunt you know, so I can track."

"Too bad you're not hunting today." Becky pulled a long leather sheath from inside her jacket. Then she removed a wicked looking knife from it. "You showing up is perfect now that I think about it. I'll bet your blood will make our elixirs even more intense. What ya think, Regan?"

Regan giggled again, but stopped when she glanced at Becky's intense frown. "You're foolin' around to scare her, right?"

Becky moved forward but stopped when LaShaun took a fighting stance. "No, I'm not 'foolin' around'.

After we had the last gathering things started to happen. Your daddy bought you that snappy sports car. My parents put a deposit on that condo for us to have our graduation trip down to Florida. Just think of what we'll have if--"

"You used poor Elliot's blood?" LaShaun stared at Regan.

"We didn't mean to hurt Elliot. That was an accident. And anyway, my daddy had already promised to buy me a car, and your parents," Regan whined.

"Will you shut the hell up? Keep talking too much and I'll leave your ass out here." Becky took a step toward LaShaun. "Now back me up. Get behind her."

"You girls really don't want to do this," LaShaun warned.

"Yes we really do, Miss LaShaun," Becky said in a sing-song voice. "I'm going to have a baby, a special child. My little boy will be even more powerful with your blood. He told me about it."

"Who told you?" LaShaun grabbed at the clue.

Becky shook her head. "Enough talk. You're tired. Feeling your eyelids get so heavy, so heavy. Just lie down on those soft leaves to take a little nap."

LaShaun gazed at Becky for a few moments. Then she burst out laughing. "Somebody lied to you, sweetie. That hypnosis trick won't work on me."

"Let's see how funny it is when I cut your ass!"

Becky lunged forward swinging the knife as she came. LaShaun moved fast and the blade missed her midsection by a few inches. Snarling like a feral cat, Becky ran full force toward LaShaun with the knife raised. LaShaun took off in long strides through the trees. In minutes she'd put distance between them. Becky screamed at Regan to go in a circle to cut off

LaShaun. When LaShaun tripped, Becky cackled. LaShaun jumped to her feet again before either of the girls could reach her. Pain shot through her left ankle.

"Hey old lady! You can't out run us." Despite her glee, Becky panted. "Jump her from behind, Regan."

"If you stop right now before things go too far I won't press charges," LaShaun said. She grimaced as pain stabbed through her ankle again.

"We have big plans for this world, and I'm going to play the most important role." Becky still held the knife firmly in her right hand. She rubbed her belly with the left.

LaShaun's arms tingled so intensely she forgot the throbbing that spread up her leg. She stood straight and pointed at Becky. "Silly little girl. You've been fooled. Greg isn't some kind of demi-god with special powers."

Regan stepped forward. Her eyes seemed to glow in the dim light as the sun set. "Becky was chosen to give birth to the next ruler of the..."

"Be quiet," Becky said with force.

"I deserve to know why I'm about to be killed," LaShaun shot back and faced both girls.

Regan seemed to blink back from the high of the chase. "No-nobody said anything about killing anybody."

Becky gripped the knife handle though the blade still pointed at the ground. "You're going to hold her down for me."

Regan backed away from LaShaun. "What for?"

"The others will know you're weak if you don't help me. And you know how we deal with the weak," Becky spoke in a deadly calm tone. "Remember who I am."

Reagan took a tentative step forward but stopped. She swallowed hard. "Mother of the new age, I know.

215

But... her boyfriend is a head deputy or something."

"The ground is nice and soft here. Great place for a grave, Miss Rousselle." Becky's eyes narrowed. "She does have some kind of supernatural abilities. Maybe we better burn her body."

"She-She's not gonna tell anybody she saw us out here, are you lady? I mean it's not like she knows where..."

"We can't let her leave here, Regan. You know that, right? I mean, with her skills she's probably figuring things out right now." Becky gazed at LaShaun, her young face transformed by malevolence into something terrible. "She knew we were out here."

"But I've never..." Regan wavered when the reality of murdering another person hit home again. "I was so drunk that night when Elliot..."

"I know," Becky broke in quickly to cut her off. "Just hold her down and I'll do it. You can close your eyes."

"Okay."

But for the fact that they were discussing how to murder her, LaShaun would have laughed. They were like two ten year olds discussing chores they'd been assigned. As the girls talked, LaShaun grimaced even more to make them comfortable that she was no threat. Meanwhile she got a firm grasp on the thick length of wood that she'd tripped over. Pretending to move in pain, LaShaun kept it hidden beneath the leaves.

Becky nodded to her friend, and Regan circled to LaShaun's right side. LaShaun stood straight and hefted the old broken axe handle. The jagged edge of wood would have to do since the blade was missing. Becky hesitated then took another step.

"Grab that bitch," Becky screamed.

Regan rushed LaShaun, swinging both fists. LaShaun shoved Regan to the ground hard with little effort, but Becky closed in with the knife. Grunting, Becky tried to get close, but LaShaun drove her back with a swipe of the pointy wood.

"We got you now," Becky crowed.

"Should you be getting into brawls with a baby on the way?" LaShaun snapped. "One kick to your tummy and no new world order."

"Blood and battle feed my baby. He's born for destruction. Let's get her, Regan," Becky replied with a snarl.

LaShaun's mind worked fast to make a decision. She ignored Regan. Instead LaShaun sprang toward Becky. The offensive move surprised Becky. The split second of uncertainty gave LaShaun time to land a solid blow to the girl's head. Stunned Becky stumbled, but she still held onto the knife. LaShaun kicked to her right fast and hard. Her boot connected to Regan's knee with a loud pop. The girl screamed as she went down. Becky struggled to recover, but LaShaun struck her arm with all her might. The knife fell from Becky's hand.

"LaShaun. LaShaun!" M.J. shouted.

LaShaun still held the old axe handle as she backed away from the two girls. Regan tried to stand but stopped when LaShaun raised her weapon. Becky lay on the ground. She rocked back and forth moaning.

"Over here. I'm in the woods," LaShaun yelled. Her voice came out weaker from exertion than she wished.

"Coming from the north," a male voice said.

Gun drawn, M.J. reached LaShaun first. Deputy Toni Ferdinand and a male deputy flanked her. Both cautiously approached the two girls. Becky spat profanity as the female deputy kicked the knife farther from her. Regan whimpered like a toddler when the male deputy walked over to her.

"She's not armed," LaShaun told the deputy. He nodded and holstered his gun securing it with several leather snaps before he helped Regan to her feet.

"Get your stinking poor white trash hands off me. You know who my daddy is? He'll have all of you fired. Fucking morons," Becky shouted.

"Becky says she pregnant," LaShaun gasped out as the pain in her ankle came back.

"I called for an ambulance crew to come out just in case," Deputy Ferdinand told M.J.

"Y'all can ride in my ATV to meet 'em on the highway," Mr. Marchand said.

"Pregnant? Damn, this just keeps getting better and better. All right then. Just keep me updated," M.J. replied and tapped the walkie-talkie on her hip.

"Will do, chief." Deputy Ferdinand hoisted Becky up with Mr. Marchand's help. They ignored her verbal abuse as they got her into the ATV. Moments later they drove off.

LaShaun swayed a little and leaned against a tree trunk. "How did y'all know to come out here anyway?"

Mr. Marchand's youngest son, Xavier, Jr., approached and offered her a canteen. "Here Miss LaShaun. I brought some water just in case."

"You're a good man to have in crisis, Xavier." LaShaun smiled at him in gratitude and accepted the canteen. Once she'd had enough, she handed it back to him.

"Thank you, ma'am," he said with a shy grin. He hopped on his ATV and followed his father's trail between the trees.

LaShaun felt steadier on her feet, so she pushed

away from the tree trunk and stood straight. "Like I said, how'd you know to come out here?"

"Mr. Marchand called the station when Sunflower came back without you." M.J. said. Her gaze swept the ground in a professional manner. Then she stepped carefully to lead LaShaun a few feet away. "We need to get this area marked off."

A third deputy appeared and handed M.J. yellow crime tape. They moved with care to mark the clearing where they'd found LaShaun and the two teens. As they methodically followed crime scene protocol, LaShaun allowed her body to relax for the first time. As she did, images and sensations assailed her. She sucked in gulps of damp, cool night air. Her stomach churned, and LaShaun felt light-headed. With great effort she gained a bit of control. Oddly she saw snatches of the Sweet Olive Bed and Breakfast. Pictures of the way the stately old home looked today mingled with sepia pictures of what it must have looked like in the nineteenth century. LaShaun shook her head and willed away the dizzying assault of images.

"Not all at once." LaShaun held her head. A touch on her shoulder caused her to jump.

"Hey, I'm taking you to the hospital, too." M.J. stood over LaShaun with a worried frown.

"I'm okay, just unwinding from the nervous tension of fighting two crazy teenagers." LaShaun gave a shaky laugh. "Really, I'm not cut or anything."

"You look like hell," M.J. said bluntly. "Like any second you're going to pass out, puke or both. You could have internal injuries from taking blows, so don't argue."

"I'm standing on my own." LaShaun tried to say more, but suddenly she felt energy drain from her limbs.

"You're sitting on the ground," M.J. replied.

"Huh?" LaShaun glanced around and discovered M.J. was right.

"One minute you were standing there looking fairly solid. The next time I look around you're halfway lying in the dirt looking several shades of green. Deputy, help me walk Miss Rousselle to my car." M.J. nodded to the tall, thin deputy.

Between them they guided LaShaun to her feet. A walk that seemed to last forever took them to M.J.'s white Chevy Tahoe. The Sheriff's Department shield was on the front doors. The deputy practically lifted LaShaun single-handedly into the passenger side of the back seat. M.J. pulled a large flannel blanket from a bag. She opened it and spread it across LaShaun.

"Hey, what is this?" LaShaun protested, though the leather seat felt welcome after the hard cold ground.

"You could go into shock easily after the night you've had. Now stretch out." M.J. satisfied herself that LaShaun was well covered up. She turned at the sound of another vehicle.

"I don't need to lie down." LaShaun relaxed against the seat back. Despite her attempt at bravado, her eyelids felt like tiny weights. She even felt too weak to close the vehicle door.

A long white RV pulled up with the Sheriff Department logo and the words Incident Command painted in large letters on it. One of the doors swung open and Dave Godchaux jumped down. He walked toward them looking like he was already in charge. LaShaun sat up on alert, her lethargy suddenly gone.

"Sheriff, anything else we need out here? Going to be too dark for an evidence search. I assigned Deputy

Thibeau to patrol out here tonight to keep the area secure as possible." Dave glanced around before he faced M.J. again.

"Thanks, Dave. That's good thinking," M.J. said.

"Yeah, yeah," LaShaun muttered as she watched them.

Though she strained to hear, their voices were low as they walked off toward the clearing. No doubt M.J. was bringing him up to speed. Dave carried a powerful flashlight with a huge lens. He and M.J. continued to walk for a few seconds only and then headed back. Their conversation became more audible as they approached.

"I agree, Sheriff. Getting her checked out is the best thing. You want to call Deputy Broussard I expect," Dave said. Then his voice went low.

M.J. answered him just as quietly before he turned around and went back to the Incident Command RV. "Okay, let's go. Deputy Thibeau, keep your eyes on anything moving out here."

"Will do, Sheriff," he replied in a deep voice. He shut the SUV's door and he looked at LaShaun. "Feel better, ma'am."

"Thanks," LaShaun replied. She started to say more but the deputy quickly strode off intent on his patrol. "Where's Chase?"

M.J. climbed into the SUV behind the wheel. After she slammed the door shut M.J. let out a noisy grunt. "Investigating leads on that last victim we found. The guy's so beat up we had to use fingerprints to identify him. Luckily he has a long criminal record. He's a felon on the run from Shreveport, a known gang member."

"Damn. Greg is running with a rough crowd." LaShaun shivered.

"We can't tie him to Greg. Remember they weren't found together. So I sent Chase up to Shreveport to look for any possible connection." M.J. turned the key and the Tahoe rumbled to life. "But mostly to get him out of town for a while."

"And you're going to tell me why," LaShaun shot back, ready to defend him despite pain and fatigue.

M.J. scowled at LaShaun. "After you get checked out at the hospital. Don't try that scary voodoo princess look on me. I'm not in the damn mood."

"Humph." LaShaun crossed her arms and glared at the world through the wide windshield. She knew M.J. wouldn't say more until she thought it was the right time.

"He's meeting with a gang task force. No interviewing gang bangers, so he's not going to be in any tricky situations," M.J. added.

"I can't wait to hear your explanation. You've gotten a lot like your mentor Sheriff Triche."

"Thank you, ma'am," M.J. drawled in imitation of the retired Sheriff's deep swamp country Cajun accent.

"I didn't mean that as a compliment," LaShaun grumbled.

M.J.'s loud laugh in response only made LaShaun more petulant. She settled in for a long ride back to town with the steel-willed Acting Sheriff. She knew full well M.J. would stay true to her word and not talk. LaShaun grunted in annoyance.

Chapter 15

The ER doctor released LaShaun after two hours of observation at the hospital. L She felt alert and jittery. Since M.J. wanted to get her statement, they drove to the sheriff's station. More than a few heads turned to watch them once they arrived. As M.J. closed the door to her office, the low hum of conversation signaled a lot of speculation was going on. LaShaun sat down on one of the imitation leather chairs in front of the wide desk. True to form papers were arranged neatly on it. One set in a stylish wooden outbox. Another set waited for attention in the matching inbox.

"See how much fun it is being Sheriff?" M.J. frowned down at the stack of messages and snorted.

"You handle the job with a lot of grace," LaShaun replied with a grin.

"Diplomacy, tact, and a quick lesson in playing politics is what this job requires. Having a level head doesn't hurt either," M.J. said and sat down in the executive chair behind her desk.

"Hmm." LaShaun could sense something more was on M.J.'s mind so she waited.

M.J. rested her elbows on the wood surface. "I'm still worried about Chase. I mean his state of mind."

"Listen, Sheriff, there is nothing wrong with Chase," LaShaun shot back. When her outburst was met with silence LaShaun sighed. "I'm sorry. This has been one helluva day for me."

"I hate bringing it up now, but his behavior is causing folks to talk. I don't think it's helping his campaign. At first he was the 'tough on criminals' hero.

Now more than a few people are saying he might go overboard. Greg's parents are whipping up sympathy with some in their crowd."

"Humph, you don't have to tell me people can turn on a dime. Funny how they were thrilled when he arrested a poor black kid. But let a privileged spoiled brat be held accountable and all of a sudden Chase is too hardnosed." LaShaun grimaced.

"He's still got his defenders. Quentin Trosclair and Neal Montgomery seem to think he's fair and honest." M.J. raised both her dark shapely eyebrows

LaShaun stared at M.J. like she'd just announced a unicorn was in the parking lot. "Is that a joke?"

"You heard me right," M.J. replied.

Before LaShaun could react, Dave Godchaux knocked firmly and opened the door. "Excuse me, Sheriff. I needed to tell you before I finish up paperwork with the guys and go home. Judge Trahan released Regan to the custody of her parents. Becky has a big knot on her head, so they're keeping her overnight for observation. So far the baby seems fine though, and they don't think Becky has a concussion. The overnight stay is precautionary."

M.J. heaved a relieved sigh. "Well that's something. The last thing we need is a charge that we caused a sixteen year old girl to miscarry."

"You might want to mention that big as hell knife she was swinging at me. The girl acted like a serial killer from one of those old slasher movies," LaShaun retorted and rubbed a growing dull ache in her right shoulder.

"The problem is her parents have influence. The judge will consider her age, no previous record. The assistant DA said something about letting her plead to assault," Dave said.

"I don't want her in jail, even though I'd love to be the one to give her a spanking she never forgets," LaShaun retorted.

"I have to agree. These privileged brats have gone way past annoying pranks. Maybe a judge can put some scare into her," Dave replied.

"Yeah, we can only hope," M.J. said with a sigh.

"I don't think that girl is scared of anybody," LaShaun muttered. When Dave cleared his throat, LaShaun looked at him.

Dave gazed at M.J. "Did you..."

"Yeah, we were just talking about Chase." M.J.'s worried frown returned.

LaShaun glared at Dave. "Look, I know you want to get elected, but don't try trashing Chase's good name to do it."

"Dave isn't trying to take advantage of this situation," M.J. said quickly.

"Sure he isn't," LaShaun replied.

"He didn't bring up the conversation. I did. Two deputies had already expressed concern to Dave since he's in a supervisory position," M.J. said.

"They didn't want to talk to M.J., I mean the Sheriff, and hurt his career with the powers that be," Dave added.

"Lord, please don't refer to me as one of the 'powers that be'," M.J. said. She pinched the bridge of her nose and rubbed eyes red with fatigue.

"You know what I mean," Dave said quietly. "I'm surprised the mayor or president of the aldermen board hasn't shown up."

LaShaun stood. "Chase was a hero just a few days ago. People in this town make me sick. I'm ready to go home."

"You're going to stop being so defensive and listen," M.J. said. When LaShaun cast a heated glance at Dave she sighed. "Thanks for the update, Dave."

Dave nodded his understanding. "I'm his opponent in the race, Miss Rousselle. But I'm not his enemy." He left and closed the door behind him.

"He's right, LaShaun. Dave has his faults, like being a real kiss-up to the 'powers that be' as he put it. But," M.J. said quickly to cut off a wisecrack from LaShaun. "He really wants what's best for Vermilion Parish."

"Sounds like you're ready to hand out leaflets for him," LaShaun said sourly. When M.J. crossed her arms and stared back at her, LaShaun lost some of the heat in her attitude. "So fine, Dave is an all round solid guy."

"The point being something is going on with Chase. Dave isn't the only one who's taking notice." M.J. gestured for LaShaun to sit back down.

LaShaun suddenly felt worn out. She dropped back into the chair. Closing her eyes, LaShaun willed herself not to blurt out all of her fears. She had no intention of sharing her true suspicions with the level-headed Acting Sheriff. M.J. had a serious skepticism about the supernatural. In her opinion most of the local legends were a big pile of nonsense superstition.

"Maybe it's the stress of facing an election and a wedding. I don't know," LaShaun said in a muted tone.

"He had some bad experiences in Afghanistan. Post Traumatic Stress Disorder can come out in some strange ways. And I hope... that he's not drinking," M.J. said.

"Chase only drinks socially with his pals and not even that often. How could you even imply he's an alcoholic? I can't believe you'd say such a thing," LaShaun said, her voice bouncing off the glass wall windows that surrounded M.J.'s office.

Outside, two deputies looked into the office. M.J. waved a hand at them and turned back to LaShaun. Her stony expression showed that she was done with the soft approach. "Stop twisting what I say. You know damn well I support Chase's campaign. More than that, we've been friends for a long time."

"Right," LaShaun said, but her spurt of outrage had fizzled at the look M.J. gave her.

"Damn right," M.J. shot back. "Chase used to party too much when he was a teenager. His daddy got him out of trouble a few times back in the day. I'm worried that seeing some bad stuff during his Army tours might push him back to hard drinking."

LaShaun let out a long, slow breath. "Chase is acting strange, but he's not drinking too much. Trust me on that."

"Okay, well what about this? Doesn't it worry you that of all people, Quentin Trosclair is on his side? Not to mention that lawyer from New Orleans trying to get crazy Manny Young back on the streets. I can tell you it's kept my mind buzzing for the last day or two since I found out."

LaShaun's heart skipped at her words. "Yeah, and Chase went to Quentin's Mardi Gras party. He said he wanted to meet voters on Quentin's side of the tracks."

"Chase didn't like Quentin long before you came to town. To say I'm surprised Chase decided to socialize with Quentin is an understatement. Even with the election coming up." M.J. blinked at LaShaun.

"It gets better. Greg's daddy made a big scene. He accused Chase of harassing his son. We didn't have much fun let me tell ya." LaShaun massaged her temples as a tension headache threatened.

"Jonathan Graham is saying Chase set up that scene at your house just so he could shoot Greg." M.J. waved both hands in the air when LaShaun's mouth dropped open. "I know it's nutty, but folks are starting to listen. Add to that we don't have any evidence that Greg killed Elliot. The other members of that little gang aren't talking. Or what they're saying doesn't make sense."

"Tell me," LaShaun said.

"I won't discuss an active investigation. All I'm saying is so far the DA isn't anywhere close to a murder charge, maybe reckless endangerment or aggravated negligent injury." M.J. slumped back in her chair.

"You don't have to tell me Elliot's parents are upset," LaShaun said.

M.J. looked at the pictures of her ten year old son. "Hell yeah. I don't want to know what that's like. Ever. I want my kid to bury me."

LaShaun put a hand over her abdomen and thought about the threat to children she might have. Correction, according to two gifted psychics, LaShaun would most definitely have children. Even worse, a demon looked forward to their birth.

"I know," LaShaun said softly.

M.J.'s eyes went wide. "Wait a minute. Are you pregnant?"

"What? No!" LaShaun burst out. "And don't start that rumor. All we need is folks saying Chase is a 'baby daddy'."

"Right, right." M.J. glanced around as though afraid someone had overheard her question. Then she lowered her voice. "A lot of us would be happy for you both."

"Not his mother, or a certain group of conservative old Beau Chene folks." LaShaun felt a tingle when she looked at M.J. "You know something."

M.J. cleared her throat. "My grandmother has been filling me in on town gossip again. The word is Mrs. Broussard, or Queen Bee as she's called behind her back, is bad mouthing you all over the parish. She says if anything is wrong with Chase... uh, it's you."

"Big surprise," LaShaun spat.

"C'mon now. She's going to be the grandmother of your kids." M.J. wagged a finger at LaShaun in much the same way her grandmother might.

"I wish y'all would stop talking about babies like they're already at the house waiting on me," LaShaun shot back. "How is Miss Clo by the way? Hope she's staying out of trouble."

"Mostly," M.J. replied with a smile. Then she became serious again. "Back to Chase."

"There's more you want to tell me," LaShaun said and stared at M.J.

"I'm sorry to say there is. The DA has one of my deputies working as a criminal investigator on the Manny Young case. He's been reviewing the evidence again, and doing more interviews. Chase supervises this deputy." M.J. paused.

"Well?"

"Chase pretty much took over. He's put together some kind of theory that could, maybe a long shot, but could help the defense." M.J. said.

LaShaun started at the sharp tingle that crawled over her body like dozens of electrified spiders. "The Blood River Ripper back on the streets with help from Chase. Damn."

***

The next day, LaShaun set out to do her own investigation. Chase sounded normal when he'd called her the night before from Shreveport. Yet she couldn't kid herself. Paranormal events were in motion. Unfortunately she had no clear images to hang onto this time. LaShaun knew her emotional stake in events unfolding made the difference. She was too close to see clearly what was ahead because it involved her.

She went to Savannah's law office after doing historical sleuthing at the museum and local library. Her friend's sunny office on Main Street didn't help lighten LaShaun's mood. What she'd learned about from her research was anything but reassuring.

"Mrs. Honoré will be with you in a minute, Ms. Rousselle," Ginger said crisply. The legal office manager seemed determined to keep a big city professional feel.

"Thank you."

LaShaun smiled at her and then took a seat. She decided to skip her usual format of reminding Ginger to call her by her first name. Besides, a suited gentleman sat across the room waiting as well. Maybe the formality would impress Savannah's potential client enough to bring more business. Minutes later, Savannah strode out holding a thick brown folder. She waved to LaShaun, but went straight to the man who stood. His officious manner and thousand dollar suit made him look out of place in small town surroundings.

"Sorry for the delay, Mr. Harold. Here you go. I'm sure you'll find the file is complete. Let me introduce you to Ms. LaShaun Rousselle. Her family owns the company in question." Savannah turned to LaShaun. Her brows arched as her hazel eyes sent LaShaun a message. "Mr. Harold is a real estate attorney specializing in mineral rights, oil, and gas leasing."

"Hello, Ms. Rousselle. Not to be technical, a family trust actually owns the company which includes the property in question." Mr. Harold gave LaShaun a smile so friendly, the sunlight outside seemed dim by comparison.

"Hello, Mr. Harold. You're correct. But since I'm the trustee no one cares about the technicalities." LaShaun beamed back at him.

Mr. Harold gave a slight nod as though saluting her smooth comeback. "True, all in the family so to speak. We'll sort it out."

"Oh I think it's sorted out already. The deed refers to all rights being included in the sale as listed in the previous deed, which includes mineral, oil, or gas. I included a copy of the previous deed issued in nineteen thirty-seven," Savannah said in her best attorney "case closed" tone. Then she flashed her own mega watt smile at him.

The attorney seemed unfazed. "I'll look over these and get back to you. Have a great day, ladies."

"Goodbye." Savannah waited until the glass door whisked shut before speaking. "We need to talk. Ginger, take messages."

"Yes, ma'am. Should I buzz you about your one thirty deposition in Lafayette? It's almost ten o'clock now and..."

Savannah pointed a finger at Ginger as she headed to her office with LaShaun in tow. "That's why you're valuable. Keep me on schedule."

LaShaun shut the office door. "Harold was hired by Quentin?"

"By Olympia, Inc., the company that is seriously interested in drilling on your land. They're looking over the geological studies. I authorized it on your behalf, remember?"

"Yeah, right." She didn't really. LaShaun had more important matters on her mind, like saving Chase.

Savannah went to the coffee maker on the credenza in her office. She poured two cups of coffee and picked up a box. "I've got pastries. We'll need both."

"So we're not celebrating," LaShaun muttered. She took the tray from Savannah and set it on the compact round conference table. They sat across from each other.

"Not so fast. The good news is once again your grandmother proved to be smart. Monmon Odette didn't miss a thing, girl." Savannah shook her head in admiration.

"Monmon Odette was smart enough to get good advice when she needed it." LaShaun selected a small round flaky treat with chocolate icing.

"Well the good news is I'm almost one hundred percent confident we neutralized the Trosclair threat." Savannah frowned. "I did some digging on Olympia, Inc."

"Pun intended?" LaShaun wisecracked and licked icing from her thumb.

Savannah blinked at her for a few minutes, focused on business. "Yeah, I guess. Anyway, Olympia's CEO and board president is the grandson of Claude Trosclair's old fraternity brother. These families stay connected across generations."

"So that's what got Quentin interested in our land. I wondered how he picked that company," LaShaun said.

"I'm certain he had his lawyers and accountants scouring documents for weeks to find some kind of opening. Your grandmother may have conducted business with the Trosclair patriarch back in the day,

232

but she was no fool," Savannah said.

"Monmon Odette knew them well." LaShaun had studied the legal papers associated with every transaction. Quentin's grandfather, Claude, wrote the book on keeping every business advantage.

"Old Claude underestimated Monmon Odette," Savannah replied with a grin. Then she grew serious again. "Now the bad news. Neal Montgomery."

"He's a respected attorney. Not one hint of anything dicey in his background. No shady clients or questionable behavior."

"But you were right about him working on cases of horrible killers. He's hooked up with attorneys across the world who are doing the same thing. It's funny, and I don't mean in an amusing way." Savannah squinted at LaShaun. "Are we about to take a stroll down Creepy Lane?"

"Why I'm sure I have no idea why you'd say that," LaShaun replied mildly.

Savannah put down her cup of coffee. "You specialize in weird, LaShaun."

LaShaun gazed back at her friend for a time. "I'm worried about Chase, Savannah. Every since that poor kid was murdered he's been acting strange. Those kids were doing more than just partying out there in woods."

"Okay, but how is that connected to Manny Young?" Savannah leaned forward.

"I don't know yet," LaShaun replied.

"One of the members of Juridicus is representing Greg Graham." Savannah sat back with a frown.

"Juridicus?"

"It's like a private social club for lawyers. Montgomery is one of the co-founders. " Savannah let out a sigh. "The club bought a historic building in the warehouse district of New Orleans in 2006. Get this; they also own a plantation home on Bayou St. John in New Orleans. Membership is exclusive and what goes on at those meetings is hush-hush. All I have is lawyer to lawyer gossip, speculation about what goes on behind those mysterious closed doors. Very strange."

"You ever see that movie The Devil's Advocate?"

"Whew, that was a while ago. But what does that have to do with ..." Savannah's expression went from surprised to stunned. "Oh come on! You can't seriously believe that Montgomery is Satan on earth. I know people hate lawyers, but that's way out there even for you."

"No, but I wouldn't be surprised if he and his friends are into some kind of high-class cult," LaShaun said quietly.

"A group of highly educated professionals are devil worshippers. Okay, I get a group of rebellious adolescents dabbling in the occult. That I get. But the list of Juridicus members is a legal Who's Who. They couldn't..." Savannah's voice trailed off.

"I'm not saying Montgomery has some hotline to hell, but more than a few adults dabble in the occult. We both know that."

Savannah fell back in her chair. "Oh shit."

"M.J. says Chase has put together evidence that could help Montgomery get Manny Young out of prison. The Chase I know would never do anything to help Manny walk free. Never."

Savannah jumped to her feet and marched to her desk. "Look at these articles I found, five cases of murderers winning their freedom. One in England, another one in Canada, two in Brazil and one in

Florida."

LaShaun gazed at the photos of the three men and two women smiling in victory after leaving prison "All of their attorneys are friends with Montgomery, and belong to Juridicus."

"I can't say for sure for all of them. Two names pop up at international symposiums on panels with Montgomery. They also co-authored articles in international law magazines." Savannah put her fists on both hips, her "feet on the ground" attorney side in evidence. "The explanation might be simple, a group of like-minded lawyers who believed those folks were unjustly convicted."

LaShaun quickly scanned the articles in her hand. The printed words dissolved into images as Savannah's voice faded away. LaShaun worked hard to shut down the slideshow of horror playing in her head. Her hands shook with the effort, which made the papers she held rustle. "Yes, except for one thing."

"I'm going to be sorry I asked, but what?" Savannah sat on the edge of her desk as though she needed the support.

"None of these people were wrongly convicted, Savannah. They committed every one of the grisly murders they were accused of. What's more, their attorneys knew," LaShaun said.

***

Chase would be home in a few hours. LaShaun kept repeating the sentence as she made preparations to greet him. He'd called on his way to the station. Miss Rose and the twins had been on a conference call. All three stressed that LaShaun should definitely not tell

Chase what was happening to him. He would be in even more danger, because the demon would step up his efforts to take over. The twins gave instructions on herbs and seasonings that would counteract bad spirits. In that way the demon would be repelled for a time, but LaShaun's window of opportunity would be brief.

"Now I don't usually encourage young people to sin when they're not married yet." Miss Rose paused to clear her throat.

Justine snorted and said, "Oh give me a break."

"This isn't 1950 for goodness sakes. Even back then people had sex whenever and wherever. They just kept it quiet," Pauline added.

"Shut up you two," Miss Rose snapped through the phone. "As I was saying, get him totally relaxed in the way only a woman can do. You know what I mean."

"In other words turn up the heat," Justine had put in bluntly.

"You got to do it, girl," Pauline piped up in agreement.

Which all explained why LaShaun had spent the afternoon saying prayers. Jumpy with anxiety, LaShaun swept through her house cleaning like a whirlwind. Her activity had a dual purpose. She badly needed to keep busy, or the tension would drive her nuts. She also used a combination of herbs traditionally used to ward off evil as air fresheners. The fragrant subtle scent soothed the frayed edges of her nerves. After a warm shower using sandalwood oils, LaShaun dressed in soft cotton wrap that draped her body. Her hair hung in thick curls to her shoulders. By the time she heard heavy footsteps on the back steps and then on the porch, LaShaun felt ready. She met Chase in the hallway with a hug.

"Welcome home, love."

"Chase gazed at her. "You look absolutely gorgeous."

"Seeing you come through my door is a beautiful sight," LaShaun replied. She walked to him and planted a trail of kisses across his cheek that ended with his lips.

Suddenly Chase drew back with a scowl. He sniffed the air. "What is that smell?"

"I've been cooking and cleaning, sweetheart. What's wrong?" LaShaun kissed his cheek again.

"Let's air this place out," Chase said. "Open the windows."

LaShaun tugged him back when he started off. "I've got a surprise. Come with me, darlin'."

"What's gotten into you?" Chase wore a smile, but his gaze darted around as though he was looking for something. "Something has been done to this place."

"Yes, come in and see the changes I've made." LaShaun took his hand, but he resisted.

"Let me get something out of my truck first." Chase tried to pull free.

"Oh no you don't, Deputy Broussard. Next thing I know you'll be on your way to work." LaShaun put a playful sound to her words. Yet she yanked him until they were in the kitchen entrance.

"I said stop this," Chase growled, except the voice hinted of another accent. His diction sounded formal in an old fashioned way.

LaShaun opened the lounger to reveal that she wore nothing beneath it. As she let it slide to the floor, LaShaun twirled around. She waved her hands hoping the scent of sandalwood would distract him from the sage used to neutralize evil. The scent worked as an aphrodisiac, especially to demons who loved pleasures of the flesh.

"Now that you're here, you don't want to be with me?" LaShaun said softly. She rubbed her hands down her breast and hips.

Chase licked his lips and let out a hissing sound. He crossed the few feet between them and pulled her against his body. LaShaun took off his jacket. When she tried to hang it on the hook for coats, Chase knocked it from her hands. Seconds later he'd pulled off the rest of his clothes as LaShaun danced for him.

"I will have you, cherie," he rasped.

Chase lifted LaShaun easily and she wrapped her legs around his waist. Kissing passionately they held onto each other. LaShaun started to unwind from around his body so they could head to the bedroom. Chase growled a protest deep in his throat. He pulled her legs back and pushed her against the wall. He entered her and LaShaun gasped at the force of his thrusts. The ferocity of his lovemaking made him seem like a stranger. Yet the smell of his skin and hair sent shudders of lust through her body each time they moved together. Fear mixed with ecstasy. The strident screams of pleasure seemed to echo inside her head until she felt senseless. He thrust once and held her tight. LaShaun felt an explosion building inside her until she dug her fingers into his flesh, greedy for every inch of him. He cried out as he came, moaning until his voice died away into gasps for air. After a few seconds Chase sighed and let go of LaShaun.

"I'm going to take a shower," he said.

LaShaun kissed his shoulders. "I put out fresh towels. Why don't you turn on the whirlpool and relax instead. I'll have your dinner waiting."

Chase playfully slapped her bare bottom. "Merci, cher."

To keep him from being distracted, LaShaun showered in the spare bathroom. She dressed quickly and finished cooking wild rice, roasted chicken and fresh snap beans. All of the dishes were seasoned with sage. Chase returned to the kitchen dressed casually in loose fitting brown cotton pants and a matching long-sleeved shirt.

"You like that outfit I bought for you? More elegant that those frayed LSU sweatpants and purple t-shirt," LaShaun teased as she spread butter on warm cornbread.

"Oui. Very elegant. This food looks delightful."

He had already begun eating in the short time it took LaShaun to turn around and bring the plate of cornbread. She felt a small prickle as she watched him. Chase looked totally at ease, but something was... off about him. The way he sprinkled French words in his conversation was uncharacteristic. He ate the food slowly, pausing at times to gaze out of the bay window at the woods beyond the backyard. Although LaShaun tried for small talk, Chase only nodded a few times as he kept eating. When the phone rang LaShaun jumped. She started to get up, but Chase put a restraining hand on her arm.

"I'll get it." He wiped his mouth on a napkin and went to the kitchen wall phone. "Hello, Sheriff. Honestly the trip was sorta boring. Those guys in Shreveport are depressingly by the book. No, I'll come in. Thanks to my sweet wife to be I'm energized."

LaShaun stood when he hung up. "Stay with me this once."

I'm running for Sheriff, so I intend to be visible. You can bet good old Dave is going to be at the crime scene when I get there," Chase said. He picked up the last bite of chicken on his plate and ate it.

"I'm surprised you care about appearances," LaShaun murmured.

Chase's hand whipped out so fast she hardly had time to blink much less react. He gripped her wrist tightly and smiled down at her. There was no warmth in his dark gaze. Instead his eyes sparkled with amusement that seemed at her expense.

"You think you're so clever. I've grown strong. The herbs only annoy me now," the voice came out slow. He pronounced his consonants in a fluid accent that didn't belong to Chase.

"I don't know what you're talking about, Chase. Stop hurting me." LaShaun tried to pry his fingers loose.

His grip tightened. "I've been chastised for falling prey to your charms. Wanting you, watching you all these years. Who was it that made your family rich? Me. When you were with that fool Quentin, who guided your hand as you controlled him for your own profit? Me. Our time is coming. You will enjoy even more wealth and power at my side. Why must you continue to fight me?"

"I know who you are," LaShaun spat. She fought to control the growing terror that threatened to leave her senseless.

"Then say my name," he said, his face so close the tips of their noses touched.

"No." LaShaun shook her head slowly.

If she said the demon's name at the wrong time he would gain power over her, and Chase might be lost to her forever. She had to set the stage for another attack plan, and say his name with her weapons ready.

"I don't have time for these games. One way or another, you'll be mine. You can choose the hard way or accept the inevitable." With his eyes half-closed, he brushed his face against hers breathing in deeply. "This weak man does not deserve such sweetness."

"Chase, please hear me. Fight against this vile thing trying to control you." LaShaun couldn't hold back the tear that slipped down her cheek. She started to pray.

"Stop being foolish woman. I..." The accented voice trailed off. Chase's eyes blinked rapidly as he kissed LaShaun's forehead. "You smell so wonderful."

"You have to resist. Do you remember coming here? The last two hours or so?" LaShaun searched his gaze, uncertain Chase was back with her.

"Of course I remember. How could I forget every tender touch from my beautiful fiancée?" Chase gave LaShaun a puzzled look. "Why are you staring at me like that?"

"You're in great danger of being possessed by evil, Chase. A beast from another realm is back and trying to take over." LaShaun wrapped Chase in a strong embrace. "Remember the good in you. Remember our faith."

"I'm just fine. In fact, I feel more alive than I have since enlisting in the Army." Chase pushed free of her hug. "Now I gotta go see about some crime. I have to look like the next sheriff of this parish, because that's exactly what I plan to be. We're gonna have a new day around here, little darlin'."

"But Chase..." LaShaun followed him to the bedroom.

He turned to face her. "LaShaun, you've gotten yourself all tied up for no good reason. This is our time."

"You never asked what I was talking about, or made fun of me for talking about evil spirits," LaShaun said.

LaShaun felt numb as Chase strode away without looking back or answering her. The sound of Chase whistling a jaunty tune seemed to mock her. She muffled the shuddering sobs by clamping both hands over her mouth. In a rush of emotion she'd done exactly what Miss Rose had warned her not to do. Because of her weakness Chase was now in even more danger.

Chapter 16

Katie and Adrianna arrived at LaShaun's house promptly at ten o'clock the next morning. She hadn't been able to convince them that a phone conversation about the wedding plans would be enough. Besides, Katie had been a force not to be denied. Exhausted after a sleepless night of self-recriminations and fear, LaShaun had no energy to resist. To her surprise, Chase's oldest sister Elaine had come with them. They sat down in her den with Katie's famous wedding notebook with all the critical details. After LaShaun served them orange spice tea and sweet potato tea cakes, Katie got down to business.

"Morning. Elaine." LaShaun gazed at her steadily.

"Uh, Sharon couldn't take off work to help Katie and Adrianna do all the measurements for the garden." Elaine gave her an anemic smile. "So how've you been doing? I hear the wedding should be beautiful."

"Did you? Well yes, I suppose," LaShaun replied in a flat tone.

"Girl, you look like a worn out dish rag," Adrianna said with her characteristic candor. She leaned forward. "Your eyes are red with dark circles under them, too."

"You're not getting sick?" Katie stopped flipping through pages of her notes and looked up.

"I think she's been crying," Adrianna said.

"Allergies. Other than that I'm fine," LaShaun lied, and not that well even to her own ears.

Katie took up the interrogation. "Where's Chase? I told him he needs to sit still for at least a couple of hours and find out about his wedding."

"He's at work. Again." LaShaun could only imagine what kind of chaos Chase might be causing at another crime scene.

"Chase is starting to get bad press over some of the stuff he's done," Elaine said. "I don't even recognize the man they're describing as my brother."

LaShaun saw traces of her future mother-in-law's disapproving expression in Elaine's face. Ironically she and Chase looked the most like their mother. No doubt Elizabeth had felt free to express her feelings about the intruder in their family. LaShaun could well imagine what had been said.

"He's trying to show how dedicated he is to making sure Vermilion Parish is a decent, safe place to live," LaShaun said, reciting the political line of bull as though she were the candidate.

Katie squinted at LaShaun. "I heard the sarcasm. You look awful because you two have been fighting."

"Gee thanks," LaShaun snapped and looked away.

Adrianna glared at her sister-in-law "Katie means you look tired is all. Isn't that right? You didn't mean she looks awful literally."

Katie stared back unfazed by the disapproval. "What? You said she looked like a dish rag."

"All right, so I didn't get much sleep last night." LaShaun stood and walked to the window. "So can we discuss the damn wedding now?"

Adrianna followed her. "Bruce and I fought a lot coming up to our wedding. This is a time when everybody's nerves get on edge. It's normal." She gestured for the others to join in.

"Uh, that's right," Katie added.

"You wanna tell us about it?" Adrianna gave LaShaun's arm a squeeze.

244

Under different circumstances LaShaun might have laughed at the irony. What if she told them she was exhausted partly because their brother had made love to her like a demon? No, scratch that. He was a demon. In fact she did start laughing, except the sound frightened the three women. LaShaun understood why. The high pitch of hysteria in her own voice scared LaShaun as well. Yet she couldn't stop. Finally she bent double and started to cry. Adrianna led her to the sofa in the den section of the kitchen. Seconds later Katie appeared with a box of tissues, a glass of water and a wash cloth. Adrianna dried LaShaun's tears like she would for one of her children as she patted her back. Katie made LaShaun drink the water. Then both women had her lean back and placed the cool towel on her forehead. Elaine said nothing, but observed them with keen interest. After a few minutes she pulled Katie aside.

"Maybe there won't be a wedding," Elaine said low.

"Shut up. She'll hear you," Katie whispered harshly.

"I did," LaShaun replied with her eyes closed." Like I said, a lot of couples go through stuff like this," Adrianna said. She held one of LaShaun's hands. "All the details of selecting the caterer, then the menu, flowers, the tables, the chairs, on and on and on. It's enough to drive anyone nuts."

"Sure, even a simple wedding like yours takes a lot of planning," Katie put in.

"You two have done most of the work," Elaine protested. She got a pair of angry frowns. "I'm just stating the facts."

"LaShaun still has a lot on her plate what with the campaign and everything," Adrianna said, springing to her new friend's defense.

Elaine seemed unfazed. "All I'm saying is maybe things are moving too fast. I mean, they don't have to get married in less than a month. They could give it more time, take some deep breaths and..."

"Yeah, and give your mother time to work on coming between them." Adrianna let out a grunt of disgust.

"How dare you," Elaine clipped.

"I'm just stating fact," Adrianna retorted, mimicking Elaine's haughty tone.

Her words caused an eruption between the three women. Elaine hotly defended her mother. Katie shouted that Adrianna might have told the truth, but this was not the time or place. Adrianna stood her ground, saying Elizabeth should spend less time judging others. A throbbing headache started between LaShaun's eyes despite the cool compress. Finally she tossed the towel aside and stood.

"Hey. Hey! Everybody calm the hell down," LaShaun shouted. "Look, let's not make this into a bad reality show. Elaine, Chase and I haven't 'rushed' into anything. We've known each other for almost a year. Remember? With my past I can see why Mrs. Broussard would have... uh, let's call them reservations. We love each other."

"Chase is grown, so he can make his own call on who's right for him," Adrianna put it. "He's been alone for a while now."

"We were worried after he came back from the war in Afghanistan," Katie said before Adrianna could continue.

"Exactly. He dated a few women, but nothing ever stuck. I've never seen him smile the way he does when LaShaun is next to him," Adrianna added firmly and shot a pointed glance at Elaine.

"I wasn't saying they shouldn't get married," Elaine replied in a crisp tone. She hissed and crossed her arms. "Of course I want Chase to be happy."

"Let's just plan the wedding," Katie said with a smile. She seemed determined to bring sunshine back into the room."

"If there's going to be one," Elaine mumbled. "Chase seems to be working non-stop, and now they're arguing, too."

Adrianna raised a forefinger. "I'm not kidding with you, Elaine. If you don't cut it out..."

"Alright," LaShaun broke in sharply before Katie could play mediator again. "Elaine is right. With the election we've gotten off track. But there is damn sure going to be a wedding." Even if I have to find a priest to perform an exorcism on the groom, LaShaun thought grimly.

"Elaine, Chase has been miserable for a long time. Right, that's what I said. He couldn't connect with most of us, let alone a woman, when he came back from the Army. You don't want to spoil the joy he's finally found," Katie said dramatically. She placed a hand on her sister's forearm. "You really want him go back to being that grim loner?"

Elaine fidgeted with her purse straps for a few seconds. "I'm sorry for acting like mama. I shouldn't have channeled her negative energy. Besides, we got over Bruce, Jr. marrying Adrianna. I think we can handle you now." She gave her sister-in-law a sly grin.

"Oh no, you didn't!" Adrianna squealed, and then they all burst into laughter.

Katie fanned her face with a napkin. "Lord have mercy, we are going to have some fun at family get-togethers from now on. Okay, y'all. Let's get back to business. Even with all these... distractions, there is some good news. The Sweet Olive Bed and Breakfast has openings for y'all to have a wonderful reception and honeymoon. We can still use the catering from the Savoie's. They don't mind that and..."

"Wait a minute, they were booked solid," Adrianna said.

"Marion Saunders called me. They've had cancellations. Seems our little parish crime wave spooked a few of the out of town folks." Katie frowned. "I didn't think we made national headlines."

"You haven't been watching Ghost Team USA. That show is huge, plus James Schaffer was on CNN. He mentioned the recent Beau Chene murders. Then one of his researchers looked up the history of the bed and breakfast. There were at least two murders in that house." Elaine nodded as the other three women stared at her.

Katie blinked hard. "Elaine, you watch Ghost Team USA?"

"Yeah, you're the one who only watches public broadcasting or The History Channel and claims everything else on television is 'garbage'," Adrianna added.

"James Schaffer is a history professor, and his shows delve into a lot of fascinating facts from the past," Elaine protested. "It's not just any reality show. It's educational."

"Yeah, right," Adrianna snorted.

"Hmm," was all Katie said. Her twin raised eyebrows spoke volumes.

Elaine lifted her nose in the air. "As I was saying, Schaffer did research on the area. Naturally, the fact that those teenagers were found on land that used to be part of the plantation caught his interest."

LaShaun leaned forward and ignored the snickering of the other two women. "What?"

"He reported on those murders and about Manny Young's grandfather," Elaine said. She cut a glance at her sister and sister-in-law. "I won't say more, but..."

"Yes, I was up to my neck in that case," LaShaun said.

"Ahem. Anyway, three guests complained of strange noises or pictures falling off the walls. One lady said she heard screaming one night." Elaine cast a sideways look at LaShaun. "Folks cut their stays short and word got out."

"Nonsense. Just a bunch of folks who let their imaginations run wild," Katie waved a hand.

LaShaun tuned out the chatter from the others as thoughts of the Metier house raced around her brain. The evening she'd stumbled on Becky and Regan they were headed somewhere. Or maybe they were on their way back. LaShaun left the table suddenly.

"Wait a minute," Katie objected. "We've got decisions to make. Marion Saunders needs to know about the reception."

"Tell her I want Chase to tour the place," LaShaun called over her shoulder.

"It should be soon. The wedding is supposed to be in a month you know," Katie yelled back.

"Call her now. See if tonight around eight o'clock is okay."

LaShaun went to her grandmother's parlor and slid closed the old wooden door. She turned on her laptop. In seconds she had an old map of Vermilion Parish on the screen. Then she used a modern app that gave her an aerial view. The tingling beneath her skin ramped up as she stared at visual confirmation of what she'd suspected. Becky and Regan's path could well have taken them to or from the Sweet Olive B&B. LaShaun jumped at the sound of a firm knock on the door.

"Really, LaShaun," Katie said through the door. "I'm out here defending you to Elaine, but you're not making it easy."

LaShaun got up and slid back the lovely paneled door. She smiled at her future sister-in-law. "Sorry, I just thought of some business my accountant asked me to take care of."

"Is your dress ready? Please tell me you've got the dress," Katie whispered.

"I'll get it," LaShaun said. "Meet you back in the den."

"Okay," Katie blinked rapidly when LaShaun quickly darted away.

Minutes later LaShaun returned with the dress in a protective plastic bag. The three women were so intent on talking that they didn't notice her at first. The soft rustle of the covering caught Adrianna's attention first.

"Wow. Es un hermoso vestido, mi amiga," Adrianna said and got up as though hypnotized.

"I agree. That is stunning." Katie stared at the dress.

Elaine's mouth hung open for ten seconds before she recovered. "Very nice."

"A New Orleans seamstress who specializes in restorations of antique clothes did alterations and repairs."

LaShaun's grandmother and great-grandmother had worn the dress. Sadly LaShaun's troubled mother had died young without having her own dream wedding. The seamstress had marveled at how the lace was so well preserved. Only a few seed pearls on the bodice were missing. Those had been easily replaced.

"Candlelight champagne. Our teal green bridesmaids' dresses will look fabulous alongside that color. It has a golden glow to it," Katie said, her voice hushed with awe.

"Wow," Adrianna repeated.

"Okay, now I'm really excited!" Katie clapped her hands together. "I can tell Mrs. Savoie about the change of plans. We can still cancel the tent rentals without forfeiting much of the deposit."

"Not just yet," LaShaun broke in. "I mean, we haven't decided on Sweet Olive as the reception site."

"We called Marion, and she sounded thrilled. Tonight at 8 o'clock is fine. They only have one room and one of the cottages rented out. She was curious why so late though," Adrianna said and lifted an eyebrow.

"I would think you two would want to appear super normal. There's enough talk going around about Sweet Olive. Just wait until they hear where your reception will be." Elaine pursed her lips. "

"We should support our local businesses, Elaine. That poor couple put a lot of money into making Sweet Olive a tourist destination. Let's show everyone those Ghost Town people are phonies. LaShaun, you and Chase need to make a decision fast," Katie said crisply. She tapped her notebook computer.

"Ghost Team, Katie," Elaine replied, correcting her. "Besides, you really think LaShaun being there will make talk die down?"

Adrianna looked up at her with a frown. "And just what is that supposed to mean?"

"We'll let Marion know something tomorrow

morning at the latest," LaShaun said quickly to head off another argument.

"Why at night?" Elaine gazed at LaShaun with a question in her dark eyes.

"Chase is working long hours. He won't be able to get away before then," LaShaun put in smoothly. She hadn't even spoken to Chase yet.

"Oh." Elaine looked dubious but said no more.

"Okay, it's settled. We have the priest, the food, and the landscape artist confirmed. Now all we need is to nail down the reception and we're set. Our small wedding of about one hundred twenty people is going to be the event of the year." Katie beamed with satisfaction.

"June Bug Landry is now a landscape artist instead of a plain ol' yard man?" Elaine asked. "Humph."

"He will be for this wedding," Adrianna quipped. "Besides, my brother in Houston gave him some tips. Carlito owns one of the most successful landscaping companies in Texas."

"We didn't leave anything to chance. Now let's go over everything one last time. LaShaun, call Chase to make sure he can go tonight," Katie ordered.

"On it." LaShaun headed to the kitchen. She shook her head as Katie started handing out assignments.

"If we live through the wedding, life should be grand," LaShaun muttered. She called Chase first and found out he would be off work. Then she called Miss Rose.

***

The bright moon hung in the indigo backdrop that enhanced its luminosity. A few stars blinked against the night sky, but the silver disc was the main attraction. Chase took a catnap while LaShaun drove them to the B&B in his truck. The intense pace of chasing down leads, keeping up a good face for the voters and dealing with routine job duties had taken a toll. At least LaShaun hoped those were the only reasons Chase had dark circles under his eyes. She stole glances at him. With his eyes closed he looked peaceful. She placed a hand on his muscular thigh.

"Hey, gettin' fresh with a sleeping man must be against some law or other," Chase mumbled. He opened one eye at her and grinned.

"You were out cold within two minutes of us leaving the house. Now you're suddenly alert?" LaShaun squeezed his thigh before putting her hand back on the steering wheel.

Chase yawned as he sat straight. "When a good-lookin' woman starts feeling me up, hell yeah I'm alert."

"Silly," LaShaun teased with a smile. "Seriously, I'm sorry you have to do this instead of going to bed. But I promise this is the only side trip you'll have to take."

"Hey, this is my wedding, too. Only right I should be dragged into... I mean consulted on some of the details." Chase chuckled when LaShaun took a playful swipe at his head.

The next fifteen minutes of the journey passed quickly as they traded jokes. LaShaun could almost believe things were back to normal. Yet she knew not to be fooled. Abiku may have gathered enough of a hold to mimic Chase's personality traits and even his gestures. After all, the demon could study Chase from the inside. LaShaun whispered a short prayer that Abiku hadn't penetrated the deepest recesses of Chase's psyche and soul yet.

Chase started awake from another dozing episode. "Did you say something?"

"Just that we're almost there." LaShaun's heart thumped at the prospect of what she intended to try.

Five minutes later they pulled into the parking lot of the Sweet Olive Bed and Breakfast. A reproduction nineteenth century street light gave the stately old home a romantic look. Chase took LaShaun's hand as they walked up the brick path. As they got to the top of the wide steps onto the porch, the door swung open. Marion Saunders smiled at them.

"I'm so glad you could make it," she said with enthusiasm.

"I know we're almost thirty minutes early, but Chase was able to break away from the station and..." LaShaun stopped when Marion shook her head.

"Don't you worry about it. Come on in." Marion moved aside and then closed the door once they stood in the foyer. "We finished serving supper over an hour ago. So we can go into the dining room. Now I was thinking we could set up the small parlor on the west side of the foyer. That way your guests won't feel crowded in here."

"We won't have a huge crowd, so I think we'll be fine," LaShaun said as they followed her.

"Oh, no extra charge dear. Spreading out will make it more elegant." Marion waved an arm out dramatically. "Deputy Broussard, what do you think?"

"Looks okay to me."

"Yes, it's beautiful." LaShaun discreetly poked him in the side.

Chase cleared his throat. "Right. Mighty fine room."

Marion Saunders laughed. "Most men don't look at decor the same way women do, Deputy Broussard. If the room has chairs and tables you're satisfied. Am I right?"

"Pretty much," Chase admitted with a sheepish grin.

"I promise we're going to charm your guests."

Marion Saunders chattered on for a few more minutes. Her husband joined them. He stood silent, hands stuck in both pockets of his corduroy slacks. Harry Saunders seemed content to let his wife do the sales job.

"So why don't you look around. We have lighting on the grounds. Go out to the two gazebos we have near the lake," Marion said. "Harry installed a solar power fountain and colored lights in the center of it."

"Yeah, you'll have the run of the place. We got only two couples, and they don't want to wander around here at night. In fact the Thompsons are leaving tonight they're so eager to get out of here," Harry said with a grim expression.

Marion shot him a look. "Now Harry, you know they have a family emergency back in Ohio."

"Yeah, sure they do," Harry mumbled.

"LaShaun told me y'all were booked solid," Chase said and glanced at LaShaun.

"Things were fine until some idiot connected the place with that kid getting murdered," Harry replied. "Damn fools."

"What?" Chase frowned at him.

"Just a lot of wild talk that doesn't mean a thing. The property those kids were found on used to be part of the original plantation, but that means nothing." Marion twisted her hands together for a moment. Then she smiled and forced her hands to be still. "Nothing to it all. Go along and savor the atmosphere. Think about if you want a room or a cottage. We'll charge you the same rate considering..."

"Yeah," Harry broke in again. "You'll probably have your pick of any room you want."

"Inspect the kitchen, dear." Marion struggled to keep her smile as she nudged him to leave. "Make sure Mrs. Dautrieve put everything away, and prepped for breakfast in the morning."

"Ella always has that kitchen spotless," Harry replied.

Marion glared at him. "Just go. I mean, it's best to double check."

"Fine, fine." Harry left.

Marion faced LaShaun and Chase. "We can finalize the arrangements when you come back. I opened the patio doors for you."

"We won't be long." LaShaun tugged Chase toward the parlor.

Chase gazed around the foyer as though seeing it for the first time. "Right."

"So what do you think?" LaShaun said. "I agree with Marion. Guests can spread out here even with the band playing in this room."

"Uh-huh. What's this about the house?" Chase brought LaShaun up short as she attempted to continue on their tour.

LaShaun closed the double oak doors to the parlor. "James Schaffer..."

"That bonehead again," Chase blurted out.

"His research learned the original plantation stretched for seventy acres or more. The woods where Greg and the others were found hanging used to be part of the Metier family land." LaShaun studied his expression closely. She felt no tingle, and no sign that a vision might appear.

"Most of this parish was owned by some old family at one time or another. Hell, the Trosclair mob owned a big chunk," Chase replied.

"Yeah, well there were two murders in this house over a hundred years ago. There are rumors that owners were into the occult." LaShaun stared hard for any sign of a change.

"How many folks around here believe in spirits and bad mojos? Only every generation for over three hundred years. Longer if you count the Indians. All I see is a lot of fancy what-nots and a few too many lace doilies for my taste." Chase faced LaShaun. "Wait a minute. It's no coincidence you came here that first time with Katie and Adrianna. Am I right?"

LaShaun sighed. "Miss Rose showed me an old newspaper story about one of the murders. Katie suggested I consider Sweet Olive as a local honeymoon spot. When I found out this used to be the Metier Mansion, I took the opportunity to get a feel for the place."

"So now you've been here twice. Are you saying there's something to Schaffer's story other than a grab for ratings? Chase stood with his long legs apart.

"Well I did see... well experienced is more accurate...." LaShaun was about to go on when a scream sliced through the calm night air. She strode to the garden doors and opened them.

Chase went around LaShaun to go outside. He walked down wide brick steps to the patio. "What the hell?"

LaShaun joined him in the cool night air to scan the landscaped grounds... "I don't see anybody on the nearest gazebo."

Harry rushed out to the patio. "Did you hear that?"

Marion pushed him aside. "There are a lot of wild animals out here. Nothing but a cat feeling romantic."

"That didn't sound like a cat to me," Harry said. He started to say more but another scream cut him off, not as loud but unmistakable.

LaShaun pointed to the nearest cottage. Light could be seen beyond the curtains. "Coming from there."

"The Watermans," Harry said, his eyes wide.

"I'll go take a look," LaShaun said and took off.

"LaShaun," Chase called out. When she didn't stop he spun around. "You two stay here."

"Okay, we..." Harry started.

When a third scream rang out Chase didn't wait to hear the rest. His long legs pumped in an effort to catch up to LaShaun. She hurdled toward the cottage. The cute postcard exterior contrasted with the grunts and screams that came from within. LaShaun tried, but couldn't see anything but shadows through the window curtains.

"Don't. Stop!"

A woman's shaky voice filtered through the walls. Seconds later LaShaun heard cautious footfalls on the grass behind her. LaShaun turned around to face Chase. He crouched low and pulled LaShaun down with him.

"What did I tell you about running into trouble," Chase rasped. He heaved in a breath and let it out.

"There's a woman inside. I think she's in trouble. I think we should..."

In a flash he strode to the cottage porch, up the steps. Chase stood to the side of the door and shouted, "Vermilion Parish Sheriff's department. Throw any weapons out the door."

"I, uh, I mean I don't..." A deep male voice stammered. "I'm not armed, not exactly."

"Throw out the damn 'not exactly' weapon and get your ass out here," Chase snarled.

Seconds later the door opened slowly. A couple of odd looking objects hit the door facing and landed close to Chase's feet. He glanced down and then up again. "Now walk out backwards with your hands up. Ma'am, are you okay? Say something if you can."

"I'm fine," came a weak reply. "Please don't hurt Teddy."

Moments later a paunchy middle-aged man backed out onto the porch wearing only a black leather thong and a mask. LaShaun blinked hard at him. Chase cuffed him to the porch railing.

"That's Ted Waterman. Oh my God, is he hurt?" Harry started across the lawn.

"Stop right there," Chase ordered. He stepped inside the cottage still holding his gun.

"Please keep him safe," LaShaun whispered as five tense minutes ticked by. She relaxed a little when she heard muffled voices.

"Uh, LaShaun come in here, please," Chase yelled.

LaShaun sprang past the cuffed man to Chase's aid. She froze at the sight before her. A tall thin redhead lay stretched on the bed, her hands tied to the bed posts. She wore a blood red bustier. She looked scared out of her mind, but not because of the man outside. The woman pressed her knees together as she stared at Chase. When she saw LaShaun the woman started to shake.

"Please, take our money. We have plenty. Don't throw us in the swamp to be eaten by alligators." The redhead started bawling.

"Ma'am, he's a deputy sheriff. We're not criminals," LaShaun shot back. When the woman continued to cry, she felt bad. "It's okay. You're safe is what I meant. Calm down."

Chase holstered his Glock. "You talk to her. I'll deal with Teddy."

LaShaun loosened the knots on what turned out to be red satin wrist straps that matched the woman's bustier. "Let's get you free from these. Are you here of your own free will?"

The redhead pulled her hands from the straps. She gasped a few times, blinking rapidly. Suddenly her expression turned into a frown of fury. "Teddy is my fiancé. Of course I'm here of my own free will. What the hell is wrong with you people in this backwoods place? Invading our privacy like a horde of terrorists or something."

"Sorry, but we heard screaming and..."

"We're in a honeymoon cottage for God's sake. You're surprised to hear moans and screams?" the woman shouted. "I'm going to sue everybody in this damn hicksville town."

Chapter 17

Two hours later things had calmed down considerably at the Sweet Olive Bed and Breakfast. Inside the cottage, Chase wound up his interview with Mr. Ted Waterman. Then he took on the infuriated future Mrs. Waterman. Mrs. Saunders promised them the moon and stars to make up for the intrusion, including a free future stay with meals included. Gina, the redhead, huffed and puffed until she got two free stays. She seemed somewhat placated after that. Harry served generous helpings of fine brandy to the shaken groom-to-be.

"Ma'am, I need to get a statement. But let me say I do apologize," Chase said to Gina. "We're investigating several murders in the area, and I wanted to make sure you were safe."

Gina glanced at LaShaun. "Is she a deputy, too?"

"No." Chase stepped over to LaShaun and whispered, "I think I might have more cooperation on my own."

"Yeah, I know," LaShaun mumbled back. She could tell Gina's taste for rough men hadn't been satisfied yet. "Be careful you don't end up tied to that big fancy bed."

Chase blushed pink. "Cut it out."

With a shrug, LaShaun walked out, but not before glancing back at Gina. The woman's eyes glittered with excitement as Chase approached her again. LaShaun joined Marion and Ted on the porch. Dressed in a robe and slacks, Ted took another gulp from the brandy glass he held.

"Look, uh, I realize we're in the Bible belt. So if

261

we've broken any laws... I'm a prominent business man with a family. So I don't want to make a fuss, never mind what Gina says." Ted looked at Harry for understanding.

Marion raised an eyebrow. "You checked in as Mr. and Mrs."

"Well, ah, my divorce isn't final. I mean, it's in the works." Ted drained the glass and held it out to Harry, who filled it again.

"I can fix that door in a few minutes so you folks can get some rest," Harry said quickly before his wife could probe more. "Come on and help me get some tools." The two men left.

"Humph, you know what that that means. The current Mrs. Waterman doesn't know about the divorce, and she probably thinks he's on a business trip. Men." Marion scowled at the retreating pair.

"I'm just happy Ted doesn't want to raise a big stink. Busting in on S & M games between consenting adults isn't exactly good campaign publicity," LaShaun said.

Chase came out of the cottage just as Harry and Ted returned. Ted carried a basket of goodies from the kitchen that included a bottle of their best wine. The two men seemed to be in a good mood, both laughing. Harry gave Chase a wink and then went to work on the cottage door. LaShaun, Marion, and Chase went back to the main house.

"Why don't you two relax here for a while? All of our nerves are shot. I've got some peach brandy to settle us down." Marion left without waiting for an answer.

"This has been one hell of a night." LaShaun yawned.

"That's one way to describe it. At least I didn't shoot those idiots," Chase retorted. He sat down on the sofa next to her.

LaShaun laughed. "No wonder they wanted the cottage way out back."

Marion returned with a tray of crystal snifters full of brandy the color of dark amber. "Here we go. I think we've all earned more than a few of these."

"Thanks." LaShaun took a sip. "Wow, that's good stuff."

"My secret recipe, but I'll tell you the basic ingredient. The brandy is made from peaches grown right here in Louisiana."

"I usually take beer, but I gotta admit it taste okay." Chase finished off his glass.

"Whoa, Deputy Broussard," LaShaun said. "You're driving, remember?"

"This tastes more like punch than a real drink. Hit me again," Chase winked at her.

LaShaun shook her head. "At this rate we'll end up spending the night so you can sleep off that 'punch'."

"Excellent idea! You can have Suite 3A and sample a room in preparation for your honeymoon stay." Marion jumped up as though the decision was made.

"All that runnin' around has made me kind of tired," Chase said. He drained his glass again and yawned.

"That alcohol your chugging is making you sleepy," LaShaun said. She turned to Marion. "Obviously we haven't had time to discuss the wedding or reception tonight, so..."

"Deputy Broussard will soon be elected sheriff. With all the crime I doubt he'll be able to get away for an extended trip," Marion replied. She continued down a hallway. "I'm going lay out fresh towels. I even have some wonderful bath salts you two can use to calm your nerves."

"But wait..." LaShaun started.

"After all the ruckus of tonight, we can all use a peaceful rest. That's for sure," Marion went on. She disappeared muttering to herself about other details.

"Here, have some more. I think this stuff is a love potion or something. I want another glass myself with a slice of LaShaun to go with it." Chase poured brandy into LaShaun's snifter. He rubbed LaShaun's thigh.

"Marion or Harry will walk in."

"The sight of leather and all this talk of honeymooning has me sweating. I'm not talking about the temperature either." Chase cupped one of LaShaun's breasts. He brushed her lips with his and smiled.

"Chase, I..."LaShaun shivered as she gazed into his eyes. She wanted to know exactly who was talking to her. Before she could go on Harry entered the parlor.

"Damn fortunate I got those two settled down and in a good mood. The Watermans, well Ted and Gina, actually bought my story." Harry heaved a sigh as he fell into an overstuffed chair.

"Exactly what did you tell them?" Chase still had a hand on LaShaun's thigh.

"Well, er..." Harry turned bright pink. "I kinda implied that we set up that scene for a little bit of local color. You know, to enhance their, ahem, experience."

"And they believed you?" LaShaun blurted out.

"Generous servings of champagne helped," Harry said. He lowered his voice. "Don't mention this to Marion. She'll say this place will become a magnet for the bondage crowd."

"I won't talk." Chase saluted Harry with his snifter.

"Thank you, sir." Harry popped out of his chair. He went to an antique bar in the corner of the parlor. "Believe I'll join you two with a glass of fine red wine."

Harry and Chase chattered about sports, cars, and more sports. LaShaun took Chase's hand, but let the men have fun. She savored the familiar warmth of Chase's voice, and the normalcy of his behavior. Maybe her fears had gotten the best of her. Certainly no trace of the awful events of this house seemed to stoke the power of Abiku.

Marion came down the staircase. "Well, I have the room ready for you. On the house of course."

"You have the floor to yourselves," Harry put in brightly.

"Yes, unfortunately," Marion added with a brief frown, but then her expression brightened. "I'm hoping to change that with more publicity. Maybe we can attract a more adventurous clientele even."

"Like the Watermans?" Harry murmured into his wine glass with a wink at Chase. The two men laughed.

"Check the doors and let's get some rest, Harry," Marion said sharply and squinted at him.

"Yes, dear," Harry replied. He struggled to stop grinning, but didn't quite succeed.

"I hope you have a good night." Marion beamed at them before she headed to their downstairs quarters. They had a master suite on the first floor in an old wing that used to be part of an outdoor kitchen. Moments later they heard Harry talking to her as he followed.

"Goodnight," LaShaun said and covered the wide yawn that followed with one hand. "What time is it anyway?"

"From the way you're eyes are drooping I'd say it's time for bed," Chase teased. He glanced at his cell phone. "Almost eleven thirty. This turned out to be quite a tour. Now let's take them up on that free deluxe suite."

"Well, since we're here," LaShaun replied as she stroked his muscular bicep. Chase scooped her up into his arms. "Hmm, suddenly I'm not all that sleepy."

"Even more reason to stay over. Hmm, did I hear her say we've got the third floor all to ourselves?" Chase traced a line of fire with his lips down LaShaun's throat.

LaShaun snuggled closer. Detecting no alien presence in him, she sighed with relief. Maybe her prayers combined with prayers from Miss Rose and the twins were working. She d delivered a scorching kiss until both were breathless.

"Yes, their other guests on the second floor checked out today," she whispered.

"Then let's not waste anymore time down here," Chase said.

He took her hand like an old fashioned southern gentleman and led LaShaun up the polished oak staircase. Along the way they admired beautiful antiques. Both second and third floor landings decorated to fit the historic period the home was built. Each floor had three bedrooms. French doors at the end of each hallway led to porches. They paused for a few moments to look at their room. Chase took both their jackets and draped them over a chair. Then they went out to admire the view from the third floor porch. In minutes they were wrapped in a kiss lying on a cushioned bamboo sofa. Chase opened LaShaun's blouse. He kissed her cleavage and then started to undress her.

"Chase, we can't, not out here on the porch,"

LaShaun murmured. Despite her words, she did nothing to stop him.

"Look around, darlin'. You see any other houses?" Chase pushed the blouse down and off her shoulders.

"Of course not, but..."

LaShaun went breathless when he unhooked her bra. His tongue snaked around her nipples in a hungry circular motion. The rouge ridges of it felt delicious against the tender, sensitive nubs. Both grew hard as he licked more insistently. She let her head fall back, but kept her eyes open. The dark shadows of tall pine and oak trees let only a few sections of the bright moon shine through. Something about the cool night air and Chase's hot touch drove LaShaun's desire skyward. Soon they were both naked. His attention to detail in kissing her entire body left LaShaun begging for more in a harsh whisper. When he'd driven her over the edge with just his tongue, Chase pulled away. LaShaun moaned in protest, but soon in bliss when he entered her slowly. As he filled her, LaShaun locked her legs around his waist. They moved in rhythm, slowly and faster, and then going slow again. The feeling of being all alone surrounded by nothing but the sounds of crickets and birdsong heightened their pleasure. They whispered words of love, desire, and devotion as their movements became more frantic. First LaShaun cried out softly, savoring the waves of a strong orgasm. Then Chase followed her over the edge with furious thrusts, moaning until he grew still.

"We're going to get sore throats and the sniffles if we fall asleep out here," LaShaun whispered. She brushed his right shoulder with her lips.

"You kidding? I'm dripping sweat like it's one hundred degrees," Chase replied hoarsely. "It's going to be worth it if I get some more of you."

"We came for the soft big bed with Egyptian cotton sheets and down comforter. Remember?" She playfully tapped his back.

"This is what I came for, cher." Chase chuckled with his mouth against her left breast.

She laughed, but then grew quiet for a few more moments. "Chase, about what we discussed the other night after..."

He went still in her arms. After a few moments Chase raised his head and looked into her eyes. "You believe someone is trying to control me."

"No, some thing."

"Strange, but it's not exactly a memory of our conversation. More like I heard your voice from a distance during the day while I was working."

LaShaun felt a surge of relief. She hugged him tight. "Your essence responded to the familiar. Hold onto those moments, honey. I can't lose you. I just can't."

Chase pressed his body to hers as he continued to stare into her eyes. "You know I don't halfway believe a lot of that demon, voodoo stuff. I've seen people act weird enough on drugs, being crazy or just plain mean as hell."

"Yes, but--" LaShaun's words stopped when he rubbed her lips with his thumb.

"Something deep inside me is all yours. The way I love you shakes me sometimes. Feels like a red hot chunk of coal burning me up until I got to have you. Not just sex. I need to hear your voice or see you smile at me like you don't smile for anybody else. Now I know you're the expert on supernatural stuff, but know this- nobody, no thing will come between us. I feel you when we're apart, so strong. So strong," he whispered again and closed his eyes. "You could never lose me."

LaShaun cradled him close for a long time. When an owl hooted several times she smiled. "I think that Mr. Owl is reminding us that we don't belong out here in nature. He's right. We'll be more comfortable in bed."

Chase unwound his brawny frame from hers. He lifted LaShaun from the chaise sofa. Together they gathered their clothes. They giggled and tiptoed inside as though they needed to escape detection. Once inside the room, they realized the night had turned chilly. To her delight, Chase started the gas fireplace that also opened onto the bathroom. LaShaun filled the tub with warm soapy water. Chase got in first, and then LaShaun joined him, seated between his legs. They talked about the wedding and debated again which house they'd live in. After thirty minutes they rinsed rich lather from each other and padded sleepily to the inviting queen-sized bed. Two cotton bathrobes with the bed and breakfast logo embroidered in dark green lay across it, but they tossed them on another chair. Flesh to flesh they curled up and drifted off. The crackle of wood from the fireplace lulled LaShaun until the golden light from it faded as her eyes closed.

Strange dreams filled her slumber. She sat at an antique dresser just like the one in their room. A lovely brush was being used by someone's hands to groom her thick hair. The same hands arranged her hair around her shoulders. LaShaun tried to explain that she preferred a braid or to have it pinned into a bun. A voice explained that flowing hair symbolized carnal delights and fertility.

In the background she heard violins, but the notes seemed oddly discordant. Still the tune seemed to pull at her. LaShaun hummed in time with the brush strokes in her hair. Everything appeared to move at the same pace as the music. LaShaun blinked slowly, entranced by the play of light on the walls. Someone told her the candlelight brought out the beauty of her brown skin against the color of her wedding dress.

"Thank you," LaShaun murmured with a smile.

How wonderful to dream of the day she would begin her life with the man she loved. As if her thought brought action, LaShaun found herself floating along. Or was she walking? Someone held her hand. The long trailing hem of her dress rustled as she moved. Pearls on her dress glowed in the flickering candlelight. An arch covered in strange dark vines with blood red flowers stood at one end of a room. A tall man stood with his back to her. Another man dressed in a long flowing black robe with strange red and gold symbols stood facing her. As she got closer LaShaun blinked to clear her vision. Everything seemed a bit hazy. She tried to rub her eyes and discovered that a gossamer veil covered her face.

"I'm walking down the aisle," LaShaun whispered. She glanced around looking for her friends. "Where is everyone?"

"The important players are here, sweetie," a voice to her right said.

LaShaun wanted to turn her head so she could see the source of the voice, but her neck felt stiff. Instead she focused on figures at the end of the aisle. In a disorienting combination of slow motion and missed scenes, LaShaun found herself repeating words. The man in the robe read from an open book. Shadows on the walls seemed to be from a crowd of people surrounding them, watching the ceremony. Yet LaShaun didn't see anyone else when she did manage to glance to her left.

"Favor your soul mate with a passionate embrace," The man in the robe said.

"I will indeed."

The tall man turned to LaShaun until they stood face to face. LaShaun's heart swelled with joy when she looked into Chase's eyes. Her lips parted to express her love, but she froze. The light animating his eyes had no trace of Chase's loving essence. She tried to move away, but his arms trapped her. The smothering kiss cut off her attempts to call his true name. All around her faded from flickering candlelight, to sepia tones and then to darkness.

***

The incessant tick-tock invaded her dreams. LaShaun twisted and turned feeling an urgent need to wake up. When she opened her eyes, the first thing she saw was cabbage roses, or rather the huge roses of the room's wallpaper. Dressed in a long cotton sleep shirt and leggings, she lay on a large bed.

"What the hell?" LaShaun sat up. Long leather straps attached to the bedposts bound both wrists. The door opened just as she started to yell for Chase.

"Ah, I told them you'd be awake by now. I have that little potion down to an absolute science." Gina stood holding a tray of food.

"You've lost your damn mind. Untie me," LaShaun shouted.

Gina placed the tray on a round antique table within reach of the bed. "We had to move up the time table because of those stupid kids. I told everyone that teenagers are a wild card. They're too impulsive to trust with anything this important. I have your favorites:

271

fluffy biscuits with honey and butter, a pile of bacon and strong hot coffee."

LaShaun ignored the food. "Where am I?"

"Make the best of it, okay? You'll get a hot husband and power out of this deal. A lot better than me, I'll tell you that. Ted's a bit of a bore to be honest. Anyway, I have to make sure you eat something."

"Hell no," LaShaun shot back.

"You can't get loose to hurt me. Go ahead, try it," Gina said with a smug expression. "Those ties have binding ciphers."

LaShaun didn't doubt Gina, but she wanted to test what she was up against. She jerked on the straps with all of her might. Her grip weakened the harder she pulled. The leather seemed to sap her energy. After a few seconds LaShaun gave a final gasp and stopped.

"What is this stuff?" LaShaun said.

"The ciphers pull the force you put into resisting from you and make the straps stronger. Brilliant little tool, right? Just one of many reasons we're going to rule the world pretty soon." Gina grabbed a slice of bacon. "No reason for me to go hungry if you're not going to eat all of this."

LaShaun sprang forward to grab Gina. The bindings yanked her back, and LaShaun's arms felt weaker. The woman's laughter enraged LaShaun even more. Against better judgment LaShaun pulled at the straps until she lay exhausted and sweating. Her eyelids felt heavy with fatigue.

Minutes later Gina stood over LaShaun gnawing on a second thick bacon slice. "Now I'm going to have to clean you up for him. Of course, he might like you all hot and helpless like this."

LaShaun steadied her breathing. "Who are you

talking about?"

"Your husband of course. Humph, they said you were so smart," Gina retorted. She started to go on, but stopped when the door opened.

"You're upsetting her," a low voice said.

"So what? She's only a tool. There isn't one thing special about her."

A rapid fire series of three loud cracks of skin on skin rang out. LaShaun's eyes flew open to see a bizarre tableau before her. Neal Montgomery stood over a cowering Gina. He wore a mild disapproving frown as he gazed at the woman. Gina's wide-eyed stare glittered with fright, and something else. LaShaun concentrated. Resentment. LaShaun filed away that knowledge.

"Get out." Neal pointed a long arm at the door as though he needed to emphasize his point. Gina rushed through the door and it shut with a solid thud. "How are you feeling?"

"Seriously? This is a low budget horror movie with dumb players and even dumber questions," LaShaun shot back.

Neal laughed. "I can see why he craves you like a man on drugs. Nothing you say or do is expected."

She was about to speak when an odd mental tug brought LaShaun up short. Words like wisps of smoke appeared before her eyes. Don't say his name. Not the right time. She stared at Neal. He cocked his head to one side and gazed at her in curiosity. He apparently hadn't seen anything. LaShaun felt dizzy. She heaved in a deep breath and let it out slowly.

"Maybe you should have a bland diet for a day or so. Gina probably got too enthusiastic with the ingredients of that drink she concocted. Jealously thy name is woman," Neal said. He looked at the tray of food, and then covered the plate with a cloth napkin.

LaShaun felt tears sting her eyes. The smoke from strong incense made them water. "What do you mean a day or so? You can't keep me here or get away with this. Being a lawyer, you know the penalties for kidnapping. You'll have to kill us because we can identify you all."

Neal sat down in a chair at the table and crossed his long legs. He seemed at ease, as though they were chatting over afternoon tea. Except LaShaun had no idea how much time had passed. She glanced around the room. The source of the loud ticking hung on the wall; a large clock with no hands. Heavy draperies blocked any view from windows.

"You think...?" Neal shook his head slowly. "I couldn't give the order to kill you even if at some point I thought it best. Three powerful men desire you. No wonder the ladies, Gina especially, are so jealous."

"I'd feel flattered except being drugged, tied up, and married to a demon has me in a bad mood," LaShaun drawled. She glanced around the room looking for clues on breaking out.

"You can't get away. No, I'm not psychic," Neal said. "Few people really are in fact. I'm only a humble servant."

"Of Satan?" LaShaun gave an exaggerated sigh. "Lord, not another annoying nest of devil worshipers. You can't swing a dead black cat without hitting one these days."

Neal laughed so hard he bent double. After a few moments, he stood and crossed to LaShaun. When his long fingers stroked her hair, LaShaun didn't move away. The contact would help her get a read on him. She tossed her head. Her thick black hair bounced away from her forehead as she glared at him. As expected, her hostility only drew him closer. His breathing grew ragged.

Neal took in a deep breath and slowly let it out. "I'm having a tough time resisting your enticing scent of magical sexuality."

"The boss would likely cut you, so be careful," LaShaun murmured as she gazed back through narrowed eyes. "Why tie me up if I'm so harmless?"

"We both know you're not harmless." Neal took a step closer when LaShaun didn't make a hostile move. Still he watched her hands.

LaShaun did something she'd sworn never to do again, not since her affair with Quentin Trosclair. She whispered a seduction chant an old woman, a friend of Monmon Odette's, had taught her. Well, Miss Dahlia had been more a colleague than a friend. The woman had been at least ninety when LaShaun was only fifteen. LaShaun remembered the words, and though she didn't have gris-gris to go along with them, she had one important ingredient. Montgomery's lust for her burned beneath his skin.

"You hid your desire well. Your lover must scare you, but since she's not here..." LaShaun let the words trail off to a whisper.

"Krystal doesn't stop me from having who I want." Neal lifted a hand to touch her just as the bedroom door opened. He stepped back quickly.

Chase stood in the opening with Gina and Krystal. "Thank you for being so attentive to our guest."

Krystal walked around Chase. "We don't want you to be burdened with all the work, sweetie. So we came to relieve you."

Neal smiled easily. "I appreciate your helpfulness."

"Leave us," Chase commanded.

LaShaun might have calculated her odds of escaping, or using the signs of friction to her advantage. But the sight of Chase tangled her mind into knots. He looked strikingly handsome dressed in a vintage crisp white shirt and black close fitting pants. In the flickering gaslight lamps on the wall LaShaun might have sworn she'd stepped back in time. Chase walked around the room. He checked the windows and tugged at the long straps bound her yet allowed her to move a few feet. Then he sat down on the bed and patted the thick coverlet.

"My sweet one," he said.

"I know who you are," LaShaun said after watching him in silence for several minutes.

Chase nodded. Or rather the being inside him did. "I admit though that I'm surprised you found out. I won't harm you. Come sit with me."

"You've harmed me already."

Her voice shook as she gazed at the man she loved. Her body ached with warring impulses to caress Chase and attack him. Her psychic instinct told her the being needed to be destroyed. Yet how could she and not fatally wound Chase?

"You don't have to choose. Your true love is right here. Every man has demons. This way you'll simply know exactly what his are. You see?" Abiku spread his borrowed arms out as though the logic made life simple.

LaShaun placed both her open palms on the broad chest. The warmth and solid flesh sent a flash of craving through her. "It's so like a devil to wrap itself in a beautiful body like my Chase."

"Think of the fun we shall have, mon petite. Let me

show you even more pleasure than he could. His love is strong, but I'm growing stronger." Abiku shivered beneath her fingers. "I've grown to savor the way human flesh joined together feels."

"I see," LaShaun replied softly.

She lifted the hem of the long shirt and straddled him. The being sighed and leaned his back against one of the thick bedposts. He inched back farther on the bed to gain more leverage. He shifted his hips beneath her.

"What could I bargain to make you leave him alone for good?" LaShaun tickled the side of his neck with the tip of her tongue. "You want power, riches... another body?"

"Hmm, all that and more," Abiku rasped, his breathing heavy. "But I don't have to bargain. I will have you both. Being in this body makes me weak to your charms. That I must admit." He fumbled to free himself from the slim slacks as his passion grew.

LaShaun used sheer willpower not to strike out when his hands went beneath her night shirt. To counter the aversion, she stared at his body and not into his eyes. Abiku moaned in a language she didn't recognize when his fingers found one of her nipples. Like a clanging bell, a string of phrases sounded clearly in LaShaun's mind.

"Seduce the seducer," a chorus sang.

She covered her startled cry by pretending to gasp with pleasure. In a quick motion, LaShaun lifted her hips and let his fingers rip the fabric of her leggings down the center seam. One more tear and she'd be wearing nothing else. Abiku bucked against her and moaned louder.

"I love the flesh," he said through gritted teeth.

"Then taste it," LaShaun replied.

Despite her actions, her mind focused like a laser on what she must do next. The chorus in her mind grew louder. Chase tore free of his pants in two quick motions. With fingers like claws, he shredded the leggings and shirt LaShaun wore. It seemed the sight of LaShaun in tattered fabric drove him even wilder. He growled in an attempt to form words. LaShaun felt repulsed even though she saw Chase.

"Be strong," a voice said.

"Yes," LaShaun murmured.

A glint to ravenous lust made Chase's eyes bright, but the glow really came from the demon. "I knew the power of his strong body would rule your senses."

LaShaun turned her head so he wouldn't see the fear in her eyes. Every part of her spirit rebelled at being in union with Chase while he was controlled. But the chorus in her head urged her on. So she lifted her body and lowered her hips on his pelvis.

"Devour me," Abiku's accented voice gasped.

He licked LaShaun's neck like a man starving for the taste of her. Through his guttural pleas as he called out her name, LaShaun heard the phrases again. She spiritually grabbed onto them until her mind cleared to the one true purpose. At first she repeated them silently, but after a few seconds she whispered the words.

"We are bound in truth and faith. Yes, we are truly joined, but not in the darkness that attempts to enslave us. We are bound by the pure love of our union before God," LaShaun said, her mouth pressed against Chase's cheek. "We are united, we are wed, but not with the unholy purpose. We did not willingly choose this way."

"Ah, ah, what is that? What..." The voice of Abiku

grew hoarse; his grunts sounded more in pain than pleasure.

"We are joined in God's love as we intended with this token," LaShaun yelled. "With these words I declare our marriage is true and..."

"Stop this defilement!" The demon roared.

The true evil essence of the thing pushed to get away from the power of her prayer. Chase's skin felt clammy suddenly. A blast of hot air swept the room causing the heavy drapes to sway. LaShaun shivered in a second sudden gust of icy cold. The bed shuddered and the rest of the furniture in the room started to move. LaShaun wrapped her body around Chase. She continued her vow despite the whirlwind. LaShaun ignored the way the room shuddered. She had no idea how much time passed, but when she finally opened her eyes Chase panted against her breast. Her left hand tingled intensely. LaShaun gazed at her engagement ring. The Ametrine sparkled even in the muted light of the room.

"Open this door," Neal called.

"I told you not to leave them alone," Marion Saunders said.

"We don't have time for your harping," her husband shouted.

The banging on the door intensified until it vibrated on the hinges. LaShaun looked for anything to use as a weapon. She intended to fight her way out no matter the odds. She pulled back from Chase. He slid down to the bed when she let go, his eyes half closed. Her feet hit the Persian wool carpet just as the bedroom door rattled ominously. Though solid the wood, it couldn't withstand much more of multiple people applying such force. LaShaun heaved in air and let it out to clear her head.

"You need to get dressed."

LaShaun whirled around to find Chase fumbling with the leather straps. He soon had one untied. With effort he grunted, sat upright and managed to get the second strap loose from her wrist. He braced himself with both hands on the bed. When Chase started for her, LaShaun raced to the table. She broke the plate and pointed the jagged piece of China at him.

"Who the hell am I talking to?" she shouted.

"What's she saying?" a voice asked on the other side of the door.

"Me, but I don't know how long before..." his voice trailed off and his dark eyes looked glassy. Then he looked at LaShaun again.

"I, I..." LaShaun fought to stay in control, but she heard it in his voice. Only Chase remained in the room. At least for now. Tears rolled down her cheeks despite her efforts not to cry. No time, a voice barked in her head. This is no time to fall apart.

Chase took a step toward her with his hands extended. "I love you, and that's forever. No matter what I said or did, we are one."

LaShaun trembled at the tenderness in his gaze. Her heart told her no demon could mimic what she saw. "Don't leave me, Chase. Please. We have to fight him together."

"I know, cher. I know. But do what you have to." Chase continued talking to her sweetly as he approached.

"No. No." LaShaun shook her head. She tried, but couldn't bring herself to attack him.

Seconds later, Chase took the improvised weapon from her shaking hands. LaShaun collapsed into his arms, not caring if he killed her in that instant. The sweet touch she knew well combed the wild hair from her face.

"We don't have much time," Chase rasped. "Once I get you out of here don't look back, no matter what."

"Chase, I can't." LaShaun shook her head frantically. "Don't ask me to."

"Listen, do you think I want to live not knowing when I'll black out or do things I despise? You might say something supernatural is happening, but... inside me is something dark. I went through hell in the war. Things I saw." Chase squeezed his eyes shut and opened them again. "Things I did, LaShaun. Don't let me become a monster. No matter why, don't let it happen. Promise me."

She gazed into his dark eyes for a second. "We're married, but not because of the foul ceremony they performed. Once we're both free we'll exchange holy vows."

"Married?" Chase gripped both LaShaun's shoulders. Before he could say more wood splintered into the room.

Chapter 18

Seconds later the door flew open and hung crazily to one side. Neal rushed in first holding a thirty-eight pistol. Harry Saunders waved an iron fireplace poker over his head. Ted Waterman hung back looking much less eager to jump in. Gina and Marion craned their necks to see around the men.

"What the hell happened to my room?" Marion blurted out with her eyes stretched wide.

Neal scowled at her and Marion snapped her mouth shut. He turned back to Chase. "Are you okay?"

LaShaun sank to her knees and whimpered. Or pretended to. She looked up at Chase. At that moment she hoped he could read her expression since he couldn't read her mind. More importantly, she hoped Chase was still Chase. He blinked a few times and then stood straight.

"I hope you have a damn good reason for interrupting our wedding night consummation," Chase said. He held out a hand to LaShaun. When she moved back, he reached down and forcibly pulled her up. Then he yanked a decorative throw from a chair nearby and draped it around her.

"We apologize for the intrusion, master," Ted Waterman wheezed.

Neal walked closer to Chase with the gun still pointed at him. "Nice try, but I've been around long enough to know better. The connection is weakened. It's not him."

Harry Saunders stepped closer with the poker still raised. "We need to speed things up then. She's still able to block his energy enough that the possession is unstable."

"I agree," Neal replied. "We're running out of time. The hearing is in two days."

"Two days?" Ted squawked. "You expect us to keep them both locked up for that long? Look at him. He's strong as a young bull."

"Hmm, yes he certainly is," Gina agreed. Her gaze roamed over Chase's body.

Marion pushed past Ted to enter the room. "And she's tricky. We don't know the true extent of her paranormal abilities. All I've heard are vague rumors and superstitious gossip."

"Manny can tell us," Neal replied.

"Then why hasn't he? He's still playing games," Marion answered sharply.

LaShaun held herself stiff as though she loathed being close to Chase. In truth the warmth from his body fed her spirit, reminding her of their love. With their captors intent on their conversation, she gently nudged him with her hip. His hold tightened and then loosened.

"The Blood River Ripper isn't some poodle I can train with treats after a few weeks," Neal growled at her. "I've been in The Fold longer than you, so don't question me. I'm not your whipped hubby. Remember who I am."

He glared at Marion first, and then his heated glance flickered to the others. The room grew still, the air heavy. A faint whiff of something burnt, something dead, snaked in like a foul invisible beast. Marion's overbearing expression dissolved as she inched away from Neal. Ted looked scared enough to wet his pants.

"Marion didn't mean to challenge you. Tell him, honey," Harry said, his voice strained with tension.

Seconds ticked by before she spoke.

"Of course not. I'm just anxious to advance our cause. Proceed as you see fit." Marion gripped her hands together.

"Thank you," Neal retorted with smile that looked deadly rather than conciliatory. He looked at Chase again. "Step away from the bride."

A hot breeze swept the room and Chase rolled his shoulders. LaShaun's stomach lurched as she watched Chase's handsome face take on a foreign look. His jaw muscles tightened until he wore a ferocious smile, his lips pulled up into a sneer. The brutish gleam had returned to his dark Cajun eyes.

"Ah, but being with you fed me in more ways than one. Sweet love," the words came from his mouth with the faint accent. Chase looked at Neal. "You're right. We don't have much time. Have the women dress my soul mate properly."

LaShaun jerked free of his grip on her arm. "I'm not your soul mate."

"You will be." The smile that Chase wore bore no resemblance to the one she loved so well. Then he turned to Neal. "We have much left to do tonight."

"We must reinforce the connection," Neal said quietly. He looked at LaShaun.

"Agreed." Chase gestured at him and strode out of the bedroom.

Neal followed him after a few instructions to the others. Seconds later LaShaun let the throw slip from her shoulders. The shredded fabric of her cotton night shirt left her breasts and thighs exposed. She brushed hair away from her face and turned to Harry.

"Don't let them do this to me. Please," she whispered. Then she looked at Ted. "Please."

"You're going to be a lot better off because he's chosen you," Harry said. His stern expression loosened once his gaze slid down to her breasts.

Ted gawked at her exposed thighs. "Listen, honey, you're actually going to have a lot of fun. I mean once you get used to us we're not so bad."

Gina came up behind Ted and slapped the side of his face. "Stop drooling and do something useful."

"She's right, Ted. I'll make sure this little spitfire is secure," Harry replied.

"Think again. Gina and I will get her dressed," Marion said. She walked around him to block her husband's view of LaShaun. "Stop fantasizing. From what I've seen, he has no plans to share her. I don't think you want to cross our new leader."

Gina barked a laugh. "Hell, I don't think you want to piss off Marion either. You two horny middle-aged dudes need to leave. Now."

"We'll be in the study." Harry avoided his wife's gaze as he left.

"Yeah, in the study," Ted echoed. Then he looked at Gina. "You're no prize you know. Remember, he didn't choose you." When Gina hissed at him, Ted scurried after Harry.

"Why do I waste my time?" Gina asked no one in particular.

"He's got millions," Marion replied in a dry tone.

"Oh yeah." Gina snorted a laugh.

"Now get the clothes in the armoire," Marion ordered. She shoved LaShaun onto the bed. "Don't try working your little charm on the men again, dear."

LaShaun pretended to be still too shaken to resist much physically. "You're all insane and evil."

"Then that's real bad news for all of you worms not

in our circle, huh? We're about to rule the world," Gina said.

"Oh please. You can barely hold on to your men," LaShaun wisecracked. "Five minutes alone with those two and they wouldn't have remembered your names."

"Shut up," Marion snapped.

LaShaun honed in on the button she'd just pushed. "Harry will be sniffing around me sooner rather than later."

"I'm going to..." Marion advanced toward LaShaun with her hands balled into fists.

Gina cut her off. "Cool it. You saw how he acted toward her. Our leader has a permanent hard on for this one. He'll eventually get tired of her though. Then we'll teach her some manners."

Marion glowered at LaShaun for a few moments then let out a slow hiss of air. "I look forward to the day."

Gina tossed LaShaun a pair of cotton yoga pants and a long sleeve T-shirt. "Here, put those on lover girl. You won't be such a temptress in that."

"By the way, don't think you can get away." Marion marched to the heavy drapes and pulled them aside. "There are bars on both windows. And we're going to keep you company while Harry fixes that door."

LaShaun caught a glimpse of a darkened landscape, but part of the sky still looked orange. "What time is it?"

"You're not going anywhere, so it doesn't matter," Gina replied with a laugh. "It's just about five o'clock in the evening. Don't worry though. Your date will be on time."

"We're prepared for you, bitch," Marion said with a feral smile.

LaShaun said nothing as Marion tied the thick

leather straps around her wrists again. She attached them to metal circles on the wall above the bed's headboard. Made to look like they were part of the decorative wall sconces, LaShaun hadn't examined them closely before now. Harry and Ted returned. They replaced the broken door. Marion and Gina kept the men from re-entering the room. Harry tried his best to get a look at LaShaun stretched out on the bed with her arms extended over her head. After a few choice curse words from Marion, he retreated. Ted called the two women over. Voices low, the three of them talked a few moments before Ted left.

Gina looked around the bedroom. She'd done the job of putting furniture back in place. "Okay, this was just a minor distraction."

"You're going to stay tied up like this if I have anything to say about it," Marion said. She laughed when LaShaun didn't answer.

"I think we've taken the fight out of her," Gina retorted.

Gina sat at the table, took out her phone and stared at the screen. Marion sat in an armchair next to the table and stared at LaShaun. The hostility in her glassy eyes gave her an unhinged look. Though tempted, LaShaun restrained her itch to taunt the woman. Instead she centered her thinking. She breathed in and out in a steady rhythm. After a while Gina put down her phone.

"Damn, wish we had a television or something in here."

"No. We need to watch her," Marion said, her gaze still on LaShaun.

Gina looked at LaShaun and then at Marion. She tapped Marion on the arm. "Hey, you need to lighten up on the jealous woman shit. Harry might have the hots for her, but he's no fool. He would slice Harry up for touching her."

Marion's eyes narrowed. "She's got some kind of supernatural thing that makes men lust after her. I say we get rid of this piece of trash."

"What we need is some entertainment," Gina replied forcing a playful tone. "Hey, I'll keep an eye on her. Go get that backgammon set and a deck of cards. Could be a long night."

"Backgammon?" Marion glanced at Gina sideways.

"It'll be fun. Besides, I can fix her some more of that special brandy," Gina said low, but not low enough that LaShaun didn't hear.

"I'm not going to fall for that one twice," LaShaun snapped.

"You'll drink it if I have pour it down your throat," Marion snarled. She started toward the bed, but Gina grabbed her arm.

"Will you calm the hell down? You don't want him to catch you threatening her. Besides, I've got a Plan B for this one. Ether. One whiff of that and Miss LaShaun will do as she's told."

"I say we skip to Plan B anyway. Be right back," Marion replied with a nasty grin. She continued to glare at LaShaun until she disappeared through the door.

A click indicated Marion locked it from the outside. Gina went to the window. She gazed out of it for a few minutes then paced the room. LaShaun felt the nervous energy radiating from her.

"You got something to say?" LaShaun raised an eyebrow at her.

"Quit keep making cracks about Harry, okay? Marion can be a little... she gets crazy when it comes to him." Gina frowned at LaShaun.

"I noticed," was all LaShaun said.

"Look, I didn't know all this crap was going down. Kidnapping, murder, a bunch of bat shit crazy teenagers. Now they're trying to get some guy with a nickname like The Blood River Ripper out of prison. I'm not ready to hang out with devil worshipers and serial killers." Gina chewed on her fingernails until she chipped polish on one. She muttered a curse word and snatched her hand down.

LaShaun watched Gina pace a few seconds more, her agitation increasing. "How do they plan to get Manny out of prison?"

Gina went to the door and put her ear to it. "Okay, before Marion comes back--"

"She's not coming right away," LaShaun said quietly.

Gina looked at LaShaun over one shoulder. "Is it true? They say you have paranormal gifts, like you know things before other people."

"Tell me what's going on."

LaShaun wondered why the demon hadn't filled them in on her skills. Then she remembered her grandmother's lessons about demons. They didn't know everything. Despite what movies or myths said, not even Satan could create. His lesser minions had fewer powers than he did. Demons took advantage of the weakness of people, appealing to their lust for power, money and pleasure. Those desires lead humans to perform dirty work for demons. With little time to spare, LaShaun had to test if Gina's fear could be used to advantage.

"Untie me and pretend you gave me ether. Get Marion to leave and I'll--"

Gina's eyes went wide with terror. She shook her head so hard her short red curls bounced around. "You must be out of your freaking mind, girl."

"Then you come up with a plan. I know you want out of this situation. We're talking heavy prison sentences here," LaShaun said.

"Let me think. Shit." Gina flailed her hands for a few seconds. Then she snapped her fingers. "I got it! I'll pretend that you had to go use the toilet real bad. When I took off one strap you overpowered me. Punch me hard a few times to make it look real."

"No problem," LaShaun drawled.

"That could work. I'll unlock the door. Take a left. At the end the hall is a window with no bars. Harry just put them on these windows for other, uh, activities we've had."

"Right." LaShaun took that to mean they'd held others here against their will. She made a note to do research on any missing persons around Vermilion Parish.

"Okay, okay. I'm going to untie you now." Gina paused as though unsure.

"You better move it over here fast 'cause Marion could be here any second," LaShaun said firmly.

Gina scurried over and tugged at the knots in the leather straps. "Damn they tied these good. I'm not sure I can get them loose. Shit, I broke a nail."

"Hurry up." LaShaun scowled at the woman.

"I got this one. There." Gina stood back, arms spread out. "Okay, slap me before I lose my nerve."

"Sure thing," LaShaun shot back. She put all her force into the slap across the left side of Gina's face. The loud crack bounced off the papered walls.

The woman let out a whosh of air. She staggered,

blinking rapidly. "What the..."

Before Gina could finish the sentence LaShaun punched her in the stomach with a closed fist. The redhead bent double as she gulped for air. LaShaun slapped her again for the satisfaction and then ran to the door. Before she could make it out, LaShaun felt pain at her temples. Gina had a handful of her hair. With a grunt of force she dragged LaShaun back into the bedroom.

"You believed that bullshit, didn't you? I didn't mention something. In a former life I was a wrestler." Gina swung LaShaun until she slammed onto the bed. "Cherry Bomb, three time Divas of The South Champion."

"Get off me," LaShaun pushed hard. Only then did she feel the solid muscle of Gina's arms and legs.

"I like it rough, baby girl. Let's have fun," Gina panted close to LaShaun's ear.

"Yeah. I'm up for it," LaShaun through clenched teeth.

Gina chuckled low in her throat when LaShaun couldn't get leverage to get free. Indeed the woman enjoyed the thrill of a physical battle. LaShaun sensed the excitement that rippled through her. Not satisfied, Gina sprang back and let LaShaun get to her feet. But seconds later she jumped on LaShaun's back. She straddled LaShaun, pinning her to the hardwood floor.

"Looks like you're not up for it after all, sweetie," Gina said between heavy breathing. She put her face close to LaShaun's. "I hope they let me have a crack at you again. Hmm, you smell good."

LaShaun stared into Gina's dark blues eyes. The woman wore a sadistic smile as she puffed hard. With a burst of red hot energy coursing through her veins,

LaShaun grunted. Gina's mocking expression slipped, and so did the pressure of her hold on LaShaun. She looked confused for a few seconds.

"What the hell is happening?" Gina squawked. She tried to maintain her grip, but pain mixed with growing alarm distracted her.

"I'm not having fun anymore, baby girl," LaShaun shot back.

She flipped Gina onto her stomach and delivered two quick blows to the redhead's jaw. Gina's body went slack, her eyes rolled back and then closed as she passed out. With her opponent down for the count, LaShaun ran to the door. She got there just as Marion appeared carrying a tray with glasses and a Backgammon board tucked under one arm. LaShaun body slammed Marion against the opposite wall and sprinted down the hallway to the window. No bars. Gina hadn't lied about that at least. LaShaun grabbed a heavy brass ashtray on her way past a table. She smashed through the glass, not willing to take time opening it. She scrambled through it as male voices shouted behind her.

For a few dizzying moments LaShaun hung onto the window sill. She looked down from the second floor. When the voices grew closer she let go. A gardenia bush broke her fall, but she had scratches from the wood. Rolling to the ground, LaShaun felt stunned. But fear and adrenaline forced her up. She sprinted straight ahead into dark woods. A full moon lit the way as she pumped her legs until she ran full speed. LaShaun made as little noise as possible despite the panic stabbing into her like daggers. With eyesight sharpened by survival instinct, she dodged trees and wild shrubbery. Shouts in the distance propelled her onward. LaShaun slowed to a quick trot. Glancing around to get her bearings, she estimated directions. Lights from the bed and breakfast appeared to her left, west. So she raced straight ahead in a northern direction. Highway 90 should be several miles ahead, if she made it that far. Then she stood still. The sound she heard meant someone or something had closed the gap between them.

"Damn."

LaShaun shot forward opening up a burst of speed as she zig-zagged hoping to confuse her pursuer. But the effects of whatever drug Marion had put in the brandy seemed to have bounced back on her. Light-headed and breathing heavily, she slowed down. A solid body crashed into her as she darted to avoid a large pine tree. They both hit the ground.

"Got you," Chase said. Or it was Abiku using his voice?

"Get the hell off me you..." LaShaun punched hard but missed when Chase snapped his head aside.

"It's me. LaShaun, it's me." Chase struggled with her. "I swear it's me."

LaShaun continued to slap at him until her will to right the man she loved dissolved. No matter what possessed him, LaShaun couldn't try to hurt Chase once she heard his voice. He pinned her hands down against a carpet of dead leaves as she sobbed until her chest hurt.

"I can't do it anymore," LaShaun cried.

"Shh..., baby I know." Chase cradled her against his body. "LaShaun, listen to me. We don't have much time."

"Oh Chase." LaShaun frantically kissed his face, hoping to wake up from the nightmare.

He pulled away and pressed keys into her hands. "I

don't know how much longer I can hold on. Thank God you ran in this direction. Turn to your right. There's an old barn. Get in the truck and go."

"I'm not leaving you with these demon worshiping psychos! No, I won't--"

"They're not going to hurt me, right? They need me to take over the world and start the new age. Until maybe we get Manny out of prison," Chase added in a soft voice.

LaShaun cupped his face with both her hands. "You just said we, Chase. Let's fight off that bastard from hell."

"I turned off my flashlight, so they can't see which way I came. Now run." Chase shoved LaShaun away from him.

LaShaun wiped tears from her eyes. Voices sounded closer and closer. "I'm coming back for you."

"Don't go home. Not tonight. But you know that." Chase turned to leave, but then faced LaShaun again. "I love you."

"We'll be together," LaShaun protested, pushing back against the finality in his voice.

Chase shook his head and shot off in the opposite direction. Seconds later a bright light bounced when he turned on his flashlight again. LaShaun bit back a cry of anguish as she followed his instructions. After ten minutes of hard running she found the ramshackle barn with the doors lying broken on the ground. LaShaun almost sagged to her knees with relief when she saw Chase's truck. She scrambled inside, fumbling to get the key into the ignition because her hands shook. Once she got the engine started, LaShaun hit the gas pedal. Five minutes of bumping down a gravel road brought her to a black top surface.

"Which way do I go?" LaShaun muttered in frustration as she looked around. Then she remembered the GPS system.

LaShaun whispered a thank you when the mechanical sound of its voice command gave her directions. Each time she saw headlights in her rear view mirror LaShaun tensed up. She didn't know which made her more paranoid, being alone on the dark highway or watching a vehicle approach. With the window down and cold air hitting her face, LaShaun's thinking cleared. Only one destination might offer safety for a time.

"Let's hope I've got enough gas to make it to Mouton Cove."

Chapter 19

Miss Rose shushed her anxious husband and three grandchildren. The oldest child, a tall lanky girl of eleven, had large eyes, round with curiosity. The next one in age was a boy who appeared to be about eight. The youngest couldn't have been older than five. She had sandy red hair, light brown skin, and one thumb in her mouth. She gazed between her grandmother and their visitor.

LaShaun hadn't expected Miss Rose to have a full house. No wonder they stared at her in fright. Leaves drifted to the floor when LaShaun raked fingers through her tangled hair. She tried to tuck the shirt into the yoga pants. Realizing that only made her appearance more bizarre, she smoothed out the shirt instead. LaShaun smiled at the five year old. The little one shrank behind her grandfather until she disappeared completely.

"Pierre, take the children over to Eloise's. They can spend the night there," Miss Rose said quietly. Then she looked at her grandchildren. "Your Tante Eloise baked a chocolate cake and has ice cream waiting. Your cousin Tremaine is over there."

"Tremaine has video games," the little boy piped up in excitement. He shot off without waiting for more instructions.

"Come with us, Monmon," the youngest girl said in a high voice that spoke of tears to come.

"Papa is going to be with you, sweetheart. We'll sing while your Uncle Ivory plays his guitar," Mr. Fontenot said. He picked her up and kissed her round cheeks. As he tickled and teased her, the little one smiled. Soon she let out a laugh as Mr. Fontenot walked off with her.

"Go on now, Isabelle," Miss Rose said, urging the older child to follow him.

"I'm not scared. I can help," Isabelle said with confidence. She gazed at LaShaun.

"Not yet, baby. I'll let you know when it's time." Miss Rose shooed her down the hallway. Though reluctant to leave, the child obediently walked away. But not without several backward glances.

"That little lady wants to know what's going on," LaShaun said when Miss Rose came back into the living room.

"Isabelle has the gift of special sight. I pray that she's not burdened by it. But Le Bon Dieu knows best," Miss Rose said with a sigh. Then she turned her full attention to LaShaun. "Well?"

"These people are playing with forces they don't understand, Miss Rose. But that's on them. I've got to save Chase."

"Sit down and tell me." Miss Rose eased into one of the chairs nearby, a rocker that matched the two sofas.

"No, if I sit down I might pass out from exhaustion," LaShaun replied. She massaged her forehead trying to think straight.

Then she told Miss Rose about the sequence of events while pacing. She paused only when Mr. Fontenot came back to announce they were leaving. With a brief wave he turned back down the hallway. The children's voices could be heard as they waited for him at the back door. The back door slammed shut and the locked clicked. Only then did LaShaun finish her account. Miss Rose asked no questions, but allowed her to tell the story in her own way. Finally LaShaun finished. Spent, she sank down onto the sofa.

"I ended up here to tell you what happened, to get advice or an opinion. Or... something. I don't know. I can't go home." LaShaun hid a yawn behind her right hand. "I've got money for a hotel."

"No, you won't go to a hotel. You stay here," Miss Rose said.

"I can't put you at risk, Miss Rose. They'll be looking for me. Chase will figure out where I am eventually and he's, well he's not responsible." LaShaun fought the urge to curl into a ball and cry her eyes out. Now was definitely not the time to collapse.

"You'll be more vulnerable alone. Besides, you say those folks are on a deadline. They won't spend what little time they have searching for you." Miss Rose looked at LaShaun with a grave expression. "They have Deputy Broussard, and as you said this evil one has control over him."

"He helped me get way, so the control isn't complete," LaShaun protested. She sat up straight.

"The fact remains that Deputy Broussard loses himself for long periods of time, cher," Miss Rose said, pressing home her point.

"I would know, if..."

"Non, ma cherie. We who have the gifts can't always tell what is happening to the ones we love. It's as if God knew what true heartache that might bring. How could we stand to be around family knowing they would be hurt or worse? How could Pauline and Justine not go insane hearing from their own deceased family members constantly? There are those of us who do. Mostly they live solitary lives with no mate, no children. They cut themselves off to have some measure of peace." Miss Rose gently rocked in the chair.

"That's who we need, someone with a powerful

connection to the other world. Let's get in touch with her, or him." LaShaun stood up.

Miss Rose continued to rock in silence for a few seconds. Then she went still and gazed up at LaShaun. "I only knew of two. Your grandmother, Odette. The other was the man Jean Paul. I haven't seen him in over thirty years, and I have no idea where he might be."

"But there must be others," LaShaun insisted. "You just said..."

"I know of others, but only secondhand. We can't just call up somebody we don't know and invite them to battle with demons, cher." Miss Rose raised a hand cutting off LaShaun's impending passionate argument to the contrary. "There is more. Sit back down."

"I don't like the sound of this," LaShaun mumbled, but obeyed much like the older woman's granddaughter had earlier.

"From your account these events have been well planned. Those teenagers have likely been performing rituals that strengthened this thing," Miss Rose spat out the last word with disgust.

"Makes sense," LaShaun agreed.

"But more cunning adult followers somehow detected the demon had grown in strength." Miss Rose stopped talking and studied LaShaun. She waited patiently while LaShaun thought for a time.

"How would Neal Montgomery know about things happening in Vermilion Parish?" LaShaun asked, but not Miss Rose.

The older woman kept quiet as LaShaun got up and paced again. This time LaShaun didn't have the feverish movements of a woman in panic mode. She turned over the facts in her mind. Suddenly images flashed before her as though a tiny movie screen inside her head.

Miss Rose nodded. "You see it."

"Montgomery met Manny Young a good five years ago. This club or group has been searching for a sign, and Manny led them to Vermilion Parish." LaShaun came to a stop in front of Miss Rose. "He and this spirit have grown stronger, thanks to me."

"No time for self recriminations. You weren't the first Rousselle deceived into opening the door for him," Miss Rose warned wagging a forefinger at LaShaun.

"I carry the same amount of guilt for this crime," LaShaun said. "But you're right. What's done is done."

"So this Montgomery and those of his group learn that a strong power rests here in Vermilion Parish. Go on," Miss Rose urged.

"They probably stumbled on Manny by accident. Nothing in the court documents would make him stand out from any other serial killer in Louisiana." LaShaun paused. "Can't believe I just said that."

"South Louisiana has been a killing ground. Three killers were caught in Baton Rouge alone. They were sentenced to death like Manny Young." Miss Rose stopped rocking and rubbed her chin in thought.

LaShaun looked at her. "There are still at least sixty unsolved murders of women in East Baton Rouge Parish. None have been connected to any of those three."

"There's another series of murders in central Louisiana, too." Miss Rose stared back at LaShaun.

"You're thinking what I'm thinking, huh? Evil has been at work. What if these lawyers and their helpers know other serial killers? They could be helping them avoid capture." LaShaun stood still as the full force of her theory hit home. "What if this demon leads them to the others? They represent them for minor crimes;

advise them on staying under the radar or how to avoid detection."

"Lord help us. Lawyers are helping vicious killers roam free? These are educated people," Miss Rose said, her voice rising. The former teacher seemed to find it hard to believe such a thing. To her education and those with advanced degrees would find only high and noble purposes.

"Education and morals are not always connected. How many educated men worked for Hitler? For Chairman Mao? Remember your history lessons." LaShaun gave Miss Rose a consoling pat on the shoulder. "I'm afraid book knowledge doesn't equate to goodness in the soul."

"Oui." Miss Rose sighed. "I sound terribly naive for my age. Of course you're right. So Vermilion Parish attracts their interest."

"Manny must have told them about his father. I don't know if Manny told him about the Rousselle family. But with even a little bit of research they could find out. If they visited the museum in Beau Chene, I know Pete would have been thrilled to give them more sources," LaShaun said. As the museum director Pete Kluger had his dream job. He would probably live at the museum if his wife allowed it.

"I haven't been there in a while. I used to take my students to the old Francois House on field trips when I was still teaching," Miss Rose put in with a smile. "That was years ago. Then it became the first museum, and a bigger, modern building was put up."

LaShaun nodded absently as she continued putting the puzzle together. "Manny gets caught. But Orin Young has his own cult of young people following him. That was the first group lured in. Orin Young is killed and the rest captured, so that little nest is cleared out."

"Protect us, Holy Father," Miss Rose murmured and made the sign of the cross. "Now these children found hanging in the woods..."

"Imagine a group of angry, bored and rebellious kids hanging out, looking for direction. These adults show up more than willing to give it to them, even if that direction leads to a nightmare." LaShaun tried to shut off the flashing images of underage drinking and sex.

"Evil. Pure evil. Giving young folks liquor and drugs," Miss Rose said with a scowl.

"They're smarter than that, Miss Rose. No, they gave the kids money. Montgomery or his pals don't have to take the risks, which is fine with the kids. Taking chances is part of the rush," LaShaun replied deep in thought.

Seconds ticked by before Miss Rose broke the silence between them. "Pauline called. There is only one way to stop him. Kill the host. I'm sorry, but--"

"I won't accept that," LaShaun shouted. She squeezed her eyes shut. "There's another way. There has to be."

"The twins consulted more than one source. The texts are clear. You must put a sacred knife of silver through his heart." Miss Rose sat very still. "Think, dear girl. Your Chase would not want his body to go on with a demonic spirit inside."

LaShaun trembled as waves of horror made her legs weak. She sank to her knees. "I can't kill the only man I've ever loved."

Miss Rose no longer looked like the kindly retired school teacher. She wore a grim and determined expression. "Satan intends to spread his influence on this earth. Think of the wars, the insidious climate of hatred between different races, tribes, and ethnic groups around the world. I don't usually talk about the end of days... LaShaun, deadly supernatural forces are at work. We of all people can't stand by knowing the source and how to stop it, but do nothing. Let us handle it."

"You've done this kind of thing before," LaShaun replied in a shocked whisper.

"We have."

LaShaun felt as though all air had been sucked from her lungs. She fought to find her voice for several seconds. "Please don't do anything. Let me try to find another way."

"Time is running out, cher. You must know this, eh?" Miss Rose sighed. She sat frowning for several minutes as LaShaun watched her anxiously. "Two more days. That's all."

"Thank you, thank you," LaShaun sprang forward to hug Miss Rose tightly.

Miss Rose held LaShaun for a few moments, then she stood. "I'm going to fix up one of my guest bedrooms for you. I might even have a big t-shirt you can wear as a nightgown. I'll wash your clothes so they'll be fresh in the morning."

"I'm going to use your phone if it's okay," LaShaun called out.

Miss Rose was already halfway down the hall. "Sure you can."

"Don't go to a lot of trouble. I'll help you in a minute."

LaShaun heard her protest as the older woman's voice faded. Then she went to the kitchen to make a call. Miss Rose had given her an idea. Savannah answered on the fourth ring.

"Girl, what the hell is going on? I've been calling you all night. Your cousin Azalei came by my office saying you're missing and..."

"Azalei? Why is she looking for me?" LaShaun frowned at the latest twist.

"She wouldn't tell me, but when she called over here looking for you, I got worried. Then I called the Sheriff's station this morning. They say Chase hasn't been in to work. M.J. is beside herself," Savannah took a deep breath.

"I'll call M.J. in a minute," LaShaun cut in before Savannah got going again. "I want you to hire a professional to do a discreet investigation. I don't want anything bouncing back on you."

"Sounds like some serious crap is about to hit the fan," Savannah said, her voice lower.

"I'll tell you about it later."

LaShaun withheld the seriously creepy facts. She asked Savannah to find out the how, when and where of Montgomery's first meeting with Manny Young, aka The Blood River Ripper. Not that LaShaun needed confirmation. Her vision had shown her clearly that Manny had played a key part in drawing Montgomery and Juridicus to Beau Chene. Knowing more would help LaShaun prepare.

Savannah finally hung up, but only after repeated reassurances that LaShaun was safe. LaShaun glanced at the digital clock on the kitchen counter. She and Chase had gone to the Sweet Olive Bed and Breakfast on Thursday evening. Now it was Friday night. LaShaun guessed M.J. might be on the verge of calling out a full-fledged search with a Louisiana State Police helicopter. She might even use the new air boat the Sheriff's office just bought. That might cause Montgomery's crew to do something desperate. Fighting the dread sitting in her stomach like a rock, LaShaun dialed M.J.'s direct office number. M.J. picked up on the second ring.

"Hi M.J. It's LaShaun. I just called to let you know I'm ok, but Chase has been a bit under the weather. He's going to need an extra few days off," LaShaun said. Then she held her breath for M.J.'s reaction.

"Chase called to let me know he needed an extra day, but he's on duty now. And he didn't say anything about being sick." M.J. went silent on the phone for a long time. "You wanna tell me the real story?"

***

LaShaun had managed to put M.J. off with a hasty explanation. Chase had promised to take more time off, but apparently changed his mind without telling her. LaShaun had improvised M.J. sounded more than a little skeptical. Luckily another call came in and M.J. couldn't press LaShaun on her story.

Despite Miss Rose's comfortable bed and motherly attention, LaShaun got no sleep that night. Aside from trying to figure out her next move, LaShaun was alert to any sound or movement. The night passed quietly. No human or spiritual attack had been directed at Miss Rose's house. Through the heart. A sacred silver knife through the heart. Those words slammed around in LaShaun's mind for hours until her head throbbed with pain.

The next morning, LaShaun put fresh sheets on the bed and carried the used bedclothes to the laundry room. At six o'clock she cooked breakfast. Miss Rose and her husband woke to the smell of coffee, biscuits baking, and grilled Cajun sausage.

"Good morning, LaShaun. My, oh my. Your new husband is one lucky man." Mr. Pierre smiled as he poured himself a cup of Louisiana dark roast. He paused to take a whiff of the rich scent before sipping.

"It's the least I can do since y'all were kind enough to let me bust in here. I'm sorry for bringing my troubles to your doorstep." LaShaun kept busy loading a serving platter with food. Then she got plates down.

Miss Rose stood in the doorway with both hands on her hips. "Girl, what you think you're doing up in here? You're a guest."

"I'm repaying your hospitality. Now have a seat." LaShaun got busy washing the pots and pans she'd used.

"You sit down and eat, too. You've done enough," Miss Rose said gently.

"I've got to keep busy. Keeps me from screaming," LaShaun said, trying to make a joke. She failed. Instead her voice shook, betraying how close she was to the edge.

Miss Rose and Mr. Pierre looked at each other. They both sat down without another word. For thirty minutes they ate in silence. All the while they stole glances at LaShaun. At some signal, Mr. Pierre wiped his mouth with a napkin and stood.

"I got to go check on those grandchildren. Promised I'd take them with me on errands today. Being it's Saturday, we might go to the zoo. Then I'll take them back home to their parents. Is that a plan, Rose?" Mr. Pierre looked at his wife.

"Sounds good, honey. Call me later," Miss Rose replied. She accepted his peck on her cheek.

Mr. Pierre grabbed his jacket from a hook in the hallway and headed for the back door, his truck keys jingling in one hand. "Thanks for that good food, LaShaun. I'll see you later."

"You're welcome, Mr. Pierre," LaShaun called back, still moving as she wiped crumbs from the granite countertop.

"LaShaun," Miss Rose started, but stopped when LaShaun whisked the dirty breakfast dishes from the table.

"I'll load these in the dishwasher."

Miss Rose watched her a few minutes and then stood. "Stop now. In a minute you'll be cleaning my entire house."

"If you need me to," LaShaun wisecracked. "I'm so grateful that you took me in and..."

"I know, baby. I know." Miss Rose took the dish cloth out of LaShaun's hands, put it down on the counter, and hugged her.

"I don't want to think, but I can't stop..." LaShaun let a few tears flow. She leaned into the caring arms of Miss Rose, but only for a few seconds. Then she stood straight and wiped the tears away. They gazed at each other solemnly for a long moment.

"The demon can only be banished with a strike to his heart. Spirits can't be killed because they're not alive in the first place. The sacred knife will dilute his strength enough to help us cast him out. Now the tricky part is finding a sacred knife made of silver."

"Miss Rose, I..."

"No, baby. Stay here and let us take care of the beast," Miss Rose said firmly.

"Us?"

She stood to her full five feet eight inches. Her dark brown face had a set expression of resolution. Gone was the worn down elderly woman. She now looked like a wise, formidable opponent. Though battle weary from years of struggling against evil, Miss Rose would take on this latest challenge. Age meant nothing. LaShaun felt her energy, her power and the force of her will. And LaShaun was afraid.

"The twins and I will do what's necessary," Miss Rose said.

"We agreed, two days," LaShaun said. "I'm going home."

"But--"

"Chase knows I'm here since I called M.J. Which means the demon knows. I can't put you and your family in danger. Besides, the sacred silver knife we need is at my house."

"So you accept that there may be no other way," Miss Rose replied softly.

"He's my responsibility," LaShaun said with a tremble in her voice.

Miss Rose nodded, but LaShaun sensed the older woman's doubt that she could carry out the ultimate solution. Miss Rose insisted on packing up a generous plate of leftovers from breakfast. She fussed over LaShaun, wrapping her in a flannel lined denim jacket. She made sure LaShaun had on warm socks. Finally LaShaun stopped her grandmotherly attention.

"I'm leaving now, Miss Rose. I need to start making preparations. Chase will get off work by six o'clock this evening," LaShaun said more to herself than to inform Miss Rose. "I have hours to be ready."

"Tonight then." Miss Rose nodded her understanding. She gave LaShaun one last tight hug before letting her go.

***

Thirty minutes later, she arrived at her house. She wasn't surprised to find her Honda CRV gone. No doubt Chase had driven it to work. An extra day off, arriving in her vehicle for work, and going about his normal tasks. None of it would have seemed unusual to M.J. or anyone who knew them. LaShaun entered through the kitchen door. She stood quietly for several minutes. Nothing came to her. She found it odd, but went through the entire house to check again. Then her heart skipped at a thought. She raced to the antique desk in what used to be called Monmon Odette's "Ladies Parlor". When she opened the ornately carved teakwood box LaShaun shuddered with relief. And dread. There it lay. The silver knife handed down from her ancestors. According to family legend, it had been used hundreds of years ago to defeat demonic forces. LaShaun lifted the knife from the blood red velvet lining that cradled it. The six inch silver blade felt warm to the touch. She put it back in the box and closed the lid.

"There must be another way. Please help me," she whispered.

For hours LaShaun read page after page. Some of the books were so old that she stopped to put on cotton gloves before touching the delicate paper. She didn't want the oils from her hands to damage them. By noon LaShaun's tired eyes felt like someone had tossed sand in them. Standing to stretch, she decided a walk might do her some good. Just as she opened the back door, LaShaun gave a yelp.

"Hey, we should have called, but frankly I didn't want to hear any excuses. We've got just one little detail to wrap up and we're done." Chase's sister Katie spoke rapid fire as she passed LaShaun on her way to the kitchen. "You'll have the most elegant wedding this parish has seen since mine. And that's saying something. You can thank us later."

"Hello, chica. Where's your SUV?" Adrianna asked. Chase's sister-in-law gave LaShaun a quick kiss on the cheek and followed Katie.

"Chase took it to work and left me the truck. Um, in case I needed to haul something real big," LaShaun said, easily slipping into the lie.

"Like a coffin? You know folks already think you're the voodoo queen," Adrianna joked. "Seriously though, the polls are getting pretty close. We're going to be biting our nails election night."

"None of that matters," Katie announced. She put down her tote bag. "Chase and LaShaun will have a happy wedding no matter what happens with the election. Their life and future together will start off with joy."

"And nobody better get in the way," Adrianna said with a grin.

"Exactly," Katie replied without smiling. "Now LaShaun, I pulled off the impossible. Lucky for you I have friends who are florists with connections. I managed to get red and lavender orchids at a great price. I just need your approval."

"I'm afraid to say no," LaShaun murmured. Instead of being annoyed at the interruption, LaShaun actually welcomed it.

Katie gave a short nod like an army officer pleased her orders would not be disputed. She scribbled notes. "Good."

"Lavender orchids are fabulous," Adrianna said. "You have to go to the right source to get the best ones. Beautiful wild orchids grow in central and South

America. Naturally I would know given my proud heritage. I have cousins in Peru who grow them for the American market."

"Yes, yes, Adrianna. It was your idea. Happy?" Katie retorted without looking up.

LaShaun gasped and grabbed Adrianna by the shoulders. "Go to the source. What's that old saying? Get to the heart of the matter. Yes! I need to get to the heart or the source."

"Are we talking about flowers?" Adrianna blinked rapidly. When LaShaun didn't answer she glanced at Katie, who shrugged and kept making notes.

"I've been too literal. I couldn't see the forest for the trees...." LaShaun stared past her future sisters-in-law to the woods outside her window.

"Absolutely," Katie answered glancing up only for a few seconds. "Details matter, girl. That's what I've been trying to tell you."

"I don't think we're talking about the same thing," Adrianna mumbled. She tried to get Katie's attention away from her notes but failed.

"I do believe we're finito, done. Every last flower petal, fabric swatch, and member of the wedding party is efficiently dealt with, ladies. High fives." Katie tucked away her tablet computer and put on her big sunglasses. "Come on, Adrianna. Let's rock and roll. Two weeks to blast off."

"LaShaun, is everything alright?" Adrianna put a hand on LaShaun's shoulders. She jumped when LaShaun slapped her hands together. "My Lord, you scared the crap out of me."

"What? Oh, sorry. Listen, I've got work to do," LaShaun started, but Katie broke in.

"We do, too. My lectures paid off," Katie smiled.

"Even Chase seems to have straightened up. He was in a great mood when I saw him a couple of hours ago. He's ready. Of course he might not win the election. It's real close."

"Katie," Adrianna blurted out and frowned.

"Might as well face facts. Mama is way off base, because being with you has really lightened him up. He was laughing and telling jokes," Katie went on.

LaShaun had no interest in the election. "You saw Chase? How did he seem to you?"

"Like I said, he seems just fine. Talk has gotten around that maybe they need somebody older, and steadier as Sheriff. Sorry, LaShaun, but he has been kind of moody lately. Even for Chase I mean."

"I'm sure the voters will realize that a younger man with a modern approach to fighting crime makes more sense." Adrianna nodded encouragingly at LaShaun.

"Hmm." LaShaun turned to Katie again. "Did he say anything about me or the wedding?"

"Only that he'd see you tonight. We have to get moving. I've got a gazillion things to do. Call you later." Katie jerked a thumb at the door as a signal that Adrianna should follow.

Adrianna hung back a few moments. "LaShaun, I feel like something is bothering you. And all this strange behavior from Chase is..."

"Adrianna, I really need to leave now," Katie shouted. "We'll have to hang out another day." Seconds later the outer screened storm door show banged shut.

"Don't worry about me, Adrianna. Now go on so Katie won't be late. I've got a ton of errands myself," LaShaun said. She tugged her down the hallway toward the door.

"We should have at least one rehearsal, don't you

think?" Adrianna tried to stop, but LaShaun kept them both moving forward.

"The priest will stand there. We walk to him. We say the vows. What's to rehearse? Thanks for everything y'all are doing. You don't know how much I appreciate it," LaShaun spoke rapidly. Seconds later they were on the back porch.

"But Jessi is the flower girl and she..."

"Just walks ahead of us carrying a basket of flowers. I know. It's going to be wonderful. I'll talk to you later." LaShaun nudged Adrianna off until she went down the steps.

"But..." Adrianna stopped when Katie tapped the horn of her SUV.

"Bye."

LaShaun darted inside before Adrianna could try again. Then she retrieved the knife. Once again she admired the workmanship of it. Specially treated cloth lined the inside of the case to keep the silver from becoming tarnished. Yet this was not a decorative item to be displayed in a museum. She took out her grandmother's shotgun, and made sure all of the windows were locked, and put the alarm on.

"I might as well be prepared in case they come at me in the day time. Right, Monmon?" LaShaun tilted her head as though expecting an answer.

Then she continued the search for answers. For two hours she read. Seated in a cane rocker with her grandmother's favorite throw across her lap, LaShaun traveled back in time. She needed to understand who and what she would be up against later. Soon she was lost in the late eighteenth century when her ancestor Alcide LeGrange began to prosper. The son of a former slave in Saint Domingue, present day Haiti, he narrated his extraordinary life. He befriended LaShaun's other ancestor Claude Alsace Rousselle. Twenty years later their children married. Yet their friendship becomes strained. Alcide heard strange tales of how Claude gained his wealth and influence. His wife, also a native of Haiti, waves away his concerns. Then he becomes suspicious that she, too, was involved in voodoo rituals.

Alcide wrote, "They have no shame in these untamed gatherings. To my horror I have learned that my wife, Marie-Claire, has been sneaking away to take part. I will not allow such ungodly behavior in my household."

His journal ended with that entry. The next account LaShaun reads refers to his untimely death and funeral. A prickle of gloom started at the base of LaShaun's spine. Alcide hadn't died of natural causes, despite what the entry by his youngest son says. LaShaun scanned two dozen pages hoping to find letters or anything written by Marie-Claire.

"Damn. I'll have to leave that mystery for another day," LaShaun mumbled to herself.

She was about to close a container when she glanced at a stack of papers again. Carefully, she un-wrapped the acid free sheets around them. These were letters written in French and English. LaShaun put her bilingual reading skills to the test as she switched between the two. Written over several years in the early to mid eighteen hundreds, the grandchildren of Marie-Claire and Alcide kept in touch. From their accounts the two families, LeGrange and Rousselle, seemed to have suffered a series of setbacks. The Americanization of Louisiana after the Louisiana Purchase made life hard for Blacks, including Creoles of Color. Therese-Claire Rousselle complained bitterly about their loss in social status.

"We must call on our spirits again, sister," Therese-Claire wrote in 1824. "Lest our lands and livestock be swept away. I know you are reluctant. Our grandfather's words contain wisdom on controlling the..."

LaShaun strained, but couldn't make out the rest of the sentence. The ink was smudged in some places, faded in others. Desperate, she sorted through the rest of the letters until she found a reference to the family cemetery. Suddenly LaShaun felt tiny needles along her forearms again. She dropped the letters and went to a framed antique map on the wall. Her forefinger traced a line from landmark to landmark. Gazing at it, LaShaun prayed she was right. Minutes later she raced to town in Chase's truck, pushing past the speed limit.

"I have to find the source," she whispered.

Chapter 20

By seven o'clock that night LaShaun had returned home and made preparations. Savannah sent an e-mail confirming LaShaun's hunch. Manny Young hadn't contacted the True Justice Project. Montgomery and Juridicus had reached out to him first. Over six weeks of visits, Montgomery had built a relationship with him. Finally Manny agreed to hire him for an appeal.

Chase hadn't called, but she was sure he would come. No doubt Montgomery and the others were waiting for nightfall. The only other reason they hadn't arrived was most likely because of orders from Abiku. All this LaShaun knew with the certainty because of her paranormal extra sense. She'd prayed about what she must do. Miss Rose and the twins called to give her counsel as well. The three women insisted that they should be present, but LaShaun did not want them in harm's way. She did her best to reassure them. When she called Chase he picked up on the first ring.

"Why aren't you here by now, cher?" LaShaun asked, her heart thumping. "You told Katie and Adrianna you'd see me tonight. I hope you're not still working. M.J. shouldn't be pushing you so hard."

Chase's rich, deep baritone laugh came through the phone's speaker. "Ah, so M.J. is to blame. No, I'm at the scene of another murder. A body was found way down near Vermilion Bay. I'll be late, but I'll definitely come to you tonight love. Please forgive the smell of death on me."

LaShaun shivered as chill bumps spread up her arms. "I won't give him up to you so easily you know."

Chase's voice changed completely. The accent and

manner of speech came from another time. "Ah, a challenge. I love the fight in you. Maybe we will make love on the ground beneath the moonlight after, eh?"

"Bastard," LaShaun hissed in reply.

"LaShaun?" Chase replied. "I'm way out in the middle of nowhere so you're breaking up. I have bad news. We found another body."

LaShaun felt no surprise that suddenly her Chase was back. She whispered a prayer into the phone. "I know. You just told me."

"I did?" Chase was silent for several seconds. "Maybe I should stay away from you until I get my head together. The last few days are a blur."

"Chase, listen to me. You have to come to my house tonight. Trust me, you're not going crazy, and it's not post traumatic stress disorder from your days in the war. We need each other to get through this."

"You know what's happening, don't you?" Chase said low into the phone. Voices of his colleagues were in the background.

"Yes. Promise you'll come to me no matter what," LaShaun said with force.

"Of course we'll be there. I would not reach my full power without my dear wife by my side," Chase said in a light tone, his voice changing again.

"Pride goeth before destruction, and a haughty spirit before a fall," she said quoting Proverbs 16:18.

"You really should stop reading that silly book, my sweet. Until we meet beneath the moonlight." A soft kissing sound followed by laughter came through before the call clicked off.

"I'm gonna kick your ass back to hell," LaShaun shouted into the phone. She tossed the handset across the room where it landed on the sofa.

For another hour LaShaun had to restrain herself. Though impatient to find answers, the fragile antique documents had to be handled with care. As she read LaShaun paced and glanced at the wall clock from time to time. A slight sound caught her attention. When she glanced out of her kitchen window LaShaun saw nothing. Only a small lamp was on in the large formal parlor. LaShaun hurried down the hallway. Through one of the three windows she detected movement just beyond a stand of trees. A bumpy gravel path led to the Rousselle family cemetery.

"Cars, three of them moving slow with their lights off. So the gang's all here," she murmured to herself.

Shadowy outlines of the vehicles inched along. Soon she couldn't see them at all. That could only mean they'd reached the curve in the path leading deeper into the woods and to the cemetery. LaShaun was in no hurry to confront the group alone. She could only guess at what they were prepared to do, these fanatics convinced they would be rulers in a new world order. LaShaun let them think they had crept onto her land unnoticed. She went to the small family parlor, knelt and prayed. Someone, or some thing, banged loudly on her back door. LaShaun armed herself with the silver knife. Next she calmly loaded silver bullets into her small derringer. She walked to the kitchen with unhurried steps. As the knob turned, LaShaun put on her jacket. Her boots were warm, sturdy and would allow her to move quickly.

"LaShaun?" Chase stood in the doorway with an uncertain expression. "I don't know what's supposed to happen but..."

"We don't have much time." LaShaun made the sign of the cross, grabbed both his hands and continued the prayer she'd been reciting for two hours. She spoke rapidly in French and then switched to Latin. She struggled over the pronunciations.

"What are you doing? I..." Chase started, but stopped when LaShaun squeezed his hands tightly.

"Say you love me, promise you'll trust me tonight. I don't have all of the answers, but we have to go anyway," LaShaun said. She checked her pockets as she spoke.

"Go where? Feels like my head is splitting apart these days, and I can't be sure what the hell is going on half the time. So I'm gonna need you to explain." Chase jerked back when LaShaun tried to lead him back outside.

"Do you remember us going to the Sweet Olive B&B?" LaShaun glanced past him to the woods. She saw flashes of light.

"Yeah." Chase rubbed his forehead. "Kinda."

"Then what happened? Think about where you were after that, what you remember," LaShaun insisted. A hint of blue appeared. "Think honey. We have to hurry."

"Then I... went to work and you... were wearing a wedding dress. Wait, that sounds crazy. Where did I get that about a wedding dress?" Chase tilted his head to one side as though listening.

LaShaun shivered, but not because of the cold air coming in through the still open back door. She wrapped both arms around his waist and pulled him close. "We love each other, no matter what has happened. Say it."

Chase smiled down at her. "I hate to interrupt this tender moment, but we need to take a walk. I will make a promise. Tonight I'll pleasure you until we are both breathless. But first, to business."

"Bastard," LaShaun screamed.

She beat her fists against his chest while Chase laughed at her. He grabbed both her wrists. In seconds the strong arms that had held her close in adoring embraces dragged her across the back lawn to the woods. A soft blue mist glimmered in the distances. LaShaun tried to dig her heels into the soft ground, but the rubber slid easily on damp grass.

"I don't know why you seem so reluctant to visit your beloved forest tonight," the demon said. The sound of his voice seemed to scrape out of Chase's throat.

"You turned it into a filthy dung heap, you and those worms you call followers," LaShaun snapped. She tried to twist free of his iron grip, but the defense techniques she knew were no match against his superior strength.

"Such hostility when I'm trying to make you a queen." Chase suddenly stopped and yanked LaShaun against his body. A pulsing heat came through the layers of his clothes. "I am going to transform this pathetic man you chose as a mate into a world ruler. You should thank me."

LaShaun pushed against him, but froze at his words. Heart pounding, she looked up into eyes that gleamed with cruelty, and triumph. "What are you talking about?"

"Your ancestors called me forth, and then left behind mewling offspring. They whined about Him," Chase spat as he pointed to the sky. "They got down on their knees and crawled begging Him to forgive. My cunning and power had enriched the LeGrange and Rousselle families, but I was ignored. Still I knew the true nature of man would win out. So I waited. Finally another one called on me. I grew stronger. And I waited again. Two generations later you came along to captivate me with your beauty, intelligence, and ruthlessness. You were the best of them all, until you crawled in the dirt on your knees as well. Lighting candles and mumbling empty words. I was sorely disappointed in you until you gave me this gift, a vessel. A body to let me enjoy the pleasures of the flesh. We can be together."

"No, we won't," LaShaun shouted back at him. She felt dizzy at the impact of what he said.

"Face the truth, ma cherie. You delivered Chase into my hands the day you ensnared him in your love. He could not fight his passion for you. Do not lie to yourself, LaShaun. You knew," the voice coming from Chase's lips now bore no resemblance to the man she cherished. "Just as you pulled other men into your sensuous web to get your way, you set just as delicious of a trap for this one. Oui?"

"Liar." LaShaun kicked his legs with as much force as she could.

Chase stumbled, but held on firmly to her. "Why deny who you really are deep inside? I'm giving you this man. Feel him; the body that brings you delight."

"Stop." LaShaun tried to pull away, but couldn't. She could feel the heat from Chase's body, and his arousal as he pressed his pelvis against her.

"Even now your body responds to him," he whispered in her ear.

Though she whipped her head from side to side in denial, LaShaun could not look away from the dark eyes that had captured her heart. Their mouths touched, and a flash of fire seemed to lick at her very soul. More than physical desire, LaShaun felt an overwhelming hunger to have him inside her. A powerful memory of the way Chase felt when they made love left her weak. Though a small part of her mind rebelled, LaShaun clutched at Chase with a moan. She kissed him greedily, raking her hands over his body. After a few seconds he pushed her away.

"Chase," LaShaun gasped.

"Sweet one, we will have plenty of time later. But right now we have one more task before we can taste the delights of human lust." He laughed and yanked her farther into the darkness.

LaShaun clawed at his arms in pure rage born of frustration. She'd allowed his filth into her mind. For a brief moment she almost gave in to the temptation. His suggestion that she accept him as Chase should have sickened her. Instead LaShaun became seduced. Anger with herself as much as with the deceiver burned like a hot branding iron.

"You don't know me," LaShaun rasped, panting with exertion against her own inner demons and the one made flesh in the man she loved.

"But I do, love. That's why you fight with such intensity. I'm a mirror, and you do not like what you see. Enough," he growled and waved an arm. Cloaked figures separated from the shadows as though they were part of the tree trunks. "We begin."

LaShaun pushed back against his effort to play on her deepest doubts and fears. She needed to stall for time. "Why didn't you inhabit Manny Young? He'd probably love to team up with you."

Chase let go of her. "I would have settled for him, but he foolishly became imprisoned. I tried to counsel him, but he has little self-control. His release could take years, if it happens at all. Poor chap."

"Like you give a damn about Manny," LaShaun spat back at him. "If he becomes useless he's dead. The rest of you better listen up because that goes for you, too. This thing will use you and walk over your dead body when he's done."

He yanked LaShaun against his chest again and put his lips to her ear. "They don't care. My followers have tasted the freedom I offer."

"Freedom? You're his slaves, his fools. You're not free," LaShaun yelled at them. The figures stood still, waiting for orders.

"Some say I'm entirely too indulgent with you. If I didn't need you awake for our ceremony, I'd knock you out myself." Chase's features twisted into a frightful scowl. He pointed a forefinger at her. "Don't push me."

"Montgomery, this is insane. Serving evil will lead to damnation," LaShaun shouted, trying to gain time.

Chase lifted LaShaun in the air in a bear hug. Then he let one hand roam over her body. His breath became ragged. The cloaked figures started to chant. Once again LaShaun felt his arousal as Chase moaned. He brushed a hand across her breasts. Quickly he reached into her jacket and took her knife. Murmurs of admiration came from the figures when he held the knife up. LaShaun counted six, but felt sure more blended in the darkness.

Montgomery stepped forward wearing a smile of victory. "Ah yes. The legendary sacred knife of purest silver. That will make a nice addition to my collection."

"You're among friends here, no weapons needed," a familiar female voice cackled.

"I'm going to cut you first, Gina," LaShaun snarled in her direction.

"I said enough." Chase nodded to someone. While

the figures moved around in some kind of purposeful activity, he whispered to LaShaun again. "We'll finish what we started once this is over. I can't wait to part your legs."

He dragged her to an older part of the family cemetery. They went through the wrought iron gate LaShaun had installed after her grandmother's burial. Her pulse quickened. Abiku headed in the direction LaShaun had seen on the old map. Moving through thick brush they came to a clearing. A large tree had been cut and only the stump remained. An iron fire pit had been embedded in it. Blue and yellow flames licked the night casting a glow in a wide circle.

"You have an awful choice. Kill the man you love, and you will banish me. Or accept the inevitable and rule by my side. Of course you must get over that unfortunate need to be good." The demon twisted Chase's features into a grimace, as though the word tasted sour on his tongue.

"I can't kill you," LaShaun replied.

"Of course you can't, dear one. I'm the man you adore, the man of your dreams. I'm your husband, bound to you by our eternal vows."

"Forever to rule this world in darkness, we claim our right to make the meek bow down. Strong is the way of the wicked. Yea, we crush them beneath our boots as we stride across this land," the cloaked figures changed on cue.

LaShaun swung a fist hoping to hit Gina first. Strong hands pulled her back to the center of the clearing. Looking down she noticed symbols drawn in the dirt. A raised mound stood opposite the fire pit. She stared hard and realized what looked like a mass of vegetation appeared more solid. LaShaun started for Chase. Three cloaked figures came toward her, but he waved them back.

LaShaun reached into her lace bra. She held up a silver wolf's head with black onyx and lapis. "Remember when I gave you this? Here, take this symbol of our commitment. You haven't worn it lately because of work."

Chase pushed the collars of his jacket and shirt away to expose his neck. The cloaked followers murmured in protest, but he chopped a hand in the air demanding silence. He then turned back to LaShaun. His eyes glowed as he looked at her. "This trinket cannot harm me because she gives it freely, a symbol of her devotion. Still warm from the heat of her flesh."

"L'union fait la force," LaShaun whispered fiercely. She cupped his face with both hands, kissed him and began a prayer in old Louisiana Creole.

Chase's eyes blinked rapidly. "LaShaun..."

"Together we fight. Always," she whispered in desperation.

When he swung away from her, LaShaun let out a cry of desolation. The cloaked figures around her closed in and resumed chanting. As their voices rose a blue light pulsated from the wall of vines, illuminating them so the leaves became translucent. LaShaun recognized the outline of a door. One of the figures, a tall masculine hulk, stepped forward. Still chanting, he swept aside the living curtain that concealed a cement crypt. A huge iron ring served as a handle. The blue light came from within.

"I want to see," LaShaun said, pretending to be in awe. Her mind raced, sorting through how and when she should make her move.

"Not yet," Chase said softly.

LaShaun looked at him closely. She couldn't tell from his voice or expression who he was in that moment. With a nod she turned back to watch the macabre ceremony taking place. She had to find a way to stop it, and stop these people. Suddenly one of the cloaked figures behind her gave a whoop.

"Why should you be the first?" came a screech of protest. "I've served him longer and better than you!"

Startled, the other cloaked figures turned in tandem to gape at their companion. The offender punched the follower closest. The hood of the cloak fell away and Allison Graham yelped with pain. Her attacker jammed an elbow into Allison's midsection. Allison's eyes rolled back in her eye as she fell. For a few moments everyone stood frozen.

With a growl, Montgomery threw back the hood of his cloak, his face twisted into a mask of hatred. "Grab the intruder."

Another cloaked figure rushed forward to obey. From the darkness a large stick landed a crushing blow on his head. The man grunted in surprised agony as he went down. Two more cloaked figures jumped into the circle of light and a battle began. LaShaun took advantage of the confusion to race away into the darkness. She desperately searched the darkness. Sweat trickled down her face as LaShaun strained to find the bag she'd concealed earlier. After what seemed like an eternity she found it. She whispered a prayer of thanksgiving as she raced toward chaos. An all out brawl raged in full force. Shouts, curses and screams of pain rang in the night air.

Gina, her red hair plastered to her forehead by sweat and blood, blocked LaShaun's path. "You won't walk away this time, bitch. I don't give a shit what anybody says."

"I'm afraid she's right, Ms. Rousselle," Neal Montgomery said. He wore a grin. "Even Abiku agrees. None of you will leave these woods alive tonight. Fresh blood will only enhance our rite."

LaShaun's heart broke at his words. She'd failed to free Chase from the hellish fate of being possessed by a loathsome fiend. Faced with making a last stand, LaShaun vowed to do as much damage as she could. She glared at them both.

"If I take anybody with me, Gina, it's going to be you," LaShaun barked and assumed a defensive position.

"You just made my night," Gina replied with a smirk.

The vengeful woman charged LaShaun. Gina faked a punch but kicked out with her left leg instead. LaShaun took the blow to one leg and stumbled. Gina barked with glee like a victorious she-wolf. She swung a fist that struck the side of LaShaun's face. LaShaun cried out as she scrambled to get away.

"You've got this under control. I'll meet you back in the circle." Montgomery strode away.

Gina panted out as she danced around, like a predator toying with her prey. She jabbed with her fists and moved in on LaShaun. "Damn right I've got this. Guess you're worn out from all the excitement. Am I right, Miss Cutie Pie? Killing you will make sex with your hubby even hotter. I'm going to ride him like the fine stallion he is with your blood still on my hands."

LaShaun stood straight in one quick motion, pressed the muzzle of her derringer into Gina's belly and fired. Gina's eyes went wide and her mouth worked but not a sound came out. Then she gave a scratchy whimper as she clutched at the wound.

"The only thing you'll be riding tonight is a magic carpet to hell," LaShaun said. She delivered a backhand slap that sent the woman to the ground.

LaShaun turned her attention back to the clearing. Her goal of stopping Abiku seemed beyond her reach. She could only hope to leave behind clues to guide Miss Rose and the twins in marshalling forces against his cult. With a certainty that she would not survive, LaShaun strode back to the clearing. She tried to make out Chase, but shadowy figures seemed everywhere. Two people locked in a struggled blocked her path to the door of the crypt. She ran full on using the energy of her momentum to push them aside.

With one strong pull of the iron ring LaShaun found herself in the opening. The door swung smoothly on oiled hinges. A polished ebony coffin lay on the dusty brick floor. Spider webs thick as rope hung from the walls. Three tombs were set in each of the three walls. The brick opening of the one in the center had been broken open. Metal lined the vault. The pieces of an ancient wood coffin lay in a pile.

"As you can see we had a new coffin built," Montgomery said quietly. His eyes looked glazed with a crazed zeal.

LaShaun spun around to face him, concealing the gun in her back waistband in the process. Chase stood to his left, his face a blank mask. "Why?"

"Because a king deserves better," Harry replied from another corner.

LaShaun brushed a hand along the wall causing years of dirt to crumble to the floor. "The maid has been on vacation for a few centuries. Why not move your king to a grand mausoleum?"

The middle-aged man's mouth curled into a sneer.

"We created a magnificent resting place made from the finest Makassar ebony from Indonesia."

"I have to agree it's beautiful." LaShaun made a half circle around the coffin.

She expected one or both of the men to stop her. Harry seemed too intent on gloating. Chase gazed at a point somewhere beyond her. The blue glow came from within the dark wood coffin. LaShaun reached for the lid.

"He grew strong here, but soon he won't need this place. The living don't need a grave," Harry said with a nasty smile.

"You're lying. He'll always need this coffin, otherwise you wouldn't have gone to so much trouble," LaShaun shot back. She placed a hand on the lid, bowed her head and prayed.

"How dare you defile the seat of his greatness by mumbling a feeble creed," Harry shouted.

"The Bible says the faith of a mustard seed can move mountains. I'm sure it can chop up a little wood." LaShaun said another line of prayer, this time in Latin mixed with Creole French. The light inside the coffin grew fainter.

Harry balled both hands into fists. He took two steps forward then glanced at Chase. "Come forth, master. Let us squeeze the life from her worthless body."

"Yes," Chase said in a hoarse voice.

"This slut doesn't realize she's defeated. You'll beg us to kill you very soon." Harry laughed feverishly as he reached for LaShaun.

LaShaun pulled the antique knife from the sheath on her belt with one hand and pushed the lid of the coffin open with the other. A black heart lay nestled in silk surrounded by a gruesome vine with leaves shaped like claws. As she stared at it, the vines began to writhe like snakes.

"Nothing can destroy the power, you stupid bitch," Harry said.

"Nothing except a sacred knife of purest silver, like the one I've got in my hand. You idiots thought I didn't have a back-up plan. The knife Montgomery took from me is harmless. I bought it at the local hardware store," LaShaun said. She raised the knife high above her head.

Montgomery stood gaping at her in shock. "Stop her, Abiku!"

Chase took two long strides across the dusty floor. He towered over LaShaun for a few seconds. Harry panted with anticipation, his eyes bright with excitement. Instead of striking out at LaShaun, Chase spun around and landed a crushing punch that caused facial bones to crack in Harry's face.

"No, no!" Montgomery started toward Chase but stopped short at the deadly look in his eyes.

Chase kicked Harry's limp body aside and confronted him. "You're next."

"You've awakened, Master. Remember who you are," Montgomery said in a strained voice.

"I know exactly who I am," Chase growled. He attacked Montgomery with a series of power blows that sent the man reeling against the wall.

"Keep him busy, baby. I've got work to do," LaShaun muttered, praying that Chase's control held.

One of the vines wrapped around her wrist. She winced from the sensation of acid eating into her skin. Searing pain shot up her arm as if sizzling poison flowed through her body. LaShaun grew weak, her mind and vision became cloudy.

"Now, LaShaun. Do it now!"

The voice jolted LaShaun back from the brink of passing out. She concentrated all of her will. In a flash she saw the brutal injuries of the teenage boy, and saw countless other bodies; the victims of vicious killers Montgomery and his cult had helped go free. With a cry of wrath LaShaun plunged the knife into the quivering slimy heart, then again, and again. A stench rose up as viscous fluid flowed from each stab wound. A roaring gust of wind slammed the heavy stone door shut. She screamed for Chase, but a sound like thunder drowned out her voice. Dust and brick shards swirled into a whirlwind until LaShaun was blinded. Then everything went black.

Chapter 21

She dreamed, or maybe she only thought she dreamed. Figures stumbled around weeping bitterly as they were led away. Some begged for mercy. Others snarled in angry defiance. Uniformed figures efficiently brought order to the pandemonium. Hands that tenderly rubbed her face pulled her attention away from the commotion. Soothing voices spoke to her. LaShaun felt sure she heard her grandmother speaking words of strength, urging her to return. LaShaun's eyes snapped open to find a cloaked figure bending over her.

M.J.'s worried frown melted into relief. She took a shaky breath and let it out. "You better wake the hell up so I can whip your behind. This is another fine mess you've gotten me into."

"Hi."

"Don't 'Hi' me like we just met for coffee and donuts, girl. I hope you can answer some questions. I got a tricked out empty coffin that looks like it costs more than my house. It's filled with some weird dead plants and what looks like a burnt human organ. "

"Chase is here," LaShaun rasped through a throat dry as dust. When she coughed, an emergency medical tech put a bottle of water to her lips.

M.J. waited until LaShaun finished before she spoke. "Chase took a blow to the head or something. He can't tell us a damn thing."

LaShaun shot upright and realized she lay on a stretcher in an emergency van. "Where is he? How bad is Chase hurt? I've got to see him."

"Whoa, you, you're not going anywhere. And Chase

is just fine. The emergency medical tech doesn't think he got hit hard enough to get amnesia. But a CT scan will rule out serious injury. He's just as worried about you." M.J. gave her a head to toe glance. "I don't blame him. You look beat to hell and back."

"You have no idea," LaShaun retorted. "Let me see Chase."

"He's on his way to the hospital. I told him you were already there. Only way I could get him into the ambulance. Don't worry," M.J. said cutting off another outburst from LaShaun. "You're on your way to join him."

M.J. nodded to the EMT, a tall black woman who nodded in response. The double doors to the vehicle whooshed shut and it started to move. The woman gently cleaned LaShaun's injuries.

"How you get this nasty burn on your wrist?" the EMT asked, her brow furrowed in curiosity.

"You wouldn't believe it if I told you. Trust me; you don't really want to know." LaShaun sank onto the stretcher again and closed her eyes.

***

Sunlight filtered through the canopy of leaves overhead. LaShaun emerged from the yellow striped tent, her heart pounding but in a good way. For once her boisterous Uncle Leo did not blurt out one of his signature hearty jokes. He strode forward with his chin up, looking every inch the dignified senior male family member. He offered his dark-suited elbow and LaShaun delicately looped her arm through his. Music from the small band swelled into the wedding march. They followed the linen and bamboo carpet down the center of two rows of chairs. The seed pearls on her wedding gown seemed to have a magical radiance. Father Vavasseur from St. Augustine Catholic church stood beneath the arch covered with flowers. Jessi, Chase's niece, beamed at the attention she got spreading rose petals from a basket as she marched ahead of them. When Chase turned to gaze at LaShaun, her breath caught.

She and Chase didn't have to discuss going ahead with the wedding despite the mayhem of the previous two weeks. Their vows of holy matrimony would wipe out the profane rite forced on them. They'd each only spent a day in the hospital to rule out serious internal injuries. Next had been the endless interviews with the state police and district attorney. Abiku's cult members had been arrested. They faced charges of battery, kidnapping, and criminal property damage. Allison Graham faced a much more serious charge for a crime that hadn't even taken place in the woods. Police had gone back to her house to find her husband's dead body stuffed in a huge antique trunk stored in the attic. Though Greg wouldn't say a word against his mother, the two younger children had given deputies enough information to paint a grisly picture. In spite of his flaws, Jonathan Graham hadn't known his wife was involved with the cult. The children hid during a violent argument between their parents. When all was quiet, Allison had locked them in their room with games and food for several hours. She'd told the kids she needed to "clean up daddy's mess".

Yet on this wonderful day of days, LaShaun pushed aside thoughts of darkness or death. Chase watched her walk slowly toward him. He smiled at her with great love in his eyes. Tears threatened to ruin the perfect make-up Savannah had painstakingly applied only an hour ago. LaShaun blinked rapidly, determined not to get watery so soon. Uncle Leo grinned as he handed her off to the groom. The priest cleared his throat loudly when Chase bent down to kiss LaShaun.

"Ahem, let's do the marrying first. Kiss on my cue, oui?" The priest raised an amused eyebrow at them.

"Right," Chase whispered and took LaShaun's hand instead.

LaShaun listened as Father Vavasseur read the wedding sermon in a solemn tone. As they got to the vows, sniffles and camera clicks came from the small audience around them. Savannah, Katie and Adrianna, dressed in light green dresses embroidered with flowers at the neck and bell sleeves, wore expressions of joy. Their husbands looked dapper in their dark suits. Chase's brother stepped forward with the emerald green velvet box holding their wedding bands.

"The bride and groom have their own wedding vows. First the bride." Father Vavasseur nodded to them.

"From this day until my last breath I will cherish you. Our hearts have been as one since the moment we touched. I stand with you through whatever happens in our lives. Before God and the world I declare my everlasting love for you," LaShaun said softly.

"Now the groom," Father Vavasseur said as he beamed at Chase. He winked. "You'll get to kiss her soon, son." The audience laughed.

Chase took a deep breath. "You know I'm not one for long speeches, or poetry. So I'll just say I'm going to be your protector, provider, friend, handyman, car mechanic and anything else you need me to be. And one day if I'm very, very blessed, I'll be the father of your children."

"That's so beautiful," a female voice said from the audience as louder sniffles could be heard.

"Chase Matthew Broussard, do you take this woman to be your lawful wedded wife before God and this assembly?" Father Vavasseur intoned.

"I do, with all my heart," Chase replied and slipped the gold band inlaid with diamonds on LaShaun's finger.

"LaShaun Gloriana Rousselle, do you take this man to be your lawful wedded husband before God and this assembly?"

LaShaun sighed and slid the matching gold band on Chase's finger. "Yes, I do."

"Now's the time, son. Kiss your wife," Father Vavasseur boomed with glee.

When their lips met, applause broke out in the crowd. Jessi gleefully tossed red and pink rose petals all around them, as did Savannah, Katie and Adrianna. The shouts and applause swelled as they clung to each other. Music played. All of the sound faded into the background for LaShaun. All she could hear was their twin heartbeats as they sealed their vows.

Thirty minutes later, the reception was in full swing. The band had the crowd up on their feet dancing like crazy to popular rhythm and blues songs. LaShaun and Chase finally took a break after doing the Cajun two-step through three Zydeco tunes. They playfully staggered to the large reception tent. The band played in one corner as wedding guests circled the tables laden with food and drinks. They sat at a long table reserved for the bridal party.

"Well, well, well. Thought I'd never see the day when this serious fella would be having so much fun. And at his wedding at that." Retired Sheriff Triche grinned down at them. He held a plate piled high with food from the buffet.

"Have a seat, Sheriff. You seem to be carrying a load," LaShaun quipped.

The old sheriff looked around guiltily. "Yeah, I'm hiding out from my wife cause I know what she's gonna say. Thank goodness y'all got a good crowd here keepin' her distracted while I stuff my face."

"I should go find her. She's trying to keep you healthy," LaShaun replied and poked his arm with a finger.

"If I can't treat myself every once in a while, then life ain't worth livin'. Hmmm, whoever did these little meatballs has a true gift. Once I polish this off I'm gonna get a slice of each one of those cakes." He nodded toward the rapidly disappearing white wedding cake, and the large chocolate groom's cake.

"Have yourself a good time, boss," Chase quipped. He stretched an arm around LaShaun's shoulders and smiled at the crowd.

"You two deserve to have a good time more than me after the hell you've gone through." The older man put his plate down and wiped his mouth. "Any of them crazy cult folks talkin'?"

Chase shook his head slowly. "Nope. Neal Montgomery managed to slip away in all the confusion. Not that we could charge him with anything more than trespassing. Even the kidnapping would be hard to prosecute based on what happened. I don't remember a lot of that night, and the Saunders couple claim we drank too much."

"What about the murder? He had to have been part of that Graham woman shooting her husband twelve times. Dang, she really wanted him dead." Former

Sheriff Triche let out a whistle.

"No evidence he was there or that he ever met Allison or her husband," Chase said, laying out the facts like a law officer. "We would like to question him, but he's disappeared."

"Well least the DA is gonna charge them other fools. Of course after tangling with you two, they're the ones with all the bruises and black eyes." Former Sheriff Triche let out a hearty laugh. "I coulda told 'em not to mess with your missus."

"She's amazing." Chase kissed LaShaun on the forehead.

Miss Rose and the twins approached. All three had plates and held glasses of champagne. Miss Rose looked around at the crowd. She shook her shoulders in time to the music. Justine and Pauline chattered away about who they recognized.

"How ya'll ladies doin'. I-- oh-oh. My wife is lookin' for me. Excuse me. I'll be back later." Former Sheriff Triche nimbly slipped from his seat to blend with the crowd. He moved away from his wife and toward the dessert buffet.

"Mrs. Triche is gonna have his hide when she finds him," Miss Rose said with a grin. She sat down in his now empty chair. "You children are a beautiful sight together."

"Your dress is a masterpiece, LaShaun," Justine added.

"Not to mention that fabulous wedding ring. Almost makes a body want to get married again," Pauline said. Then the twins turned to each other in tandem. "Not even close," they tittered in unison.

"I'll be right back, honey. Excuse me ladies." Chase made his way around the room, stopping to chat with several guests.

"He's going to talk to his mama," Justine said with certainty.

"I'm surprised she showed up. Mrs. Broussard hasn't spoken to him for over three months." LaShaun felt the brightness of the day dim a little.

Miss Rose patted her hand. "Don't you worry, cher. She'll have to come around. Being hard-headed won't get her anywhere."

LaShaun turned to the three older women. "Speaking of hard heads, what in the world were you thinking showing up in the woods that night? Dressed up in cloaks and everything. And how did you manage to get away when the cops showed up?"

Pauline and Justine giggled like naughty kids. They glanced at Miss Rose to explain as they stuffed cake in their mouths. Miss Rose shrugged. She stopped in the act of biting into a spicy chicken wing.

"I'm not a helpless old lady. I used to kick-box back in the day. Oh yes I did," Miss Rose added at LaShaun's open-mouthed expression.

"You needed back-up no matter what you said," Pauline said. She sipped champagne. A handsome gray-haired gentleman at the next table smiled at her. She lost interest in the conversation.

"Exactly," Justine replied. She daintily dabbed frosting from her lips. "We knew you could handle yourself, but we decided to even up the odds. Good thing we did, too. We knew they'd be cloaked. Most of the old cults favor that get up."

"Yes, Lord," Miss Rose said. "The twins came over that afternoon you left my house. We formed a circle and could see dark cloaks moving among trees. We knew what it meant, that they were in your woods."

"Why didn't you stay to tell the police what happened though?" LaShaun gazed at them with new admiration.

Miss Rose smiled slyly. "And how would we explain being there? We don't advertise our gifts, cher. We've had to do more than a few spiritual rescue missions over the years. By the way, we made sure your sacred knife was safely returned to its resting place. So no worries on that front."

Justine leaned forward and lowered her voice. "We may need it again someday."

"This time we didn't need more of us." Miss Rose continued on enjoying the food on the plate, but LaShaun placed a hand on her arm.

"This time?" LaShaun asked.

Miss Rose shook her head. "We're scattered around the state, country and the whole world. A network of those who fight evil." Her expression grew solemn. "I'm afraid we're going to hear more from Montgomery and his crew."

"We've alerted the network. Our group will track him when he pops up on the radar," Justine said.

"Tell me more," LaShaun started to ask a question, but Miss Rose cut her off.

"No, cher. Let's not talk about a gloomy subject on this day of happiness. Good will win," Miss Rose said with a gentle smile.

"I didn't kill Abiku," LaShaun replied.

"No, you only destroyed the vessel that kept him anchored to this world. He's been forced back into one of the deeper levels of hell. I imagine Lucifer is very displeased with him." Justine's voice took on an ethereal tone as she spoke. Then she seemed to snap back to her sunny mood. She noticed her sister was chatting up the gray-haired man. "You'd think Pauline would have learned after three husbands."

"I want more wings," Miss Rose announced.

"And cake," Justine agreed. The two women stood at the same time. "I'm enjoying your wedding almost as much as I enjoyed my own!"

"We have such beautiful weather, too. As if the angels are smiling down on you," Miss Rose exclaimed.

LaShaun accepted hugs from the women and watched them drift away. Chase made his way back to the table, but smiled without mentioning his mother. He took her hand and laced his long fingers through hers. LaShaun studied his face and spoke to him softly.

"Everything okay?" She asked.

"Perfect," Chase replied without a trace of upset or anger.

LaShaun sighed and leaned against him, shoulder to shoulder. Seconds later Dave Godchaux walked over. Dave nodded to the crowd. Some gaped at him in surprise. Several of LaShaun's extended family members squinted at him to show their displeasure at his presence. Chase rose to greet him and shook his hand.

"Sorry, I'm late you two. Here's to your happiness." Dave lifted a goblet of champagne.

"Thanks, Dave. The better man won," Chase said with a wide grin.

"We ran a good race, Broussard. No mudslinging or below the belt jabs. We'll work together to make sure Vermilion Parish is safe," Dave said, ever the politician even after the election.

"No argument here," Chase replied.

"I'm going to say hello to a few of these good people." Looking every inch the man in charge, Dave strode off. In minutes he was working the crowd with smiles and handshakes.

When Chase sat down again LaShaun leaned against him. "You're not upset about losing the election," she said. LaShaun knew the answer so it wasn't a question.

"Nope. I'm no politician, and that's what the job is mostly about. I enjoy the action out in the field. All in all, things worked out for the best. Dave made it clear we would be a team. I'll still be chief of criminal investigations. M.J. will head up the property crimes and traffic division. Dave gets to rub elbows with big dogs." Chase laughed. "Yep, I'm thinking I got the best job in the world."

"I'm happy you're happy." LaShaun winked at him.

"And now I've got the best woman in the world by my side," Chase said and pressed his lips to the back of her hand. His deep brown eyes clouded over. "Thank you for saving my life. Is it finally over? I don't want to be a danger to you or anyone. If I thought..."

LaShaun pressed her finger tips to his mouth. "You're free, baby."

"But that didn't answer my question completely. Is that thing and the cult that follows him destroyed?"

"No, but at least they're scattered to the winds. That's the best we can do, beat back evil before it takes root," LaShaun said quietly.

"Yeah, like being a law officer. We'll never get rid of crime, but we can control how much it spreads and the damage crooks do." Chase sighed and smiled. "At least for today we kicked evil in the butt and sent it packing. That's good enough for me. Now come on and dance with your husband, Mrs. Broussard."

"I'd be delighted, Mr. Broussard," she replied with a grin.

LaShaun allowed him to pull her to her feet. A slow

tempo song played as Chase took her into his arms. They swayed to the music as a spring breeze brought the sweet scent of magnolias in bloom. Laughter floated around them. Chase hummed, his rich baritone voice soothing to her ears. She relaxed fully into is embrace. Yet a flutter of anxiety rose up out of nowhere. LaShaun held Chase closer as if to shield the precious life growing within her. And she tried not to hear echoes of Miss Rose's warning that evil might stretch its icy skeleton fingers toward their child.

Read More Lashaun Rousselle Paranormal Mysteries

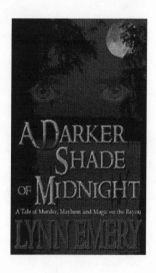

Lashaun returns home to Beau Chene to say goodbye to her grandmother. Instead of peaceful closure, she becomes a murder suspect. Will Deputy Chase Broussard ask her out on a date or arrest her? Together they unravel dark secrets in Beau Chene to find a killer.

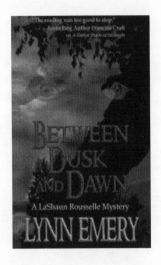

LaShaun and Deputy Chase Broussard investigate a series of gruesome murders. Whispers of something demonic stalking the bayous of Vermilion Parish has everyone in Beau Chene on edge. Are they dealing with a human serial killer of a nightmare from Cajun legends? LaShaun and Chase battle both human and supernatural evil.

Lynn Emery's novels explore Louisiana's exciting present and exotic history. From the big cities to the stunningly beautiful and mysterious swamps, stories of intrigue, secrets and murder play out on the pages. A native of the state, her knowledge of folklore, the uniquely colorful politics and crime combine to spice up each tale. For a complete list of Lynn's novels and to read more about her visit:

www.lynnemery.com

Made in the USA
Charleston, SC
26 December 2014